OUT OF BREATH

OUT OF BREATH

Rebecca Donovan

SKYSCAPE

Text copyright © 2013 Rebecca Donovan

Published by Amazon Children's Publishing
PO Box 400818
Las Vegas, NV 89140

ISBN-13: 9781477817186
ISBN-10: 1477817182

DEDICATION

For my loving friend and
life-sister, Emily
~ You are my happiness, and the
choice I never had to make. ~

PROLOGUE

I don't even know why I bothered picking up. Yeah, maybe I'll talk to you about it eventually, after you stop acting like such an ass." I stood at the top of the stairs with a heavy box of textbooks balanced in my arms. Sara released a frustrated groan, so I assumed she'd hung up.

I made some noise as I neared the door so she'd know I was coming and could hold her temperament in check. She'd told me about her decision to end things with Jared, and I'd listened. But I was basically incapable of offering any guidance. Sara didn't confide in me too much lately, afraid something would upset me. It wasn't that I was that fragile. I just refused to talk about...anything.

"Is that it?" Sara asked, her smile brighter than usual, overcompensating for the annoyance that still lingered in her eyes.

"You can tell me, you know," I offered, trying to be the friend that she needed right now.

"No, I can't," she said, redirecting her attention to the boxes stacked all over the room. "I don't have much space to work with. This room is tiny."

I let her avoid the topic, since that's what she preferred.

"I don't need anything. Really. No need to bother."

"I thought you'd say that," Sara replied with a small smile. "That's why I only brought one thing to decorate your room." She reached for a purse so big it could honestly be called a duffel bag, and pulled out a frame. Flipping it around, she held it up under her chin with a beaming smile. It was a picture of us at her house, the large bay window overlooking the front yard in the background. Anna, her mother, had taken it during the summer I'd lived with them. From the gleam in our eyes, it was apparent we were on the verge of laughing.

"Omigod," Sara said with a shocked seriousness. I tightened my eyes in confusion. "Is that a smile I see on your face, Emma Thomas? I was wondering if I'd ever see one again."

I ignored her, straightening my lips, and turned toward the built-in desk in the corner of the small bedroom.

"Perfect." Sara set the photo on the dresser, admiring it. I pulled out the textbooks and tucked them on the shelf under the desk. "Okay, let's unpack you. I'm so happy you're out of the dorms now. And I've always loved Meg…and Serena, even though she won't let me do a makeover. I'll work on it. But what's up with Peyton?"

"She's harmless," I said, breaking down an empty cardboard box.

"I guess every house needs drama," Sara noted, laying a stack of folded shirts in an open drawer. "And as long as Peyton's the only drama in this house, I can live with that."

"That's what I was thinking," I replied, hanging clothes in the minuscule closet.

Sara plopped a black boot box on the bed. "Should we keep the boots in the box or set them in the closet?" She began to slide the cover off, but my hand slammed it shut. She jumped and looked up at me in alarm.

"They're not boots." I could hear the edge in my voice.

Sara's mouth opened in surprise as she took in my intense expression. "O-kay. Where do you want it?"

"I don't care. I'd actually rather not know," I answered. "I'm getting something to drink. Do you want anything?"

"Water," Sara requested, her voice quiet.

When I returned with the two bottles of water a few minutes later, Sara was making the bed and the box was gone. Setting my shoes on the bottom of the closet floor was the final step. There was a benefit to not owning much.

I sat on the rolling chair at the desk while Sara lay on her stomach on the bed, scattering the display of decorative pillows she'd just masterfully assembled. I knew I'd stuff them on the top shelf of my closet after she left.

"You know I ended it because I can't do the distance thing, right?" Sara asked. I spun the chair around, surprised she'd decided to open up.

"I know it's hard for you. It always has been," I replied. She'd had the same challenge in high school when we were in Connecticut and Jared was attending Cornell in New York. But she made it work by visiting him practically every weekend for the last part of our senior year.

"I'll be in France, there's no way I could do that to us," she continued. "It doesn't seem fair to make him wait."

"But would you want him seeing anyone else while you're gone? Because that's basically what you're giving him permission to do. And then what happens when you get back?"

Sara was quiet, resting her chin on her hands with her eyes focused on the floor. "I just don't want to know about it. And if I meet someone in Paris, he doesn't need to know about that either. Because in the end, I know we're supposed to be together. But I'm not sure either one of us is ready to admit that."

I still didn't understand her logic, but I wasn't about to challenge her.

She sat up suddenly, not allowing me the chance to say anything in return. "So, do you think...since I'm going to be gone... that I can let Meg know a little about you? Not everything, just enough so she'll be here for you while I can't be. I hate the thought of being so far away without someone—"

"Looking out for me," I finished.

"Yeah," she replied, smiling gently. "I don't want you to be alone. You have a tendency to shut yourself off for days at a time. It's not good. I'll still call you every day, of course. But I hate not being close…in case you…" Sara looked down, unable to finish the sentence.

"Sara, I'm not going to do anything," I promised feebly. "You don't have to worry about me."

"Yeah. It doesn't mean I won't."

1. PANDORA'S BOX

Bonne Année!" Sara shouted through the phone. Music and voices exploded around her, making it difficult to hear her clearly. It could also have been that she was calling from Paris, and the reception wasn't the best.

"Happy New Year to you too," I replied loudly. "Although it's still last year here for another nine hours."

"Well, I'm telling you next year is looking pretty frickin' fabulous from where I'm standing! This party is insane. Designer drunks," she giggled, her own sobriety in question. "And I designed my own dress just for tonight."

"I'm sure it's impressive. I wish I could see it." I wondered if we really needed to keep yelling to be heard, but she didn't retreat to anywhere quieter. I sucked it up because I wanted to hear her voice, even in her current giggly mood. I hadn't heard it enough since she'd started the exchange program in France in the fall.

She'd spent last summer and every break during our freshman year in California with me. Knowing I was going to see her every few months almost made life bearable. So far, my sophomore year sucked. If it weren't for my roommates, I wouldn't do anything outside of soccer and school.

"You're not going to lock yourself in your room like you did last New Year's Eve, are you?"

"The door won't be *locked*, but I am staying in my room," I confirmed. "Where's Jean-Luc?"

"Getting us a bottle of champagne. I'm sending you a picture of my dress as soon as we hang up."

"Hey, Em—" Meg poked her head in my room, then noticed I was on the phone. "Sorry. Is that Sara?"

 I nodded.

"Hi, Sara!" Meg screamed.

"Hi, Meg!" Sara screamed in return.

"Umm, I think she heard you," I told Sara, wiggling a finger in my ringing ear, "but now I can't." Meg smiled.

"Well, I have to go," Sara yelled above a roar of laughter. "My man and champagne have arrived. I'll call you tomorrow. Love you, Em!"

"Bye, Sara," I replied. God, I missed her. I wasn't sure if she realized how much. It wasn't like I told her. But I did. I missed her…a lot.

"It sounds like she's having an incredible New Year," Meg remarked, sitting down on my bed. "I could hear the party all the way across the room."

"What time are you leaving?" I asked, knowing she was meeting up with some friends in San Francisco to celebrate.

"In an hour. We're all supposed to go out for dinner before the party."

My phone chimed, and an image of Sara filled my screen. She looked stunning, of course, in a shimmery dark green sleeveless dress that had a twenties flapper-girl flair, her shoulders dramatically exposed before it swept up into a high collar. Her wavy red hair was twisted back at the nape of her neck. She was puckering her shiny red lips, her eyes smoldering as Jean-Luc kissed her on the cheek while clutching a bottle of champagne.

I shared the picture with Meg. "Sexy. Did she design that dress?"

"Yup," I replied.

"That's incredible."

"Agreed."

I placed the phone on my desk next to my laptop as Meg asked, "Do you mind if I borrow your black boots?"

"Go for it." I turned back toward my screen to continue downloading the required reading for the next quarter. "They're in the box under my bed."

"You can still change your mind and come with me," Meg offered. I could hear the box sliding along the carpet.

"Thanks, but I'm all set," I told her. "I'm not really a New Year's fan." I tried to keep my tone flat, not allowing the reasons why to reflect in my voice. The last time I'd celebrated, the year had held promises of happiness and a future I wanted to be a part of. Now, it was just another page torn from the calendar.

"Em, I'm begging you one more time, please, please, please go with me tonight," Peyton groveled within my door frame. "I really don't want to go with Brook. You never go out with me and it's *New Year's*. Make an exception this *one* time!"

I spun around in my chair to decline for the thousandth time. Before I could utter a word, her eyes lit up, with her attention direction toward Meg. "Ooh, what's that?"

I followed her inquisitive expression as she walked into the room. Meg had just removed the cover to the box that was set on my bed. The *wrong* box. A vapor of memories and unfathomable heartache was released into the room as the box opened. I couldn't breathe.

Meg ripped the white T-shirt with the blue handprints out of Peyton's hands as she held it up.

"Stop it, Peyton!" Meg scolded. I remained paralyzed as she flaunted my past in front of me.

Still not doing a very good job fading. His voice flitted through my head, sending a chill down my back.

"I love this," Peyton admired, shaking out my pink sweater. "Can I have it?"

"No! Knock it off, Peyton!" Meg snatched the sweater and placed it back into the box. "Sorry, Em."

A rush of painful emotion coursed through me, forcing me to feel more than I had in the past year and a half. I couldn't utter a sound. It was as if I was being flayed, every nerve exposed.

Before Meg could slide the cover back over my past, Peyton removed a jewelry box.

You can't have it. Please, I'll pay you. But you can't take that from me.

The desperation echoed through me, and the memory of cold, hard eyes triggered a flash of panic, releasing me from my silent torture.

I sprang from the seat and grabbed the blue box from Peyton's hand. My sudden movement forced her to take a step back. I threw it in the box and slammed the cover back on. My heart was beating so fast my hands were shaking. I gripped the edge of the cover, waiting for the pain to subside. But it was too late. The simple act of opening that box had unleashed the wrath of guilt and despair I'd hidden within my darkest depths, and now it wasn't going to be confined by a lid.

"Sorry, Em," Peyton whispered. I didn't turn around. I slid the box under my bed and took a deep breath. My heart singed around the edges like a burning piece of paper, the flames slowly creeping toward the center. I closed my eyes and tried to extinguish it, but couldn't.

"I'm going for a run," I murmured, barely audible.

"Okay," Meg responded cautiously. Afraid of what she might see in my eyes, I didn't dare look at her as she ushered Peyton out of the room. "I'll see you when you get back."

I threw on running gear and was out the front door within minutes. With my iPod blaring music in my ears, I began to run.

Picking up the pace until my thighs burned, I cut down side streets until I reached the park. I stumbled to a stop, unable to fight back the onslaught of emotion. I clenched my trembling hands into tight fists and released a guttural cry, until I feared I'd collapse.

Without looking around to see whose attention I'd drawn, I took off into a sprint again.

By the time I returned home, my face was dripping with a mixture of tears and sweat. The exhaustion from the run had helped ease most of the fire, but I couldn't extinguish it all, as much as I tried. My insides still burned. I considered what I could do to push the torment back into the dark and return to my numb state. I couldn't do it on my own. I needed help. I was desperate.

"Peyton!" I called out from the bottom of the stairs. She turned down the music in her room and poked her head out.

"Hey, Em. What's up?"

"I'll go with you." I heaved, still trying to catch my breath.

"What?" she asked, unsure that she'd heard me correctly.

"I'll go to the party with you," I repeated more clearly, my breath beginning to even out.

"Yes!" she exclaimed. "I have the perfect tank top for you to wear too!"

"Great," I grumbled, heading toward the kitchen to get a drink of water.

"You have no idea how happy I am that you changed your mind," Peyton chirped when we stepped out of her red Mustang at the end of the car-lined street. Even from here, the music carried down the block.

"No problem," I replied absently. I needed to be distracted from the voices that were suddenly whipping around in my thoughts. I needed to find my way back to being numb.

"You cannot wear that sweatshirt," Peyton scolded before I could shut the car door.

"But it's cold out," I argued.

"Not where we're going. It's only a short walk to the house. Come on, Em. Suck it up."

I reluctantly removed the sweatshirt to reveal the glittery silver tank top beneath and shivered as I tossed it into the car.

"Much better," Peyton admired with a vibrant smile, joining me on the sidewalk and sliding her arm through mine. "Let's go party!"

Peyton strode alongside me in her strapless red dress, her golden blond hair lying in a glossy sheet down her back. Her greenish-blue eyes were lit with excitement as she escorted me toward the music that grew louder with each passing house. I was surprised the police hadn't show up yet. But when I looked around, I realized the party was surrounded by college housing. Most of the residents were probably away for winter break or at the party.

We approached the side of a beige house with a large white tent in the backyard. A couple of guys were handing out tiaras and top hats as we passed through the entrance. Peyton slid the tiara on her head and I took a top hat. A guy ladled red liquid out of a trash can and set the cup on a table in front of us.

Peyton's eyes widened when I took the cup. "You know that has alcohol in it, right?"

"Yes, I do," I replied casually, taking a sip. It was…sweet. It reminded me of an overly sugared fruit punch. This wasn't going to be as difficult as I thought. Why had my mother opted for the dreadful taste of straight vodka when this was an option?

"But you don't drink," Peyton countered in obvious shock.

"New year, trying new things," I explained dismissively, holding up my cup.

She grinned and tapped it. "To trying new things!" As Peyton took a sip, I opted to down the contents of my cup, needing the effects to kick in sooner rather than later. After all, it was the reason I was here.

"Em!" Peyton scolded. "I know it doesn't taste like it, but there's *a lot* of alcohol in there. You may want to pace yourself."

I shrugged and grabbed another before we entered the tent crammed with bodies. We made our way to the stage where a band was performing, drowning out any possibility of a conversation—which was fine by me.

"Hey!" Peyton hollered, recognizing a tall guy with wavy brown hair dressed in typical college plaid.

"I've been waiting for you," Plaid Guy replied.

"I told you I was coming," she returned playfully. She turned toward me and said, "Tom, this is Emma, the roommate you haven't met yet."

"Wow," Tom said. "I can't believe you're actually here."

I feigned a smile, wondering what Peyton had told him about me. I could only guess.

"And this is Cole," Tom said, directing my attention to the blond guy with broad shoulders standing next to him.

"Hi." Cole responded with a nod and slight smile. Peyton elbowed me. I ignored her and barely nodded in return, taking a sip out of my cup instead.

Insistent, Peyton grabbed Tom's arm and said, "I need another drink." Tom eyed her full cup in confusion, but let Peyton drag him away. I glared at her as she smirked back at me.

"Having a good time?" Cole yelled over the screeching coming from the stage. He didn't appear concerned about the forced pairing. I cupped my ear to indicate I couldn't hear him. Instead of repeating the question, he bent down and said, "I was beginning to wonder if you were real. I kept hearing about you, but I've never actually seen you out." I leaned back, not wanting to encourage him to get so close, and began scanning the crowd around us. "Don't say much, huh?"

I shook my head and took another large gulp of my drink to drown the inferno still burning beneath the surface. Why had I thought coming to this party was a good idea?

You're amazing.

What did I do?

Just you, everything about you—you're amazing,

My back straightened, the clarity of our voices invading my head. Images of the last New Year's party I'd attended threatened to surface, and I swallowed them down with another sip.

"Are you going to say anything at all?" Cole asked, pulling me out of the painful remembrance of being wrapped in Evan's arms while watching fireworks explode overhead.

"Huh?" I finally looked up at him. "What would you like me to say?" I challenged.

"Well, that was a start," he taunted, not fazed by my rudeness. "You go to Stanford?"

I nodded my head, then caught myself when he accusingly widened his eyes. "*Yes*," I stressed. "And you?"

"Yeah, I'm a junior," he answered.

"Sophomore," I responded, pointing to myself. I preempted the next predictable question: "Premed."

He appeared impressed. "Business." I nodded in return. "Do you play soccer with Peyton?"

I sighed, and took another gulp, not loving the mundane exchange. "Yup. Are you on a team?"

"No. I played lacrosse in high school, but nothing here."

I didn't come to the party for small talk or to get to know someone new. I needed to get away from this guy. And I really didn't care what he thought of me. I swallowed the last mouthful of the drink.

"I need another," I announced. "I'll see you around." I turned and walked away before he could respond, dodging through the crowd in search of the drink table. The band stopped to take a break, and a DJ started, igniting a movement of dancing energy toward the small stage.

I was still *feeling* too much. I'd never drank more than a couple of sips before, so I didn't know how long it would be before it took effect. I also had no idea how it would feel when it finally did. My mother turned to alcohol to numb her pain, and even though I swore that I'd never drink, there was only so much a person could endure before breaking that promise. And I didn't want to be in pain anymore.

I squeezed through the crowd toward the far side of the tent, where a table was lined with filled cups.

"Need a drink?" a voice asked close to my ear.

I turned to find a guy with a thin, muscular frame, a mop of black hair, and a dark line of facial hair down the center of his chin. From the tattoo behind his ear that crept down his neck and the few guys with similar attire of T-shirts and ripped jeans, I deduced that he was with the band.

"Are you talking to me?"

"Yeah," he replied with a cocky grin. "I'm Gev. I noticed your empty cup and thought I could help you out."

"Well, you don't have a cup at all, so maybe I should be helping *you* out."

He laughed, but I left him and kept walking toward the table. When I turned back I had two cups in my hands. He stopped short and smiled when I offered him one.

"I like your name. It's different."

"I'm attached to it," he said with a quick raise of his brows, making me roll my eyes with a low laugh.

"Are you going up again?" I asked, nodding toward the stage, deciding I might as well talk to *someone*, and he seemed interesting enough. At least he wasn't predictable.

"Nope. We're done for the night. And now I have some catching up to do." He downed the cup with several large gulps. I looked on, amused and handed him another, which he accepted with a flashy smile.

"What's your name?" he asked, moving away from the crowd forming in front of the table.

"Emma."

"How are you feeling?"

A minute ago I would have answered, *On fire*. But now I realized the fire was gone. In its place was a dull hum. A swirling calm ran through me, casting a veil of numbness over my senses.

"Calm," I answered with a deep breath, relieved that the jacked-up Kool-Aid had finally kicked in.

He laughed at my answer. "I've never heard that one before."

"You've never met me before."

"True. But I like that—I mean that you say what you're thinking. No bullshit. That's cool."

I shrugged.

"Well, here's to no bullshit," Gev raised his cup, and I tapped it with mine before we both took several large gulps.

"Do you go to—"

"No bullshit," I cut him off.

"Okay," he said, considering my request. "What color underwear do you have on?"

I was caught off guard by his forwardness. "I can't remember." I pulled my jeans by the belt loop to take a look. "Purple."

"Nice." He nodded in approval.

"And you?" I asked, liking this "no bullshit" conversation. It was more interesting than talking about majors and sports teams.

Gev was more daring, unbuttoning his pants to show the top of his boxer briefs. "Black."

"I can see that." I pursed my lips to keep from smiling.

I tipped my cup back and finished it, embracing the haze that continued to creep in.

Gev's hand slid along my back as he leaned in to ask, "Who are you kissing at midnight?"

"How much time do I have?" I inquired, not that it made a difference.

He looked at his watch and answered, "An hour."

"I guess whomever I'm closest to."

"Then I'd better stay next to you," he replied with an arching brow.

"Emma!" Peyton exclaimed. I turned toward her voice and squinted to focus as she neared me. "Where's Cole?"

"I don't know," I replied when I finally recognized her beside me. She looked from me to Gev and scrunched her eyes in confusion.

"Come over here," she demanded, grabbing my arm and dragging me away from him. I stumbled after her, not prepared for the sudden movement. "Who is that?"

"Gev. He's with the band," I answered and waved back at him. He raised his cup in return.

"What happened to Cole? He's hot."

"He's boring," I huffed. "Gev's much more interesting."

"How many drinks have you had?"

"Three." I grinned proudly at my accomplishment. "And I'm numb."

"Three?! Em, we've only been here an hour! You can't drink anything else, or you'll be on the ground before midnight. And I don't think Gev's a good fit for you."

"So?" I wasn't looking for a "good fit." I was just looking for someone interesting to talk to, or drink with. But I didn't want to waste my words trying to explain that to her.

"Omigod. You're already drunk."

I considered her accusation and smiled widely. I was numb from head to toe, except my lips felt tingly. I didn't mind being drunk. It wasn't what I expected, but it wasn't bad.

"Okay," I answered, accepting her assessment as true. "I'm going to find Gev now." I was done with the lecture. She wasn't being fun. I turned, and the quick motion made everything blur past me. I remained still for a moment to allow the world to settle back in place before searching for his dark hair among the faces.

"Fine. I'll find you at midnight," she called after me.

I felt a hand grab my arm, and I turned my heavy head to find his dark blue eyes. "Still next to you," he declared, clasping my hand.

"Tell me something interesting," I requested, taking the cup he offered me.

"I think *you* are the most interesting person I've met in a long time," he responded. He slipped his hand around my waist and leaned in to say, "Dance with me."

I was about to open my mouth to explain that I didn't dance, but the next thing I knew, we were squeezed in among the sweaty bodies and his hand was pressed against the small of my back, pulling me against him. I flopped my arms around his neck to steady myself and let him do all the dancing. He even danced for me, swaying my hips along with his.

Time moved fast, and the next thing I knew, I was yelling along with everyone else as this year ticked away into the next.

"Happy New Year!" we all chimed in unison. Gev turned me around and made certain he was the one closest to me. I allowed his wet lips to slide along mine, followed by the force of his tongue. My head buzzed louder when I closed my eyes, propping myself against him. He pulled me closer, making me stumble slightly. Gev gripped me tighter and continued to kiss me aggressively. I didn't stop him. I kept thinking about how strange it felt. I couldn't feel my lips, or maybe I couldn't feel *his* lips. Either way, it didn't seem like we were really kissing, and I was more focused on this than the fact that I was kissing at all.

"Wanna get out of here?" Gev offered, his breath tickling my neck. "I live a few houses down, and we have a hot tub."

A hot tub sounded good. Besides, I wanted to sit down. My legs weren't doing a good job holding me up.

"Sure," I replied, and he led me through the heat of the crowd and into the cool night. It must have warmed up after we'd arrived because I didn't need my sweatshirt anymore. He kept a hold of my hand and led me down the sidewalk.

I could've sworn he said he lived a few houses down, but I felt like I saw a million sidewalk cracks before we were finally in his backyard. But then I didn't remember seeing his front yard. Maybe his house really was close by. Either way, we were here, and I couldn't wait to sit down.

Gev uncovered a hot tub tucked next to a fence. As he turned on the jets, I studied it, trying to figure out how I was supposed to lift my leg over the side. It seemed so... tall.

Gev stripped down to the black boxer briefs I'd gotten a sneak peek of earlier. I followed his lead, dropping my jeans and tank top on the ground. I discovered I didn't have any shoes on, and I couldn't remember where I'd put them.

"I love purple," he declared, pulling me toward him and nuzzling his face into my neck. He was distracting me from solving the hot tub dilemma. I was about to push him away when I finally spotted the stairs. I smiled proudly.

He led me to the hot tub, and I slipped in, breathing a sigh of relief now that I was finally off my feet. I closed my eyes and leaned my head back. Everything started to spin.

I could feel Gev's hands on me and his mouth on my shoulder. I opened my eyes, and he was right there, eager for more kissing. I tilted my head toward him and connected with his greedy lips. I still couldn't feel them, but I couldn't feel anything anymore, so I didn't care.

Caught up in the kissing and the hot swirling water, everything suddenly ceased to exist. My head mimicked the motion of the water, and the steamy air closed in around me. Gev was there again, pushing up against me. I was too distracted to participate, trying to keep the world from spinning out from under me. That's when I felt the tightness in the back of my throat and knew I had to get out.

I pushed past him and staggered down the stairs, just in time to find the bushes and release the red contents of my stomach. The world spun faster, knocking me to my knees before I heaved again.

"Are you okay?" Gev asked from behind me. I shook my head, giving in one more time. I took a deep breath of cold air and pushed myself up to stand, leaning against the fence to steady myself.

"I need to lie down," I told him, not even knowing where he was.

He grabbed my hand, and I stumbled after him. Everything flashed by in a blur. I concentrated on keeping my feet under me as I tried to keep up with him. We were in a house; then I saw a door. The door opened, and a light revealed a bathroom.

"I'll get you shorts and a T-shirt to put on," he said and disappeared.

I gripped the edge of the sink and closed my eyes, trying to find center. The scales of calm had tipped to swirling chaos. And I had an awful taste in my mouth. I opened the cabinet above the sink and grabbed the toothpaste. Squeezing it along my finger, I scrubbed my tongue before rinsing my mouth with water.

Folded clothes appeared in front of me. I removed my wet bra and underwear and slid them on. The warm, dry T-shirt smelled good as I slid it over my head. Then Gev's hand found mine again, and I trailed after him into a dark room.

Gev stood before me in a pair of shorts. I leaned against him for balance, my hands pressed against his bare skin. He took this as an invitation and bent down to taste the toothpaste on my lips. His hands gripped my hips, and he kissed me hard. The numbness that I had so desperately wanted to possess me kept me from caring when his hands groped my back under the T-shirt. I didn't care when he thrust his tongue into my mouth. I didn't care when he ground his hardened body against me and groaned in my ear. And I didn't care when he slipped the T-shirt over my head and let me fall back onto his bed.

2. NO DO-OVERS

My head splintered into a thousand pieces as I slowly opened my eyes. I placed my hand against it to keep it steady while I propped myself up on my elbow.

Where was I?

The slightest movement intensified the lightning storm inside my skull. Glancing around the musty room, I tried to remember what I'd done and why I was here. There was someone lying next to me. I noted the dark hair on the unmoving form under the blue plaid comforter.

I tried harder to recall last night, but was only met with flashing images of the party—and a guy. It must have been *this* guy. I looked under the comforter. I didn't have any clothes on. My stomach churned as I sank back onto the flat pillow. I looked over at the nightstand and saw the torn package. I was about to be sick. What had I done?!

I lifted the blanket and examined his lean, naked body beneath it. A winding tattoo along his back finished behind his ear. Who was this guy? I knew he'd told me his name, and I searched through my broken memory to find it. Gev. That was it.

All I wanted was to leave and never see him again. But I didn't know where my clothes were. Flinching in agony, I crawled along the bed, trying not to disturb Gev, who was breathing heavily with his mouth open. It didn't look like anything would wake him.

I found a T-shirt and shorts on the floor and slipped them on. Moving gingerly, to keep the fit of axes from slicing through my head, I glanced around the small room. The full-size bed took up most of it. The walls were papered with rock posters, and clothes hung out of the half-open drawers of an abused bureau.

I opened the door leading to a small hallway, peeking out to listen. A hum of voices carried from a television, but otherwise it was quiet. Passing the bathroom, I suddenly stopped—recognizing my purple bra and underwear hanging on the doorknob. Unable to remember removing them, I sighed and shoved them under my arm before continuing down the hall.

A sprawled figure lay on the couch with the remote in his hand and a bag of chips spilled on the floor next to him as the morning news program aired on the television screen. I crept past him, flinching as the screen door squeaked and I entered the frigid morning air. The grass was coated with dew, chilling my bare feet as I stepped across the back lawn. My clothes caught my eye, lying next to a hot tub. I pulled my phone out of my jeans pocket before flinging them and the tank top over my arm.

Hugging my body to quell a shiver, I listened to it ring as I walked toward the sidewalk. Sitting on the edge of the front lawn, as if waiting for me, were my shoes. I blew out an exasperated breath as I hung them from my fingers and kept walking.

"Emma?" Peyton rasped, still half asleep. "I lost you. Where are you?"

"I don't know," I whispered, though my voice still sounded loud in the predawn quiet of the sleeping neighborhood. I began to notice clear plastic cups strewn along my path. "I think I'm near the party. Where are you?"

"On the couch," she muttered. She groaned and continued with, "Let me find my shoes and I'll meet you outside."

I spotted Peyton's red dress several houses down and continued to move slowly in her direction.

"Hey," I croaked when I finally reached her.

"Hey," she uttered in return. She plopped a top hat on my head and slid her tiara in place before wrapping her arm around mine. With her head on my shoulder, we drudged toward her Mustang, which felt about a million miles away.

I carefully lowered myself onto the passenger seat, trying not to jostle the few brain cells I had left while Peyton positioned herself on the driver's side. She slid on her oversize sunglasses and sighed in relief—even though it was barely light enough to see without headlights.

When we arrived home we crept silently up the stairs and closed our bedroom doors behind us. I stripped out of the T-shirt and shorts, not wanting them touching my skin a second longer, and tossed them in the trash before slipping on a pair of boxers and a tank top. I pulled the covers over my head and passed out.

"Emma?" Peyton beckoned softly. I was jarred slightly when she sat down next to me. "Are you alive?"

"No," I grumbled from under my blankets. "I was hoping for death." I pulled the blankets tighter around my head. "Drinking sucks."

Peyton chuckled. "The way you drank does. It's almost noon. Let's get breakfast. It will make you feel better."

"I don't believe you," I griped without moving. "I think a decapitation is the only thing that will make me feel better."

"Grease is a hangover miracle cure," she promised.

I peeked out from under the blankets. Peyton's hair was a tangled mess, and her puffy eyes were smeared with mascara. I could only imagine what I looked like. Glancing in the mirror above my dresser, I ran my fingers over the nest that was once my hair and wiped the black streaks under my bloodshot eyes. My mouth was pasty with the lingering taste of something putrid.

"Let me take a shower first," I conceded.

Peyton stood up and headed toward the door. "I need one too. I'll meet you downstairs when we're done."

I grabbed random clothes from my drawers and faltered blindly toward the bathroom, unable to open my eyes beyond a squint. I turned on the water until it was almost scalding and stood under the cleansing streams. The night was slowly coming back to me as the water pelted my skin, turning it red.

You're fucking disgusting. Carol's hateful voice rang through my head. With my eyes clenched tight, I forced her away and scrubbed harder.

I tried to scour away the feel of his hands on my body and the taste of his tongue in my mouth. When I turned off the water, I was still repulsed with myself.

After dressing in jeans and an oversize grey hoodie, I tucked my hair under a baseball hat and found Peyton slumped on the couch. She stood up, and just as we turned toward the door, Meg walked in. She looked tired, but not near death like we did.

Her eyes flipped from Peyton to me, and then back to Peyton.

"You got her drunk," Meg accused.

"She did that all on her own," Peyton countered. "We're getting breakfast. Wanna come?"

I lowered my head in avoidance. I could still feel Meg looking at me when she answered, "Sure."

"Good." Peyton held up her keys. "Then you can drive."

A line awaited us when we pulled into the parking lot of the local breakfast spot. The busy restaurant was occupied by a mosaic of pale faces, trying to piece together their New Year. Thankfully, the line progressed quickly, and we slid into a booth fifteen minutes later.

Meg studied me from across the booth and shook her head. "I can't believe you drank. I mean, you *never* drink. What happened?"

I shrugged and mumbled, "Pandora." As Meg's eyes dipped in sympathy, I redirected my attention out the window.

"What does music have to do with getting drunk?" Peyton questioned, not understanding my reference. "Do you mean the musician you hooked up with last night? Were you trying to be cryptic or something?"

"Wait. You slept with someone?!" Meg's voice rose, drawing the attention of a couple of guys walking by. I sunk into the booth, pulling my hat over my eyes when I heard them chuckle.

"Meg!" Peyton said sternly. "Why don't you just announce it to the whole diner?"

"Sorry," Meg grimaced. "But I—"

"I don't want to talk about it," I interrupted firmly. They both opened their mouths, and then closed them again. Our food arrived, thankfully, allowing us something to do other than dwell on my drunken indiscretion.

"Where did *you* end up, Peyton?" Meg interrogated.

"On Tom's couch," she stated. "*Alone.* He disappeared around three, and I couldn't find Emma, so I fell asleep on his couch."

Meg filled us in on her night as we ate our bacon and egg sandwiches—it wasn't nearly as eventful. And, as it turns out, grease really does have miraculous effects. At least my body felt one step closer to rejoining the human race when we left the diner.

My phone rang as we reached the front steps. I knew what was about to happen, and I wasn't ready. I took a deep breath and answered the phone anyway. "Hi, Sara."

"Happy New Year!" she bellowed. I winced and pulled the phone away from my ear.

"Not so loud," I begged.

"Uh, okay," she replied in confusion. "Wait. Did you go out last night?"

"Yeah," I answered softly. "But I'm not talking about it."

Sara was quiet for a moment. "Does Meg know?"

I sat down on the couch and rested the back of my head against the cushion. "Yes."

"Can I ask her about it?" she requested cautiously.

I paused and swallowed hard. "As long as you promise we'll never have to talk about it."

I could hear her thinking on the other end of the phone. "I promise." She hung up on me, and within thirty seconds Meg's phone rang. She shot a glance at me from the other end of the couch.

"Sara wants to know what happened to me last night, and I told her I wasn't talking about it."

"But I can tell her, right?" she confirmed.

"Not in front of me."

Meg stood and began to climb the stairs as she answered her phone. "Hi, Sara."

"I'm coming with you," Peyton called after her, taking two steps at a time. She was obviously feeling better.

I chased two aspirin with a Vitaminwater and remained on the couch, watching movies all afternoon.

I slunk away to my room in the early evening, leaving the girls with some horror movie that I really had no interest in. Sleep and I had taken way too long to finally find each other, and I didn't want to jeopardize that with a movie.

Someone knocked lightly on my door. "Come in," I answered.

Meg poked her head in. "Hey." She sat at the end of my bed. "Still feel like shit?"

"Tell me it goes away," I begged, my eyes closed.

"You'll be better tomorrow," she assured me. "Peyton told me how much you had to drink, or what she saw you drink anyway."

I remained silent. Then she finally said it. "I know you don't want to talk about it, and we won't. I promise to never bring it up again. But before you drown in shame, know that everyone makes mistakes. And as far as I'm concerned, Ev—"

"Don't," I shot out before she could finish his name.

"Sorry," she said, biting her lip. "I meant that it didn't count. It was a mistake, and it doesn't count."

I'd never told Meg about my life in Weslyn. I didn't explain why I almost never went out or why I refused to drink—or had, before last night. But I let Sara tell her when she came to visit after I'd moved into the house this past summer. She never mentioned what Sara had told her, but it helped her understand why I kept everyone at a distance. I trusted Meg.

I'd met her on the first day of soccer conditioning during our freshman year. She'd flown in from Pennsylvania, so we were both transplants. Meg accepted my withdrawn demeanor, and instinctively felt the urge to look out for me. This reminded me of Sara, and we bonded instantly.

Over the season, we found Peyton gravitating toward us. Truth be told, Peyton gravitated toward everyone. She was in your face and refused to be ignored. People either hated her or loved her, and she couldn't care less either way. I think her brazen attitude is what made me like having her around.

And then there was Serena. She was from California, as was Peyton, and she was currently spending winter break with her family. But when she was with us, she completed our mismatched quad perfectly. Serena was genuinely the kindest person I'd ever met, but it was laced with a straightforward attitude that could tell a priest where to go if he crossed her. I responded to her cutting-edge Goth lifestyle with equal measures of intrigue and respect.

As much as I was grateful for Peyton's and Serena's patience with me and acceptance of who I was (although Peyton did have moments of being a little too…well, Peyton), it was Meg who I trusted with the truth about a past that we'd never actually talked about. Meg became my voice of reason, vying to keep me sane. When I was tiptoeing along the edge, Meg was there to make sure I didn't fall over.

So when she told me that my one-night stand could be erased, I wanted to accept her assurance and swallow it whole, letting it salve the guilt like an antacid. But I knew there was no use in trying—everything had begun to crumble the moment she opened that box. My shameful encounter was just one more destructive choice I'd made that couldn't be undone.

3. NEW YEAR, NEW EXPERIENCES

Classes for the next quarter began the following week, allowing me to continue into the New Year consumed with books, lectures and studying. Everything seemed back to how it had always been. But it really wasn't the same, and I knew it.

Meg and I drove to school together. Since we were both angling for acceptance into the School of Medicine, we shared several classes, but while she was gearing toward the hospitals, I was seeking refuge in the labs.

Peyton flitted through the house as usual, not knocking when she entered the bathroom or bedrooms. She wasn't bothered by what she could be potentially walking in on—except with Serena, the only one of us with a boyfriend. Serena had little tolerance for Peyton's invasion of privacy—not to mention that Peyton annoyed the hell out of her.

"Okay, listen." Peyton approached me while I was in the kitchen making a sandwich before heading to the soccer field with Meg. "I know the party a few weeks ago was a bit of a disaster, but I think you should go out with me again. I promise to keep a better eye on you and help you gauge your level of drunkenness."

I laughed at her absurd proposal. "Peyton, the drinking was a onetime thing. I'm all set, thanks."

"Em," she implored passionately, "you had *one* bad night. It doesn't mean that you should give up your entire social life. We're in *college*. This is the time when we discover who we are…and flirt with our tolerance for alcohol. I swear to you, there is a way to have a few drinks and not end up in some random guy's bed."

I whipped around and threw a piece of bread at her. "Shut the fuck up, Peyton."

She deflected the bread to the floor. "Sorry. Really, that was stupid. I'm sorry," she groveled. "I shouldn't have said that." Before she walked away, she begged, "Will you at least *think* about it?"

"Fine," I responded impatiently, just wanting her to stop. "I'll think about it."

"Great! There's a party this Saturday," she chirped, and whipped around before I could object.

"You're going to that party at College Green?" Meg questioned as she rounded the corner, a soccer ball tucked under her arm.

"I'm not—"

"You're going too, right?" Peyton interjected before I could finish.

"I guess so." Meg shrugged, then looked to me. "Don't worry. We'll have fun."

I blew out a defeated breath. "Okay," I caved.

Peyton produced a triumphant smile, and proceeded to bang on Serena's door.

"What?!" Serena hollered from the other side.

"Are you going to the party with us on Saturday? Emma's coming too."

Serena poked her head out and raised her eyebrows in my direction. "You are?"

"I guess so."

"Okay. I'll go," she replied and slammed her door in Peyton's face.

———

"Please tell me that's not what you're wearing." Peyton scowled at my worn jeans and faded concert T-shirt over a long-sleeved shirt.

"You want me to go?"

She huffed before returning to the bathroom to finish her makeup while I went downstairs.

When I reached the bottom step, Serena walked through the front door with a paper bag in her arms, wearing formfitting black pants, a black tank top under a cropped leather jacket, and black combat boots. Her short black pixie hair flipped out stylishly around her powder-white face. Dramatic liner framed her large brown eyes. Serena's look was more than a style; it was a statement.

She returned from the kitchen with a beer in each hand and offered one to Meg, who was leaning over the coffee table, painting her nails.

"I'm driving," Meg told her with a shake of her head. Serena eyed me and held out the bottle.

"Umm, I can drive," I offered.

"That's okay," Meg said. "I don't mind. Go ahead if you want to drink. You're going with *us*, not just Peyton, so we'll watch out for you."

"Hey!" Peyton shouted down the stairs in offense.

I contemplated the bottle in Serena's hand carefully. The first time I drank had nothing to do with the alcohol. And I never wanted to be that drunk again…ever.

"Okay," I agreed, taking the bottle. Meg flipped her eyes to me in surprise. But she went back to painting, trying to appear unfazed by my decision.

Serena acted like we drank together all the time. But then again, Serena was pretty accepting of just about everyone and everything, taking all that came her way without blinking. I'd yet to witness anything that surprised her.

I took a sip and grimaced. Yeah, I didn't like beer. "This tastes horrible."

Serena grinned. "It's an acquired taste."

"Why would anyone want to acquire a taste for something that tastes like ass?" I scrunched my nose in disgust.

Serena laughed. "I'll make you a drink," she said before disappearing into the kitchen.

"I'll drink your beer," Peyton declared, appearing at the bottom of the stairs. Her shiny golden hair hung down her back, not a single strand out of place. She was very mindful of her appearance, intently assembling herself from her shiny pink lips to her polished toes. She'd never let anyone other than us see her less than picture-perfect. Just thinking about what she had to go through to keep this up exhausted me.

"You'll drink anything," Meg teased, twisting the top on the polish. "I think you've probably tried just about everything there is."

"Funny," Peyton sneered, tipping the bottle back into her mouth.

"Here, try this." Serena handed me a glass with red liquid in it. My stomach instinctively clenched. Noticing my cringe, she assured me, "It's cranberry and vodka. I made it pretty weak too."

I accepted the drink and took a sip. It tasted mostly of cranberry with a hint of something else. "Thanks."

While Meg finished getting ready in the upstairs bathroom, we sat in the living room—drinking. Something I quite honestly never thought I'd ever do.

Was I supposed to keep holding the glass, or set it on the coffee table? I watched Serena and opted to hold it. I took a *sip*, not wanting to drink too fast. I knew I was being paranoid; I just needed to relax already.

"So, where's James tonight?" I asked Serena, needing to distract myself from internally freaking out.

"He's working," Serena replied, finishing her beer and getting up. "Peyton, you ready for another?"

James was a bouncer at one of the clubs that showcased local rock talent. With his shaved head, his broad frame, and the tattoo on the back of his skull, he fit the persona. On the other hand, he was a dedicated student at Stanford, pursuing an education degree. The thought of James reshaping the minds of adolescents always made me smile.

"Sure," Peyton called.

I'd barely finished half the glass, and they were already on their second. Maybe I was drinking *too* slow. Or maybe I just needed to get a grip and stop obsessing.

"There's a great show coming up in a few weeks," Serena informed me. She handed Peyton another beer.

Serena was my direct line to the best shows in the area. I was thankful to have a roommate who understood my need for fast beats and heavy guitar. Meg and Peyton didn't appreciate the genre, preferring head-bopping or hip-swaying music, although I'd recently taken Meg to a few shows, with encouraging results.

"Let me know when, and I'll check if I have tests or anything due." I took another sip.

"Em, you spent all break reading the upcoming assignments for the next month," she accused. "You'll be fine regardless. It won't be a late night."

"Ready to go?" Meg announced, bounding down the stairs with her spiraling auburn curls bouncing around her. We finished off our drinks and followed her out the door.

It was obvious when we'd arrived at the party, because there was nowhere to park. After circling the block a few times, we were finally able to creep into a spot as another car pulled away. We followed a small group of people through a gated archway into a courtyard.

Meg nudged me playfully. "There's a pool."

"You wouldn't," Peyton threatened.

"Relax, Peyton," Meg snapped. "We wouldn't do that *here*." I smirked.

Two floors of apartments wrapped around an inner courtyard. People were mingling on the balconies and throughout the central area. A half dozen apartment doors were open to grant access, and a sound system was set up in the open space, blaring the most recent hip-hop music.

"We need drinks!" Peyton announced, raising her hands in the air and moving her hips to the beat.

We followed her form-fitting green sweater through the crowd. She turned heads as she wiggled by, but she was too focused on her mission to take notice.

We continued up the stairs and into the closest open door.

"Wait here," she instructed. "I'll get us something."

I didn't think we could squeeze in any farther if we tried; the room was packed. Peyton reappeared, her fingers dipped into small plastic cups of Jell-O. She handed one to each of us. I looked down at the cup, trying to figure out how to eat it without a spoon. Squeezing the edges, I tried to slurp it.

"Don't chew. Just swallow." Meg laughed as I licked at pieces of Jell-O still clinging to my lips.

"Always excellent advice." Peyton giggled.

Meg grimaced. "Eew. We're only talking about *Jell-O*, Peyton!"

It took me a moment to figure out what the hell they were talking about, and I scowled in revulsion when I figured it out. Peyton took note of my delayed reaction. "Oh, Emma. Are you sure you had sex with that guy from the band? 'Cause I swear you're a virgin."

"Let me get another round so you can try again," Meg offered, dragging Peyton with her.

When they returned, I took two little cups and awaited instructions.

"Swipe your finger around the edge to loosen it and then pop it in your mouth." Peyton demonstrated with ease. I made another attempt and got *most* of it in my mouth. My Jell-O shot ineptitude made Meg laugh. But I did better with the next one.

"Now you let it settle and wait for The Tickle before you drink anything else," Serena explained.

"A Tickle?" Peyton questioned Serena with her brows raised. "Serena, you are so weird."

"Whatever." Serena said, turning away.

"Tom!" Peyton suddenly hollered across the courtyard to the opposite balcony. To my surprise, he heard her and waved. She grabbed my wrist, causing me to stumble after her, though she didn't seem to notice, or care, as she forced our way through the crowd.

"We'll wait right here," Meg called out behind us.

"I was hoping you were going to be here," Peyton exclaimed when she reached Tom, giving him a hug.

"You'd know if you'd actually *call* each other," I mumbled under my breath. Tom and Peyton had a strange relationship. I kept hearing about him and how they'd meet up at parties. She was obviously interested in him. But we didn't think they'd even exchanged phone numbers yet. We were all confused by it.

"Hey."

I looked up to find Cole standing in front of me. Gritting my teeth, I forced a smile, suddenly realizing why Peyton had been so adamant about bringing me along.

"Wow, two parties. I'm impressed," Cole taunted.

"Parties aren't my thing," I countered in annoyance.

"Obviously," he stated. "Otherwise I would have seen you before."

"True," I admitted with a slight nod. "Well, it's a new year, so I'm trying new things."

"What's next on your list?" Cole inquired, his clear blue eyes focused on me. I avoided his gaze and studied the crowd around us.

"Umm…stage diving," I answered without thinking. I really didn't have a "new things" list. I was making it up as I went. But now that I'd said it, I actually wanted to try it.

"Nice. You'll have to let me know when so I can witness that."

"We'll see," I answered, not wanting to commit to seeing him again, no matter what he looked like. When he turned his head in the other direction, I slipped away. I heard Peyton call my name, but I ignored her.

When I squeezed my way to where we'd left Serena and Meg, they were nowhere to be found. I scanned the crowd and spotted them by the pool, then ducked into an apartment and grabbed something grape-flavored and bubbly. I could barely feel The Tickle, so I figured I was still safe.

Meg saw me at the top of the stairs and waved. I nodded and followed the line down the steps. When I reached the bottom, an arm swept around my waist and pulled me to the side.

"Hey, gorgeous," Gev murmured in my ear, kissing my neck. "I was hoping I'd see you again."

"Uh, hi," I stuttered, my entire body stiffening at his touch. I looked around in a panic, but I couldn't locate Meg or Serena. Then Meg's spirals came into view, and I connected with her. Her eyes flipped from me to Gev, and she pushed through faster, not caring that she was pissing people off.

"So, how are you?" I asked, my voice cracking slightly.

"Sober," he complained. "I'm going up to get a drink. Wanna come?"

"Emma!" Meg exclaimed, her bright smile not entirely masking the concern flashing in her eyes. "There you are. We thought we lost you." She noticed Gev's arm around my waist and the tightness in my shoulders as he squeezed me against him. "Hi. I'm Meg, and this is Serena." Serena just nodded and didn't even bother faking a smile.

"Gev," he responded. "Guess I'll find you later," he said, kissing my cheek before disappearing up the stairs. I tried to smile while swallowing the sour taste of disgust that rose in the back of my throat.

"Are you okay?" Meg asked, taking me by the hand and leading me away.

"Yeah, I'm fine," I responded meekly, taking large gulps of the purple stuff from the cup in my other hand.

"He's awesome looking," Serena noted from beside me. "Too bad he's a complete dick."

I laughed, almost spitting out my drink.

Meg smiled. "We won't let him near you," she promised, stopping near the pool.

"Hey!" Peyton exclaimed dramatically when she found us a few minutes later. "Em, why'd you take off like that *again*? Seriously, I think you should give Cole a chance."

"He's not my type."

"Wait, are you talking about the guy you've been trying to set her up with for like forever?" Meg clarified.

"Uh, I just met him at the New Year's party," I countered.

"But I've been wanting you to meet him for way longer." Peyton sighed. "I need an in with Tom, and they're never apart, so I figured you'd be a good fit for Cole."

"You obviously don't know me very well."

"Come on," Peyton said, sulking. "Cole is *everyone's* type." She eyed Serena in contemplation and corrected with, "Well…except for Serena. He's lacking the freak factor."

"Fuck you, Peyton," Serena bit back. Meg laughed at their banter. They were always throwing snide comments back and forth. I sometimes wondered if they liked each other at all.

"Seriously, Em," Peyton continued. "He's gorgeous. He's intelligent. He's a surfer."

"I don't go for the surfer type. Just drop it—okay?" I felt a sudden twist in my chest and swallowed the last of the grape alcoholic soda to be rid of it. "Um, I could use another drink. Anyone else?"

"I'll go with you," Serena offered, leading me toward another apartment. "She's just being selfish as usual," she consoled. "Don't let her force you."

"I'm fine," I said quietly.

I waited for Serena on the balcony while she got our drinks. I kept scanning the crowd around me, fearful of running into Gev again. She returned a few minutes later and handed me a red plastic cup.

"Jack and Coke," Serena explained.

I took a sip, and my stomach lit up. "Whoa." I shivered. "That's strong."

"Sorry," Serena grimaced. "I didn't make it. Do you hate it?"

"It's not my favorite," I admitted as my mouth filled with saliva, "but I'll drink it."

We noticed Peyton and Meg dancing in a crowd by the pool.

"Great," Serena grumbled and directed me to stand on the outskirts, where it was less crowded. I leaned against the rough exterior of the building, under the overhang of the balcony, slowly sipping the Jack with a touch of Coke. The Tickle was turning into a slightly dizzying haze.

"Someday we'll go to a party where there'll be music *we* can dance to," Serena promised. "This music is shit." I laughed.

Two guys came up behind Meg and Peyton, pressing up against them and putting their hands on the girls' hips. Peyton turned around with a flirtatious smile and swung her arms around the guy's neck. Meg scooted away from the other guy, and he eventually got the message and disappeared into the crowd. I grinned in amusement.

"I'm getting another drink," Serena announced. "Will you be okay here, or do you want to come with me?"

The party was now at capacity, and I didn't want to fight through the crowd. "I'll wait."

"Don't go anywhere," Serena stressed. I nodded and took another sip. She glanced back a few times on her way up the stairs, making me roll my eyes.

"I found you," Gev announced, appearing in front of me out of nowhere. He leaned in and pressed his lips to mine. I froze, not returning the kiss. He pulled back, confused. "Are you mad at me?"

"Uh, no," I responded, not expecting the question.

"Is it because I passed out on you last time?" he continued. "You know, before we could have sex. I promise not to drink that much tonight."

My breath stilled, and I stared at him. *We didn't have sex. Oh. Dear. God. We* didn't *have sex!*

"No, that's not it," I said, feeling my shoulders ease up. "I just think you got the wrong impression."

"Ah." Gev nodded in understanding. "You're not that into me."

"I'm not into *anyone*," I stressed, not wanting it to sound so harsh. "Don't take it personally."

"Not a problem." He shrugged. He really didn't take it personally—he honestly didn't seem to care at all. "Well, have fun, and if you ever need to relieve some of that tension, find me."

"Uh, will do," I responded flatly, watching him walk away.

"Oh shit, Em," Serena groaned. "I'm sorry! I totally forgot about Fuckhead. What happened?"

"We didn't have sex," I told her.

"Well…obviously," she replied. "I mean you're in the middle of a party." Then she examined me. "Oh! You meant…before?"

I nodded. I'd held on to the guilt so tightly, I was having difficulty letting it go. But I couldn't deny I felt a hell of a lot lighter learning it had never happened. Or maybe the Jack was starting to kick in. I spotted Meg still dancing along the pool's edge and smirked.

"Watch this," I said to Serena, dropping the empty cup on the concrete and shimmying my way toward Meg. Her back was toward me as I glided up behind her. Just as I was within reach, she turned toward me and smiled. Then she saw the devilish gleam in my eyes and her mouth opened in surprise as I pushed her over the edge of the pool. Just as I let out a triumphant laugh, she grabbed my wrist and we both crashed through the water's surface.

"This makes us even," Meg sputtered, blowing water from her lips and grabbing the pool's edge.

"For now," I jeered.

Everyone was looking at us, some in amusement, others in annoyance. When we dragged our wet bodies from the pool, we discovered Peyton glaring at us with her arms crossed. "Let's go," she snapped. "They're kicking us out."

"Why?" Meg laughed in confusion. "Because we were in the pool?"

Peyton released an exasperated sigh and stormed off toward the gate.

"I guess the building manager doesn't care about the parties," Serena explained with a smile, "but he doesn't want to put any extra effort into cleaning the pool, so no one's allowed in during the parties."

The crowd parted to let us pass, staring and snickering. When we made it to the sidewalk, we heard the announcement, "No one is allowed in the pool! If anyone else goes in, the party's over."

Meg and I started laughing.

"Well, you definitely made an impression," Serena said, laughing alongside us.

"I can't believe you did that," Peyton scolded. "You promised!"

"*Meg* promised," I countered. "Don't worry, we won't get your car wet. Do you still have the trash bags in your trunk?"

"Of course," Peyton said, annoyed. "I still can't believe you got us kicked out."

As we were peeling off our wet jeans and socks to place them in the trash bag, Serena announced, "So, good news! Emma never slept with the sleazebag!"

"What?!" Meg and Peyton shot out in unison.

"He passed out before it happened," I explained, averting my eyes.

"I don't understand," Peyton said, shaking her head. "How did you not *know*?"

I looked at her without understanding what she was asking.

"I mean, couldn't you feel that you didn't?" She sighed. "Wow, Em. You're seriously clueless."

"Peyton!" Meg reprimanded as we entered the car.

"I've only had sex once," I defended. "I had no idea I was supposed to be *sore* every time."

This made them all laugh. "Not...*sore*," Serena tried to explain. "But you definitely can tell when someone has trespassed."

"Serena!" Meg said, her mouth dropped open. "That sounds so...awful."

"I get it," I stated quietly, not wanting to reflect upon my first time any more than I wanted to think about what I'd *almost* done with Gev.

"Oh, by the way, Em—I gave Cole your number," Peyton announced. Everyone in the car was suddenly quiet.

"What the fuck, Peyton!"

4. BLIND LEAP

As my hands searched blindly under the bed for the shoe I'd been frantically trying to find, I caught a glimpse of a photo half hidden beneath my nightstand. I remained on my knees, staring at *his face*, unable to touch it.

I'd taken this picture. We were in the woods behind his house. I'd stolen his camera away from him and started to snap pictures of him. He'd always been the one behind the camera, so he was a reluctant subject. He chased after me, trying to get the camera back. The image was a black-and-white photo of his hand reaching for the camera. But I could see his eyes behind his outstretched fingers. They were grey and translucent on the paper; there was a shine to them, reflecting light. He was smiling. I didn't have to see the rest of his face to know that.

I love that picture. My heart squeezed tight as his voice whispered to me, reminding me of just how much I missed him.

I hadn't allowed myself to feel anything since I'd left him in that house. But now I was barraged with more emotion than I could handle. And I was finding it impossible to breathe.

"Emma, you ready to..." Serena's voice faded away.

I forced myself to exhale, to find the strength to look away from the image.

"Yeah." My voice cracked as I stood on unsteady legs. "I'm ready."

Serena studied my face when I turned toward her. Her eyes flicked to the picture on the floor, but she didn't say anything. I pushed out another breath and stilled the quake of my hands by clenching them into tight fists.

Shoving my foot in my shoe, I tied the laces hastily and said with a forced smile, "Let's go." The black hole of emptiness that had protected me all of this time refused to shroud me in its shadows like I needed it to. I couldn't shut everything off anymore.

The contemplative look in Serena's eyes disappeared with a blink. Her face lit up with a wide smile. "Okay, c'mon!"

When we arrived at the club, there was already a line of eager fans forming along the sidewalk.

"Hey, Guy," Serena greeted the bouncer with bright eyes. He stood without expression in front of the entrance, his muscles heaving beneath a shirt that looked like it was about to burst. He was primed for ass-kicking.

"Serena," he acknowledged and stepped to the side to allow us to enter. There were groans behind us as we slipped though the front doors.

Serena liked to arrive early to watch the last-minute bustling as the club prepared for the show. She also wanted to see James before he had to take his post in front of the stage.

He found us at our usual spot, seated on the crushed velvet couch on the second level. He sat between us and leaned into the crook of Serena's arm after he kissed her hello.

"James, will you let Emma stage dive tonight?" Serena asked, stroking his smooth-shaven head affectionately.

"You really want to stage dive?" he asked me with a skeptical crooked grin. "Girls usually get groped when they do that. It's not pretty. And then I may have to fuck the douchebags up."

"Maybe not then," I replied. Desperate to try anything that would allow me to breathe again, I hadn't considered the groping part of stage diving. I figured adrenaline was a better choice than alcohol. If I couldn't be numb, I could at least get my heart pumping to temporarily dull the pain. But having strangers fondle me didn't sound very appealing. I slumped back into the couch.

"What if she falls backward?" Serena suggested. I jerked my head up at this option.

"You can try. Not many people do that because they can't see who's going to catch them, and it's a trust issue. Your ass will definitely be grabbed no matter what. Why don't you crowd-surf so you don't have to fall?"

I considered it, but knew that wouldn't be the same. "I need to fall," I explained. "And I can live with the ass-grabbing."

James wrinkled his forehead in confusion. "Why do you want to do it?"

"Because I can't breathe," I stated flatly. Their eyes steadied on me.

James released a laugh, shaking his head. "I don't get you. Is that why you don't go out with guys, because you're…"

"James!" Serena scolded, smacking the back of his head with the palm of her hand.

"I didn't mean it like that," he said defensively. "She's just…different, that's all. It's not a bad thing." He turned toward me. "You know I think you're cool. But I still don't get you." Serena eyes tightened at his honesty.

"It's okay," I replied unaffected. "I don't get me either." James grinned.

"They're about to let in the masses," he reported, his hand covering his earpiece so he could hear better. "I need to go. I'll see you after the show." He kissed Serena and walked off toward his post.

"Are you really going to fall backward off the stage?" Serena questioned, her dark eyes scanning mine.

I looked away. "Yeah." My heart skipped a beat at the thought of it, countering the pain for a split second. I *needed* to do this, to feel something, anything else.

"Maybe we should do a few shots," she suggested. "That way if you hit the floor you won't feel it." She left and approached the bar along the side wall, talked to the girls attending it for a few minutes, and returned with two brimming shot glasses rimmed with sugar and two lemon wedges.

I hadn't *planned* on drinking. But in order to get up on that stage—

"To breathing!" Serena raised her shot glass to mine. My chest tightened with her words. I clicked her glass and threw back the shot, swallowing it as I'd seen done so many times in my life. I coughed in protest, and my body shuddered. The lemon did a little to cut the distinct vodka bite. My stomach ignited as the alcohol seeped into its walls.

"Didn't love that," I admitted, puckering my lips at the sourness of the lemon.

"It gets easier," she promised, smiling softly. I had a feeling she wasn't talking about the shot. "Let's find a good spot in front of the stage before it gets too crowded." She leapt up from the couch and pulled me after her.

Serena fed me a few more shots as we listened to the opening act. I kept thinking I was fine, that the alcohol wasn't really taking effect. But I honestly couldn't tell.

The headliner took the stage, and the crowd squeezed in around us. We jumped to each song, rocking our heads and pumping our fists in the air. Serena appeared with another shot. I was so lost in the music, I hadn't even noticed she'd disappeared.

"This is it, Em!" she yelled as she held up the shot. "It's now or never!" We tossed the liquid back easily—I seemed to have acquired a taste for it.

Serena shouted encouragements as I walked toward James. Without a hint of emotion, he nodded his head slightly, letting me know the stage was all mine. My heart thrust to life, and my body buzzed with nerves. He murmured "Good luck" just before I hopped onto the platform.

I shuffled to the center of the stage and saw a few people pointing at me out of the corner of my eye. Another bouncer from the opposite side started moving toward me, and I knew I didn't have much time. If I was going to do this, I had to do it fast. My breath quickened. I could feel the adrenaline pump through me until everything else was gone, and it was all I could feel.

I turned my back to the audience, hoping they had their arms outstretched behind me. The lead singer continued belting out the lyrics. I glanced at him as his eyes twitched curiously. I grinned at him ever so slightly…and I fell back.

My stomach opened up, and I let out an excited yell. Hands gripped, jostled and guided me across the crowd. Music bellowed around me. People hollered beneath me as I passed over them. The lights flew by in a blur of color. I rode along the turbulent sea of hands until I was gently lowered to my feet. I stood in the spot for a moment, orienting myself as faces flashed before me. The crowd rocked in unison, their energy gliding over my skin like a hot breeze.

I thrust my arm in the air, bellowing out the lyrics while jumping with the crowd. Serena burst through the bodies and screamed, "That was so fucking awesome!" We leapt side by side until we were drenched in sweat, and there was no more music to keep us on our feet.

We collapsed on our couch as everyone filed out. I had a permanent smile on my face, and all that pulsed through me was elation. The room swirled, and images shifted before my eyes. I blinked heavily, having a hard time holding my head steady.

"I'm going to find James and get us some water," Serena told me. I think I nodded. If I didn't, I meant to.

A moment later, the couch jostled beside me. I flopped my head to the side and found a lean guy with tightly trimmed deep auburn hair and a chin capped with a buzz of whiskers.

I smiled. Or maybe I hadn't stopped.

"Hi," he said, throwing his arm along the couch above my head. "I'm Aiden."

"Hey, Aiden," I greeted loudly. "I'm Emma."

"Emma, you shouldn't be sitting here all by yourself. You need to come to a party with me and my friends."

"I do?" I laughed.

"Yes, you do," he confirmed with a charming smile.

"I'm waiting for my friend," I explained. "I don't know where she is." I couldn't remember where Serena had disappeared to. The fog in my head was too thick to recall her words. "But then we'll go…with you…to the party." I smiled again—or I continued to.

"You're cute," he said, scooting in a little closer.

"You're not so bad yourself," my mouth said. He leaned over and thanked my mouth with a kiss, and I let him. I realized again that I couldn't feel his lips. Or maybe it was my lips I couldn't feel. I really needed to figure that out. I realized I was drunk. And I was okay with that too.

"Emma!"

Aiden pulled back. I was confused by his retreat, and when I opened my eyes, Serena was standing in front of me. She looked mad. Why was she mad?

"Serena!" I yelled enthusiastically. "There you are! This is Aiden. We're going to a party with him."

"Hi," he said.

"Uh, no we're not," she snipped. Wow. She was *really* mad. "Get lost, Aiden."

Aiden pushed up from the couch. "See you later, Emma." And then he disappeared.

"Where's he going?" I asked in confusion.

"Who cares," Serena muttered. "Let's go home, Emma."

"Are you mad at me, Serena?" I asked, my smile lost.

"No, Em," she sighed. "I just screwed up and fed you too many shots. You're drunk, and you need to go to bed."

"Yeah, I'm tired."

I felt dizzy on the ride home, so I kept my eyes shut, but everything kept spinning. I pressed my head against the window, begging for it to stop. And then we did.

"Em, we're home," Serena announced.

"Huh?" I tried to lift my head, but it was so heavy. I blinked my eyes open as Serena appeared next to me by the open door. I stumbled to the front porch, leaning into her. My feet were clumsy, almost as bad as my head.

"Help me," Serena said.

"I'm trying," I muttered.

"How did this happen?" Meg asked. Her arm slid around me.

"My fault," Serena said. I followed the stairs up to my room, but I wasn't sure if my legs were moving.

"There you go, Em," Meg said as I felt the pillow cradle my head.

"I fell off the stage," I told Meg, my tongue lazy and uncooperative.

"You did what?"

"She did a backward stage dive," Serena clarified.

My eyes wouldn't stay open, so I couldn't see Meg's reaction. There was a tornado in my brain that kept the room spinning beneath my lids. I groaned and flopped my arm over my eyes to try to keep myself pinned down.

"Just get some sleep," Meg said, pulling a blanket over me.

When I woke the next day, my head was trying to split itself in half. Serena was overly apologetic, claiming she'd been so nervous about my stage dive that she thought she was helping take the edge off with the shots. I couldn't connect the logic of how getting *me* drunk helped *her* nerves, but the knife plunged into my head distracted me from arguing the point. I vowed to never drink again...again.

5. NOT BORING

I felt a presence hovering above me as I bent over my Anatomy book with music blasting in my ears. I raised my head to find Cole standing across the communal table. I eyed him curiously, not expecting to see him standing across from me after I'd ditched him…twice.

I removed the earbuds without a word and looked at him in expectation.

"How's the list of new things coming along?" he whispered. "That was an impressive stage dive at The Grove a couple weeks ago."

"You were there?" I wasn't certain I liked that he'd witnessed the next thing on my list. The list that hadn't existed before I'd met him. "I didn't figure you for the type to like that kind of music."

"I'm pretty open to anything," he answered casually. "Can't always judge by appearances."

It was true. I *had* judged him the moment I saw him. "I'm surprised you're talking to me."

"Me too," he replied. "I didn't call you for a reason after Peyton gave me your number. A guy can only get blown off so many times before taking a hint."

"So, why are you talking to me now?"

"Maybe a part of me is convinced you're not a total bitch," he answered, his eyes crinkling wryly.

"Just most of me." My mouth quirked slightly.

"Well, I'll let you get back to studying. I think my time's about up." He adjusted the strap of his backpack on his shoulder and turned to leave.

"What's that supposed to mean?"

"Before you walk away—it's usually about now." He gave me a crooked smile.

"Nice," I smirked.

Cole strode away without another comment, or a good-bye. I found myself following the untucked white T-shirt that hugged the contours of his muscular back until he was out of sight. I shook off the distraction, replaced the earbuds, and dove back into studying the ventricles of the heart without giving him another thought. Mostly.

———

I was packing up my laptop to head to the library and finish typing my Sociology paper when my phone rang. I noted the California listing on the screen and was prepared for a wrong number.

"Hi. It's Cole."

My lips twitched in amusement. "I thought you weren't going to use my number," I teased.

"I decided to take a chance," he responded. "Not sure why, but I'm calling you anyway."

I released an offended laugh. "Well, maybe I should let you go then."

"Wait," he said quickly. "Don't hang up."

"I'm not much of a phone talker. And I'm on my way to the library."

"It's Saturday night." He sounded confused. "Why aren't you going out?"

"Despite my resolution to try new things, I really don't party much," I told him. "You just happened to be at every party and show I went to this year."

"Lucky me," he replied, making me scrunch my forehead and wonder why I hadn't hung up on him yet. "Meet me out."

"What?" I was stunned by the directness of his statement, like he was telling me versus asking. "Did you not hear the part about going to the library?"

"Meet me on your way," he proposed. "Fifteen minutes, that's it."

I drew in a deep breath while considering his request. "Okay."

"You're not going to blow me off, are you?" he asked bluntly. I stifled a laugh.

"No, I won't blow you off."

"I'm at Joe's."

He hung up. The abruptness of it left me staring at the *Call Ended* time flashing on my screen. Why had I agreed to this? Glancing at my image in the mirror, I shrugged, not bothering to make an effort before slipping my canvas flip-flops on my feet. I really wasn't concerned if this guy saw me without makeup and wearing a holey T-shirt and cargo pants. I zipped up my hoodie before heading toward the stairs.

Peyton peeked out of her room, her hair in hot curlers. "Where are you going?"

"To Joe's, then the library," I answered without looking back as I tromped down the stairs.

"Why are you going to Joe's?"

"To meet Cole," I hollered back before closing the door behind me.

It was past the dinner rush when I entered the sports bar, and way too early for the college drinkers. Various sizes of flat-screen TVs suspended at every angle broadcasted different athletic events to the virtually empty room. Cole was poised on a stool at the bar, watching a college basketball game on the large screen. I sat down next him without a word, my eyes on the TV.

"Wow, you're here," he gawked, shifting toward me.

"Fifteen minutes," I reminded him, inspiring the return of that crooked grin.

"Fair enough." He took a sip of the beer he had clasped between his hands, and I remained quiet, watching the game. "Oh, you're still going to make me do all the talking, huh?" he noted with a chuckle.

"I'll talk. But you'll probably be disappointed, because I don't have a lot to reveal."

"If you're too boring, I just won't call you again." One side of his mouth curled up when I raised my eyebrows in offense.

"I'm anything but boring," I retorted, focused on his clear blue eyes.

"I had a feeling," he murmured, not breaking the connection. I redirected my gaze back to the game, even though I had no idea who was playing and couldn't concentrate enough to figure out who was winning. I fidgeted on the stool and tried to contain the impulse to get up and walk out the door, knowing it was what I *should* do.

"So, have you thought about the next new thing to add to your list?"

"Um…" I cast my eyes toward the ceiling in thought and said the first thing that came into my head. "Skinny-dipping." Granted, I'd never had the desire to strip out of my clothes and swim before, but I hadn't done it yet—so I blurted it without considering whether I would.

"You don't have anything small on your list, do you? It's all or nothing?"

All in, huh?

A hot spear shot through my chest as his words echoed a voice from my past.

"That's the point," I responded calmly, despite the tension along my back.

Cole chuckled with a small shake of his head. Evidently he found me entertaining. "As long as you don't go skinny-dipping at a party—that would be a little too much."

"That's not my style."

"But jumping in the pool completely clothed is?"

"I wasn't supposed to get pulled in," I explained. "But I had a little too much to drink, and I wasn't fast enough when she grabbed me."

"So, you *were* pushing your roommate in?" he clarified. I nodded.

He laughed. "You're crazy."

"Yeah, I think am."

Cole held the amused expression on his face for a moment longer, and then he noticed that I wasn't joking. His eyebrows pulled together. "You're serious?" I shrugged in admission.

I stood from my stool. This seemed like the best time to make my exit—he was way too intrigued.

Cole looked at his watch. "Uh, we still have six minutes."

"Not anymore," I replied and headed toward the door with a committed stride. I thought I heard him let out an exasperated breath, or it could've been the air in my lungs that I'd been holding in since I sat down. I shouldn't have come here to begin with. I'd hoped I could convince him that I wasn't worth his time. Not even fifteen minutes of it.

"You promised fifteen minutes," he declared, jogging up next to me on the sidewalk.

"Wow, you're either the most stubbornly determined person I've ever met, or you love the abuse. Because I know it's not my charming personality."

The corner of his mouth lifted. "I think it's morbid curiosity, because no, you're not all that pleasant to be around."

I sighed in exasperation. "I don't understand you."

"What do you want to know?" he offered, seeming sincere. "I'll tell you anything."

I quickened my pace toward my car.

"Walk with me," he suggested. "For"—he glanced at his watch— "another four and a half minutes."

"Fine. I'll feed into your twisted curiosity and give you your four minutes," I said sharply. "Tell me something about you worth knowing."

"Worth knowing? Wow, that's pressure," he pondered. As I glanced at my watch he blurted out: "I surf."

"And that was more predictable than the sun rising every day," I scoffed. "Is there anything you do that most of the state doesn't?"

"Well, I'm not exactly adrenaline-driven like you," he countered. "I don't live my life in quest of the next adventure; sorry to disappoint."

He should have been pissed. He should have turned around and told me to fuck off. But he didn't. He was seriously considering my question. He stopped along the sidewalk, next to a house with an ill-fated garden.

"Umm…okay." He paused in contemplation. "I listen to silence." With this, he started walking again. I stared after him. At first I thought he was antagonizing me with his cryptic response, but then it struck me that he was serious. I caught up with him.

"I'm pretty good at it too. It might have something to do with having four sisters and never getting a word in. I became a sort of expert at listening to what no one said. I could tell when my older sister was fighting with her boyfriend, or when my younger sister was mad at my mother, or when my youngest sister was frustrated when she couldn't run as fast as she wanted to in track. I knew my parents were getting a divorce way before it happened, even though my sisters swear they had no idea." Cole stopped and turned to face me. "I listen to silence. And you"—his mouth pulled into a smirk—"you have a lot to say. Although I haven't quite figured out what it is yet."

My brow creased as I stared back into the depths of his eyes. I *didn't* have anything to say. I didn't want to be this puzzle he was trying to solve, or *listen* to.

"Time's up," I announced, starting back toward my car. Something stirred inside me, something I wasn't comfortable with.

Cole jogged to catch up. "I think we should hang out again," he concluded as he followed me down the sidewalk.

"You do? Why? Wasn't this disastrous enough?"

He just laughed in response.

"I promise not to delve into what makes your silence so loud, if you promise not to walk out on me."

I should have said no. I should have kept walking and let him go on with his life, without my interference. But I didn't.

I crossed my arms and released an impatient breath. "Fine. Let's see how interesting you really are."

He shook his head with a wry grin before replying. "You're not going to pressure me into coming up with something crazy to do. We'll just hang out—plain and simple."

"I will limit my expectations," I goaded.

He ignored my remark and said, "I won't be around much, since I have a big paper due next week. But how about after?"

"Maybe I'll see you at the library. I pretty much live there." I stopped walking, and he eyed me curiously. "Uh, I can make it to my car from here."

"Right. Time's up." He turned in the opposite direction and walked away without saying good-bye...again.

———

Cole didn't say anything when he pulled the chair away from the table and sat across from me in the library the next night. I looked over the top of my laptop as he began pulling books out of his backpack, then returned my attention to the screen and kept typing.

He didn't acknowledge me in any way, just concentrated on his work. This continued throughout the week. Each night I'd sit at the same table, and he'd sit across from me. I wouldn't have known he was there at all except that his hair was so shockingly blond that it would catch my eye as he bent over his books, taking notes. We didn't talk, or attempt conversation. When he was done, he'd close up his books and leave without saying a word—it was a little strange, but I dismissed it easily enough.

"Do you want to get something to eat?" he whispered across to me on Friday. I was calculating a Statistics problem and erasing—a lot. I hated Statistics.

Shocked to hear his voice, I glanced up into translucent blue eyes that awaited my answer.

"Are you hungry? I'm getting something to eat, and was asking if you'd like to come along."

"I'm not quite done. I need to stay a little longer." I bent over my notebook and figured he'd walk away like he usually did.

"How about tomorrow?" he persisted. I raised my eyes inquisitively, wary of his motives.

"I don't date."

"I wasn't asking you on a *date*," he clarified, his neck turning slightly red. "I was just asking you to get something to *eat*—you need to eat, right?"

"That I do." I deliberated. "But no, I don't want to get something to eat with you tomorrow."

"Are you trying to be cruel, or is it just me?"

"It's just you." I continued to work out the math equation in front of me.

When he remained silent, I looked up to find him watching me intently. His eyes narrowed in on me for a silent moment, as if trying to read whether I was sincerely messing with him. Then he stood up to walk away.

I let out a breath and said, "Fine. I'll meet you at The Alley at seven tomorrow night…for food."

"Yeah, just food." His annoying crooked smile now flustered me because I had no idea what it meant. I found myself looking after him as he walked around the corner. I couldn't be cruel enough to make him stay away, but I was certain that he should. I bowed my head and returned to the misery of my assignment.

6. A THOUSAND WORDS

My ears picked up the musical chime coming from my nightstand before my brain could understand what it was hearing. I hit the *Snooze* button, but the notes continued. I squinted an eye open to peer at the clock. It was after three in the morning. The chiming stopped, and I fell back into my pillow.

My phone started ringing again, insistent that I pick it up. I groaned and grappled with the device, pulling it in front of my face.

"Sara?" I grumbled, my voice still lost in the world of sleep.

"Emma!" she sobbed, her voice broken and full of pain. I bolted upright.

"Sara, what is it?" I demanded urgently, sitting in the dark of my room with my heart pounding. I tried to remain patient as I heard her strain to catch her breath. "Sara, please tell me."

"He's engaged!" she screamed in piercing agony. My entire body stilled. A moment passed, and all I could hear were her deafening cries.

"Who's engaged?" I whispered, knowing the answer.

"Jared," she whimpered. She collapsed into something that muffled her cries. I waited until she finally said, "I saw it…in the *Times…*"

And then there was nothing.

"Sara?" My phone displayed the lost connection message. "Shit." I dialed her back, only to hear the blaring of a busy signal. Frustrated and still confused, I pushed my blankets back, flipping on the bed-side lamp.

I tried to call her back again, but was blocked by the same bleeping signal. I scrambled to my desk and booted up my laptop.

I searched "Mathews" and "New York Times" and was directed to a link. The page opened to the engagement section of the *Times*, featuring a large black-and-white photo of Jared and a girl. I stared at the screen in disbelief.

It wasn't a professionally posed engagement photo. They were surrounded by formally dressed people at some kind of function. The photographer captured an image of them walking hand in hand. Jared was grinning slightly, while the girl next to him was simply glowing with a vibrant, open-mouthed laugh. Her dark eyes twin-kled, even in the colorless image. Her brown hair was swept up into a loose style, with elegant wisps framing her undeniably stunning face. She held a hand up, as if to cover her laugh, and there it was… the ring. A *huge* square diamond on her left hand.

I couldn't focus on the words announcing their engagement. I didn't care when they were getting married. I didn't even care what her name was. Sara's heart was being torn out of her chest in another country, without me there to console her. I called back again, and just as the phone started to ring, my eyes shifted. And I saw Evan.

He was in the background, within the crowd of partygoers. Most of his face was cut from the picture, though with the dis-tinct structure of his jaw and the sharp lines of his mouth, there was no denying it was him. I did, however, have a full view of the girl draped around his left arm. It was hard to forget the detest-ably smug grin of Catherine Jacobs, the same girl who'd practically thrown herself at him at the dinner we'd attended years ago at her parents' house. She looked very comfortable on his arm, like she thought she belonged there.

"Emma?" Sara answered. "Are you there?" But I could barely hear her.

My insides had fallen into a bottomless pit, and my throat had closed up.

"Emma?"

I dropped the phone and rushed to the bathroom, crashing the door against the wall, just in time to reach the toilet before expelling the contents of my stomach. I broke out into a cold sweat, gripping the rim of the seat tightly as my entire body convulsed.

"Emma?" Meg's soothing voice came from the open door of the bathroom. "Are you okay?" Then I heard her say, "She's here, Sara. But she's sick."

"No," I coughed, shaking my head. "No, I'm here." I dropped the tissue that I'd used to wipe my mouth into the toilet before closing the lid and flushing it. I flopped onto the floor with my back against the wall, my muscles trembling as if I were sitting outside in the middle of a snowstorm. "Let me talk to her." I reached out my unsteady hand.

Meg studied me for a moment, then stepped into the small bathroom and handed me her phone. She didn't leave when I put it to my ear, opting to sit on the edge of the bathtub.

"Sara?" I rasped, my throat raw. "I'm so sorry." I ran the back of my hand across my upper lip, clearing the ledge of sweat. I couldn't stop shaking. My shirt was damp, and my hair was plastered to my face like I'd just woken up from a nightmare. But I was very much awake.

"You saw," she whispered knowingly.

"Yeah," I returned quietly. "I wish I were there, with you."

"Me too," she whimpered. My eyes blurred. Hot tears streaked down my cold, clammy skin.

"But I'm here. I'm not going anywhere. Just close your eyes, and it will be like I'm right there next to you. We're facing each other, and I'm holding your hand. I'm there, Sara."

"I don't understand," she cried. "I don't understand why he didn't tell me. Why did I have to see it in the fucking newspaper?" She released a scream full of anger and pain. I remained silent. "He knew I'd see it. He knew how much it would kill me." Her voice cracked, and she broke into heart-crushing sobs. I closed my eyes, and tears continued to cascade down my face.

I'd almost forgotten Meg was in the bathroom with me until I felt her hand in mine. I laid my head on her shoulder and listened to Sara cry. My back ached from holding in my own sobs. But I couldn't do that to her. She needed me. I had to push away my pain so there was room enough for hers.

"Emma?" she whispered.

"I'm still here," I answered softly. "I just don't know what to say."

"You don't have to say anything," she replied, sniffling. "Stay on the phone with me, okay?"

"For as long as you need me," I promised.

"Emma," Meg beckoned to me, pulling back my thin veil of sleep. I blinked my eyes and realized I still had the phone to my ear, but it was quiet on the other end. I sat up from Meg's lap and stretched. My neck felt contorted and cramped.

"Sorry," I muttered.

"It's okay." Meg stretched her hands over her head and yawned. "I fell asleep too."

"What time is it?" I asked, slowly pushing myself off the bathroom floor.

"Almost seven," she groaned, standing too. I handed back her phone. "I'm going to bed. Em, will you be okay?" I blinked at her through bleary, bloodshot eyes.

"I'm fine," I answered automatically, not giving myself a second to consider otherwise. But I knew I wasn't. The acrid reminder still burned the back of my throat. After dragging my feet to the bedroom, I picked up my phone from the floor and sent Sara a text to call me whenever she needed. Then I climbed into my bed, pulled the blanket over me, and shut everything out until I was forced to face it again.

I picked up the phone on the first ring a couple hours later. Before I could ask how she was, she hollered, "He keeps calling me! What the fuck?!"

"Did you talk to him?" I asked cautiously, struck by the venom in her tone.

"Hell no! He can't call me the day the announcement hits the papers and expect me to listen to an explanation. Fuck that! I'm so pissed, Emma. So, so pissed!"

"I can hear that," I noted sympathetically. "And I understand."

She continued as if I hadn't spoken. I knew there weren't any words to console her. She just needed me to listen, and that's what I did, as helpless as that made me feel.

"She's some fucking socialite from New York. I don't even think she went to college. How pathetic is that? What the fuck can he possibly see in her? I mean, she is, I guess, attractive or whatever, but what the hell? She has a jewelry line that she puts her name on and claims to be a *designer*. Yeah, right. I can't fucking believe that's who he's marrying! What the—"

Her voice broke off, indicating she was receiving another call.

"Do you need to get that?" I offered gently.

She hesitated. "Omigod! He's fucking calling *again*. I need to block his calls and e-mails, so I gotta go. I'll call you later." And then she was gone.

Her raging fit, coupled with my role as the mute bystander, left me exhausted. I wanted her to feel better. To go back to the exuberant, energetic person I loved like a sister. Sara was stronger than I was, so I had hope that she'd recover from this. But wanting something didn't always make it happen.

Every choice had a consequence. I'd earned every aching beat that pounded in my chest.

Emma!

The sound of him calling me, lying battered and abandoned on the floor of my mother's house, echoed within me. I was the only one to blame for my desolation.

I looked down at my hands and flexed them. They still trembled ever so slightly. I closed my eyes, and the tears were there waiting, dammed by my lids. I clenched my teeth and breathed in quick bursts, demanding the numbness to return.

"Em, we're going for a run," Serena announced, poking her head in the door. I opened my glassy eyes. Without reacting to my tortured expression, she calmly directed me, "Get dressed and come with us."

I didn't argue, knowing the run would be more therapeutic than sleep.

Meg was in the hall, tying her running shoes, when I exited my room.

"Hey," she greeted with a comforting smile. "Get any sleep?"

"Some," I responded. She didn't mention the picture from the *Times*, which was no longer on my computer screen. I knew she'd closed it. Just like I knew that either she or Serena had picked up the photo that was missing from under my nightstand. I wasn't oblivious to their protective gestures, even if we never talked about them.

"How's Sara?" she asked.

"Lethal. Jared better hope he never bumps into her."

Meg smiled, probably picturing Sara in all her vengeance.

"Ready?" Peyton bounced out of her room, her blond hair swinging in a ponytail.

"Yeah," Meg and I answered in unison, following her as she hopped down the stairs.

Serena and Meg were quiet during our run. I wondered if Meg had told Serena what happened, but I wasn't about to ask. Peyton remained oblivious to the strained silence. She proceeded to recap the fraternity party she'd attended the night before, with detailed descriptions of how each room was decorated in a different book theme, with corresponding drinks.

"I think I drank every book." She laughed. "I mean drink."

"Shocking," Serena scoffed. Peyton ignored her.

"When are you going out with Cole?" Peyton interrogated, jogging faster to catch up with my pace.

"What?" Her voice was droning in my head like a rhythmic buzz.

"What's going on between you two? I never got to ask you, what happened when you met him at Joe's?"

"Umm…nothing really," I said evasively. "It was…nothing."

"Are you going to see him again?" she pushed.

"I…uh…"

I couldn't form a sentence, forget about a thought. I was concentrating on not collapsing and bursting into flames right there on the sidewalk.

"Are *you* ever going out with Tom?" Meg intercepted. "I mean, you two have been flirting for forever. Does he even have your phone number?"

"*Yes*," Peyton snapped. "He has my phone number. We're just… taking our time."

I lengthened my stride and left them behind, pushing myself around the next corner until I was sprinting, needing to extinguish the inferno before it consumed the limited air I had left. Serena remained right behind me, her face set and determined.

This only drove me to push harder toward the house, now in sight. My thighs screamed and my lungs burned. I let up and slowed to a walk after passing our front steps. Serena was hunched over with her hands on her thighs, sweat dripping down her flushed face.

"Fuck, Em," she panted. "That was intense."

I continued to walk around, taking long breaths, waiting for my heart rate to come down and the calm to take over. I closed my lids; the flames still danced beneath them, relentless, leaving me out of breath.

"Serena?" I said, frantic for relief.

"Yeah?" She sat on the bottom step with her elbows propped on the step behind her.

"Will you do something with me?"

She stood up. "Anything."

"Will you go with me to get a tattoo?"

"Today?" she asked, her eyes scrunching ever so slightly to inspect the smooth expression on my face.

"Yeah," I replied calmly. I knew what I asked her was drastic, but I figured if anyone would understand, she would.

"Definitely." She smiled brightly. "I would love to be there for your first tattoo. Maybe I'll add one to my collection."

"Thanks."

After we'd showered and changed, Serena and I left for the tattoo parlor without saying anything to Peyton or Meg.

"What are you going to get?" she asked, the excitement dancing in her dark eyes. Her enthusiasm to be a part of this was exactly why I needed her to go with me.

I pulled the paper out of my pocket and handed her a drawing I'd created about a year ago, when I was still fighting with the nightmares. I hadn't sketched it with thoughts of having it permanently inked on my body, but it seemed appropriate.

"Wow," she admired. "You drew this?" I nodded. "I didn't know you could draw. This is amazing, Em. But with all that delicate script, it's going to take a while. Spider would be the best to do this. Where are you going to get it?"

"Here." I gestured to my left side, above my hip.

She cringed. "That's going to hurt like hell."

That's what I was hoping.

I never made it to The Alley to meet Cole. I probably should have called him, but I didn't. And he didn't call me either.

7. WORLDS COLLIDE

ow are you feeling today?" I asked Sara a week after our meltdown.

When Sara ended her relationship with Jared the summer before she left for Paris, I knew she'd never expected him to move on, at least not like this.

"Fuck him. He and his little skank can go to hell. I don't care anymore."

"Um, okay." I'd spoken to Sara every day since she'd discovered the announcement. She'd explored every range of emotion during that time, and this bitterness was the closest she was going to come to acceptance. I knew she didn't want to talk about it. I could respect that.

"So Jean-Luc and I are going to Italy next week for break," Sara revealed excitedly, as if we'd previously been discussing the weather.

"Oh, okay," I responded, adjusting to the sudden change of conversation.

"His friends have a place right on the water in this small village in southern Italy," she continued. "I can't wait. I need to get away from the city for a while. Doesn't your quarter end in a couple of weeks? What are you doing during the break?"

"Uh, nothing."

"Are the girls going away?" Sara inquired.

"Yeah, I think so," I tried to recall. "Serena's going to Florida with her sister. Meg just started dating some guy a few weeks ago, and he's taking her to Tahoe. And I'm not sure what Peyton's doing, but she's going somewhere."

"So, you'll be by yourself?" she confirmed.

"Yeah."

"Are you going to be okay?" I knew she worried about me. And I knew she and Meg talked about me more than they led me to believe.

"I'll be fine," I responded without conviction.

———

The week of final exams for winter quarter, Peyton let herself into my room and plopped down on my bed to announce, "You're going with me to Santa Barbara during break."

"Excuse me?" I spun around in my chair. "Why am I going with you to Santa Barbara?"

"Because I don't want to stay in my aunt and uncle's place alone, and you don't have plans, so you're coming with me."

"You're not asking me?" I clarified, recognizing that it had all been discussed and decided.

"Nope. We're leaving after your last exam on Thursday." With that, Peyton bounced off my bed and left my room. I stared after her with a baffled look on my face. This had to be Sara's doing.

———

"Have so much fun!" Meg gave me a hug before I ducked into the car.

"And don't let Peyton drive you crazy," Serena added with a taunting grin.

"Screw you, Serena," Peyton shot back, her voice overly sweet but laced with a bite. "Don't scare the little old ladies in Florida," she sang before rolling up the window. Her smile beamed when Serena flipped her off.

"You two kill me," I laughed with a shake of my head.

"Whatever," Peyton stated, driving away.

I plugged in my iPhone and started scrolling through my music selection, finally settling on a playlist that I considered a compromise. Peyton and I preferred music at opposite ends of the spectrum. She didn't complain, so I assumed she approved.

"I know this isn't the wildest spring break spot, but I'm hoping we can find some decent parties," she said as she pulled onto the highway. "Especially if it's too cold to lay out on the beach."

"I'm sure you'll find something to do."

"No...*we* will find something to do. Don't think you're getting out of partying that easily."

I saw it coming. I knew she was going to expect me to go out with her. I sighed. A moment later, I asked, "How do you do it?"

"Do what?" she responded, obviously having no idea what was in my head.

"Party like you do, play soccer and still maintain your grades. I mean, you're prelaw. You have to be doing well."

Peyton chuckled. "Emma, just because you don't see me study, doesn't mean I don't. You're usually at the library anyway. I don't have a perfect grade point like you, but I have no doubt I'll get into law school. And it's called *balance*. Ever heard of it?"

"I may have heard of it."

"Seriously, Em, I would die if I didn't let off some steam during the weekends. I mean, soccer is what I do to help me stay focused, and we don't get to go out *ever* during the season. School is a necessity to get what I want in life. So when I actually have free time, I want to have fun. You don't have to get wasted and be ridiculous. This is college. I know I keep saying that to you. But when else will we get away with this? It's the only time in our lives we aren't judged for fucking up. It's expected."

"I think I have the fucking-up part perfected."

Peyton laughed. "Give me a chance, and I'll show you a side to college life you haven't seen yet. I know there's a part of you that's actually fun."

"Wow," I replied, feigning offense. "I've always wondered why we're friends."

"Because you can actually be pretty entertaining when you aren't being miserable."

"That was rhetorical, Peyton. But thanks." I shook my head at her unfiltered honesty. A moment later I conceded, "Fine. You have a week." I should have felt anxious agreeing to be a pawn in Peyton's "balanced" world. She was more dedicated to it than Sara had been. But then again, that was in high school, and Sara had limitations called parents. So maybe it was time I had some fun. I didn't want to be miserable anymore.

———

"We're going to a party tomorrow night," Peyton declared the next morning, before I'd even had a chance to have breakfast.

"Wow. That was fast," I noted, searching the cabinets for a cereal bowl.

"Tom told me about this party that's happening down the street from him," she continued. "I guess these guys throw the best parties, and the family's loaded, so sometimes hundreds of people show up."

"Tom?" I questioned. "I didn't know he was going to be here."

"He got here his morning," she answered casually, ignoring the edge to my voice. "We're going to dinner tonight. It's our first official date."

I ground my teeth, trying not to show I was bothered by this revelation. "Where is he staying?"

"In Santa Barbara," she answered, pulling a box of cereal out of the cabinet. "When the fog burns off, I want to get some sun. I don't care if it's a little cold. I cannot go back to school without any color."

We were staying in Carpinteria, a beachfront town about fifteen minutes south of Santa Barbara. Peyton's aunt and uncle had a quaint three-bedroom house two blocks from the state beach.

"Whatever." Being agitated with Peyton was pointless, and too exhausting. I now knew that Tom was her motive for being here. I'd been dragged along as an obligation, but I wasn't about to be the third wheel. I'd much rather sit around, look at the ocean, and read for a week.

And that's exactly what I did when Peyton left for her date later that night. We'd braved the chilly temperatures on the beach for the afternoon and surprisingly walked away with pink cheeks and tan lines. Peyton was dedicated to sun worshipping, while I was fidgety, needing to get up and walk around every once in a while. Staying still for too long made the voices in my head restless, and that was the last thing I needed this week.

I received a text from Peyton around midnight. Going to spend tonight at Tom's. See you tomorrow!

They'd been flirting for forever, so I wasn't surprised they'd hit it off on the "first date." But I *was* surprised that she was already moving in. I had a feeling that was the last I was going to see of her for a while.

———

At beach w Tom. See you at party later. Use my car. WEAR A DRESS! was the text I woke up to.

I don't own a DRESS! I responded.

I have plenty. Wear what you want. YOU WILL BE AT THIS PARTY OR I WILL FIND YOU!!

It looked like I was going to the party after all, but…I was *not* wearing a dress. Peyton texted me the address and then disappeared for the day. I flipped through her closet, only to find formfitting or barely-covering-my-butt dresses. Since I'd vowed to *try* to have a good time, I decided to drive to Santa Barbara to search the local shops for something that I could actually wear.

I inspected the reflection of the girl in the full-length mirror. The white capris with the colorful embroidered halter top were fun and summery, even though it was not technically summer. The outfit highlighted the color I'd picked up the past two days on the beach. I liked it.

Liner accented the almond shape of my eyes, which were dusted with a soft neutral shimmer. I applied a layer of gloss on my lips and grinned at the feminine girl in the mirror. A complete contrast to the one who typically wore T-shirts and jeans and refused to mess with makeup. Pleased with myself, I grabbed my light-blue cardigan, scooped up the keys to the Mustang and headed out the door.

I'd spent the entire day mentally preparing for this. These people didn't know me. I could be a fun, outgoing girl, and maybe even talk to people. I could fake it for just one night. What did I have to lose?

I parked along the car-lined street and looked at myself one more time in the mirror above the visor. I connected with the brown eyes looking back at me. "Okay, Em. You *can* do this. You're going to have a good time. Deep breath." I flipped up the visor and inhaled, filling my lungs, and then exhaled quickly. I got out of the car and started walking toward the music with the droves of other partygoers, shifting my shoulders back, trying to appear confident—like I did this all the time. On the inside, my heart was pounding frantically, and I was afraid I might start sweating.

As I neared the door, a group of girls stood in front of me on the sidewalk. I slipped in behind them, smiling like whatever they were saying was funny. They gawked at the large home. But I was unfazed by its grandeur, having seen similar houses where I grew up in Connecticut.

There was way too much giggling within this group of girls. I wasn't *that* good at faking it. So I headed downstairs while they continued into the open great room, their necks twisted awkwardly to take in the epic scale of the space.

I followed the hallway past several closed doors until I entered a game room. It had the essentials all wealthy families seemed to have—pool table, foosball, large flat-screen TV suspended on the wall with an assortment of gaming equipment beneath. I went out the sliding glass doors and stepped out onto a patio that was crowded with even more people. Upbeat music echoed from speakers set around the pool, tiki torches blazed along the perimeter and I caught a glimpse of a bar on the other side of the patio.

I eyed the plastic-cup-carrying multitude of scantily dressed girls—skin on display despite the chilly night—trying to locate Peyton amongst the blondes. But this was California, so that was a daunting task.

I pulled out my phone to text her but couldn't send; the estate, carved into the hills with the ocean in the distance below, apparently had made my cell signal sketchy.

Instead of searching for the right spot to send the text, I headed toward the bar in hopes of spotting Peyton. A guy in a multicolored tropical shirt stood behind it. He paused a second after handing a beer bottle to the guy in front of me. I stepped up to the bar and looked behind me, confused by the recognition that flashed across his face. When I turned back toward him, he produced a charming smile and asked, "What can I get you?"

"Vodka with something," I requested. Not expert enough to know what I liked, I decided to fall back on my mother's liquor of choice.

"I can do that." He began scooping ice from a bucket. "Who do you know here?"

"No one," I answered, fidgeting awkwardly. He kept looking at me with this ridiculous grin, like he knew an inside joke that I wasn't privy to. "I'm supposed to meet a friend, but I haven't seen her yet."

"Well, I'm Brent," he stated, holding out his hand for me to shake. "This is my friend's place. I'm staying here with him and a few other guys for the weekend." He handed me the drink.

"I'm Emma. And now I know *you*. So if anyone asks, I'll tell them that you and I are friends."

"We *are* friends," he replied adamantly, as if this was a known truth. I wrinkled my brow at his peculiar answer.

"I think I'm going to go find my *other* friend," I told him, glancing around the pool. I took a sip of the clear bubbly drink with a lime floating in it. It didn't taste bad. I turned back toward Brent and asked, "What am I drinking?"

"Vodka soda. I kept it simple," he answered while preparing a drink for a girl leaning against the bar. "I didn't figure you for the supersweet girly-drink kind of girl."

"Good call," I noted with a small laugh.

"I *will* talk to you later. I'm not at the bar all night. We need to catch up, since I haven't seen you in…ever," he stated with a gleaming smile. I nodded and couldn't help but smile in return before walking toward the stairs.

"Emma!" I heard my name above the noise as I was midway up the steps. I tried to turn around, but was forced to keep moving up, caught in the line of people going into the house. I looked over the railing and spotted Peyton waving frantically below. "I'll come up!"

I moved to the corner of the large upper deck to wait for her. "How long have you been here?" she asked when she finally made it to the top of the stairs.

"Not long," I told her. "This party is pretty huge." The crowd continued to grow around the pool, and inside it was packed with people dancing.

"I know, right?" she responded. "You look amazing." I smiled uncomfortably. "But…that's not a dress."

"I don't wear dresses," I told her. "Where's Tom?"

"Getting us drinks." She nodded toward the bar on the patio, but it was difficult to spot him from the aerial view. However, she seemed to know exactly where he was. Her gaze lingered, and her lips drew up dreamily.

"I take it you had a great date."

"You have no idea," she gushed. Then she waved, and I saw him nod his head in our direction.

Tom handed Peyton a drink when he joined us and slid his arm around her shoulder. Peyton nestled into him, her arm snug around his waist. I tried to act casual, but the amorous energy they were emitting was making me uncomfortable.

"So…Tom, I heard you're staying in Santa Barbara," I finally said, feeling like I should say something to distract from the awkwardness.

His eyes twitched slightly, and he looked down at Peyton. I heard her mumble, "I didn't tell her." I stared at Peyton, silently demanding her to spill whatever she was keeping from me.

"Yeah," Tom answered hesitantly. "The place is right down the street from here. The house isn't very big, but it's right on the beach. It's pretty sweet."

"Great," I forced, still watching Peyton, who refused to look at me.

Then I heard, "You've got to be fucking kidding me." I looked past Tom, and there stood Cole, staring at me in disbelief. *Shit.*

I couldn't speak. My eyes shifted from Cole to Peyton, who still refused to look at me. I downed the last gulp in my cup and announced, "I think I need another drink," quickly slipping into the house. After navigating my way through gyrating hips and flinging hair, I arrived at a bar on the far side of the cleared-out living room.

The bartender at this bar wore a blue tropical shirt. His brown hair was full of dreads and pulled back into a low ponytail. He scanned me casually, and his mouth tightened into a subtle smile. I was beginning to wonder if I had something stuck to my face. "Can I get you a drink?" he offered. I requested the same concoction that Brent had prepared; then he asked the question of the night: "Who do you know here?"

"Brent," I answered automatically.

"Really?" He handed me the drink.

"Yeah, we're friends," I continued, the side of my mouth quirking up slightly.

"You do look familiar," he noted with a deliberating nod. I thought he was playing along, but he really looked like he knew me, which threw me off.

"What's your name?"

"Ren," he told me, continuing to examine me, probably mentally rolling through the list of Brent's friends, searching for my face.

"You do know me, don't you?" I teased, hoping to confuse him more.

"I do actually," he said sincerely. Before he could continue, an overly excited group of girls approached the bar, demanding shots. I slipped out of the way, through the crowd and onto the deck.

I considered avoiding Cole all night, but knew the universe was just too cruel and we were going to keep bumping into each other if I tried to stay away. So I thought if I approached him, he'd leave and I could resume faking my good time. I stood next to him as he leaned against the railing, looking out at the ocean in the distance. He refused to acknowledge me, but he didn't leave either.

"I haven't gone skinny-dipping yet," I announced, leaning my forearms against the rail next to him.

"You'd better get to it," he snapped, still not looking at me. "The year's slipping away." He gripped the cup tightly in his hand, as if he were about to crush it. I considered walking away. And I probably should have. But I didn't.

"It's not even April," I contradicted. He shrugged. We stood in silence for a moment. I sipped my drink and waited. And then...

"What the hell, Emma! Why are you even talking to me? You obviously don't give a shit. So why don't you go torture someone else and make him feel like a jackass."

His angry rush of words startled me, and I swallowed each one whole, letting them sink like rocks in my stomach. I deserved every one of them. So I accepted his ire without blinking.

"Do you want a drink?" I offered. "The bartender by the pool is a friend of mine. He makes a mean vodka soda."

Cole stared at me in disbelief. "I don't understand you." He shook his head, still staring. After a moment of silence he caved. "Yeah. I'll get a drink. God knows I'm going to need one with you around."

"I'll take that as a twisted compliment." I smirked and led the way down the stairs.

The bar by the pool had a new guy attending it. He had dirty blond hair that was neatly trimmed, combed forward, and stylishly pushed up in the front. He was sporting a red Hawaiian shirt, evidently this was the dress code for the guys staying at the house.

When I approached, his eyes narrowed in recognition. I was beginning to get a little freaked out.

"Hi," he said cautiously. "You're Emma, right?"

"Yeah," I replied, assuming that Brent had said something to him when he took over the bar. "And you are?"

"Nate." He raised his eyebrows in expectation. He was waiting for me to react, but I had no idea what I was supposed to be reacting to. I held up my hands, at a complete loss.

"Wait. Are you guys messing with me?" I accused, concluding I must be the victim of an inside joke. "Did Brent tell you and Ren to give me a hard time or something?"

"No," Nate said, appearing confused. "You don't know who I am? But you're Emma Thomas, right?" The fact that he knew my last name alarmed me.

"Yeah, I am. Why? Should I know you?" I asked, studying his face more closely. I glanced over at Cole, who was observing the exchange curiously. Nate didn't seem to care that there was a line of thirsty people piling up behind me.

"No way!" A guy with shaggy blond hair approached. Nate gave him a warning glare, but he didn't pay any attention. He was too focused on me. Now I was beyond freaked out. I didn't like this game anymore. "Emma! You really are here!"

I remained still, glancing from this guy to Nate and back again.

"Come on, TJ," Nate implored. "Don't do it, man. Leave it alone."

"What's going on?" I demanded quietly. I could sense Cole behind me, but he didn't say a word.

"*You're* Emma Thomas? Evan's Emma?" TJ laughed in disbelief.

I couldn't speak. I flipped my eyes toward Nate, who grimaced in apology.

"He was here over his break," TJ chuckled, not understanding what was happening in front of him. "Seriously, he just left last weekend. That is so crazy."

These were *his* friends. His California friends he went to school with when he lived in San Francisco. The friends he went on trips with during breaks.

I ran my eyes over Nate's face, allowing it to all click into place. And this was Nate. *His best friend.* And this was the place where he'd planned to take me when he wanted to leave together our junior year. My knees felt like they were going to buckle. I grabbed the edge of the bar for support.

"Can I have a shot?" I choked. TJ started helping the other patrons, who were becoming irritated. I was in the way of their good time.

"Sure," Nate replied, watching me carefully, like I might combust in front of his eyes. "What do you want?"

"It doesn't matter," I answered, having difficulty breathing. I tried to hold it together so Nate wouldn't see what was erupting on the inside. "And can you fill this up again—vodka and soda?"

"Okay," he agreed, nodding slowly. He searched the bottles in front of him. "Uh, looks like I'm out of soda."

"Just vodka works," I muttered, trying to swallow. He handed me a plastic shot glass filled with a clear liquor and placed a lime on a napkin. The smell of it made my mouth salivate. "What's this?"

"Tequila," he answered slowly, like he was surprised I didn't know.

I swallowed the liquor and bit into the lime, with a shudder.

"Thanks." I took the cup and walked away, my knees quaking beneath me. I knew Cole and Nate were watching me. I started hyperventilating now that my back was to them. But no matter how quickly I drew in air, I was suffocating. I feared that I wouldn't be able to gain control over the burning pain, and I couldn't lose it here. I needed to calm the fuck down. Fast.

I pushed my way up the stairs and into the house, bumping into people dancing, annoying everyone in my path until I arrived at the second bar.

"Hi, Brent," I greeted.

He produced a dazzling smile. "Emma, my friend! How are you doing?"

"Great," I answered. "Can I have a shot? Actually, would you like to do one with me?"

"Sure," he accepted emphatically. "What did you have in mind?"

"Your call." I tried to maintain a smile. Wanting to keep up my casual appearance, I took a sip of my drink, but was unable to hide the tremor that sloshed the vodka around as I raised the cup to my mouth.

Brent selected tequila as Nate had done, and poured us each a shot.

He raised the plastic shot glass and toasted, "To friendship." I swallowed it down without hesitation, sinking my teeth into the lime immediately afterward to contain the cringing.

"How about one more?"

He raised his eyebrows at my request, then shrugged. "Sure. Why not?"

This time, I raised my cup and toasted, "To yesterday." His eyes flickered in confusion, but he didn't ask. I wouldn't have explained if he had. I tried to suppress the shudder as the tequila passed down my throat.

"Thanks, Brent. I'll talk to you later."

"Wait," he called after me. But I kept walking like I didn't hear him.

Cole was standing on the deck with a drink in each hand. He offered one of the cups to me without saying anything. We stood on the deck, watching the people below for a few songs.

"Are you going to be all right?" he finally asked.

I shook my head. He continued to stand by me in silence, glancing at me every so often without a word. I concentrated on breathing, dumping the contents of the cup he'd given to me into the one I already had. I took slow sips and waited.

And then my head began to swirl, and the numbness settled in over the winding fire. I closed my eyes, inviting the induced calm.

"Emma!" Peyton called to me, making me spin around, which was not such a good idea. I steadied myself with a hand on the railing.

She eyed Cole next to me and grinned widely, probably figuring we were talking again. Which technically wasn't true.

"Peyton!" I hollered in return and grappled her into a hug.

"Are you drunk?" Peyton accused in shock.

"I hope so," I responded, breathing deep through my nose, savoring the hum of nothingness.

"Did you do this?" Peyton asked Cole.

"Nope." He shook his head, holding up his hands in defense.

"Well, don't do anything stupid," Peyton advised. "We're getting another drink. Come find me." And just like that, she disappeared.

"Where are you going?" Cole called after her, but she was already lost in the crowd.

"You don't need to babysit me." I looked up at him. "I think I need another drink anyway." I looked down at my cup, which was still half full.

"Really," Cole challenged.

"Yup." I put the cup to my lips and drained the rest. "See?" I tipped it toward him. Cole took a step to follow me as I started toward the inside bar. I turned to tell him not to come with me, but my ankle faltered slightly. I still wasn't used to heels, even if they were wedges. "Stupid shoes."

I bent down to try to unstrap them, but stumbled.

"Need help?" he offered.

Before I could answer, he squatted in front of me and unbuckled the sandals. I stepped out of them, relieved to have my feet flat on the ground. He stood up with the sandals swinging from his fingers. He looked so *tall*, all of a sudden.

"Wow," I gawked. "You grew."

"Or you shrunk," he replied with a crooked grin. "Let's go." He nodded toward the house.

I turned and examined the obstacle course between the deck and the bar across the room. There was a lot of movement with the dancing and arms swaying—it was going to take a lot of concentration. I took a deep breath in preparation.

Cole grabbed my hand, and I looked up at him in surprise.

"You look like you could use some help."

"Yes, that I do. I definitely need help." Cole escorted me through the obstacles without incident, and I emerged on the other side unscathed. I considered raising my arms in victory, but he still had my hand, and I didn't think he would join me.

"Emma!" TJ hollered joyously when he spotted me.

"TJ!" I returned enthusiastically.

His expression changed, and he appeared perplexed. "Are you leaving?"

Without my realizing it, Cole had directed us toward the front door.

"See you later, TJ," Cole said to him, opening the door for me to pass through.

"We're leaving?" I questioned in confusion, as TJ said, "Later, Cole."

That's when I picked up on it. "Wait. You know them?"

"Yes. And yes," Cole responded patiently as we continued along the walkway to the street. "My dad has a house down the road."

"You've got to be kidding me," I griped, frustration pushing through the calm. Why was this happening to me? This had to be a sick and twisted joke. "Of course you know them! Of course I had to come to *this* party. You probably know *him* too, right?"

"You mean—" He opened his mouth to say his name and stopped when I cut him down with my glare. "I've met him."

I screamed up at the sky, "Fuck you, karma!"

But I couldn't yell and walk at the same time, so I stopped. Cole looked on in baffled amusement.

"Fucking stupid karma," I grumbled under my breath with my arms crossed.

"You're seriously pissed?" he chuckled.

"Shut up, Cole," I snapped. "Fucking karma."

"You'd better stop telling karma off, or she's going to kick your ass." He laughed.

"Oh, she can bring it. Come on!" I screamed at the stars. "Give me everything you've got!"

The corner of Cole's lip rose. "Okay, champ. Calm down."

I suddenly felt drained. With my shoulders curved forward, I sat down on the side of the street.

"What are you doing?" Cole inquired, towering over me.

"I'm tired," I moaned, drawing up my knees and plopping my head down on my folded arms.

"Come on," Cole encouraged, offering me his hand. "We're almost there. And then you can pass out." I took his hand, and he lifted me from the ground. My footing faltered, and I grabbed on to his arm.

I continued walking with my head slumped against him, holding myself up with his arm. I was so tired…and dizzy. The ground wouldn't stay still, and it was messing with me. I bit my lip, concentrating. Then I realized I couldn't feel my lip, which made me think of kissing.

"Cole?"

"Yes, Emma."

"Will you kiss me?"

"Uh, no," he responded bluntly.

"But I want to know if you can feel my lips," I urged impatiently.

"Still, no. I'm not kissing you."

"Why?" I sulked.

There was silence for a minute. Then he said, "Because I'm not even sure I like you."

"Good reason," I noted sleepily. "But you don't have to like me. You just have to kiss me. I can't feel my lips."

"Stop biting them," he instructed. I blinked heavily and noticed we were walking toward a house.

"Cole?"

"Yes, Emma."

"I'm sorry I'm a bitch." He took out a key and unlocked the door. I was having a hard time holding my body upright. "And I'm sorry you don't like me." He opened the door.

"There's a spare—"

But I was already moving toward the couch that I'd zoned in on when he'd opened the door. I fell on it with a heavy sigh and let the world spin me to sleep.

8. CAPTURING THE SILENCE

I moaned as the sound of metal clanging reverberated through my head. "Sorry," I heard a male voice say.

Fuck!

I squeezed my eyes shut and ran my hands along my hips— exhaling with relief when I felt fabric. Peeking out from under my lashes, my face pressed against a pillow, I noted a blue fuzzy blanket laid over me. Beyond the foot of the couch was an open kitchen, and *him*, with his back to me. The taste of tequila still lingered in my mouth—probably seeping through my pores as well.

I pushed myself up to sit, expecting pain, but it didn't come. Instead a swirl rocked me. I blinked, trying to focus. The stark white room forced me to squint against the intense brightness.

"Hey," Cole greeted me, busy with something in the kitchen. "Hungover?"

"No," I rasped, running my fingers through my hair, feeling one side all pushed up. I attempted to smooth it down and tuck it behind my ear. "I think I'm still drunk."

Cole chuckled. "I wouldn't doubt it. I'm making pancakes, if you want some."

I looked around the small open space, with its wall of shelves filled with books, pictures, boxes and ocean paraphernalia. There was an oversize beige chair, complementing the couch I had awoken on. Behind the couch was a square wooden table with a couple of chairs. The kitchen was separated by a peninsula that had three wooden stools pushed against it.

I stood up and shuffled over to the sliding glass doors to admire the ocean view, then opened the door and walked out onto the wooden deck. The clouds hung low over the water, casting gloom over the barely visible islands that lay in the distance. Wrapping my arms across my chest, I braced myself against the chill of the breeze. I closed my eyes and breathed in the damp air, settling the dizziness.

Cole stepped out and stood beside me, placing his hands on the railing, watching the seagulls flying across the water before landing on the beach, scouring for food.

"Crappy day," he observed, glancing at me. I turned toward him, blinking lazily through the clouds in my head.

"Feels like me," I groaned, earning a grin. He went back inside while I continued to stare out at the dark water. There was something inviting about the rhythmic surf intermingling with the grey sky. I wanted to float along its surface, breathe in the mist.

When I looked back into the house and saw that Cole was preoccupied with cooking, I crept down the steps, easing over the rocks that were smooth and cool under my bare feet, until I reached the coarse sandy beach. The bordering houses were dark and seemingly unoccupied.

I stared out at the water, and my heart convulsed. I took one more glance at the house without seeing a sign of Cole. Releasing a settling breath, I slipped out of my pants and peeled off my top, dropping them on the sand along with my bra and underwear. Before I could change my mind, I waded into the frigid water until it pushed up against my thighs, and dove beneath an oncoming wave.

I broke the surface, gasping at the freezing cold water. A wave crested above my head, and I ducked under it, re-emerging on the other side. All around me the fog was thick, blending the surrounding houses into the shadows. I lay back on the rolling surface and kicked my feet, pushing farther away from shore. My thoughts were quiet as the water lapped around my ears, dissolving the world around me. The buzz in my head was replaced with a calming hush. Nothing mattered.

Some rational part of me knew I needed to get back before the water sucked me under—but I stayed on the surface a little longer, not wanting to give up the stillness. I tried to imagine what it would be like, to let it swallow me up, and surrender to the silence forever.

With a quivering inhale, I slipped under the water. A wave captured me and pushed me to shore. I broke through the surface and inhaled the cool air, filling my lungs. I continued to glide toward shore with the waves, until my knees scraped along the sand.

"Are you insane?" Peyton scolded, standing on the beach, holding a towel in her hands. "Your lips are purple, and you're *naked*. What the hell are you thinking?"

I glanced around before I stood up, making sure it was just the two of us.

"Right now?" I paused. "Nothing." Then I smirked, which irritated her more. I took the oversize beach towel from her and wrapped it around my shivering body. Even with the towel, my muscles were rigid, aching with cold. Peyton picked up my clothes when we approached them.

"I brought your bag, so you can put something dry and warm on," she explained.

"You brought my bag?" I looked over at her, and she averted her eyes.

"I was hoping you could stay here and let Tom and me have some time alone for a day or two," she replied sheepishly. I raised my eyebrows. "Cole doesn't mind, despite how strange you're being."

"He thinks I'm being strange?" I inquired curiously.

"No, but I do. He just said that you were trying 'something new' and handed me a towel."

I laughed.

Before we entered the house, Peyton stopped me to make certain I had covered everything I needed to cover, since Tom was sitting on the couch. I rolled my eyes, and brushed past her into the house.

"Your bag is in the bedroom on the right," Peyton informed me.

Tom asked, "How's the water?" as I passed behind the couch.

"Shut up, Tom," Peyton snapped. Cole was leaning against the counter, watching me. I glanced at him, and my mouth shaped into a subtle grin as I entered the bedroom and shut the door.

I stayed under the shower's hot stream until I finally defrosted. My grogginess had dissolved in the waves. I took a deep breath, satisfied with the invigorating clarity the experience had unleashed. When I walked into the kitchen, dressed and with dry hair, I could feel my skin glowing.

"Hungry?" Cole asked as I seated myself at the island.

"Starving." He set a huge plate of pancakes in front of me.

I looked around the small space and realized we were alone. "Where's Peyton and Tom?"

"They went back to her place," he answered, washing a bowl in the sink. "Was it everything you expected?" Cole glanced back with a gleam in his eye.

I swallowed a mouthful of pancakes. "What's that?"

"Skinny-dipping."

I shifted uncomfortably on the stool. "It was better," I replied softly. I heard him release a breathy laugh without turning around.

Cole selected some music and disappeared into his room to shower.

The fog had thickened outside. I was suddenly very aware that I was going to be spending the entire day with Cole in this house… alone. I looked around and realized there wasn't a television, so I considered shutting myself in the spare bedroom to read all day.

That's when I noticed the boxes of puzzles stacked on one of the shelves. I'd never done a puzzle before, and I was intrigued by the thought. It seemed like a thousand pieces would be distracting enough. I wouldn't have to think about anything other than finding the right ones to fit together.

I chose a box with a scenic mountainscape and sat down, pulling the coffee table until it was flush against the couch and spreading the pieces out before me.

Cole emerged from his room smelling like a cool breeze, his wet blond hair swept back, like he'd just run his fingers through it to style it. I shifted my eyes down when he caught me looking at him and continued flipping the pieces picture-side up.

"I haven't done a puzzle in years," Cole said, standing beside me and picking up the box cover.

"I've *never* done one," I admitted without looking at him.

"Really?" He sounded surprised. "Want help? Or do you feel like putting together a thousand pieces all by yourself?"

"You can help if you want."

Cole settled in on the cushion next to me with his legs crossed. He began separating the edge pieces from the middle pieces. When he leaned forward, his knee brushed my thigh, sending a shiver along my skin. Suddenly I wasn't sure if this was such a good idea.

"You okay?" Cole asked, noticing my stiffened posture.

"Uh, yeah." I choked, coughing to clear my throat.

"Want something to drink?" He stood on the cushion and jumped over the back of the couch, so he wouldn't disturb the coffee table.

"Sure," I replied, taking the opportunity to shift farther away from his side. "Whatever you have is fine."

"Coke?" he offered. I nodded without looking, concentrating on sorting through the pieces.

With the fog veiling the ocean, we spent the afternoon shrouded in silence except for the music filling the room. We slid pieces around the table, working in unison without an utterance of communication. I was very aware of his every move. Heat floated off him when he reached across the space between us, his long, slender fingers connecting pieces, pausing to press the edge of one against his full lips as his eyes narrowed in contemplation, searching for its placement. The skin along my arm hummed when he'd brush against it, reaching around and over my hands as we shuffled through the pieces.

"Hungry?" His voice broke the stillness, making me jump.

"Uh, yeah, I could eat." I raised my arms over my head. My back was stiff from being hunched over for hours.

Cole eased the table away and stood, stretching as well. His shirt crept up to reveal a hint of the defined muscle beneath. I caught myself and turned my head. I had done so well avoiding him, convincing myself I wasn't interested in him, that I couldn't be interested in him. But here I was, trapped in this house with him, and I was about ready to pass out from trying to control my involuntary responses. I needed to call Peyton and get the hell out of here.

"Okay?" Cole asked, pulling me from my escape plan.

"Huh?" I shot my head up, not certain what he'd said.

"I asked if Mexican was okay?" He paused to study me. "Are you sure you're all right? Are you hungover or something?"

"No, I guess I'm just a little dazed from staring at the puzzle all afternoon. Sorry. Mexican's great."

I went into the spare-bedroom bathroom to splash cold water over my face and give myself a moment to pull it together. Then I found my phone and sent Peyton a text. Can't stay here. Come get me.

She responded shortly after. Why? Are you fighting?

No

Come on, Emma. One night. PLEASE!!!! I glared at her response and clenched my teeth in frustration.

One night. That's IT. Come get me in morning.

Thanks!! appeared on my screen. I sat down on the bed, running my fingers through my hair. Maybe I should go to bed early. Like right after we returned from dinner. Which brought on a new onslaught of dread. What the hell was I going to talk to him about during dinner?

"Ready?" Cole called from the living room.

I blew out a deep breath. "Yup."

"So…you have four sisters, right?" I asked after we'd placed our orders, hoping this would let him know that I was open to conversation. There was no way I could sit across from him in silence while we ate.

"Yeah," he confirmed. He was quiet a minute, and then realized I was waiting for him to continue. He appeared…relieved. "Missy is the oldest. She's twenty-seven. Then Kara is twenty-five. Liv is twenty, and Zoe is sixteen. Yup, five girls, plus my dad and me—it was very…dramatic.

"But everyone's all over the place now. Zoe's with my mom in Seattle. Liv goes to Florida State. Kara's in Oakland. Missy's in DC, and my dad's in San Diego."

"All over the place," I confirmed. He nodded. I prepared myself for questions about my family.

"Who's your closest friend?"

Not what I was expecting.

"Sara," I answered easily. "She's in Paris right now as part of an exchange program with Parsons in New York. But she's like an extension of me, more important than a vital organ."

"Wow. That's close," he noted with a rise of his eyebrows. "Does she ever make it out to California?"

"Every break, except now that she's so far away. But she'll be here in May for the summer."

He continued to describe his family, painting their charms and quirks so vividly that I could almost picture his sisters in my head. And I talked about Sara in so much detail that I could almost hear her voice. I missed her.

"So Liv decided one day that she would be a vegetarian," Cole shared on the drive home, "except when we went to her favorite restaurants. And since my dad doesn't cook, we ate out all the time, so every restaurant became her favorite, and essentially she isn't a vegetarian. But if you ever meet her, she'll *say* she's a vegetarian, and she'll give me crap for being insensitive if I don't mention it."

I laughed, thinking I would like this girl if I ever did meet her. We'd spent two hours at the restaurant, talking. I eyed the door of the house warily, my nerves twisting—because I actually liked talking to Cole. And worse than that, I liked *him*. And that couldn't happen.

I wondered why he never asked me about my family. Or about my behavior at the party the night before. But I felt like I owed him some sort of an explanation, especially since he had escorted my drunk ass home.

"I'm sorry about last night," I blurted out as he set his keys on the kitchen table. "I was—"

"Coping," he finished for me. I laughed softly at his choice of verb. "You don't have to explain. I kind of figured it out."

"Oh, so you were *listening*," I teased, recalling his self-proclaimed talent.

"I was," he confirmed without embarrassment. "And yeah. I got it. No worries."

"I should probably fine-tune my coping skills and not resort to shots."

"That'd probably be in your best interest." He chuckled.

"Well…thanks again for putting up with me," I replied seriously, meeting his translucent blue eyes.

"You weren't that bad," he responded, not looking away. Lingering a little too long.

"Um," I said suddenly, breaking the connection and forcing a stretch. "Dreary days make me tired. I think I'll go to bed early and read until I fall asleep."

"Okay," Cole said with a slight shrug.

As I was opening the bedroom door, I heard, "Emma?"

I turned toward him hesitantly.

"I've decided that you're okay."

My mouth quirked at his teasing tone. "So you don't think I'm a bitch?"

He smiled wider, his eyes lighting up. "I didn't say *that*."

"Nice," I jeered.

"Good night, Emma."

I bit my lip with a small smile. "Good night, Cole."

9. FEELING AGAIN

I rose late the next morning. It had taken me most of the night to fall asleep. All I could think about was Cole sleeping in the room across from me, and well…that was *all* I could think about.

I took my time showering and getting ready, hoping Peyton would arrive any minute. I packed my things so I'd be ready to just grab them and go.

Cole was on the couch when I finally opened the bedroom door. He was engrossed in the puzzle, which was only about a third complete.

"Good morning," he said without turning my way. "I'm addicted to this stupid puzzle. Are you hungry?"

"I can get something," I told him. "You keep at it. Do you have cereal?"

"Yeah. But I have eggs and English muffins, if you'd prefer."

"I don't cook." I opened the cabinets in search of a breakfast I was adept at preparing.

Cole was quiet. Eerily quiet. I turned toward him and found that he was watching me with a curious look on his face. "You don't cook?"

"No."

"Huh. That's not what I expected." He turned and went back to working on the puzzle. Why did this small fact continue to surprise most people who knew me? Dismissing it, I poured the flakes into a bowl and doused them with milk.

I sat on the arm of the couch, eating and examining the pieces. Every so often, I'd notice a fit and lean over to put it in place.

"You can sit down, you know," Cole encouraged.

"Uh, I think Peyton will be here soon," I stated awkwardly, walking to the kitchen to set the bowl in the dishwasher.

"No, she won't," Cole countered.

"What do you mean?"

"She and Tom went to Catalina for the day."

Panic began to rise in my stomach. That meant I was staying here…with Cole…again.

"Come help me," he begged. When he noticed the pallor of my stunned face, his eyes tightened. "She didn't tell you?"

I shook my head.

"If you don't want to hang out, that's totally fine," he said in a rush, trying to sound unaffected. "I mean, I was planning to go surfing in a bit anyway."

"I'm sorry." I felt horrid for not hiding my reaction. "I just had expectations, that's all."

"I'm not sure what that means, but I'm not insulted." He smiled and turned his attention back to the puzzle.

I took a breath and tried to relax. Approaching the sliding glass door, I strangled my hands, trying to decide what to do. I looked out at the hazy skies and knew it was too chilly to be comfortable sitting outside, at least until the clouds burned off and the sun cut through.

I climbed over the arm of the couch and crossed my legs beneath me, leaning as far away from Cole as possible.

"What's next on your list?" he inquired, pressing the edge of a puzzle piece against his lower lip. And for that moment, I couldn't focus on anything else. He turned his head toward me, and I tore my eyes away from his lips to meet his gaze. His eyebrows rose in expectation.

"I don't..." I faltered. "I don't know. How about you come up with something for me?" And that wasn't the best thing to say either.

"What do you mean? I thought there was a list. You know, like a bucket list for the new year?"

"Not really," I confessed. "When you ask me, I just say the first thing that comes to mind. I never wanted to do those things until you made me say them. And then I actually wanted to do them. So I figure you can pick the next thing. It's your fault I have the list to begin with, and you seem to always witness whatever it is anyway."

Cole inspected me, uncertain if I was serious. Then he began laughing.

And he kept laughing.

"Stop," I demanded, trying to be upset as I shoved his shoulder. But the more he laughed, the more difficult it was to stay annoyed, and my lips eventually curled up. "Okay! Don't choose. I don't need to add to my stupid list anyway."

"What qualifies?" he finally asked after he'd gained control again.

"Huh?"

"What's worthy of the list? What's the criteria?" he specified.

"Well..." I contemplated carefully for a moment. "It has to be something that gets my blood pumping, my adrenaline surging."

"That's a given," he goaded. I rolled my eyes.

"It should be something that's all-consuming and makes me forget everything else. Strips me of every thought and whisks away the pain."

"Pain?"

"I mean, uh…" I cringed, silently cursing myself for being so honest, "anything that's bothering me. You know, if I'm having a bad day and just need to forget about things. Something that makes everything go away. Make sense?"

"I get it." Cole's eyes flickered across my face, like he wanted to ask me something, but he held it in. "I think I can come up with something. Give me time to think about it?"

"Sure," I shrugged, freaking out on the inside.

We continued to work on the puzzle for another hour. But this time, Cole brought up music, and the conversation flowed from there. I soon discovered we had more in common that I'd initially surmised.

"Aren't you supposed to go surfing?" I asked, noticing the sun had finally burned away the cloud cover.

"I can go tomorrow," he answered casually. "I'll hang out with you today."

I stared at the puzzle without moving a single muscle. I didn't want him to hang out with me today, because I very much *wanted* him to hang out with me today.

"And why do you look like you're about to throw up?"

"I, uh…" I stuttered. "Um…" I really wanted to jump off the couch and leave. But I didn't have a car, and I didn't have anywhere to go. "I, um…"

"It's okay," he assured me with an amused shake of his head. "If you prefer to be by yourself, just say it. I felt bad leaving you alone, since Peyton won't be back until tonight. But I have friends I can visit."

"Sorry. I'm being stupid. I guess I haven't figured out how to act around you yet."

"You honestly say the strangest things. No wonder I can't read you," he said with a low chuckle. "Just be yourself, Emma. Relax. I'm not going to hurt you."

But I may hurt you.

Peyton would be back tonight. How much damage could I do in one day? He barely liked me, so I could ignore the pull I was feeling toward him for a day. Just one day.

"Okay," I conceded with a breath. "What did you have in mind?"

He jumped off the couch. "Let's go to the zoo."

"The zoo?" I questioned with my brows pulled together.

"I'm not the skydiving, drag-racing kind of guy, Emma. I told you that. Let's go to the zoo."

We returned to the house hours later, full of French fries and ice cream.

"That wasn't so bad, right?" Cole prodded, tossing his keys on the table.

"No." I laughed. "I never thought I'd feed a giraffe, so thank you." There was a pause, and Cole grinned at me with that ridiculous lopsided grin of his. With those lips that made me want to…

"I think I'll go for a run." I needed time to detox from being around Cole all day. My skin was still humming from the number of times he'd inadvertently brushed his arm against mine as we strolled along the paved path. And of course it had to be one of the prettiest zoos ever, making the urge to hold his hand that much more intense. My head was spinning, along with my moral compass. I needed to get away from him.

"I'll throw something on the grill," he announced. "We'll eat when you get back."

I disappeared down the beach, leaving him on the deck, heating up the grill.

I hadn't let anyone close to me since I'd moved to California. Even my roommates didn't really know me.

My freshman year I'd basically been a recluse—shutting out everyone and disconnected from any emotion. This year, I'd struggled to maintain control, and I'd lost it several times already. This all happened to coincide with the night Cole had entered my life. And now…I was feeling again. Way too much. And I was afraid. So very afraid of what might happen next if I wasn't able to tuck everything back into the darkness, where it belonged.

We're just as bad as they are, with our lies and deceit. We destroy people's lives.

I dug deeper into the sand and forced myself forward, needing to silence the voices that reminded me of every reason I wasn't worthy of letting anyone get close to me. My own voice among them. I fought for the control that continued to evade me with each pant, but even as I stumbled to a stop, I knew I couldn't outrun who I really was.

"You really push yourself," Cole noted as I stood below the deck, breathing heavily. I looked up with a start. "I'm cooking chicken. Thought we could make sandwiches. Is that okay?"

"Sure," I responded, trying to recover. I trod up the steps and pushed my sandy sneakers off on the deck. Continuing into the spare bedroom to shower, I hoped to rinse away the emotions that were twisting inside me.

We sat on the deck with our attention on the ocean. Not talking. And it occurred to me how much of our time together had been spent that way. Cole didn't ask me about myself. He just allowed me to tell him whatever I wanted. He was comfortable in this silence. I was not.

Sitting next to him without the distraction of a conversation made me all too aware of everything about him. The quiet contemplation that reflected in his tranquil eyes as he looked out at the sea. His relaxed posture, leaning back into the chair with his feet resting on the lower railing of the deck. The effortless strength his body exuded. There was an energy between us, wrapped in silence, that communicated in a way I had never experienced before.

We returned to the couch after we ate, hovering over the puzzle, which was beginning to resemble the mountain scene on the box cover, with wisps of clouds stretched against blue skies.

"There *is* something addictive about this." I joined another cluster of pieces together. "I don't get it, but I can't quit. Maybe it's the challenge. Needing to see it completed, no matter how tedious."

"Maybe it's because once you put all the pieces together, you end up with something beautiful." A light shiver trailed along my back when I found his soothing blue eyes soaking me in.

"I think I've figured out what your next thing should be," he said softly, capturing me in his gaze.

"You have?" I whispered.

"Something that will make your heart beat fast," he murmured. "Something that will make you forget everything else around you. I could be wrong, but I think I know what that is."

"Yeah?" I said softly, my pulse erratic. The air between us had stilled, and he was inches away. I remained focused on the intense hue of his eyes, unable to move until I felt the tickle of his breath on my face. I closed my eyes, and his lips pressed softly, ever so gently, against my mouth. Everything ceased to exist except the tenderness of his kiss and the slow movement of his full lower lip over mine. I wasn't breathing. I wasn't thinking. I was filled with a tingling current that sent a rush through my body. When he pulled away, I kept my eyes closed, enraptured.

My lids slowly rose, and he was waiting for me, the corner of his mouth raised teasingly. I exhaled and melted against the couch.

"That was list worthy." My voice sounded fragile. The tingling buzz gradually dissipating. "I'm going to have a hard time coming up with something after that."

Cole laughed.

When I went to bed that night, I lay awake for a long time. *I can't do this*—the words repeated over and over in my head, the panic building with each moment of inaction. I sat up and stared at the door.

Running my fingers through my hair, I bit at my lip in contemplation. I needed to go. To leave here. To get away from him... and that kiss. That kiss that ignited a craving I didn't know how to suppress. A craving to feel. To fill the bottomless void that had splintered open when I left Weslyn. I yearned to feel something... *anything*. Even if it was wrong.

I crawled out of the bed and decided I'd ask Cole to drive me to Peyton's. She and Tom were getting back late from Catalina, but they must be home by now. I didn't care that it was the middle of the night. It was only a fifteen-minute drive.

I dressed and dropped my bag in the living room before approaching his door, staring at it for a full minute, my chest heaving dramatically as I summoned the courage to knock. I raised my hand and rapped lightly.

"Cole?" I called to him. If he didn't answer, then I'd just turn around and go back to my room. I was a wreck with nerves, waiting in front of his door. What the hell was I thinking?

"Yeah," he answered, "you can come in."

I swallowed hard and opened the door. "You awake?" This was the dumbest thing I could have said, since he had just answered me.

"What's wrong?" he questioned. I could barely make out his silhouette, propped up on his elbow in the bed. I didn't move any closer than the two steps I'd taken into his room.

"Can't sleep," I explained feebly, pulling at the hem of my T-shirt. "And um..." The one sentence that I'd repeated over and over in my head—*I need to leave*—never escaped my mouth.

He inspected me silently for a moment. "Come lie down, Emma."

My eyes widened.

"You can stay on top of the blankets," he suggested. "We'll talk, and maybe you can fall asleep."

"Okay," I rasped, cautiously moving closer to his bed. It smelled of his crisp, fresh scent. Cole shifted over to allow me plenty of room. Ignoring my protesting conscience, I smoothed the blankets and settled down on top.

The sheet was draped across his waist, allowing a full view of the contours of this broad chest as he rolled on his side to face me. I opted to lie on my back and stare at the ceiling, so I could form sentences while we spoke. I was afraid I'd lose my nerve if I was looking at him.

He didn't say anything for a moment, and then whispered, "Or we don't have to talk."

I knew he was waiting for me to begin the conversation. After all, I was the one who'd knocked on his door.

"Sorry," I muttered. "I'm confused."

"Confused?"

"Cole, I don't want you to like me," I confessed in a single breath.

He didn't respond. I suddenly felt very vulnerable. Turning toward him, I saw that he was waiting for me to explain. The intensity flickering in his eyes forced me to look away.

"I'm…I'm afraid," I breathed, clenching my jaw at the honesty I'd just expelled.

"That I'll hurt you?" he asked, his voice low and soothing.

"That *I'll* hurt *you*," I responded. "I'm fucked up. I'm so fucked up. I can't…I can't date you. I can't let you in. I can't get close. And—"

"Emma," he interrupted. "It's okay."

I shifted on my side, feeling the need to see his face as my body trembled.

"You don't understand," I continued desperately, clutching my arms against my chest. "I shouldn't be here. It's taking everything I have not to walk out that door. That's all I've thought about since we've met, that I need to leave you alone. Because that's…that's what I *should* do." I tensed against the tightening pain in my chest. "I'm a horrible person."

"I doubt that," he whispered in return. "But if you need to walk away, then go ahead. Emma, I'm not asking for anything. I like what this is. There're no expectations. So, if you can…just for this week, I'd like it if you didn't walk away."

I wanted to touch him. To run my hand along his strong, square jaw. To nuzzle my face into his neck and become intoxicated by his scent. To allow him to wrap his arms around me so my skin could come alive with the buzz that his touch incited. But I didn't. I remained contained and rigid on my side, unable to look away from him.

"What do you think? Will you stay, Emma?" he whispered, reaching over and running the back of his hand along my cheek so gently. I closed my eyes, and my entire body shivered.

"I'll stay," I responded, barely audible. I lay beside him, absorbing the energy between us.

10. PREDICTABLE

I knew I should open my eyes. I could feel the light shining in from the other side of my eyelids. But I was so comfortable under the warmth of the blanket, in my restful place, with him next to me, waiting. I squinted at him, lying across from me. He didn't say anything. He just lay there watching me with a hint of a smile.

His skin was luminous with the light peering in through the large glass door behind him, the ever-present subtle flush of color across his prominent cheekbones. I wanted to press the palm of my hand against the ruddiness, expecting to feel heat—but I resisted.

I was still on top of the comforter, but I'd been covered with the blue blanket from the couch. And he was still under the blankets, without a shirt on.

"Can I ask you one thing?" His minty breath floated to my nose. I shook my head, clamping my mouth shut. "You need to brush your teeth first?" I nodded. He laughed. "Bathroom is right there."

I considered getting my toothbrush from my bag in the living room, but after a moment of deliberation I opted to stay in his room. I used my finger to brush my teeth, then returned to the bed, nestling under the blanket. Cole continued to wait patiently.

"Go ahead," I encouraged, resting my head on the pillow.

"Why did you stand me up that night?"

I paused a moment. It seemed so long ago. "I got a tattoo." It was as close to the truth as I could get.

"And it couldn't have waited until the next day?"

"No."

He focused on my eyes, reading me, and nodded in acceptance.

"Can I see it?"

I slid my shirt up to reveal the image along my side.

Cole studied it intently. His fingers traced the crescent, over the resting eyes and along the peaceful masculine profile. His touch left a tingling trail. My breath quivered.

"What does it mean?"

"There was a time I needed to be reminded," I explained.

"It looks like it must've hurt," he said without taking his eyes off it, trying to decipher the script that ran along its edges.

"Not enough," I murmured breathily.

"You say the strangest things." He said it almost admiringly, resting his hand on my bare skin.

I shrugged shyly.

"Will you do something predictable with me today?" The heat from his hand coursed under my skin. My body hummed. *Anything.* But I knew the real answer to his question.

"Yes, I'll go surfing with you."

He laughed, sitting up in the bed, taking the electric charge with him when he removed his hand from my waist—leaving me dark and empty once again.

I barely made it into the water that day. Cole spent most of the time showing me techniques on the sand before he would allow me to take a board in the ocean. When we finally did get in the water, it was all about how to lie and sit on the board, along with instructions on how to paddle at the right time to catch the wave. He wouldn't let me even *attempt* to stand at all that day. But the "predictable" piqued my interest, so I agreed to do it again the following day.

When Peyton called me that night to arrange a time to pick me up, I shut myself in the spare bedroom and told her that she could spend the week with Tom. I played it off like I was doing her a huge favor. I tried to sound bored and disinterested when she asked how Cole and I were getting along. I knew it wasn't the right decision. But I wasn't able to walk away. Not yet.

Cole would teach me to surf in the calmer waves for a few hours each morning, and I'd insist afterward that he go where he usually surfed so he could get some riding in. By the third day, I was able to pop up and keep my balance for…not very long.

We'd spend the afternoons working on the puzzle, reading, or I'd go for a run. Then each night, I'd lie next to him on top of the blanket. Before he'd close his eyes, he'd rest his hand on my side, over my tattoo, like he could hold my words in his hand. Every so often, he'd trace the outline of it with his fingers, branding me with the charge of his touch. The sparks it created flickered light back into the darkness. I did all I could to hold on to the tingling after he'd pulled his hand away.

Once he was in the depths of sleep, I'd slip away to the spare room. I never woke next to him after that first night. It was my way of staving off the guilt. Too bad it didn't work. I should have walked away.

Cole never questioned my retreat each night. And he didn't attempt to kiss me again.

———

"You were pretty good today." We were pulling into the driveway after spending most of the day in the water. "Don't be so hard on yourself; it takes a lot of practice."

"I see how much more intense it can be when I watch you and the other guys. And I just want to be there already."

"Patience," he advised. "Or do you know what that is?"

"Oh, you're hilarious," I said, making him laugh.

"Emma!" Peyton called, when I stepped out of the car. I turned to watch her approach from the walkway, with Tom a step behind. "Where'd you guys go? We stopped by earlier, but you weren't here."

"Surfing."

"You're teaching her how to surf?" Tom asked. Cole nodded, unstrapping the boards from the roof of his SUV.

I noted Peyton's bronzed skin. She *was* determined to return from break with a tan—despite the cool weather.

"We wanted to see if you were up for going out tonight, since it's our last night here. There's a party on a private beach near my place."

"Sure." I shrugged indifferently.

Tom glanced over at Cole, who nodded in acceptance.

They followed us into the house.

"So, you've been surfing and…putting together a puzzle," Tom observed in bewilderment, sitting down in the chair. "Sounds *exciting*."

"I'm going to shower," I announced. Peyton followed me into the spare bedroom.

"So…you two are getting along really well," she sang, a knowing smile creeping across her face.

"It's not what you think," I huffed, pulling clothes from my duffle bag.

"Then what is it?"

"We get along," I responded flatly.

"I'm sure you do," she said with a gleam. I rolled my eyes and entered the bathroom, shutting out Peyton and her obnoxious smile.

The party was crowded, loud and a shock to my system after the quiet week I'd had. After I'd been bumped into one too many times, Cole looked to me and asked, "Wanna go for a walk?"

"Yes," I answered without hesitation.

We followed the edge of the surf away from the rowdiness and loud music. This was it. Our last night. And neither of us had the nerve to talk about it.

Cole's arm brushed against mine, and I shivered. I could've sworn I saw a spark. He stopped suddenly, like he'd felt it too.

"Wanna sit?" he proposed. I could only nod.

Sitting there in the stillness, I allowed my shoulders to relax. Silence enveloped us in a comforting embrace.

"Do you ever get the urge to get in your car and just keep driving?" I asked, focused on the water shimmering in the light of the moon.

"How would you know when to stop?" Cole challenged, sitting next to me so our arms barely touched.

"I guess when you find something worth stopping for," I answered, acutely aware of the heat swirling between our skin.

"I wonder how far you'd travel before that happened." Cole pondered. Then asked, "Why do you do the things on your list, especially since you don't really have one?"

I smiled lightly before giving serious consideration to his question. "So that I know I'm alive."

"You're the most alive person I've ever met," he replied softly. I turned my head up to find that he was intently focused on me.

The flickering of the dim light in his eyes drew me in. The charged hum between us intensified, and my chest rose with an exaggerated breath, drawing it in.

"Why haven't you kissed me again?" I whispered, wanting him to lean a little closer.

"I'm afraid to kiss you," he confessed, his words floating through the air in the hush. "I'm afraid that if I kiss you, I won't want to stop. I can feel you tense every time we touch, and I don't want to do anything that will make you walk away from me. I'm afraid when we get back to school, this will all be over. I know we're both avoiding talking about it. The same reason we haven't finished that puzzle that should've been completed three days ago. Because then it'll be over. Are you ready for that?"

I tried to inhale, but nothing moved. I uttered not a sound. I could only stare into his eyes, pleading with me to say *something*.

"What are you doing over here?" Peyton exclaimed. The beers she'd consumed had amped up her boisterous volume. Cole and I practically jumped, before turning in her direction. "Oooh, was I interrupting something?" She held her finger to her mouth like she was telling herself to be quiet. Too late.

———

We drove home in silence the next morning, the tension intensifying with each mile. Our week had to come to an end. But I still couldn't bring myself to say it. I could feel Cole glancing at me every so often. Doing the right thing was going to be so difficult.

As we drove through town, the looming clouds opened up. I rolled down the window and stuck out my arm to feel the warm spring raindrops upon my skin. I breathed in the scent of the moisture in the air, mixed with fresh-cut grass and earthy blooms.

When Cole stopped at a red light less than a mile from my house, I opened my door to step into the rain.

I won't destroy your life too.

My parting words echoing in my head carried me across the street to the sidewalk, not looking back. The rain intensified, saturating my shirt instantly. I took off my shoes and walked in the fast running water, letting the coolness wash over my toes, cascade down my hair and drip from my chin.

I was a few blocks from the house when I heard thumping footsteps splashing in the water behind me. I turned to find Cole stopped a short distance from me, breathing heavily. My mouth curved faintly at the sight of his shirt clinging to the curves of his chest, the water darkening his blond hair. He approached me with an unasked question in his eyes.

I watched the water drip down his nose and over his beautiful full lips. I knew what I *should* do. But with him so close, looking down at me intensely, I wanted more than anything to allow the spark he contained to possess me and fill up the chasm that had left me so empty all this time. I was craving the warmth of his touch. The rush of our connection. Regardless of whether I deserved it or not. Regardless of whether he was wrong for me. I couldn't resist it any longer.

I stepped closer, covering the flush of his cheeks with my hands to feel their heat, and pressed my lips firmly against his, until it almost hurt. Cole gripped my waist and pulled me into him, sealing the space between us. I secured my arms around his neck. As our lips slid over each other's, I was overwhelmed by the electric current coursing through me.

Desire poured into the shadows, and I didn't let anything else matter. Not the voice that told me this was wrong. Not the guilt. Not the warning that crashed through my head. I pushed it all away and let the desperate craving overtake me.

Panting, I pushed away and grabbed his hand, pulling him after me as I ran the remaining distance to the house.

I stopped in front of the door and turned back to him, kissing him with such want, my entire body pulsed. His mouth was still finding mine as I opened the door. He blindly shut the door behind him, concentrating on me, touching me. I broke away to rush up the stairs, Cole in pursuit.

My shirt was over my head before I opened the door to my room. Cole removed his while shutting the door behind him, then thrust me against it. I let my shoes slide from my fingertips as he ran his lips along my slick neck, teasing with his tongue, forcing a low, breathy moan from my throat. He slipped a hand around my back to unfasten my bra. Our wet bodies slid together as our mouths found one another over and over again, unable to get enough.

Cole kicked off his shoes while I ran my tongue along his neck. His strong hands braced my face, and he bent down to kiss me. I parted my mouth as his tongue slipped in, teasing my bottom lip. His hands ran down my sides to my hips and inside the waist of my jeans as I forced the zipper down. Cole peeled them off my legs, and I kicked them aside. I stood before him, exposed. In a quick motion, he lifted me, and I wrapped my legs around him, my back colliding against the door with a gasping grunt.

Cole carried me to the bed, gently laying me on my back. His eyes danced over the length of my body, and I bit my lip, waiting as he searched his pockets before letting his shorts drop to the floor. He returned to me after he tore off the wrapper. Pulling me up by my hips, he pressed his knees against the edge of the bed. I inhaled deeply as we connected, clutching his hand as he lowered himself over me. I gripped the tense muscles along his back as he moved into me, exploring me deeper. The charge intensified, possessing my senses. It became all that I could feel, all that I needed, as it streamed through every inch of my body. The emptiness was swept away, and I would give anything not to be devoured by it again.

My entire body quivered with his escalation. My legs tightened, and I moaned in release. The air was lost to me with a swirling rush, and I liquefied into nothing in a single breath. He gave in with the slightest audible groan, tensing until every inch of him became rigid and then folding onto me. We lay in our breathless embrace, still entwined. Cole raised his head to look at me. The ruddiness of his cheeks had spread down his neck. I ran my hand along it.

"So…you like the rain?" he inquired with a gleam in his eye.

I laughed, not expecting those to be the first words out of his mouth since we'd left Santa Barbara. "Yes, don't you?" I asked, brushing my lips along his jaw, my pulse still thrumming.

"No," he replied with a chuckle. "I think I *love* the rain." He gave me the softest kiss before laying his head on my chest. "I'm not ready for this to be over yet, Emma."

"Em," Peyton bellowed, interrupting my response, "are you home?" I heard the doorknob jiggle.

I froze beneath Cole, and he raised his head in alarm.

"Don't you dare!" Serena hollered from the bottom of the stairs. Cole and I stared at each other, waiting.

"What?" Peyton replied in surprise.

"She's not alone."

11. WHAT ARE YOU AFRAID OF?

Are you looking forward to the float trip this weekend?" Sara asked from my computer screen, her smile vibrant and her eyes twinkling with the excitement I was lacking. "Didn't you say it was supposed to be pretty huge?"

"That's what I've been told," I answered with a slight nod. "I guess students from Stanford and some other colleges take over a campground for the weekend. It's exclusive, by invitation only. I don't know how they figure out who gets invited, but yeah, it's going to be…huge."

"What's wrong?" Sara asked, picking up on my dread. "You're not freaked by the crowd, are you? I thought you were over that. Wait…is it Cole?" Her questions flew at me without pause.

"Nothing's wrong." But I could feel my throat constrict just saying it.

"You can't lie to me, Emma. I can always tell when you're lying, even when you think you're getting away with it. It *is* Cole, isn't it?"

I looked away from the screen, pressing my lips together.

"Em, things have been going so well for the past two months," Sara continued soothingly. "It's okay to be happy. It's okay if you move on. You don't—"

Before she could continue with her reassurances, I interrupted with, "We're supposed to sleep in a tent."

I reluctantly returned my focus to the screen. Sara was still and silent.

"I can't sleep in a tent, Sara," I continued, my voice edged with panic. "That night with..." I couldn't go there. I couldn't think about it. It was the last time I'd been truly happy. "I just...I can't sleep in a tent with Cole."

"I know." Sara's eyes shone with understanding. "Then don't sleep in a tent. Tell Cole you want to sleep in his SUV. You can fold down the back and put a blow-up mattress in it. It works, I've done it before." A devious smile spread on her face as she reminisced.

"Really, Sara? I didn't need to know that!"

"What? It's not like you don't get naked with Cole every chance you get!" she snapped back teasingly.

"I knew I should never have told you."

"It's the only way it's real," she responded, reminding me of the oath I'd given her in high school, that it didn't really happen unless I told her. I wished that were true; so much of my past would've been erased. "I like this. That you're dating again...and having crazy bunny sex!"

"We're not *dating*," I stressed, "and we're not always...I mean, we surf too." I couldn't finish, because in fact that's how Cole and I spent most of our time together. We were either studying in our comfortable silence, surfing or having "crazy bunny sex." I sighed.

"Whatever. You keep saying you're not, but it's okay if you are," Sara said emphatically. "You *can* move on, Em. I like him. Don't give up on him."

My entire body tensed, and I stared back as her mouth dropped in realization.

"I'm so sorry. I shouldn't have said it like that."

The last time Sara had said that same exact thing to me, we were sitting in her driveway, and she was convincing me to give Evan a chance.

"So, you'll be here next Friday, right?" I was trying to recover, but my chest remained tight.

"Yeah," Sara responded, watching me carefully. "I fly back to Connecticut on Monday and to see the fam before I spend the summer with you in Cali. I cannot wait to be there!"

I tried to smile, but couldn't. "I can't wait for you to be here either. I don't have to take classes this quarter, so I'm all yours."

"So fucking fantastic!" Sara exclaimed, her natural jubilance returning.

"I should get going," I told her. "I need to pack."

"This weekend will be good for you, I just know it. Call me when you get back."

"I will," I replied, forcing a smile, "Bye, Sara."

"I love you, Em!" Sara proclaimed before the screen clicked off. I sat in the chair and stared at it for a moment before pushing away from the desk.

"But, how about you stay the night? It's supposed to be pretty nice tonight. We can sleep outside."

"Like camping?"

"That's a better idea. I think I have a tent in the garage. We can sleep in the backyard, or we can go to the meadow. The sky will look incredible out there, away from the lights. What do you think?"

"Emma! Cole's here!" Peyton yelled.

Her voice startled me out of my memory. I scanned the sky, focused on collecting myself. I blinked the tears back and took a deep breath.

"She's *where*?" I heard him ask. Before I could make an attempt to move, he was scrambling up on the roof. I lifted my head to search for him.

"What are you doing?" I ran my finger along the corner of my eye, struggling to tuck the emotion away.

"Uh, besides trying not to fall off and kill myself?" Cole scooted next to me, his breathing slightly labored. "I came up here to find you."

"I was going to come down."

"Well, I'm here now, so let me catch my breath." Eyeing the distance to the ground, he shifted back and bent his knees to rest his arms over them, trying to appear casual, but his back remained tense. "Why are you up here?" he asked. Then he noticed my amused expression. "Oh, you think it's funny that I'm hating this right now, don't you?"

"Yes," I teased with a low laugh. "Lie down next to me."

Cole lowered himself so his body lined up against mine. My senses heightened even with this slight touch. He gazed up at the dark sky with his hands behind his head.

"It's quiet," he observed after a moment.

"Exactly."

"So, it's not about the height? It's the silence?"

"Yes."

Unfortunately I couldn't find it. I shivered as I forced Evan's voice out of my thoughts.

We let the quiet surround us and soak into our skin with the coolness of the evening breeze. Lying next to Cole stirred thoughts of the conversation I'd had with Sara earlier. *What the hell was I doing?* I'd struggled for the past two months to end this. But every time I tried, the thrilling sensation he provoked would overwhelm me into submission, leaving me weak and unable to quit him.

"Why do you want to stay with me, Cole?" I whispered, focusing on the blinking lights of a passing plane.

"Other than the fact that I'm extremely attracted to you?" he taunted. I elbowed him. "Ow," he said, laughing.

"I'm serious."

"I know you are." He collected himself, then continued. "So you want to know why I want to be around, knowing that on any day you could just walk away?"

"Well…yeah," I responded, surprised by his candor.

"I guess I just wake up each day hoping that it isn't the day you decide to walk," he answered. "I'm not an overly emotional person. I don't talk about my feelings, and you accept that. We don't have to speak at all, and it's comfortable. Most girls need to know what I'm thinking, feeling, wanting…constantly. You don't."

"But I'm so messed up," I argued, knowing too well the destruction I was capable of.

"You keep saying that. But I don't really see you that way. Yes, you're a little reckless. You do these extreme things every once in a while just for the rush. I don't get it, but I'll go with it. It's not like you're expecting me to join you or anything. I don't know enough about you or your life to say you're fucked up. And if you ever want to tell me, then I'll listen. Because, as much as I don't talk, I *can* listen. Whenever you're ready, I will hear you out. But I like being with you. Does that answer your question?"

"But whatever *this* is, I can't give you more," I warned. "We aren't dating. We're just…"

"Hanging out," Cole finished lightly.

I propped myself up on my elbow and grinned down at him. Cole's eyes flickered across my face. He added with a devious smile, "And since I am *very* attracted to you, sometimes, we can hang out… naked."

I opened my mouth in feigned offense, but before I could say anything, he pulled me down and captured my words with his soft lips. And just like that, I surrendered to him and the questioning thoughts disappeared.

I positioned myself so I was leaning against his sculpted chest, and his mouth started moving faster. I clutched his shirt in my fist, overtaken again by the charge rushing through my body. Cole tilted my head up and caressed my neck with his lips, tasting my skin. I released a moan. He started to turn me onto my back, but then suddenly stopped.

When I opened my eyes, Cole wore a panicked look on his face, suddenly aware of where he was. I bit my lip to keep from laughing.

"We're on the roof," he announced, more to himself than to me. He noticed I was trying not to laugh. "You would have loved to have sex up here, wouldn't you? We're on the fricken roof, Emma!"

I started laughing, unable to contain it any longer.

"Come on," he urged with an exasperated sigh, scooting across the shingles toward Meg's window. I followed after him, still laughing.

———

Cole didn't question me when I asked to sleep in his SUV instead of the tent. In the end it provided more privacy—privacy that we took advantage of the first night we arrived at the campground.

The campground was as crazy as I'd expected. There were camps for each college, Stanford's being the biggest. From what I'd learned, a group of friends from our university started this trip years ago, and it had gotten progressively bigger each year since. The size had been capped in recent years, to keep up the exclusivity, but there were now participants from USC, UCLA and Berkeley, blaring their school pride with jackets and sweatshirts, banners strung between trees, and even chairs and tents staking claim to their university.

The next morning I peeked out the SUV's window and observed the groggy faces making their way to the bathrooms with disheveled hair and pained, squinty eyes. As Cole slept I pulled the sleeping bag up to my nose and snuggled into my pillow, staring up at the trees around us.

You're beautiful. My heart seized as the memory invaded. I closed my eyes to quiet his voice. To force away the feel of his fingers brushing my cheek and the intensity of his steel-blue eyes looking into me.

I love you.

My lip quivered.

"What's that?" Cole groaned from behind me, his voice heavy with sleep. I froze, cursing myself for letting the words slip from my mouth.

Cole rolled over and slid his arm around my waist, pulling me into him with his face pressed against my hair. "Good morning," he murmured. My body eased as the warmth of his skin caressed me, his touch a soothing sedation.

"Good morning," I replied, squirming back so I could feel the firmness of his body.

Cole slid his hand over my hip, slipping my sweatpants down. I kicked them off, my breath erratic. I ground back against him, his hot breath in my ear. He moved into me, causing me to gasp in pleasure.

Being this close to him, filled the emptiness that had corroded my insides over the past two years. I needed him. I needed him in a way that probably wasn't healthy for either of us. He was my fix. Even if he could never *fix* me.

His grip on my hip tightened. As his muscles contracted, Cole pushed deeper with a grunting breath. My erratic pulse was replicated by my breath, as a moan escaped. I gripped his hand as I tensed around him. My body shuddered. He held himself against me, squeezing my hand, the tension in his muscles slowly releasing. I could feel his heart beating against my back.

"It *is* a good morning," he finally said. I let out a light laugh.

We emerged from the SUV a few minutes later, greeted by the crisp air, and…beer cans strewn across the ground. Remnants of the previous night's bonfire still swirled in the brisk morning breeze.

After returning from the bathrooms, prepared for the day, we met up with Peyton, Tom, Meg, and the guy she'd been dating, Luke. "You two slept in," Meg remarked. Then she flashed me a knowing grin when she noticed the lingering flush along Cole's neck. My face flamed as I looked away, aware that she'd already heard way too much through our shared wall at the house.

"Ready to go?" Peyton asked perkily as Tom dumped ice into the cooler full of beers. "The shuttle is picking us up in ten minutes."

Cole adjusted the backpack that contained our beach towels and other essentials for our canoe. "All set," he answered for the both of us. He slipped his hand in mine, and I stiffened. His grip released instantly, and he started walking ahead of me without any other reaction.

I grimaced guiltily. We weren't affectionate in public. We didn't hold hands, or…well, any *couple* things. We weren't *dating*, as I continuously reminded everyone. Last night was the first time we'd spent the night together since Santa Barbara…for a reason. And now, I was afraid this might get *complicated*, even after our talk on the roof.

I picked up my pace and caught up with him, walking close enough so our arms brushed.

"Want me to steer?" I offered teasingly.

"Yeah, so we end up in the rocks?" Cole responded, his expression easing into a smile. "I'll steer. You just sit up front and…I don't know. Don't fall out."

"Funny," I jeered. "I'll only fall out if you tip us."

Cole laughed and nudged me gently. I smiled, relieved to be rid of the awkwardness.

We were floating down the river within a half hour. The splashing, hollering, laughing and music blaring from random canoes contrasted with the natural beauty surrounding us. I tilted my face up to the sun to absorb the warmth, feeling peaceful, despite the distractions all around me. I was startled when water sprinkled across my face. I opened my eyes to find a water fight ensuing between two canoes.

"Want a beer?" Cole offered, flipping open the lid of the cooler that sat on the floor of our canoe.

"I still don't like beer," I told him. "I should've packed something else, I guess. I'm fine with water or soda." He pulled out a bottle of water and handed it to me.

The temperature began to rise and I took off my T-shirt, revealing a colorful plaid string bikini. I heard Cole choke on his beer.

"What?" I demanded, turning quickly to face him, suddenly fearing he'd seen the trace of the faded scars along my back. I knew they were faint, resembling flesh-toned scratches, but I was still all too aware of them.

"I, uh…" Cole faltered. "I don't remember that bathing suit." His cheeks grew red as his lips curled up.

I laughed. "I take it you like it."

"I do," he confirmed. "Kinda wishing we were back in the SUV right about now."

Before I could respond, Tom hollered, "Cole! Let's go to that spot we found last year to have lunch."

"Sure," Cole yelled back, following Peyton and Tom's canoe. Meg and Luke trailed behind ours.

We steered around a narrow bend that was virtually concealed by arching tree branches. The canoe traversed several winding curves before the water opened up into a large pool surrounded by jagged cliffs of rust-colored rock. It was like we'd entered a cave with its roof blown off. The walls pressed in around the crystal water where people were wading and floating, while others sat up on broken slabs along a makeshift beach, drinking and eating.

We stepped out of the canoe into chilled water that sent a rush of goose bumps over my skin. A holler cut through the air. I turned quickly just as a body plunged into the water with a huge splash, making the girls around him squeal from the cold spray. I looked back to the top of the ledge, where a line of people awaited a turn. My heartbeat sped up its pace at just the thought of jumping.

"Are you coming?" Cole called to me.

I pulled my attention away from the cliff. "Huh? Yeah, I'll be right there." Cole continued wading through the water carrying the cooler. I glanced up at the cliff again, and a charge thrummed under my skin.

What is it that keeps you up at night? What is the source of all of your nightmares? What are you afraid of? I could hear Jonathan's voice as if he were standing right next to me. I squeezed my hand into a fist to ward him off as I continued to stare at the cliff.

"Emma!" Peyton hollered. I turned my head with a jerk. She and Meg were standing on a slanted slab, calling to me. "What are you doing out there? Come eat!"

I made my way to them and climbed up on a chunk of rock. The guys popped open cans of beer while Meg handed out sandwiches. Peyton searched through her iPhone for music to blare through the small portable speaker.

A conversation started about the trip thus far and the ridiculousness witnessed along the way. The buzz of voices faded as my attention drifted back to the cliff.

Jump, Emma. My heart skipped a beat. *Emma, you're either going to jump, or I'm going to push you.*

"I'll be right back," I murmured. Not caring whether they heard me or not, I stepped across the broken slabs of rock toward the path that led to the cliff. As I neared the yelling and laughter, I noticed that the path continued around a bend. I couldn't see the destination from this vantage point, but it wound up, and so did I.

The path crumbled beneath my feet, causing my steps to falter several times, until it unveiled a narrow ledge jutting out over the water. I cautiously stepped closer to its edge and was overcome with a rush of dizziness when I looked down. There was only the crisp blue beneath me.

The water's surface appeared smooth, reflective as glass, the light from the sun bouncing off it. My quickened pulse made my hands shake as I inched closer, working up the courage to take the devastating step.

Emma, what are you afraid of?

12. OVER THE EDGE

I feared that if I turned around, Jonathan would be there, awaiting an answer. I closed my eyes and inhaled, calming my racing heartbeat. When I opened them again, the jitters were gone and the vertigo had dissipated. I took in the coppery stone wall across from me.

I craned my neck over the edge again. "What are you afraid of, Emma?" I asked in a murmur, repeating Jonathan's words from that day on the cliff.

Nothing.

I knew…I wasn't afraid. I was carved out and scraped clean, a shell of my former self standing upon the ledge. There was only something to fear if I had something to lose. And I had nothing.

My head was quiet. I stared down at the water that was inviting me to take the last step over the edge.

"Emma?" Cole's voice broke through the silence. Rocks scattered along the path with his approach. I knew I was running out of time. I glanced back over my shoulder as Cole came into view. His eyes widened in shock. "Emma, what are you doing?" I turned away. Everything blurred beneath me as the tears filled my eyes.

"Emma, what the hell are you doing?!" Cole demanded again in a panic behind me. "You can't jump! You'll kill yourself from this height."

I didn't look back. I took that final step and disappeared over the edge. Instantly swallowed up by the rushing wind as I plummeted toward the water. My entire body rippled with adrenaline. My stomach opened up as the gust of air hugged me tight, stealing my breath. Nothing mattered in those few seconds. Not Jonathan. Not Evan. Not Cole. Not even me. Everything was lost, and I surrendered to the stillness that overtook me.

The moment of peace ended abruptly as my feet slammed through the water. My insides ricocheted violently on impact. The velocity of the fall forced me down until I collided with the rocks lining the bottom. Horrific pain shot through my leg as it grated against the unforgiving surface. I restrained a scream.

Kicking off the rocks, I propelled myself toward the light. My lungs burned for air as I fought for the surface with each desperate kick.

An enticing whisper told me to stop. To stop fighting. To stop trying. To just...

I gasped and coughed as I broke through the water. It took me a moment to orient myself as I sucked in bursts of air.

I looked back up to the top of the jagged rock from which I'd just taunted death. Cole was hovering over the edge, but I couldn't see his expression from this distance. The scraped skin below my knee shrieked as I trod water, drawing my attention away from Cole's face. I was afraid to find out how bad it was.

When I glanced back up, Cole had disappeared.

I could hear laughing and hollering around the other side of the cliff. I gritted my teeth as I kicked toward the boats, coming into view of the other swimmers. Meg and Peyton were still on the rock, soaking in the sun. When I neared the boat, I heard Cole plummeting into the water to reach me.

"Holy shit, Emma! I can't believe you jumped. Are you okay?" he demanded, water splashing around him. All he had to do was look at me. "You're hurt. Where?"

"I scraped my leg," I murmured, shrinking away, holding the edge of the canoe. "I'll be fine. Can we go back to the camp?"

Cole didn't answer me right away. "Yeah," he finally replied. Turning toward the beach, he shouted, "We're taking off. We'll see you back at the camp."

Meg's forehead scrunched in confusion. Before she could question us, Peyton yelled back, "Okay. See you there."

I gingerly lifted myself into the canoe. My entire body was starting to ache from the impact. I wrapped my leg with a towel before Cole could see the gouge below my knee, but I couldn't prevent the blood from trailing along the bottom of the boat as he paddled out of the cove.

"Let me see it, Emma," he requested sternly. "Let me see how bad it is."

Hesitating for a moment, I slowly turned toward him and unwrapped the towel.

He sucked in through his teeth. "Shit. You cut it up pretty bad."

I quickly wrapped the towel back around my leg, clenching my teeth against the stinging burn.

Cole didn't speak to me as we paddled past canoes full of drunken, laughing students. When we finally arrived at the load-out, my leg was pulsing, and blood had seeped through the towel. Cole helped me out of the canoe, and I limped over the rocks to the van, where he lifted me in.

"There's a first-aid station at the campground," the driver announced, eyeing the bloody towel. "I can drop you off there if you want."

"Thanks," Cole said, responding for me.

We continued in tense silence until we arrived back at the Stanford camp, my leg thoroughly cleaned, bandaged and throbbing profusely.

"Emma," Cole demanded, the uncharacteristic strain of emotion in his voice making me raise my head. "Do you even know how fucked up that was?! You could've seriously hurt yourself, or even died. I can't believe..." He ran his hands through his hair and backed away. He shook his head in angered disbelief. "I don't understand you."

I remained silent.

Cole tightened his jaw, running his hands through his hair again. "I need to clear my head." He turned away from me and walked off down the gravel road.

I watched after him as laughter poured out of a van that pulled up to unload. He deserved an explanation. But I didn't have one that would satisfy him. Or one I understood myself.

I closed my eyes and sank back into a folding chair.

Somewhere behind me a couple guys were talking in the obnoxiously loud voices specially reserved for drunk college guys. "Hey, dude, thanks for hitting me up last night. That party was sick!"

"Were you at Reeves's party last weekend?" a second guy asked.

"Jonathan's?" My eyes shot open. "Yeah, that was the best party I've ever been to. What school did he graduate from again?"

"Architecture, I think. He was a grad student, though." My heart slammed against my chest.

I twisted around to see who was talking. Several guys were sitting at the picnic tables, stuffing their mouths with burgers.

"Whatever it was, he must've landed some killer job in New York or something because that party must have cost him a ton," the in the grey T-shirt contributed.

I bent over with my elbows pressing against my thighs, trying to calm my frantic pulse. There was no way it was *him*. But when I turned back and saw the USC hat, I knew—

Don't wait for me. I don't want you to be there for me, not ever. Stay out of my life.

My caustic words turned my stomach. I hadn't thought about him since that night I'd driven him from my life. Until today. Now, with just the mention of his name, every thought of him I'd pushed away came rushing back.

We trust each other with secrets no one else knows.

I covered my face with trembling hands. I kept his secrets as my own, despite the weight they had on my conscience. I'd never told anyone what he'd confessed to me that night. And I'd tried to shut it out, to forget the horror he'd inflicted on so many lives. But that was impossible.

"When did he say he was leaving?"

I stilled, listening closely.

"I don't know—either today or tomorrow, I think."

"Back to New York?

"Yeah, I guess he's from there or something."

Giving in to an impulse, I stood up and approached the table.

"Hey," I said at the end of the table. "Were you guys talking about Jonathan Reeves?"

The guy in the grey T-shirt produced a half smile and said, "Yeah. You know him?"

"I do," I responded. "I wasn't able to make the party last weekend. But I wanted to say good-bye before he left. Except I can't find the e-mail he sent. Do you still have it?"

The guy with the hat pulled out his phone. "Yeah, I have it right here. Want me to forward it to you?"

"That'd be great." I smiled faintly. He handed me his phone, and I typed in my address and sent it. "Thanks."

"Can I e-mail you sometime?" he asked with a wink. I cringed.

"Uh, I didn't come here alone," I told him with an apologetic shrug, quickly backing away. "Thanks for the info."

I continued across the Stanford site and sat in another chair at the far end, away from the guys. I pulled out my phone and went to my e-mail, opening the forwarded invitation.

The invite announced a graduation/going-away party. It was pretty straightforward—a date, time and location…and a phone number. I stared at the number displayed on my screen.

My world had been crumbling around me every day since that box was opened five months ago. There wasn't anyone who could understand the feeling of being consumed by a darkness that I didn't have the strength to fight. No one would be able to comprehend the overwhelming feeling of hopelessness that was slowly unraveling the threads of my soul. Except for Jonathan. He was the only one who'd ever understood. Which was why I'd never told anyone about what he'd done, because *I* understood. We'd both done terrible things in our lives, and we would always be bonded by our destruction.

I feel like I can tell you things…things that I usually keep to myself. Most people don't understand.

I inhaled as his voice echoed through my head. My chest tore open, knowing how I had betrayed that trust. I'd taken his fears and insecurities and sliced him open with them. I knew why he'd never sought me out while we were both living in California. I'd made certain of it.

No one could ever love you.

I shuddered in disgust at the resonance of my own voice. I'd chosen this desolation when I'd betrayed them both that night. Now I was being given a chance to make things right. And if Jonathan couldn't forgive me, then no one would.

I anxiously flipped the phone over in my hands in contemplation. Every time I got up the nerve to dial his number, I'd see his face, beaten and defeated, and erase it. He probably hated me for what I'd said. But if there was a chance he didn't, I needed to find out.

Hi. It's Emma. Wondering how you are?

I hit *Send*, and I felt like I might be sick. After a few minutes of barely breathing, my phone vibrated.

Emma? Wow. Never expected to hear from you.

I exhaled in a rush. The sight of his response made my shoulders ease up.

Can't say it was easy to text. But I was thinking about you.

I bit at my lip as I waited.

I think about you all the time. Thought about finding you, but didn't. Thought you never wanted to see me again.

A shudder ran through me. Before I could respond, he followed up with another text. So much has happened over the years. I've had time to think. Make some decisions.

When he didn't continue, I asked, What kind of decisions?

I need to make amends. So it means a lot to hear from you. Wish I could hear your voice, but can't talk now.

I typed, Why can't you talk?

I was tempted to call him. My heartbeat picked up at just the thought of his voice on the other end.

Leaving soon. Just know that I'm sorry. I never meant to hurt you.

His words had a finality that made my insides writhe. Where are you going? I suddenly feared there was more to this trip to New York than a career opportunity.

To make things right. Owe it to my family. It's time. Done destroying people's lives.

I stared at the screen in alarm. Was he about to do something that would ruin his life...and mine?

I pressed the *Call* button and tried to control my frantic breaths as I waited for him to pick up. After several rings, I got his voice mail.

Please talk to me. What are you planning to do? I typed quickly, my fingers fumbling with the letters.

Sorry Emma. It's too late. Need to go. Please forgive me.

I called again, and this time it went straight to voice mail.

Jonathan. What are you going to do?

I couldn't sit still. I began pacing, waiting for his response. My stomach twisted in on itself while I stared at the blank screen. He never responded.

I walked to the SUV, where I found Cole sifting through his bag in the back. Still upset with me, he didn't look up when I approached.

"I need to leave," I told him. "I have to go, and I need to borrow your car. Please." I didn't even try to hide the panic in my voice.

"What's going on?" Cole demanded, examining my distraught face.

I looked down and paused a moment. "You'll get your car back, I promise. There's something that I have to do, and it's important. I just…please trust me, Cole."

He stood before me, studying my face as I shifted, unable to hide my desperation. "Take it." He removed the keys from his pocket and dumped them in my hand. I opened my mouth to thank him, but he turned away from me, zipped up his bag and slammed the back shut.

"Thanks," I whispered, knowing he couldn't hear me.

I climbed into the driver's seat of the SUV and drove away, gripping the steering wheel tight to keep my hands from quaking. I glanced in the side mirror to find Cole watching me, his hands clasped behind his head. I had to look away as the guilt spread like acid in my stomach.

I sped through the campground, leaving a cloud of dust behind me, determined to find Jonathan.

13. TOO LATE

Emma, where the hell are you? Meg called and said you took off yesterday, but no one knows where you went. I'm about to board a plane and you have me completely freaked out. I'd better have a voice mail from you waiting when I land or I'm going to lose it."

Just thinking about what I *should* tell Sara made my chest hurt. Instead, I called and said, "I'm fine. I'm at the house. Hope you had a good flight and call me when you can." Simple. Factual. But avoiding the truth.

Feeling like my insides were filled with cement, I climbed out of the SUV and walked toward the house. I had been up all night and I was too tired to get my bags from the trunk. When I got closer, I found Cole waiting for me on the front step. Evidently he'd received my text letting him know he could pick up his SUV anytime after eleven. I kept my eyes on the sidewalk, not wanting to face him until I had to.

Standing in front of the stairs, I slowly raised my head. His face was smooth and emotionless. His blue eyes scanned my limp face.

"I owe you an oil change," I said flatly, holding out the keys and dropping them in his outstretched hand.

"Where'd you go?" he asked, his voice carefully neutral.

"To try to fix things with a friend," I answered, focused on the fading paint on the bottom of the stoop.

"Did you fix things?"

"No," I whispered, swallowing the failure in the back of my throat. "I was too late." My lip quivered, and I closed my eyes to keep the tears from escaping. But they fell along my cheeks anyway. I could've blamed my emotional vulnerability on exhaustion, but that wasn't true. I hurt, much deeper than the tears rolling down my face could ever reveal.

"I'm sorry," Cole offered with sincerity. He rose from his perch and stepped toward me, wrapping me in his arms.

I could only nod, afraid to open my mouth because I didn't want to let out all that was trapped behind it. My failure to find Jonathan, to stop him and to make things right before he disappeared, crushed me. He hadn't responded to a single message I'd left, begging him to call me.

The final voice mail message I'd left at five o'clock this morning, before I drove back home, still echoed through my head. *"It's me again. This is my last message. I've been up all night driving, and thinking about what happened that night. And I wish I could take it back, every word I said. Because I was wrong. I wish I could've told you in person, but I don't know where you are. Please don't leave. Call me."*

Jonathan was gone. Staring into the window of his abandoned apartment, seeing that it had been completely cleared out, hit me harder than I was prepared for. I wanted to see him. I missed him.

I missed talking to him, missed the way he could make me laugh at the times I needed it most. I missed our late nights, both of us unable to sleep and making fun of infomercials in the early hours of the morning. Wanting more than anything to hear his voice one more time on the other end of the phone, waiting for me to call him...no matter what time or for what reason. Now he was no longer waiting.

I screwed up. I screwed up so bad. The acrid guilt ate at me with each mile I drove. But I was too late. I always realized the truth too late.

Cole stroked my hair as the tears continued to cascade down my cheeks, soaking into his shirt.

"I'm sorry I left like that yesterday." My voice was muffled against his chest. "I was panicked, and I didn't know how to explain…"

"It's okay," he murmured in my ear. "I'm sorry I got so angry. I just…I don't want anything to happen to you. And you scared me when you jumped. You didn't even think twice, you were just… gone."

I lifted my head and peered up at him. His eyes were heavy with concern. I ran my hand along the coarse blond stubble lining his jaw.

Cole brushed the tears from my cheek with his thumb. "I don't like seeing you so sad."

His words tugged at my heart. Then he lowered his mouth to mine and kissed me ever so gently, the brush of his lips igniting the charge between us.

I gripped the back of his neck and pressed my lips against his so hard it almost hurt. I needed to feel him, to taste him, for his hands to touch me so I could release the ache—even if just for a little while.

Cole pulled me against him, answering my silent plea with a heavy breath of want, gripping me so tightly I could feel his heart beat. He clutched my hand and led me into the house and up the stairs without pause. Shutting the door behind us and securing the lock, he turned toward me and ran his fingers into my hair, overwhelming me with a kiss that shot through my entire system with a shocking jolt.

His muscles tightened along his back as I ran my hands up under his shirt, digging my fingers into his flesh. He pulled his shirt over his head and continued kissing me—my mouth, my neck, my shoulder after stripping off my shirt—like he could kiss away the pain, wanting to make me whole. I knew that even if he kissed me every second for the rest of my life, I would still be broken. But I didn't want him to stop.

I devoured him as if he were a drug, desperate to push away the sadness. The taste of him, the cool scent of his skin, the heat of his flesh pressed against mine, fed the addiction and filled the void for the moment.

We lay on our stomachs under the covers, our faces pressed against the pillows, looking at each other. I leaned over and kissed his jaw.

"Why do you put up with me?" I questioned, my voice slightly above a whisper.

"Maybe I like being tortured," he responded playfully.

I laughed.

"I like making you laugh." His mouth formed that adorable tilted smile. "It's not easy, but it's worth the effort. And I like getting you naked." He leaned in and kissed me, running his warm hand along my back. "I didn't like what happened the last two days. I really thought…we were over." He pulled away so he could look me in the eye. "Is that what you want? To be over?"

I shook my head ever so slightly. It wasn't the answer I should have given, but it was the truth. "But I can't let you in, and that's not fair to you."

"Let me decide that."

I released a resigned breath. "Promise me one thing."

"What's that?"

"That you'll leave, that you'll walk away when I'm too much. Before I hurt you. I don't want to hurt you, but I'm not strong enough to give you up."

"I won't let you hurt me, Emma. I swear." He held me captive in the depths of his blue eyes, before leaning in and pressing against my lips. Cole rested his head back down on the pillow. I watched him close his eyes and eventually drift to sleep.

As I watched Cole beside me I found my thoughts drifting toward Jonathan. *No one could ever love you.*

I squeezed my eyes shut against the hate that had spewed from my mouth. He wasn't going to call me back, and I didn't blame him.

My search for redemption was futile. Words couldn't be unspoken, and the damage they did was irreparable. I knew that better than most.

But there was something more that kept me from falling asleep. Jonathan was planning to do something he could never undo—I needed to find him. I had to go to New York. If that's where he was, then that's where I needed to be.

———

I was roused by the sound of my phone vibrating. Lifting my heavy head, I peered at the clock. It was after four in the morning. I was about to roll back under the protection of Cole's arm when panic set in. *Jonathan.*

The phone fell silent. I slipped out of the bed and knelt on the floor, frantically searching the clothes abandoned on the floor in the dark. I slid a T-shirt that smelled of Cole over my bare skin and located my shorts just as my phone started up again. Seated next to the bed, I held it up and paused at the sight of the McKinleys' number on my screen.

I sighed, bracing for a lecture on the other end of the phone, assuming Sara had arrived home and called me as soon as it was daylight, not caring about the three-hour time difference. But just as I said, "Hello," it struck me that it wasn't possible for Sara to be home yet, and dread crashed into my stomach like a large stone thrown from a cliff.

"Emma?" Anna confirmed. "Emma, honey, it's Anna."

I couldn't breathe.

"Hi, Anna," I managed to choke out. Her voice was alarmingly distraught, even in the few words she'd said.

"Emma, something awful has happened," Anna continued, her voice cracking. "It's your mother." She paused. "She took her life late last night."

I was in the dark, deep in a hole that chilled me to the bone. I couldn't see. I couldn't hear. I couldn't feel anything except the cold. I clutched my knees to my chest and began rocking my trembling body.

"Emma? Are you there?"

Her voice was a distant buzz in my ear. "Honey, can you say something?"

"She's dead," I muttered, my voice sounding foreign, like it was coming from outside of my body.

"Yes. I'm so sorry." Anna's voice wavered. "We're going to get you home as soon as we can. I'm making arrangements now, okay?"

Her voice disappeared, and I was isolated in the dark again, unable to hear her. I lowered the phone and braced against the frigidness that enveloped me.

I hate her, Sara, I hate her so much...I wish she were dead.

"Emma?" Meg broke through the voices. I squinted up at her in confusion. The room was so bright with the overhead light, it felt like I was staring into the sun. "Emma, can you hear me?" She knelt down next to me, slowly coming into focus. Alarmed, I glanced around and noticed that there were more people in my room. Peyton was sitting on the bed, and Serena was on the floor on the other side of me, holding my hand.

I glanced up and saw Cole, watching me from within the open doorway. Luke and James were in the hall, talking softly.

My eyes flicked from face to face in confusion. Then I remembered. The air was expelled from my lungs as if my chest had been punctured. "Did I wake you?" I questioned, focusing on Meg's sorrowful green eyes.

"No, you didn't wake us," she assured me. "Sara's mom called me. Emma, I'm so sorry."

She wrapped her arms around my shoulders as Serena squeezed my hand. I patted her on the back gently, trying to console her. I was still in the dark, unable to connect with what was happening. So I let her hold me for as long as she needed.

———

"I'll see you when I get back." I hugged Meg and Serena at the curb of the airport drop-off. Then I turned to face Cole. He examined me as if I were made of glass that was slowly cracking, fearing I'd shatter with the slightest pressure. "I'll see you in Santa Barbara before you know it."

"I wish you'd let me go with you," he said, lightly running his thumb along my cheek.

"I know," I responded in a hush. "But *I* don't even want to go back. I have to. Besides, you have to get ready for finals, and you can't miss classes. It's better this way. Sara will be there, so I'll be fine."

"Will you call me?"

I nodded. He leaned in and brushed my lips with his.

I left them behind me, my face masked with a faint smile of assurance, trying to make them feel as if I were more held together than I was. Then I turned toward the entrance, walking through the electric doors, and panic swept through my stomach like a turbulent storm. I concentrated on breathing as I rolled through security, half expecting to be pulled aside for suspicious behavior as beads of sweat spread across my forehead.

I sat in a chair facing the runway, uncertain how I was going to force myself onto the plane to fly to the one place in the world I'd never intended to return. I hadn't set one foot in Weslyn since the day I'd fled two years ago, and I was on the verge of sprinting back out of the terminal to keep it that way when my phone rang.

"Hi," I answered faintly.

"How are you doing?" Sara asked.

"Really?"

"Yeah, I know. Stupid question. I'll be picking you up from the airport. I'll help you get through this."

"Thanks," I said, wanting it to be over already. I'd kept myself busy contacting my professors to explain why I wouldn't be in classes this week and arranging to make up the final exams later in the summer. I hadn't stopped for a moment to think of anything— not until I stepped through the airport door, and the reality of what was happening became unavoidable.

"Sara, I'm not staying in Weslyn."

"What? What do you mean? My parents are expecting you to stay at our house."

"I can't." My voice was strained. "There's a motel along the highway, right outside town. I'll stay there. I really…can't."

"Okay," Sara soothed patiently. "Just concentrate on getting on the plane. We'll figure the rest out when I see you."

The airline representative announced that they were about to start boarding.

"I have to go," I told her. "I'll see you later."

"I'll be here," Sara assured me.

I boarded the plane and tucked my carry-on in the bin above before taking the window seat, excusing myself past two middle-aged men dressed in business suits. I gazed blindly out the window as my breath shot out in short bursts.

"Don't like flying?" the man next to me asked, eyeing my hands twisting around each other in my lap.

"It's more about the landing," I murmured honestly.

"I fly all of the time," he assured me. "There's nothing to worry about."

I nodded, trying to push my lips into a smile, but failed to look anything other than terrified. I closed my eyes and clenched my hands into fists, willing myself to calm down. I was on the verge of a full-on panic attack.

"You could use a drink," he observed with a slight chuckle.

"Too bad I'm only nineteen."

He eyed me like I was losing my mind. Which wasn't far from the truth. "If you're going to be like this the entire flight, I'll buy you a drink."

"Sure," I responded, desperate to be rid of the anxiety.

Once we were in flight, the two men each ordered a vodka and soda while I requested a water. I was surprised when they both handed me their drinks. I guess I wasn't the best flight companion.

"Thanks," I responded, reaching for my wallet to pay them back.

The man beside me held up his hand, "Don't worry about it."

I sucked the drinks down with a frantic thirst and returned them to the gentlemen's tray tables with the ice barely melted. They chuckled, and about an hour later, when I was still gripping the arm of the seat like I expected the plane to go down any minute, two more drinks were set in front of me.

"Miss," I heard through the fog in my head. "Miss, we've landed." A hand gently touched my shoulder. I peeled my face off the window and looked around in confusion. It took me a few blinks to recognize where I was.

"Shit." I sighed, making the flight attendant with the bright yellow hair raise her eyebrows in surprise. "Uh, thanks."

I unbuckled and tried to concentrate on getting out of the seat without falling over, the vodka still dancing in my head. Thankfully the plane was practically empty, so I didn't have to fight with passengers to get my luggage. I pulled it down from the overhead compartment and nearly knocked myself out when it hit the top of my head.

"Can I help you with that?" the male attendant offered, eyeing me nervously.

"No, I got it," I insisted, flushing with embarrassment. "Thanks." I took a deep breath and rolled the suitcase after me, trying to convey some semblance of sobriety.

I continued up the jetway toward the terminal, pausing once because I was convinced my knees were going to buckle and I'd fall on my face. The buzz in my head was fading, and the panic was forcing itself to the surface. If I was going to make it through this airport without collapsing, then I needed a little help.

14. JUST LIKE YOUR MOTHER

M y phone vibrated in my hand as soon as I switched it off airplane mode, just as I'd anticipated it would.

"Hi," I said, closing my eyes and leaning my head back against the wall.

"Where are you?" Sara asked, her voice steady but with a hint of unease.

"Umm..." I paused, swallowing the lump in my throat. "I don't know. Outside a bar."

"You were drinking?"

I remained quiet, waiting for the vodka to coat my insides with its numbing potency.

"I'm sorry," I whispered, biting my lip, which refused to stop quivering. "I can't do this Sara. I...can't..."

"It's okay. I'm here. Just tell me where you are."

"Uh...still in the terminal," I looked around, ignoring the glances shot in my direction.

"Follow the signs to baggage claim. I'm here," she instructed, her voice calm and soothing.

"Okay," I choked, grabbing the handle of my suitcase and standing up from the bench. I paused for a moment to steady myself. My feet haphazardly carried me toward the rolling sidewalk. I realized I still had the phone against my face. "Sara?"

"Yeah, I'm still here," Sara responded. "Are you coming?"

"Yeah," I breathed, closing my eyes. My insides tightened, and I feared I was going to collapse as I leaned against the railing that moved me along the conveyor. "I…can't…"

"Yes, you can," she encouraged me. "I'm going to get you through this."

"Fuck," I uttered, stumbling off the end of the moving sidewalk. I stood off to the side to collect myself and let other gawking passengers pass me. "I'll be right there."

Sara was at the bottom of the escalator, impatiently awaiting my arrival. As soon as I stepped onto the carpet, she pulled me in to her. I squeezed my eyes shut, determined not to cry.

"I've missed you so much," she murmured in my ear, holding me firmly to keep me upright. I wavered on my feet when she let go. She looked me up and down. "You look like shit."

I released a broken laugh. "I feel worse. Actually…" I hesitated, thinking. "I'm starting not to feel anything right about now."

"Oh, Emma." She shook her head, looking concerned, "I leave you for a few months, and you become a lush. What am I going to do with you?" She grabbed my hand and my suitcase, dragging us both toward the exit. "You need to sober up, or at least act sober, because we're meeting my mom right now."

"Shit, really?" I groaned. "I didn't know…I'm sorry."

"It's okay." She sighed. "But let's try not to self-medicate with alcohol for the next few days, alright?"

I didn't promise anything, but continued to let her lead me toward her car. Being by Sara's side, in combination with the drunken swirl that was overtaking me, eased my nerves…momentarily.

The hour drive wasn't long enough. It wasn't long enough to sober up. It wasn't long enough to prepare myself for the reason I'd returned to Weslyn.

We pulled into the small parking lot alongside the light blue Victorian house. It looked so warm and inviting from the outside, but on the inside I knew it was filled with death. I shivered.

"We won't be long," Sara assured me, pulling me away from staring at the sign—LIONEL'S FUNERAL HOME—posted on the lawn. "Come on, Em. My mom is waiting. Charles is with her too, to help with the details."

I couldn't really say what happened after that. I swear I blacked out, because the next thing I knew, we were back in the car.

"Told you it would be quick," Sara said, buckling her seat belt.

"Yeah," I inhaled, feeling like it was the first breath I'd taken since we'd pulled up.

"I just need to stop by the house to pick up my bag," Sara explained as we pulled away.

"What? No!" I exclaimed a little too loudly.

"What's wrong?" Sara questioned in alarm.

"I can't go any farther into Weslyn," I said passionately. I was grateful that they'd hidden the funeral home along the borders of the town, so the residents could remain blissfully ignorant of the pain in their backyards. "Please, Sara, take me to the motel."

Sara was quiet a moment and finally said, "Okay. I'll drop you off and then come back to get my things."

"Thank you," I said, relieved. I pressed my head against the glass and watched the trees blur by. The numbness was subsiding, and exhaustion settled in. "Maybe I'll lie down for a while."

"That's not a bad idea."

Minutes later, it was like we'd crossed an invisible line and were instantly transported into a world of billboards and neon lights, with the roar of traffic flying by on the highway overhead. Sara pulled into the broken asphalt parking lot.

"This is where we're staying?" Sara asked. It was obvious she was skeeved out by the place. Admittedly, it wasn't much to look at. The blue paint was faded and chipping, and the numbers on some of the doors had been replaced with numbers that didn't match. There was a pool with a chain link fence around it. The water was an unnatural hue of green that reminded me of a sci-fi movie where alien eggs incubated at the bottom of the pool.

"Are you sure this is what you want to do?" I knew it was her way of begging me to change my mind.

"You don't have to stay," I told her, opening the door.

"Yeah, I do," she replied, her voice resigned. "I'll check us in if you want to grab your bag out of the trunk."

After she returned, I followed Sara up the cement stairs with the rickety metal railing and allowed her to open the door to room 212, with the second two slightly askew. The room smelled of chemicals, stale cigarettes and…age, like it'd been festering for too long within its decaying walls.

Sara yanked back the thick dark blue drapes to let in the sun. It didn't really matter; the room still felt dark. It shrank away from the light in permanent shadows. I didn't mind. I felt an instant connection with its darkness, preferring it to the bright May sunlight outside.

I sat on the bed farthest from the window and removed my shoes, contemplating lying down to recover from the fog that floated through my head.

"I'll be back in a little while," Sara promised, standing by the door, inspecting me. "I'll bring back food too."

She hesitated, conflicted about leaving me alone.

"I'll be fine," I said, providing the assurance she needed to walk out the door. She smiled faintly and left. I stared at the closed beige metal door.

Emma, I'm so sorry.

I blinked away the feel of Anna's arms around me and the image of her red, teary eyes.

You look so thin.

I squeezed my eyes shut tighter, fending off the voices. Fragments of my time at the funeral home were surfacing now that I was sobering.

Rubbing the grogginess from my eyes, I pushed off the bed, walked over to the large window and looked down at the pool with the plastic lawn chairs scattered around it.

We picked out pictures to display tomorrow. Do you want to look through them to tell us what you think?

Your mother requested to be cremated....Which urn would you prefer?

I shuddered and wrapped my arms tight around my chest, shaking my head violently, not wanting to hear them, to see the shiny boxes and the ornate vases.

Where would your mother have preferred to have her tombstone?

"Stop!" I yelled, clutching the sides of my head. "Shut up!" I slammed my hand against the glass, and it shook under my palm.

A small shack across the street drew my attention—faded cardboard signs propped up in the windows advertised beer and liquor.

I breathed in heavily through my nostrils with my teeth clenched, trying to hold it together. But I knew it wouldn't be long before I lost it completely. I eyed the liquor store again. A place like that probably wouldn't card, but I didn't want to risk it. I needed a sure thing.

I scanned the parking lot, and settled on a figure by the pool. A guy in a white tank top and faded jeans sat on a sagging chair, smoking a cigarette, wearing oversize headphones. He looked like he was easily over twenty-one. I took in a breath, committed to silencing the noise.

Grabbing my tote bag with my wallet and room key inside, I didn't bother covering my bare feet. He didn't seem the type to pass judgment. If anything, approaching him barefoot might win me some points. With that in mind, I clipped my bangs back, shook my fingers through my hair and stripped off my light sweater to reveal a fitted tank top beneath. I flipped a strap so it dangled off my shoulder and allowed desperation to provide the courage I needed to walk down the rough stairs toward the pool

It didn't take him long to notice me, and he wasn't subtle about it either as he scanned every inch of my body, sliding the headphones around his neck. I contained the shudder as he molested me with his eyes.

"Hey," I smiled flirtatiously. "What are you up to?"

"Not much," he responded, running a grease-stained hand through his mop of sandy blond hair. "You?"

"My friends and I are throwing a party in our room later," I explained, trying to sound as flighty as I could, "but I can't buy. I was wondering if you could help me out? You can invite your friends over too if you want."

"Oh, yeah." He grinned, licking his lower lip. I swallowed the bile rising in the back of my throat. "I suppose I could help you out. What do you want?"

"Vodka," I said, almost too quickly. I grimaced, hoping he hadn't picked up on the desperation in my voice. I dug in my wallet and produced a handful of twenties from the cash Charles Stanley had provided me earlier while we were at the funeral parlor.

"Nice," he said admiringly. "You want the good stuff?" I shrugged indifferently as he took the bills, his fingers sliding along mine in the exchange. I fought the urge to pull away. "Do you want anything to mix it with?"

"Uh, not really," I responded, knowing I needed it as potent as I could get it if I were going to survive the next couple of days. "How about a couple of limes?"

"Sure thing, sweet cheeks." He winked. "I'm Kevin by the way."

"Well, thanks a lot for helping a girl out, Kevin," I responded, trying my best to flutter my eyes, as pathetic as it felt.

"I'll be right back," he assured me, swatting me on the ass as he passed. I released a small yelp that made him laugh.

In his absence, I filled a bag of ice and found a couple wrapped plastic cups. I returned to the pool just as he strutted across the parking lot with a paper bag teetering on his arm.

"Here you go." He presented me with two bottles of vodka. "I bought one for me too."

"That's fine," I responded, unscrewing the top and letting the clear liquid flow over the ice cubes, almost sighing as I gulped down half the cup. My stomach ignited upon contact, sending a shiver through me with a rush of saliva in the back of my throat.

Kevin lowered himself onto the lawn chair on the other side of the plastic table, grabbed a cup and scooped ice out of the bag, an unlit cigarette dangling from his mouth. He started talking. I had no idea what he was saying. I just nodded and stared at the green water, sipping the chilled vodka, waiting for the numbness—impatiently filling the cup two or three more times.

Near my father. She'd want her headstone in the same place as my father's.

I crushed my teeth together, fighting against the persistent buzz of voices penetrating the numb barrier. I swallowed down the rest of the vodka and dumped more on top of the cubes of ice.

It would be nice for you to share some moments you had with your mother.

I was at the edge of the pool, staring into its murky green depths. My body was numb, but the voices kept talking. They wouldn't stop. I slowly shook my head, needing to be rid of them.

I closed my eyes and took a step. The water was cool, and the chlorine burned my nose as the water rushed in around me. I pulled my knees up into me and sank to the bottom, my feet thumping against the rough concrete. I kept my eyes closed. And finally, there was… silence. I hugged my knees tighter against me and absorbed the quiet.

I released small bursts of air through my nose. After a time my lungs began to burn, but I didn't move. I let the cool water keep me captive. The panic never set in, like in my dreams. I'd drowned many times in my sleep. I was always so afraid, frantic to breathe. But here…there was calm. Inviting me to stay.

I ignored the need to inhale and the growing pressure in my chest. The water murmured around me. I opened my eyes and listened. It sounded like…yelling. I jerked my head up and saw two figures looming over the edge of the pool, Sara's red hair hanging above the water.

I pushed hard off the pool's hard bottom and inhaled deeply as I broke through, swallowing water with the air. I began choking on the chemically tainted water, coughing until I thought I might vomit. My breath eventually evened out as I clutched the side of the pool. That's when the yelling cut through, as if I'd just released the mute button.

"Holy shit, Emma!" Sara bellowed. Her shoes were kicked off, like she was about to jump in. "What the hell were you doing down there?!"

"She's a fucking psycho, is what she is!" Kevin shouted behind her. "She looked like a fucking zombie who just kept walking into the water. Your friend's a wack job, sister."

"Shut up!" Sara yelled over her shoulder as I pulled myself up to sit on the edge of the pool. "Just get the fuck away from us!"

"You don't have to tell me twice," he said. "Fucking psycho." He continued rambling as he walked across the parking lot with the paper bag in his hand.

"Are you okay?" Sara asked as I coughed again, spitting up water.

I nodded. Sara sighed heavily. "Emma, that was messed up." She helped me to my feet, shaking her head.

Sara waited by the pool's gate as I collected my tote bag. I was about to grab the nearly empty bottle of vodka when she demanded, "Leave it." I released my grip and silently followed her into the motel room.

Puddles of water trailed from my wet jeans as I walked through the motel room and into the bathroom. I stripped off the sopping clothes and stood under the blast of hot water in the shower until it turned cold. I still couldn't feel a thing. No emotion. No sensation. No thoughts. And the voices were vanquished.

I fumbled for a towel to wrap around my head and another to cover my body. The scratchy white material barely covered me. Sara sat at the small round table on a stained fabric-covered chair. She raised her head when I emerged from the fog-filled bathroom, clouds of vapor billowing out after me.

I avoided eye contact as the room swirled around me. My feet were finding it difficult to hold me up. I plopped down on the edge of the bed and pressed my palms against my eyes.

"I know you don't want to be here," Sara said quietly, fighting her emotions. "I can only imagine how hard this is for you. But Emma, you're not alone. And you have to realize that you have people who care about you. Who want to help you."

I blinked heavily and raised my eyes to focus on her.

"You can't keep pushing everyone away." She stood up from the chair, her body tense. "You can't keep doing this, because one of these days, you'll wake up and have no one."

I squinted my eyes up toward her, her words echoing in my head. "What?"

"I'm not going to let you," Sara's passionate plea took on strength with each word. "I won't let you push me away too." When I still didn't react, she pressed her lips together, and her eyes watered. "Do you hear what I'm saying?! Emma, look at me!"

I lolled my head to the side, having difficulty balancing it on my shoulders.

"Goddammit, Em!" she cried, shaking her head. Her jaw tensed, and her fingers curled into fists. "I'm not going to let you do this to yourself! No matter what. I won't let you end up like your mother!"

I froze. My eyes steadied on her. Sara's face paled when she realized what she'd just said. "Get out."

"Emma, I'm sorry," she cried. "I didn't mean that."

"Get out!" I screamed, making her jump.

Sara brushed away a tear and nodded slightly. Taking the room key and her purse, she moved toward the door. She gave me a sorrowful glance before closing it behind her.

My whole body quivered. I fell onto my side on the bed and folded the stale white sheets around me. I stared at the wall as the room swirled around me. Everything inside remained quiet. Eventually I closed my eyes and succumbed to the nothingness.

15. DIFFERENT

I stood in the corner of the main parlor in the funeral home, withdrawing from the mourners swarming around me. A shimmer of light caught my eye across the room. I stared out at the soft blue sky and wisps of clouds as they drifted past the small rectangular window at the top of the wall. The clouds appeared so white against the pristine sky, floating as if carried along a river. A bird fluttered across the scene occasionally, making me wish I were soaring alongside it—away from the whispers, the consoling words, the hands that jostled me and arms that clutched me to unfamiliar bodies. I needed to escape the sorrowful faces and teary eyes.

Did you hear she hanged herself?

I blinked, my blissful retreat interrupted. I scanned the room filled with faces. Faces that wouldn't stop watching me.

"Emma, I am so sorry." A slender older female stood before me, startling me. I pressed my lips into a tight appreciative smile. She hugged me. I stiffened against her. "I worked with Rachel, and she was always so happy. I'm going to miss her."

I nodded absently. "Thank you."

Tied the rope around the banister and jumped. Broke her neck instantly.

My eyes jumped from face to face, looking for the source of the whispering. Pain catapulted through my head with the movement, repercussions from the poolside vodka. My vision blurred slightly. I raised my hand to my head, convinced I was hearing things.

"Emma, have you eaten?"

"Huh?" I jolted to attention. It was the first time I'd heard Sara's voice all day. We hadn't spoken since she returned to the motel room sometime in the night.

"Emma?" Sara inspected me carefully. "What's wrong?"

"Um…nothing." I tried to breathe evenly. "I think…I think I need a break."

"You should eat something," she encouraged. "My mom's fixing you a plate in the kitchen."

I nodded absently, my eyes still twitching from face to face. I felt like I was losing it. My head was in so much pain, I could have heard anything and not understood a word.

I tried to slip through the bodies, but was stopped with hugs and words of condolence along the way. I'd perfected "thank you" so much so that it slipped from my mouth automatically, without truly hearing the sentiment that prompted it.

You've never thought about anyone other than yourself my entire life! You're not a mother, you never have been!

They didn't know the truth about the woman they were mourning. I knew too well, and seeing the captured seconds of happiness displayed around the room was enough to put me over the edge.

I slipped into the kitchen at the end of the hall, unnoticed. I found a tall glass and filled it with ice before retreating back into the hallway and easing open the door to the office I'd been in yesterday. Behind the large desk was a closet, and in that closet was my tote bag, which contained the only thing that could cure my headache and erase all of these people from existence.

I unscrewed the bottle and tipped the vodka into the glass, taking a few sips with a shudder. With a small tin of Altoids in my pocket, I left the room clutching the glass firmly in my hand, slinking back to my corner and setting it behind me within reach. I remained there, staring out the window, uttering "thank you" to the droves of people gathered to pay tribute to the woman who had never been my mother.

I didn't want to be here. I probably didn't want to be here any more than she did. But I wasn't here for Rachel Walace. I maneuvered through the crowd when we entered the funeral home filled with pictures and flowers. I didn't give the images a second glance, trying to blend in, to stay out of her sight until I was ready. I wasn't convinced that would be any time soon.

"She's in the other room."

I looked down to find the kind face of Ms. Mier in front of me.

"Hi, Ms. Mier. It's nice to see you." I smiled warmly at the woman who had always taken the time to understand, and often understood more than we realized.

"It's nice to see you too, Evan. I wish it were under better circumstances. I hope you're doing well at Yale." She patted my arm, and just before she passed me, she said quietly, "She's in the far corner in the other room. You should talk to her."

"Thank you," I replied, nodding appreciatively.

I did want to talk to her. I'd been waiting for two years to talk to her. But I knew this wasn't the place to do it.

"Evan—" Sara confronted me with a stern look on her face. "What are you—" She released a heavy breath. "I know you had to be here. Really, I do. But she shouldn't see you."

I was expecting this reaction, but it didn't mean I liked it.

"Hi, Sara," I responded. "Can I do anything to help?"

She sighed. "No, we're okay. But Evan, just know that... she's different," *she murmured before disappearing into the crowd. I looked after her, struck by her words.*

I continued down the hall that ended at the kitchen and allowed entry into the grand parlor. I scanned the room, filled with familiar faces from high school, and others I didn't recognize. *Searching for her—needing to see her, whether I was ready or not.*

"Emma dear." Her voice stilled my breath. "I am so sorry for your loss."

I stared right into the vibrant blue eyes of Vivian Mathews, unable to speak.

She ran her cool, thin hand down the side of my face. "You are such a strong young woman. I wish you didn't have to go through this."

I shifted my gaze, before she saw that my "strength" was barely holding me up.

"I'm sorry about your mother, Emma," Jared's deep voice offered in condolence. The need to escape seized me. I nodded slightly.

Vivian wrapped me gingerly in her arms and said soothingly in my ear, "If you ever need anything, I am here for you."

My hands shook as I feebly returned her embrace.

And then they were gone, lost in the crowd. I looked around for them, certain that if they were here, so was he. I turned toward the glass set in the corner and took several large gulps to ease my nerves. I wasn't ready. I didn't think I'd ever be ready to see Evan again, but it didn't stop me from looking around the room, searching for his steel-blue eyes.

Then I saw her. At the same moment she saw me. Her light brown eyes froze as if she'd been ensnared. The hints of the California sun suited her, but she looked drained and fragile in her dark dress. She'd cut her hair so it rested against her jaw, her bangs sweeping along her brow. She was thinner, the roundness of her face replaced by slender angles and jutting cheekbones. I almost could've convinced myself it wasn't her, but then I saw the blush rise to her cheeks, and I felt my mouth turn up slightly. She was still breath-takingly beautiful. Except for the vacancy in her eyes.

"Evan, I can't believe you're here."

I pulled my eyes away from Emma.

"Hi, Jill. How've you been?" I fought every desire to ignore the insensitive girl, and smiled politely in her direction.

I stole a glance back to where Emma had been. But she was gone.

"Have you spoken to Analise lately?" she pried, never one to respect personal boundaries.

"Not in a while, no," I responded, looking around for an escape.

"She would die if she knew you were here," Jill continued to harp. "Have you seen Emma? I swear she's hungover."

"Her mother just died, Jill," I said sternly, trying to conceal my anger.

"I still don't understand why you're here," she repeated. "I mean, after what she did to you… omigod."

I refused to react to her comment. "It was good seeing you again, Jill. But I'm going to see if Mrs. McKinley needs my help."

I pushed farther into the room, peering over and around the mourners, but Emma had disappeared.

"I thought you weren't going to talk to her," Jared said, coming up beside me.

"I'm not," I replied guiltily. "I was looking for you."

"Yeah, right," he scoffed. Then his attention was drawn toward the red hair that weaved through the crowd.

"Are you going to talk to her?"

He glared in response.

"What the hell do I say? Besides, this isn't exactly the best place to talk." I knew exactly what he meant. His eyes continued to follow her. As if sensing him, Sara looked up and they made eye contact. Jared looked at her dumbly. I nudged him to pursue her, but she whipped herself around and strode aggressively in the opposite direction.

"That went well," I said sardonically.

"Shut up," he muttered. "Emma was looking for you. As soon as she saw Mom and me, she looked for you. So what are you going to do?"

"I don't know yet," I admitted, still searching the faces for the girl who had broken my heart.

Once I saw Vivian I knew he'd be here. I shook my head and paced the office. I couldn't go back out there. Not until I knew Evan was gone. I felt like my heart was going to pound out of my chest. I looked down at the silver box I'd tucked under my arm on my way out of the room.

"What the hell is he doing here?" I asked the object. The panic continued to build; I couldn't calm down. I could hear people talking on the other side of the door, and recognized the funeral director's dreary tone. Not wanting to explain why I was in his office holding my mother's ashes, I rushed to the closet behind his desk and hid inside.

I held my breath, waiting for the voices in the office to disappear. When the light clicked off and the door closed behind them, I exhaled and rested against the wall. I reached above my head and found a string. An exposed bulb illuminated the long, narrow closet. My jacket, along with Sara, Anna's and Carl's, hung on the metal pipe secured into each side of the wall. At the far end was a stack of brown metal folding chairs. My feet bumped the tote bag on the floor.

"I might as well," I murmured. "I mean, it is *your* memorial."

I slid down the wall and kicked off my shoes. The glass I'd emptied in the parlor had taken the edge off. But it wasn't enough. I unscrewed the bottle.

"Cheers, Mom." I tapped the metal box with the bottle before taking a large swig and embraced the swirl that rocked through my head.

I stared at the shiny silver container, taking a few more gulps of the numbing elixir.

"Did you really hang yourself?" I paused as if she'd really answer. "Why? Why would you do that? Were you really that unhappy?" I released a heavy breath and rested my arm on the top of the box. "Well…I hope you got what you wanted. I hope the pain's gone."

"Sara," I interrupted her while she was speaking with some parents I only recognized by sight. "Do you have a minute?"

Sara excused herself and approached me. "What is it?"

"Have you seen Emma?"

Sara stopped to think. "Umm… not in a while, actually. She was supposed to go in the kitchen to get something to eat. But that was like a half hour ago."

"Where do you think she is?" Sara avoided my eyes, which made me even more concerned. "Sara, do you think she's okay?"

Sara couldn't look at me. Instead she started scanning the thinning crowd.

"I'll look in the kitchen," she told me. "Let me know if you see her."

Sara was more concerned than I was anticipating. I didn't know why, but I knew we needed to find Emma before anyone else did.

"Cole!" I exclaimed loudly when he answered the phone, my voice echoing in the enclosed space. "Oops, that was loud. Shhh!" I pressed my finger over my lips.

"Emma? What's going on? Where's Sara?" He didn't sound too happy to hear from me. I wondered if he was still mad at me.

"I don't know," I answered simply. "She's out there somewhere. Cole, are you still mad at me?"

"What?" He sounded confused. "No. But right now I'm worried about you. Where are you?"

"In a closet. With my mom. We're drinking."

Cole was silent for a moment. "Umm…what did you say?"

I started laughing. "That did sound funny, huh?"

"Emma, where's Sara?"

"Do you not want to talk to me?" I asked in confusion. "Why do you want to talk to Sara?"

"I'm kind of going crazy, because I'm in California, and I have no idea what you're going through right now. And the fact that you've locked yourself in a closet to drink doesn't sound good."

"Omigod, is the door locked?" I asked in a rush. I reached up and turned the handle and cracked the door slightly. "It's not locked." I laughed.

"Emma." Cole sighed. "I can be there tomorrow."

"No!" I shouted back, then said firmly, "I don't want you here. You don't belong here. I don't belong here. I'm stuck. I'm stuck in yesterday, and you're tomorrow. And I'll see you in two more tomorrows. Okay?"

"I have no idea what you just said."

I leaned my head against the wall with the phone pressed against my face and the nearly depleted bottle between my legs. "Cole."

"Yes, Emma?"

I closed my eyes, and I couldn't open them again.

"Emma?"

I heard him through the fog, but I couldn't find him. "Emma?"

"Emma?" Sara whispered into the office. Light seeped out under the closet door. "Shit."

I followed her into the room, shutting the door behind us before flipping on the light. I was suddenly concerned about what we were going to find behind that door.

Sara opened it and then shook her head. "You've got to be kidding me."

I stood behind her, and it took me a moment to interpret what I was seeing. Emma lay slumped against the wall with what was left of a bottle of vodka spilled on the floor next to her and a cell phone in her hand.

"Is she drunk?" I asked in shocked disbelief.

"I told you she was different." Sara leaned over and pushed the hair out of Emma's face, tucking it behind her ear. She removed the cell phone from her hand and listened.

I could only watch; I was having a hard time coming to grips with this image. My brow furrowed with the roll of anger rippling through me.

"Hello?" Her eyes widened in surprise when she heard a voice on the other end. "Cole. Hey. Yeah, I found her." She listened. "She's... passed out.

But I'm going to take her back to the motel now, and I'll have her call you in the morning." She hung up the phone and tossed it in the blue striped bag that was on the floor.

"Shit," Sara muttered again, inspecting Emma's limp body. "How the hell am I going to get her out of here without my mother seeing this?"

"Did you just say you were staying in a motel?" I asked. "Why aren't you staying at your house?"

"Because Emma wants nothing to do with Weslyn." Sara's answer made perfect sense, but it still felt like someone had punched me in the gut. "She had a hard enough time being here, obviously." She waved her hands over her.

"She's not staying at a motel, especially that dive along the highway, if that's the one you're talking about."

Sara flashed her eyes up at me in frustration. "Do you have a better plan? Because I can't let my mother know she did this. She'd lose it."

"She can stay at my house." I said it before I'd really given it much thought. "She can stay in the guest room."

"No. Way." Sara retorted firmly. "That is the worst idea ever."

"If you want my help getting her out of here, then she's staying at my house."

"Evan, why would you want that?" I didn't say anything. But after seeing Emma like this, I knew there was more going on than I understood. I was already about to split open with the questions that I'd been left with two years ago, and this was more than I could handle.

Sara didn't push for the answer that I didn't have. She kept shaking her head, at a loss for a better plan.

"Then I'm staying too," Sara insisted.

"Fine. You can stay in the other guest room."

"And you know she's going to be beyond pissed when she wakes up," she warned me.

"I think where she wakes up will be the least of her worries." I nodded toward the passed-out girl on the closet floor, unable to connect her to the girl I used to know. It seemed impossible they were the same person.

"Pull my car around to the back," I instructed. "Come in and get us when the path through the kitchen is clear. I think most people have left by now anyway."

Sara stared at me, the disapproval heavy on her face. "One night, Evan. That's it."

I shrugged. "Fine. You'll have to convince her to stay with you tomorrow, because that motel's not an option."

Sara reached out and took the keys from my hand. She walked forward a few steps, then hesitated, turning back to take the silver box with her.

I leaned against the door frame, listening to the deep breaths pass through Emma's full lips. I wasn't prepared for any of this.

"Emma, what happened?" I pulled out my phone to check the time, waiting for Sara to return, and stared back down at the unconscious girl on the floor with a disgruntled breath.

"We're all set," Sara declared. I turned away from the unrecognizable figure. Sara picked up the shoes and retrieved the bag from the closet. I knelt down next to Emma, sliding an arm beneath her thighs and wrapping the other around her ribs. Her body fell into me, her arm dangling by her side. I stood, the movement not stirring her at all. Sara tucked the skirt of her dress in between my arm and her legs before leading me out the door.

I could feel her breath against my neck and my shoulders tightened, not comfortable having her this close to me. I swallowed against the tension in my jaw and followed Sara quickly through the kitchen into the cool spring night.

I set her on the passenger seat, and Sara closed the door. "I'm going to the motel to get our bags. I won't be long." I shook my head with a half grin, knowing she didn't want Emma to wake up without her there.

I sat in the driver's seat and looked over at her again. The pale light of the night softened the lines of her face, reminding me of the girl I once knew. She could have easily been just sleeping, hiding her haunted eyes under her lids. Watching her peaceful face, something roused inside me, and I knew I was in trouble.

16. YESTERDAY

"Could use a little help here," I hollered through the screen door. I heard loud footsteps approaching from inside the house.

"What the hell?" Jared exclaimed.

"Just open the fricken door, Jared." He propped the door open and let me pass.

"What happened?" he asked, following me through the kitchen.

"Vodka happened," I grumbled. "We found her passed out in a closet."

"Holy shit." Jared gawked, remaining a step behind me as I climbed the stairs. "And you thought bringing her here was the best idea?"

"It's only one night." I waited for Jared to open the door, but he just stood there and stared at me. "Come on. Open the door."

He shook his head in disapproval. "I can't believe you're carrying Emma into our house… passed out." Jared pushed the door open and followed me into the room, flipping on the lights.

"You sound like Sara," I mumbled, then added, "Who is staying here too." I grinned, awaiting his reaction.

"What?" Jared's eyes stretched wide. "Evan, are you fucking serious?!"

"Fold down the bedding," I instructed with a light chuckle. "Now you'll get the chance to talk to her." I gently laid Emma on the crisp white sheet.

"This isn't exactly how I'd prepared to talk to her."

Emma's black skirt spread on the bed, and I noticed the large bandage below her right knee. Blotches of blood were seeping through. I remained *standing above her, scanning her body for other injuries with a knot in my stomach.*

"And you kidnapping Emma wasn't the best way for you to talk to her," Jared snapped.

I leaned over and brushed the hair from her cheek, then eased the covers over her unmoving body.

"I didn't kidnap her," I countered, facing my brother. He led the way out of the room. I glanced back at her one more time before turning off the light and shutting the door behind us.

"Yeah, because I'm sure if she had a choice, this is exactly where she'd want to wake up," Jared scoffed.

"I couldn't let her sleep in that sleazy motel on the outside of town. It's not exactly the safest place to stay."

Jared laughed at me. "I think she'd prefer it."

"Shut up, Jared."

"Evan? Did I hear you?" my mother called to us from below the landing. She must have been in her office when we'd arrived.

"He brought Emma here," Jared blurted. I whipped my head toward him and glowered. I would have shoved him if our mother wasn't watching.

"Evan, could you please come downstairs?" she requested quietly, but with a seriousness to her tone that made my back straighten. Jared shot me a now-you're-going-to-get-it look. I swore under my breath as I passed him.

I followed my mother into the kitchen. She might have only come up to my chest, but she had a way of reverting me back to a five-year-old boy with a single glance.

"Have a seat," she encouraged, standing before the kitchen counter. I settled on a stool and set my hands on my thighs, preparing for whatever disapproving lecture she was about to unleash.

"Why is Emma here?" She studied my face carefully. I knew the only way through this was to be honest.

"Sara and I found her passed out in a closet. I couldn't leave her there. And Sara didn't want to upset her mother. So I brought her here."

My mother nodded thoughtfully. "And what's going to happen tomorrow when she wakes up?"

I swallowed and shrugged. My mother shook her head.

"Evan, it's important that you realize what you've started. This one decision is now going to force you to make a succession of harder decisions. "

"I don't understand."

"You had to intervene when you saw her like this. I understand that. But what's going to happen when it's time for her to board the plane back to California? Are you going to be able to let her go, not knowing what will happen to her? You need to think this through."

I nodded slightly, weighing her words.

"You have a decision to make. And this time… it's yours to make. I won't stand in your way."

A tap at the door drew my mother's attention. I jumped up from the stool. "It's Sara."

I pushed the door open for her, and Sara came in, wheeling two suitcases behind her, with a garment bag draped over her arm and a large canvas bag hanging from the other shoulder. I took the bags from her and set them on a dining room chair.

"Sara, love," my mother greeted her with a warm smile. "I understand you'll be staying with us this evening." She rested her hands on Sara's shoulders and leaned in to kiss her cheek.

"I hope you don't mind." Sara smiled at my mother, flashing me a dagger-driven glare out of the corner of her eye.

"Not at all. You are always welcome here," my mother assured her. She then turned toward me, her sharp blue eyes connecting with mine in warning. "Evan and Jared will get you anything you need." As if on cue, Jared appeared in the doorway. "If you would excuse me, it's getting late, and I'm going to my room."

My mother approached me, and I leaned over to kiss her on the cheek. "There's not just your life to consider," she whispered in my ear before leaving, patting Jared on the cheek as she passed him.

When she was out of sight, Sara snapped impatiently, "Where is she? I want to see her."

"She's upstairs," I informed her. She stormed past me, not giving Jared a second glance as she whisked by him.

I followed her with a sigh. "Get the bags," I told Jared, who shot me a look, but continued into the kitchen to retrieve the girls' luggage.

"What happened to her leg, Sara?" I asked before Sara could open the door.

Sara paused. I could tell she wanted to tell me, but she fought with what to say. She ended up just shaking her head dismissively and opening the door. Without turning on the light, she sat down on the edge of the bed next to her best friend. I watched from the doorway as she ran her hand over Emma's short brown hair soothingly.

That's when Emma stirred and rolled over. I remained perfectly still as she squinted her eyes up at Sara. "Hey."

"Hey," Sara said in return, smiling gently down at me. "How are you feeling?"

"I think I'm drunk," I slurred, blinking the sleep out of my eyes, trying to focus, but the vodka was making it difficult.

"I think you are too," Sara nodded. "Not a good day for you, huh?"

"Not a good life." I chuckled humorlessly. I pulled the sheets up to my nose and inhaled. They smelled so good. So...clean. I sat up in a panic.

The dark room started to fall into shape around me. I looked down at the white bedspread with the pink flowers.

"Oh hell no!" I yelled. "Sara, what the fuck am I doing here?!"

"Relax, Em." Sara tried to calm me, setting her hands on my shoulders to settle me back into the bed. "It's just one night."

"Oh, no, no, no," I repeated, shaking my head. The room started to spin, and I couldn't hold my head up any longer. I collapsed back against the pillow. That's when I saw his silhouette at the door. "I'm not supposed to be here," I cried. "I'm not supposed to be in yesterday."

"I know," Sara whispered gently, smoothing my hair behind my ear. "It'll be okay. I'm right down the hall if you need me."

I fought to keep my eyes open, to insist that she take me away. But I couldn't think. I needed to stop the spinning. I shut my eyes.

Sara sat by Emma's side for a moment longer to make certain she was truly asleep. Then she whipped around and stared at me angrily. I ducked back into the hall.

Sara closed the door behind her and turned toward me. "I told you this was a horrible idea." She ran her hands over her face, suddenly looking exhausted. "Why did I let you talk me into this? This is the last thing she needs."

"The last thing she needs? What the hell happened to her, Sara?! How could you let her drink?!" I spat fiercely.

"What? I know you've taken the last two years out on me, but don't you dare blame me for this! If you brought her here to get back at her in some way, then we'll leave! I won't let you fuck her up any more than she already is, Evan!"

I bowed my head. "I'm sorry. I shouldn't have said that." I inhaled deeply, trying to calm the anger that kept my muscles straining. "And I'm not doing this to hurt her."

Sara released a tense breath.

"Has she talked to you about it?" I asked cautiously. "Rachel's suicide?"

"Does she ever say anything?" Sara countered with an exasperated sigh. "And we haven't told her the details yet. She wasn't exactly… with it when I picked her up from the airport yesterday."

"So this drinking thing isn't new?" I inquired, studying Sara's blue eyes as she avoided mine, seeing more than she was saying. "Do you think she has a problem?"

"A drinking problem?" Sara shrugged. "Evan, Emma has a life problem." She shook her head and started to turn away. "I shouldn't be talking to you about this anyway."

"Why not?" I challenged her. "Why can't I know? Don't I deserve at least that much? Tell me what happened to her, Sara!"

Sara looked back over her shoulder, her sad eyes brimming with tears. "She's just…broken." Her voice cracked. "And I'm not sure how to help her." She turned away with her shoulders slumped forward, disappearing behind the guest room door. I remained standing in the hall, looking after her, allowing everything she'd just said to echo through my head.

My fists clenched, I fought the pain and anger coursing through me. I turned toward Emma's door and set my hands on either side of the door, bowing my head. "I don't understand. Why'd you leave with him, Emma?" I whispered, then walked toward my room at the end of the hall.

I lay on my bed most of the night with my hands folded behind my head, staring at the dark ceiling, trying to decide what I was going to do when the sun pushed us all into a new day.

I squinted my eyes open. The room was still dark. I considered closing them again, but I had to go to the bathroom. I groaned and pushed the thick blankets back. I was in Evan's house. In the guest room with the flowers. *Shit.* I groaned again and eased out of the bed. My feet pressed against the cool wooden floor.

I knew exactly where the bathroom was without having to turn on the light, although my legs weren't very steady with the vodka still pumping through my system.

When I came back out, I stared at the bed.

How's your knee?

You did not come in here to ask me about my knee. I could practically feel his hand slide across my leg.

There was no way I was getting back in that bed.

I crept along the floorboards and eased the door open, peeking out into the hall. It was dark and quiet. I paused in front of his door. My heart convulsed at the sight of it.

"I shouldn't be here." I muttered as I continued past it and down the spiral staircase.

The stairs creaked on the other side of my door. I sat up and listened. She was awake. I slid off my bed, careful not to make any sound. I thought I heard her talking, but it was so faint, I could have imagined it.

Opening the door slightly, I saw her shadow disappear below the landing, down the hall. I followed her.

The familiar scents of the Mathews home filled my senses, and my heart betrayed me with a flutter. I needed out of this house. Now.

I entered the kitchen and unlocked the door that led out onto the back porch. The breeze rustled the tall blades of grass that stretched across the backyard to the woods. As soon as I turned toward the steps, my vision filled with the magnificence of the large oak tree. And there, rocking from its branch, was the swing.

My throat tightened as a small gasp escaped. I blinked back the tears and let the damp grass brush against my bare feet, drawn to the tree. I ran my hand along the coarse bark and searched up through the branches that danced above my head, the light wind rushing through them.

"I've always loved this tree," I heard myself say aloud, comforted by its touch.

I've always loved that tree, I thought to myself as I watched her run her fingers around the trunk. Her eyes lifted to take it all in. She had always connected with that tree too, making it the perfect location for the swing I'd made for her.

The swing that I'd hoped would keep her coming back here. Back to me.

I held my breath when I saw her grab each rope in her hand and lift herself onto the unsteady board. For a moment, in the reflective light of the moon, I thought I saw her smile.

I fought the urge to go out there, to talk to her. Despite the joy that radiated from her as she pumped her legs, I had to remember that she didn't want to be here. That her expression would change if she saw me. So I remained on the sun porch, watching as she flew higher into the branches.

I breathed in the crisp night air, the crickets chirping in the field while I savored the rocking rhythm, increasing my acceleration and height. My hair blew into my face and quickly swept back as I continued my ascent. I closed my eyes and leaned back, straightening my arms and dipping my head so it dared the ground to touch it. A flitter catapulted through my stomach. My cheeks pushed up into a smile.

She continued to glide in the shadows of the oak tree, leaning back so far it looked like she was going to tip over. The wind billowed the skirt of her dress as she extended her legs in front of her. I grinned at the familiar sight. A warm shiver running through me. I leaned against the open door of the sunroom, crossing my arms.

This was the girl I knew. This was the girl I'd loved. And although I didn't know what had happened to her, I knew I had to find out.

17. NOT THE SAME

*T*he sun was blinding me when I woke on the wicker chaise. I needed a minute to figure out where I was, but as soon as I did, I jumped up. Emma! I pushed the door open and walked quickly to the other side of the patio, past the pool and through the wooden gate.

I stopped. She was curled in the grass under the oak tree. Her skin aglow in golden light filtering through the trees. Her skirt spread around her with her legs tucked under it, and her hands were folded under her cheek. She took my breath away. I tensed, not wanting to start looking at her the way I once had. She wasn't the same girl. And I wasn't the same either.

I walked over to her. I couldn't leave her out here on the damp grass. I crouched down and gently lifted her into my arms.

She groaned slightly, but didn't wake as I took her back to the guest room and placed her on the bed. I didn't linger to watch her sleep. I knew I had to prepare myself for her reaction when she finally awoke, sober and... unpredictable.

I was back in the bed. My body ached with the slightest movement. I was convinced I'd slept on rocks. I groaned and ran a hand over my face.

My phone buzzed. I searched blindly for it, reaching over the edge of the bed, into the tote below.

"Hello?" I grumbled.

"How are you feeling?" Cole asked from the other end.

"Shoot me now," I croaked, flopping my arm over my eyes. "Isn't it super early for you?"

"I knew you'd be heading to the church soon," he explained. "I wanted to check on you. Do you remember talking to me yesterday?"

I couldn't think. Nothing penetrated through the shards of pain splintering through my head. "Did I say anything stupid?"

Cole laughed lightly. "I'll pick you and Sara up at the Santa Barbara airport tomorrow. The girls packed your things for you and they'll meet us there tomorrow night. Call me later if you can."

"Okay," I responded in a rasp, not really following along. "Tomorrow."

I dropped the phone in my tote, afraid to move from my sprawled position on the bed. Then a rush of saliva filled my mouth, and my stomach turned. I fought to get on my feet and stumbled to the bathroom in time to heave into the toilet, collapsing onto my shaking knees.

I rested my head against the cool porcelain, keeping my eyes closed to prevent the dim light from stabbing through my pupils and into my shrieking brain.

"Emma?" Sara called to me from the other room. "Emma?" I heard the bathroom door creak open. "Oh God, Emma." I heard her gasp, but I couldn't raise my head to look at her. "We have to get you ready."

"Just let me lie here and die," I pleaded. Another swirl of nausea rushed through me with a chilling sweat, and I leaned my head over as my stomach convulsed.

Sara was beside me, running her cool hand along my damp forehead.

The guest room door was slightly ajar. "Sara?" I knocked lightly, hearing Sara's voice in the distance. "The car's here to take you to the church."

"We're in here," Sara called to me. I continued into the room cautiously, not certain what I was about to walk in on.

"Shit." The word escaped unfiltered when I saw Sara cross-legged on the bathroom floor with a ghostly pale Emma lying on her lap. "Can she get up?"

"Shh," Emma pleaded, wincing. "Not so loud."

I exhaled and said quietly, "Sara, what do you want to do? You're supposed to be at the church in forty minutes."

"I know," Sara said with a pained face. "Umm... let me get her in the shower. Can you call my mother and tell her we need a little more time?"

"Sure," I replied, taking in the scene one more time before walking out of the room. I shut the door, gripping the handle tightly.

"Come on, Emma. Let's try to get up," Sara coaxed gently, moving slowly to her knees. I forced my body to follow her, my hands shaking as I grabbed the edge of the bathtub.

Sara helped slip off my dress and removed the bandage from my leg as I settled into the bathtub, too weak to provide any assistance.

"My head hurts so bad."

"When was the last time you ate anything?" Sara questioned, easing my bra from my shoulders.

I shrugged, because I honestly didn't recall eating a single thing since I'd boarded the plane in California.

The warm water startled me as Sara ran the showerhead over my body.

"Here." She handed me a bar of soap. I flipped it in my hands before blindly pushing the lather over my skin.

"I called your mother," Evan hollered from the other room. "She said to call her when you're on your way. I'll see you at the church."

"Evan," Sara called to him, abandoning me in the tub with the shower head dangling, spraying my legs.

"I realize you have no reason to do this, but I need your help," Sara said in a rush, sadness dulling her usually bright eyes.

"What do you need?" I asked, controlling my tone.

"We need to get her into the church, and I'm not convinced she can do it on her own, or that I can by myself. Will you stay? Will you help me?"

I nodded, unable to form words. My jaw tightened, realizing Emma was in far worse condition than I could have imagined. I finally said, "I'll be in the hall. Let me know when you need me."

"Do you think you could find something for her headache, and maybe something to eat? She hasn't eaten in a couple days." Sara's voice sounded so fragile. I nodded again and left the room.

As I shut the door, I was blindsided by the anger that had been building since we'd found her on the closet floor. I wasn't even sure who I was angry with, but I couldn't deny that from the moment I saw her, everything had felt wrong.

I went down the stairs into the kitchen, to find Jared helping my mother into her jacket. I stopped short and tried to ease my clenched fists open.

"Analise, what are you doing here?" I asked, eyeing the petite girl standing in the doorway.

She looked up at me with big, sad eyes. "I came here for you." Her eyes flipped toward my mother, not wanting to have this discussion in front of her.

"Is everything okay upstairs?" My mother's voice was calm, but her brow quirked, letting me know she was very aware of the predicament I was in.

"Yes," I answered carefully. "It's under control."

"Well, Jared and I need to make a stop on our way to the church. We'll see you there?" She leaned toward me so I could bend down to receive a kiss on the cheek.

"I won't be long," I told her, glancing again in Analise's direction, trying to maintain my composure.

Jared kept his eyes to the ground as he and my mother left the house. I could only imagine the thoughts passing through his head.

I turned to Analise. "I'm still not sure why you're here—today, especially."

"I'm sorry I wasn't at the wake last night," she said softly, taking a step toward me. She raised her hand as if to touch me, but lowered it again when she noticed my shoulders pull back. "I didn't expect you to go."

"Really? I never even considered not going."

She lowered her eyes, the realization of what that statement meant not sitting well. "I thought… I thought you didn't want anything to do with her?"

I didn't say anything. That had been the truth, once. And Analise knew that better than anyone. It was hurt and anger wrapped in confusion that had me repeatedly saying that I was over Emma. That I didn't care if I ever saw her again. But…

Right around the time my mother started letting me travel again, allowing me to be within hours of Emma without her knowing it—those thoughts started to change.

"Analise, really, what do you want?" She lifted her head in surprise at my tone. "We haven't even spoken since last summer. I don't understand why you're here other than the fact that you know Emma's in Weslyn."

Analise's eyes glistened as her lower lip jutted out slightly. "I didn't want you to get hurt again. I was worried about you, and thought… I thought you might need a friend. Because I still care about you, Evan. And I was hoping to be that friend for you, like I used to be."

I suddenly felt guilty for my impatient tone. I believed she did have my well-being in mind, but that didn't mean I wanted her here. "I don't think we can be friends again, Analise. Not after what happened. I'm sorry."

She nodded, trying to hold back tears. "She's going to destroy you, Evan." She turned from me and fled out the kitchen door.

Evan appeared in the doorway with a coconut water in one hand, and a bottle of aspirin and a muffin in the other. He paused when he saw me sitting on the bed while Sara zipped up the boots that hid my skinned leg. I was afraid they would hurt the raw skin, but the compression actually made it feel better.

I watched him as he placed the items on the bedside table. He didn't look at me. If my face was any reflection of how I felt, then I must've looked worse than death.

"Ready?" he asked Sara.

Sara stood up to inspect me, like I was an inanimate object. "I think so. I don't know what to do about your eyes, Em. They're so puffy and bloodshot." She contemplated for a moment. Then she reached for her purse and removed an oversize pair of black sunglasses. "Here, keep these on."

I slid them on my face and instantly felt relief from the pain-inciting glare. Sara handed me two pills, which I washed down with the coconut water. She held out the muffin, but I shook my head with a grimace, feeling my stomach roll just at the thought of eating it.

"You're going to have to eat eventually," Sara said sternly.

"I can't." I cringed, swallowing the nausea back down.

"Can you stand?" Sara asked.

I nodded, rising to my feet gingerly, holding on to her arm. Evan made a move in our direction when I faltered, but stopped when I regained my balance. He led the way out of the room as I held Sara's arm.

As much as I tried not to, I couldn't stop looking at him. A part of me was convinced he wasn't real. He looked the same, except maybe a little more...built. But essentially, perfectly the same. Composed and mature in a three-piece suit that fit his tall frame in a way that belonged on the cover of *GQ*. Maybe that's what was going on. I was sitting on a plane, reading *GQ*, and this was all a dream.

Then the flash of pain brought me crashing back to reality. I was here, in Weslyn—to bury my mother. My knees buckled, and I fell to the floor. Sara screamed out, and Evan rushed back up the stairs, sliding his arm behind me to prop me up.

"Are you okay?" Sara asked her. Emma's body felt limp and frail, leaning into my arm.

"Yeah," she muttered, sitting up. "I just got dizzy all of a sudden. I'm sorry."

"Emma, you're scaring me," Sara stated, offering her hand. "Are you sure you're okay?"

Emma nodded slightly. She kept looking up at me, but with those large black glasses covering her eyes, I didn't have any idea what she was thinking. I slid her arm through mine for added support as she grabbed Sara's arm again, and we managed to get her down the stairs.

If the only thing she'd consumed in two days was vodka, then she was probably dehydrated, and her blood sugar was way off. How the hell were we going to make it through an entire church service without her passing out?

"Emma, do you think you could at least drink that coconut water before we get to the church?"

It was the first thing he'd said to me since I'd arrived. I nodded slightly, trying to keep my heart beating normally as I felt his arm tucked under mine. I didn't want to be this close to him, to touch him, to smell the sweet, clean scent that rolled off him and made me even more lightheaded. But I also knew that my body was shutting down, rebelling against the abuse I'd subjected it to the last couple of days, and I wouldn't be able to stand up if Evan let go of me.

The town car pulled up in front of the picturesque white church with its steeple and stained-glass windows. The funeral director approached the car when the door opened. Every muscle in my body refused to budge so I could enter the historic New England church to witness the sermon memorializing my mother. Panic held me captive in the confines of the car.

Sara climbed back in the car and grabbed my hand. "Are you going to be sick?"

I shook my head. Evan leaned into the car.

"What is it?" Sara asked gently.

"She's dead." My voice quivered. I gripped the sunglasses with my hands, pressing them into my eyes, trying to hold back the tears. "Oh my God, oh my God, oh my God. She's dead." The lump in my throat grew, and I thought I was going to choke on it.

I closed my eyes to keep the tears trapped. Sara squeezed my hand. I inhaled deeply through my nose and released the air through my mouth to force it away. The panic began to fade.

"I'm okay," I told Sara, encouraging her to get back out of the car.

"You can get through this," Sara assured me, taking my hand again when I emerged from the car. "I'll be right next to you the entire time." I could only nod.

Evan offered me his arm again, and I slid mine through and held on tight.

It was the first time I'd seen her react to her mother's death—and I couldn't do anything about it. I just stood beside her and helped her up the stairs to where Mr. and Mrs. McKinley awaited us. Anna hugged Emma and whispered into her ear before leading the way into the church.

Emma's grip tightened, and I could feel the panic rippling off her as we stepped over the threshold. Instinctively, I covered her hand with mine and concentrated on each step she took, wanting to be her strength as her own continued to slip away.

I slid in beside her in the first pew, with Sara on her other side. Sara's parents sat at the end. Emma leaned away from me, releasing her hold of my arm and leaning into Sara, resting her head on Sara's shoulder. I bowed my head in realization of who I was not to her in this moment of need.

The sermon began, and the murmuring stopped. I didn't look over at her as the reverend offered a prayer and strangers said kind words about a woman who hadn't earned them.

The reverend returned to the pulpit and said, "At this time, I'd like to invite Rachel's daughter, Emma, up to say a few words."

I froze and turned my head toward Sara, whose mouth hung agape as she stared at me in shock.

Emma slowly rose and made her way to the stairs that led to the pulpit.

"Oh no," Sara murmured beside me.

"Do you know what she's going to say?" I asked, unable to breathe properly.

"I'm afraid to find out," Sara whispered, not taking her eyes off Emma.

My hands shook as I positioned myself behind the black-draped pulpit. I glanced in Sara's direction and was suddenly rocked by the memory of her impassioned plea.

She hurt you, Emma, over and over again. You can let her go now. Don't let her hurt you anymore.

I redirected my attention out at the drawn faces awaiting my words. Words that I hadn't prepared. So I decided that in this moment I would be...honest.

"I don't want to be here." My voice came out strained and barely audible. "None of us should be here." I cleared my throat and again looked toward Sara, whose large unblinking eyes followed my every movement as she gripped the pew in front of her.

She can't keep hurting you and using you like an emotional punching bag. How many times do you have to forgive her before she destroys you?

"I wouldn't be able to begin to list the ways my mother has shaped me. I am the person I am because of her, and I awaken each day reminded of how she has contributed to my existence. I blame her..." I paused, clearing my throat again as I gnashed my teeth together. "...early departure on an unforgiving fate. Tragedy was too familiar to us both. It claimed my father many years ago. She lived so much of her life in pain. A pain that I witnessed helplessly for years. In the end she couldn't live with it, and didn't know how to let it go. Maybe now she will find the peace she spent so much of my life searching for, now that she is finally with him."

This is about you. It's always been about you—what you want, how you feel, who you want to be with. Why do you keep obsessing over a man who never loved you?

I pried my hands open from their frozen grasp of the pulpit. My entire body shook as I walked down the steps toward the aisle. The McKinleys rose to allow me access to the pew, but I lowered my head and kept walking.

"Where's she going?" Sara whispered in a panic.

"I don't know," I responded, looking after her along with everyone else in the church as she headed toward the large double doors at end of the aisle, and pushed them open. They sealed shut behind her.

"Go down the side aisle," I instructed Sara. There was a stir in the pews as the mourners whispered in speculation.

I followed Sara down the dark carpet toward the back of the church as the reverend's authoritative tone redirected the attention back to the pulpit, where he began reciting scripture.

We pushed through the heavy wooden doors, out to the stone steps. The sun seemed impossibly bright after the gloominess of the church. I shielded my eyes to look for Emma.

The town car was gone.

18. STILL HERE

I eased open the door and gently closed it behind me. She continued to stare out the large window, her legs drawn in to her, sitting on the window's ledge.

I bumped into a stool, not paying attention to anything but her. Emma turned toward me, her eyes reflective and full of a sorrow that tore at my heart.

"You're not supposed to be here," she said, her voice coated in pain. "It's not you who's supposed to find me."

The bite in her tone kept me from moving forward. "But I'm the only one who knows you'd be here."

Emma closed her eyes, and I could see the muscle in her jaw flex as she fought to contain the emotions bubbling to the surface. I wanted to tell her to let them out. To stop fighting it.

"I know why you needed to leave," I told her.

She began shaking her head, like she could force it all away.

"I won't cry for her," she croaked. "I won't cry for her." She swallowed hard. "She doesn't deserve my tears. She did this. She chose this. She doesn't get to make me cry for her." Her entire frame recoiled in pain and anger, quivering to fend off the unwanted sorrow.

I stepped closer, fighting every instinct to hold her, to comfort her. Instead, I remained out of reach. That's not why I was there.

Emma became still, burying her face in her knees. She lifted her head with her eyes closed, breathing in the scents that floated through the Art room. I waited for her to open her eyes, to find that I was still here.

"Are you here to drive me to Sara's?" she asked, her voice calm, her eyes blank. I nodded, startled by the transformation.

"I sent the town car back to the church to pick up Sara."

"Okay." She exhaled. *"Let's go."*

I rushed through the front door without looking at a single face that crowded the first floor. I gripped the white paper bag in my hand and hurried up the stairs.

"You stopped for burgers?" I heard Sara snap at Evan.

"What? She hasn't eaten in two days. So yes, we stopped for burgers." His voice faded as I climbed.

I collapsed on the white leather couch in Sara's entertainment room, rummaging through the bag for the burger and scooping a few fries from the bottom that I hadn't eaten in the car. I couldn't recall ever being this hungry.

"Feeling any better?" Sara asked as she reached the top of the stairs.

I nodded, my mouth full of the greasy burger that I could've sworn was the best thing I'd ever tasted. I wiped the ketchup from my lip and took a sip of the soda.

"I'm sorry," I told Sara as she sat down next to me.

"For what?" she asked, like she had no idea what I was talking about.

"Are you serious?" I scoffed. "I've been a selfish lunatic the past two days. And you've had to drag my sorry ass around the entire time, taking care of me every minute. I'm so sorry that I'm an awful friend."

Sara shook her head, nudging my shoulder with hers. "You needed me. And I was there for you. It's that simple. But I'd prefer it if you didn't drink…ever again."

I laughed lightly. "I will never touch vodka again, that's for sure."

"Me neither." Sara smirked. "And I'm sorry about…you know…" She eyed me cautiously, having a hard time finishing. "About what I said at the hotel…and staying at Evan's."

"We don't need to talk about it," I told her, taking another bite of the burger, unable to stop wondering where he was. Whether he'd stayed and was downstairs, or if he'd already driven home.

"Thanks. I really appreciate you helping me out," I said before hanging up. I turned to find Jared behind me.

"Who was that?" he inquired, eyeing the untouched plate of food Anna had handed to me when I arrived. "Are you going to eat that?"

"Go for it," I encouraged him. "I'm surprised you're here." I diverted the conversation from his initial question.

"What is that supposed to mean?" he asked, sitting down at the glass-topped table on the enclosed porch, stuffing his face with garlic bread.

"That you're in Sara's house," I clarified. "That's… bold of you. To show your face here."

"I think her dad was about to slam the door when he saw me."

I laughed.

"What, do you think you're going to earn points by sticking around and helping them clean up?"

"I'm not going to push it," he said, working on the lasagna slice.

"So… do you mind driving me to the airport tomorrow?"

I crumpled up the paper bag and rested my head back against the couch.

"There you are," I heard Anna say from the landing. I turned my head to find her walking toward us. "Sara, could you give us a minute, please?"

My stomach swirled uncomfortably at her request.

"I'll be downstairs," Sara told me, letting her mother take her place on the couch.

"Come here, Emma." Anna invited me to lean against her, her arm spread wide. My heart twisted as I leaned in to her, allowing her to wrap her arm around me. I inhaled her elegant floral scent and closed my eyes as she ran her fingers through my short hair. "You've had a hard time the last couple of days, and I'm so sorry."

I swallowed, unable to form words.

"We'll take care of you," she murmured into the top of my head, kissing me gently. "I think you should talk to someone about what's going on inside of you, though. I can only imagine what you must be feeling."

I remained silent, not at all tempted to explore the explosive range of emotions shredding my insides.

"I worry about you all the time," she continued. "I don't know how to make you feel safe. And as a mother, that's all I ever want for you and Sara. For you to feel safe and loved."

"I do," I whispered. "I always do when I'm in your house."

"I wish you could feel the same when you leave it."

We sat in silence for a moment longer, my head resting against her chest, listening to her heart. Her thin arms held me with a strength that did make me feel safe and loved within them.

"Can I ask you something?" I said in a hushed tone.

"Of course," she encouraged me.

"Did she...did she really hang herself?" I closed my eyes, bracing for her answer.

"Yes, she did," Anna answered, gentle but firm.

"Where?"

"At the house on Decatur Street."

Air rushed from my lungs. "From the banister?"

"Yes."

My chest felt tight, like there wasn't any room left to breathe. Like I was suffocating in pain.

"Did she suffer?"

"No," I heard Anna whisper, her voice breaking.

I pulled back to look at her, and tears trailed down her face.

"Why?" I asked, my eyes stinging with each blink.

Anna just shook her head. "I don't know. She didn't leave a note. But even if she had, I don't know if she'd ever be able to truly explain why she chose to end her life. I'm so sorry, Emma."

"Thank you," I replied, my chin quivering. Witnessing Anna's pain was almost too much to bear. "You were always so good to her…through everything. And thank you for everything you've done the past week. I know I haven't been much help, and I'm sorry."

"Do not apologize," Anna insisted, wiping her cheeks and blowing out of her pursed lips. "Carl and I care about you. And we'll help you through this."

"Thank you," I repeated.

"Do you have to go back to California tomorrow?"

I nodded.

"I know," she responded with a saddened understanding. "But will you consider speaking to someone, like I asked?"

I nodded again, knowing that I wouldn't.

"I appreciate everything you did today," Sara said to me as she sat down beside me on the large wraparound sectional in the McKinleys' entertainment room. "I know it was hard for you too."

I sat quietly for a moment. "Yeah, it wasn't easy," I answered carefully. "So will you do one thing for me in return?"

"What's that?" she asked, her eyes narrowing suspiciously.

"Let Jared and me drive you two to the airport tomorrow."

Sara stared at me, trying to figure out if there was a hidden agenda behind my request. Of course there was.

"Why?" she asked suspiciously.

"I just want to make sure she's okay before she leaves again." It was a fairly honest answer.

"I guess," she answered hesitantly. "But Emma and I sit in the back... alone."

I was trying hard not to smile. "That's fine."

———

"What are you doing here?" I heard Carl practically growl at the bottom of the stairs. I trotted down the last flight and stumbled over a couple of steps when Evan came into view. His eyes drifted up toward me, at first in alarm, but when he saw that I'd caught myself from falling, his lips spread into that heart-stopping grin—the one he'd greeted me with at the bottom of these stairs more times than I could count.

"Hey," he said, his eyes flicking away as I continued to gawk at him.

"What's going on?" I asked, my attention diverted to Carl, who looked just as surprised as I was to find Jared and Evan in his entryway.

"Our bags are in the sitting room," Sara announced as she hopped down the stairs, ignoring my scrunched eyes and her father's questioning expression. "Oh, I forgot to tell you, Dad. You don't need to drive us to the airport."

"I can see that," he responded, still wary. "Are you *sure*?"

"Yeah, it's fine," Sara said lightly, kissing her dad on the cheek with a smile. Then I heard her lean in and tell him, "It's *just* a ride to the airport."

He kissed her back, then redirected his attention to Jared, his eyes narrowed in warning.

Jared smiled uncomfortably and rushed past him to retrieve our bags.

"What the frig are you thinking?" I murmured to her as she slung her carry-on tote over her shoulder.

"It's a ride, Emma. Don't worry. It won't even be an hour." She smiled assuredly, but my insides curled into knots, knowing something was up.

I slipped by Evan, and followed Sara out the front door after hugging Anna and Carl good-bye.

The color had returned to her face, and although any expression in her eyes was still elusive, she looked… beautiful. I had a hard time keeping the smile off my face when she practically fell down the stairs upon seeing me. It was one thing to convince myself I was over her and needed to move on, but it was another thing when she was standing right in front of me.

The drive to the airport was quiet, so I selected music to fill the silence. I noticed Sara watching Emma out of the corner of her eye when I turned toward Jared. Sara was worried. There was something I didn't know, something Sara wasn't telling me. Was I really ready for this… even if I ended up hurting worse in the end? But then again, I didn't think that was possible.

My eyes kept drifting to the back of his neck, tracing his neatly trimmed hairline. He'd shift slightly and steal glances at Sara, and I'd catch a glimpse of his perfectly chiseled profile with his long slender nose, angled cheekbone and defined brow. My heart would convulse, and I'd quickly look away to keep the heat from rising in my cheeks. I could survive this for one hour…maybe.

When we pulled up along the curb at the airport, Jared and Evan got out to help remove our bags. That's when I saw the other bags stacked in the trunk.

"Are you kidding me?!" I practically yelled at Sara, convinced that she was in on this. She stared back at me just as confused.

We both turned toward Evan, glaring at him accusingly.

"I told you this was a bad idea," Jared murmured. "You seem to be batting a thousand with those lately."

"Shut up, Jared," Evan said under his breath, before shrugging toward Sara and I. "What? I'm spending the summer with Nate in Santa Barbara."

Sara's mouth dropped open. "Are you serious?"

"What's the big deal?" he questioned, feigning innocence. "You're going back to Palo Alto, right?" I knew he wasn't being completely honest. He was a terrible liar.

Sara huffed and grabbed her bags. "Come on, Emma."

"This can't be happening," I said to her, rolling my suitcase after her.

"Don't worry," she assured me, "it's going to be okay."

"Smooth," Jared teased, shutting the trunk as the girls stormed off. "Could you have been any more obvious?"

"Well... they'd find out eventually, wouldn't they?"

"Do you have any idea what you're getting yourself into?" he asked, shaking his head.

"Not really," I confessed, even after spending the entire night convincing myself I was doing the right thing. "But I never do when it comes to her. So why should that change?"

Jared sighed. "I'll be there in a couple weeks. Did you tell Nate you were arriving early?"

"Yeah, I talked to him last night. No one will be at the house, but I know where the key is, so it's not an issue."

"Good luck," Jared offered, leaning in for a quick embrace and smack on the back. He looked at me again before getting in his Volvo with a short laugh and shake of his head.

I didn't try to find the girls. I knew we'd be on the same flights all the way to Santa Barbara. I'd made sure of it after I saw their itinerary hanging on the McKinley's refrigerator. What I didn't know was where they were staying while in Santa Barbara... or who else would be there.

"Nate's house is down the street from Cole's," I told Sara, my nerves wreaking havoc. I thought I was about to be sick all over again.

"What?!" Sara exclaimed, drawing the attention of the passengers seated around us. "Why didn't I know this until now? And how do *you* know this?!"

"Uh…I ended up at a party at Nate's over spring break, the week I spent with Cole. He kind of got me through a night of tequila when I found out I was at Evan's best friend's house."

"Holy fuck!" Sara gaped. "I'm trying to get over the fact that this is the first time I'm hearing this. But…holy fuck. So…Cole knows Nate?"

"Cole knows *Evan*," I admitted, staring out the window.

"No. Way!" she gasped. "Emma, this—"

"Is going to be the worst summer of my life," I finished, thumping my head against the glass.

"We don't have to stay," Sara suggested. "Maybe we head back to Palo Alto when Cole goes back for the summer quarter in a couple weeks."

I sighed, disappointed that I might not have the quiet summer alone with Sara I'd hoped for. "Maybe."

"We'll get through it," she assured me. I didn't really believe her.

When we rolled to a stop on the landing strip at the small airport, the passengers started to stand and grab their bags. Sara and Emma were seated a few rows ahead of me, so they were off the plane before I was. I adjusted my backpack on my shoulder as I walked across the pavement, toward the canopied baggage claim. I breathed in the warm air. I'd missed California.

Sara's hair was hard to miss. I caught sight of the girls just as I heard, "Hey, Emma." I stopped short, nearly making the guy behind me run right into me.

Emma approached him, and he leaned in to kiss her.

"Oh, fuck." I stopped breathing for all of a minute, then eventually found the strength to keep moving toward the baggage area, unable to avoid them in the small space.

"Evan?" I looked over and Cole was eyeing me curiously. "I didn't know you were coming back too."

"Hey, Cole," I responded, trying to keep my voice even and pleasant. "Yeah, I'm spending the summer at Nate's." I looked from him to Emma, who wouldn't meet my eyes, and said, "I didn't realize you and Emma knew each other."

Cole's brows twitched, starting to put this entire scene together. "Yeah," he said, picking up her bag. "We do. Uh, you need a ride?

"What?!" Emma blurted, her cheeks crimson.

"He's staying right down the street. So… do you need a ride?"

"Sure," I responded, surprised by his nonchalant demeanor. I glanced at Sara and thought she was about to fall over.

Cole slipped his arm around Emma's shoulder, and she jerked her head up in surprise.

This was about to be the worst summer of my life.

19. GIVE ME A REASON

I slammed the car door and yanked my bags from the back, practically knocking myself over. I stormed to the front door and turned the handle. It was locked. Of course it was locked! I tapped my foot impatiently and waited for Cole, who was taking his fricken time walking over from the car.

I stared at the door. I didn't look at Cole, who had betrayed me *again* during the drive by inviting Evan over for burgers. I didn't look at Evan, who accepted without hesitation. And I didn't look at Sara, who couldn't seem to keep her mouth from dropping open every time the guys spoke to each other, like they were great friends and couldn't wait to catch up. I just stared at the door and waited for it to open.

When Cole *finally* unlocked it, I cut him off and rolled my suitcase into the spare room. Sara scooted after me.

"Umm…are we sharing this room?" she asked, examining the full-size bed and flipping her eyes back toward me in confusion.

"Uh…" I fumbled.

"Emma," Cole poked his head into the room. "You can put your stuff in my room."

My breathing faltered. I nodded and rolled my suitcase back into the open living room.

"Want a beer?" Cole asked Evan.

"Sure," Evan responded casually, looking around, running his fingers along the puzzles on the bookshelf.

Unable to stand seeing him touch the boxes, I tucked my suit-case by the kitchen table and continued out onto the deck, turning a chair around to sit facing the water with my arms crossed.

"Hey," Sara said cautiously, sliding the glass door closed behind her. "I'm sorry this...sucks."

"That's an understatement," I said between clenched teeth. "Why is he here? Why couldn't he have stayed away..." I clamped my eyes closed. "This can't be happening." My world was so far off balance, I could barely stand upright.

Sara leaned against the railing in front of me, sliding over so I could still stare at the waves rushing toward shore.

"Why did you automatically go into the guest room with your things?" she asked.

I looked up at her in surprise.

"I, uh, that's where I stayed before," I explained. "We don't... *sleep* together. Sara, we're not *dating*. You know that."

"Right." She nodded. "It didn't look that way to me at the airport."

I didn't really even remember what had happened between Cole and me at the airport. I'd been way too consumed by the awareness that Evan was somewhere behind me.

"Maybe you should—" Sara stopped. Her head jerked to attention.

"I should what?" I asked in confusion.

That's when I heard, "So why weren't you at the funeral?" I practically choked.

"She didn't want me there," Cole explained, still remaining much more relaxed than seemed reasonable. "I wanted to be there, but I respected her wishes. So I stayed here."

I nodded.

"And I take it you were there?" he asked, raising his eyebrows slightly.

"I was," I answered. I hadn't let Emma's wishes keep me from attending.

"And she was a mess," Cole concluded, like he expected as much.

"That's one way of putting it." I nodded carefully, wondering exactly where this conversation was headed.

"They're talking about me," I sputtered in disbelief. "Why are they talking about me? Don't they know I can hear them?"

"Shh." Sara hushed me, listening intently.

"Is that why you came back with her?" Cole asked Evan. I couldn't move. Every cell in my body anticipated Evan's response.

"I had plans to spend the summer here," I told him, evading the entire truth. "I just thought I'd come a little early, that's all."

"Really?" Cole returned skeptically. "Look, I know you have a history with Emma. I get it. She was a mess at the funeral, and you're worried about her. It makes sense. And I also know you didn't realize I'd be here for her either. But I am, so you don't need to be."

I took a swig from the beer bottle and glanced out at Sara and Emma on the deck. I caught Sara's eye, and she dropped her gaze quickly, appearing to be in conversation with Emma.

"Shit," Sara muttered. "Evan just caught me listening."

"I can't believe we *are* listening to this. I mean, this shouldn't be happening. He shouldn't be here. They should not be talking about me. Shit. Don't they know I can hear them?" I squeezed my fists, my pulse racing.

"I'm not going to interfere," I said, turning toward Cole. "I just…was hoping to…get closure. Things didn't exactly end well between us."

"I figured as much," Cole said with a shrug.

"She told you?" I looked at him curiously, wondering exactly how much Cole knew about Emma and her life in Weslyn. I couldn't figure out how close they were; their body language was all over the place. But I hadn't come here prepared for her to be involved with anyone.

"Not exactly." He laughed lightly. "Let's just say I figured it out." He paused. "So, does she want you here?"

I hesitated, knowing that I could make things difficult if I said the wrong thing.

"I never asked her," I replied honestly. "We didn't have an opportunity to talk when she was in Weslyn."

"Then maybe you should ask her," Cole advised, his forehead creasing in warning. "And if she doesn't want you here, you need to leave her alone."

"Emma, where are you going?" I heard Sara yell from the deck. I immediately headed toward the glass door.

"Don't they know I can hear them?!" I screamed, stomping down the stairs and practically tripping over the rocks in my haste to escape their conversation.

"Emma!"

My feet pressed defiantly into the sand, leaving a dent in the firm surface with each forceful step.

"Emma, wait!"

My heart beat frantically. I shook my head.

"Please, Emma!"

I whipped around, the wind blowing my hair in my face. "Leave me alone, Evan!"

"Come on, Emma. Please. Stop," he pleaded, jogging to catch up.

"You're not supposed to be here!" I yelled at him, my eyes filling with tears.

I stopped. A tear escaped and rolled down her cheek. She was so tense, she was practically shaking.

"I'm sorry I didn't tell you I was coming," I said. "I should have."

"You should be back in Connecticut!" she yelled at me. "You shouldn't be here at all! Just go back! Just... go away." *Her voice faltered as the strain of emotion broke through.*

I closed my eyes. Her words were difficult to swallow.

"I can't," I said, my voice almost lost in the wind gusting off the water. "Not yet."

"You're supposed to hate me!" I couldn't stop the tears from flowing or my body from shaking. "Why don't you hate me, Evan?!" My lip quivered.

He appeared…crushed by my explosive words. Evan's chest caved slightly, and his eyes twitched in pain. *Hate you?* he mouthed.

I collapsed to the sand and stared at the ocean with my knees hugged to my chest, my face slick with tears.

"Why would you ever think I could hate you?" he asked so quietly I could barely hear him. Evan lowered himself beside me. I could feel him looking at me, but I couldn't bring myself to face him.

She kept her teary eyes fixated on the water. "Emma, I could never hate you. I've told you that before, and it's still true." Her expectation that I could made me feel like she'd just punched a hole through my chest. "But I need closure, so I can move on."

Emma turned her head toward me. A tortured expression flashed across her face. "It'd be easier to hate me."

I scanned her eyes, and the pain held within them cut me open. She looked away, knowing I'd seen too much. She had always been protective of her emotions, keeping them locked up. But her eyes always told the truth. My jaw clenched. She wasn't who I hated. But I hadn't exactly forgiven her for leaving me that night… with Jonathan.

"Give me one reason why I should hate you," I asked her, not truly expecting an answer.

Her face became smooth and her eyes sharp when she said, "How was your birthday, Evan?"

His eyes flinched. I knew I had hit a nerve, as I'd intended. He had to know. He had to understand why he should hate me. And I needed to remind him, as difficult as it was to watch his face flicker with the remembrance.

But I wasn't expecting his expression to change and the cocky grin to emerge when he said, "It sucked actually. Yeah, you kinda ruined those for me."

My brow knitted in confusion. Why wasn't he angry?

Evan laughed with a shake of his head. "Well…you ruined chocolate for me too."

"Chocolate?" He wasn't reacting the way I expected. But then again, he never did.

"The house, it smelled of chocolate that night," he reminded me. "So…I can't eat chocolate."

"That sucks," I said, redirecting my gaze back to the water, wiping my wet cheeks with the palms of my hands.

"You have no idea." His voice was sarcastic.

"As much as you'd like me to hate you, I can't. And I'm not here to ask for you back either."

Emma's shoulders tensed. I hadn't expected this to bother her. Especially after she'd just begged for me to hate her. I thought she'd be relieved.

"Will you let me try to forgive you?" I asked her.

"I think it's easier to hate me," she stated firmly. "It's easier than you think."

She believed it. It reflected in the confidence in her voice. And that disturbed me.

"Let's make a deal," I offered, wanting the answers I came here to get.

Emma shook her head.

"Wait, hear me out."

"Fine. Go ahead." She swiped her tear-streaked face, and looked to me with a sigh.

I grinned. "Nate and the guys arrive in two weeks. So let's say you have two weeks to convince me to hate you. But you have to talk to me. Answer my questions. All of them. Let me try to forgive you."

"All of them?" I asked cautiously, my heart skipping a beat just considering the questions he could ask.

"Yes," Evan confirmed. "And you have to tell me the truth. In the end, I'll either hate you, like you insist I should, or I'll have the closure I came here for."

I was quiet, looking into his eyes, questioning if he was truly serious. He held the slightest smirk on his face, challenging me, which only baffled me more.

"Why is this so important to you?" I asked.

"Emma?"

I looked up with a start, not realizing I'd been staring into Evan's eyes, waiting for him to say…whatever he was going to say. Cole's approach broke me free from his gaze, and I took in a deep breath to rid myself of the shivers that trailed down my neck.

"Everything okay?" Cole asked, inspecting our faces.

"Yeah," Evan answered for both of us, standing up and brushing the sand from his jeans. I offered a tight smile. Evan turned toward me. "So…I'll see you tomorrow?"

I knew this was his way of asking if I agreed to his proposal. Even though I still didn't understand why, I shrugged in agreement. "See you tomorrow."

I watched him walk away 'til my attention was redirected abruptly by Cole, who sat down next to me, blocking my view.

"Are you sure you're okay?" Cole asked, taking my hand in his. My back tensed at the gesture.

Walking away was more difficult than I'd imagined. And it sucked that I'd left her there with Cole. But she'd agreed to tell me the truth. I could finally find out what happened. Why she chose Jonathan. Why she trusted him when she couldn't trust me. I bit back the anger I could feel rising at just the thought of him, wishing he'd never set foot in her life.

I was about to venture into the unknown. But that's what life with Emma had always been. The truth might be more than I could handle, but I knew it would change everything.

I walked up the steps to the deck and slid the glass door open, stopping short. I hadn't anticipated a room full of girls.

"Where's Emma?" Sara asked, sitting on the chair across from me.

I thumbed back toward the beach, meeting one set of eyes after another.

"Hi, I'm Serena," the girl with powder-white skin and dark-lined eyes said cheerily. She jumped up from the stool and offered me her hand. Her frail, thin hand got lost in mine as she stared up at me with a broad smile.

"Nice to meet you," I said, still having no idea who she was.

"These are Emma's roommates," Sara explained, reading my confused expression.

"Oh," I said, still thrown. I'd always pictured Emma living by herself, for some reason.

"I'm Meg." The girl with the curly auburn hair and cautious green eyes waved from the couch, clearly not as thrilled to see me as Serena.

The petite blond just glared at me.

"That's Peyton." Serena leaned toward me. "She doesn't like you very much."

My mouth opened in shock at the honesty.

"Shut up, Serena," Peyton snapped, obviously overhearing her.

"O-kay," I said slowly, not exactly comfortable with the judging eyes. "I think I'm going to go now."

"I'll drive you," Serena offered in a rush. "Peyton, give me your keys."

Peyton rolled her eyes, but tossed the keys to Serena anyway.

"I'll see you later, Sara," I said, uncertain why I was a little afraid to get in the car with Serena. Sara nodded. I picked up my things and followed the girl dressed all in black out the front door.

"So you went to the funeral," Serena said, hopping in the red Mustang parked on the street. Her voice was upbeat and friendly, not at all reflective of the Goth persona I'd expected.

"Yes, I did," I answered cautiously, very aware this was more than just a polite offer to drop me off.

"And she was a disaster, right?" Serena sounded like she already knew the answer.

I nodded, eyeing her apprehensively.

"We should've gone. I told the girls we should have gone, even though Emma told us not to."

"I don't really know if that would've helped, if that makes you feel any better."

"But still. We should've been there." She appeared upset by this.

Nate really didn't live far from Cole. I was actually surprised at how close the houses were. I could have easily walked.

Serena pulled the car to the curb and turned toward me. "I'm glad you went. I'm glad you were there for her. Thank you."

I nodded in acceptance, still wary of her friendliness. "Thanks for the ride." I removed my bags from the backseat and started to walk toward the large beach house.

"Evan," Serena called to me. I turned around. "We're going to fix her."

A bright smile full of certainty spread across her face before she spun the car around and headed in the opposite direction.

I watched her drive off, and a smile crept onto my face too.

20. GUILT TRIP

Good morning," Cole murmured with his head against the pillow. He was alert and waiting for me.

I groaned, still half asleep.

"I was a jerk yesterday," he confessed, running his eyes along my face in concern. "I'm sorry."

Cole hadn't touched me when I crawled in bed last night, after the girls had left and Sara had gone to her room. But I knew he wasn't asleep either as he lay with his back to me.

I went to say something, and then clamped my mouth shut with a grimace.

Cole chuckled. "Go do your bathroom thing and come back here."

I slid out of the bed and emerged a few minutes later, a little nervous to hear what he was about to say.

"So," I started us off, "last night was beyond awkward."

"I guess I was...jealous," he admitted. "I wanted to be there in Connecticut, but you asked me not to. And...*he* was there. I'm not the jealous type...and I hated how I was last night. So, I'm sorry."

I could feel his discomfort. It wasn't what he did, expressing himself.

I smiled and set my hand on the red of his cheek. He closed his eyes to my touch, absorbing the charge. I felt it running along my arm, speeding up my pulse. It soothed me, momentarily erasing the torment I'd been through in the past few days. I needed it…him… to help me forget.

I scooted closer, and he slid his hands along my waist.

"I didn't want you there," I whispered, leaning closer to his lips. "I wanted you here, for when I got back." I ran my tongue over his lower lip, and he inhaled quickly.

Cole's grip on my waist tightened as I ran my hands over the definition of his chest, tucking my nose into his neck and brushing my lips along his pulse. "Don't be jealous." I continued to whisper. "There's nothing to be jealous of. Please don't be like you were last night again. I didn't like it."

"I know," he said breathily into my hair, running his warm hands up my back, peeling my T-shirt off. "I'm not that guy."

"No, you're not," I said with a slight gasp as his tongue trailed down my neck. He pushed the shorts over my hips, and I kicked them to the end of the bed. His mouth made its way toward mine, consuming me.

Suddenly I couldn't get enough of him, pushing my hands through his hair, and kissing him fervently.

I could feel his boxers slip away, and I pushed him onto his back. A moan escaped as I slid my leg over the top of him. His hands caressed my body, making me arch my back as I lowered myself on top of him, inhaling quickly at the intensity.

"Emma," he gasped in pleasure as I worked into a slow rhythm. I closed my eyes and gripped his thighs behind me as he guided me with his hands on my hips.

My entire body was on fire with a tingling heat. I could feel it spread through me, igniting my flesh. Every fiber taut. Cole sat up, and I wrapped my legs around him, our rhythm slower and deeper. I opened my mouth to gasp as he slipped his tongue in, capturing my breath. My body tensed around him, and he held me tighter. My back arched, peeling me away as he ran his lips down my chest.

I groaned loudly and he grunted beneath me, his fingers pressing into my back. I waited for his body to ease before sliding back down to the bed, my head on his chest.

"Good morning," I said with a contented sigh. Cole laughed.

"Spend the day with me?" he requested, running his hands along my bare back.

"What did you have in mind?" I asked, though I knew the answer.

I was anxious to talk to her. I waited as long as I possibly could, but there was only so much Xbox I could play. I walked over to the small white house down the hill and followed the walkway, pausing at the door, hoping Cole wouldn't be the one to answer it. I knocked, and a few seconds later it swung open.

"Hi," the girl with the auburn hair said to me. I ran through the names introduced to me last night and came up with...

"Meg? Right?" I gave her a small smile, trying to put her at ease, since she continued to look at me like she didn't trust me.

"Yeah," she said, not making any move to invite me in. "Emma's not here."

"Evan!" Sara hollered from the other side of the room. "We're sitting on the beach. Come on in."

Meg stepped back to allow me access with a tight-lipped smile.

"Emma's not here, but you can hang out with us if you want," Sara offered, a beach towel slung over her arm and a magazine in her hand. I could hear the music coming from the deck as she continued out.

I wanted to ask where Emma was and when she'd be back. But I knew who she was with, since all of the girls were here. Now I wasn't sure I wanted to be here when they got back.

"She's with Cole," a chilled voice spoke behind me. I turned to find Peyton glaring at me with a malicious smirk. She wasn't exactly hiding the fact that she didn't like me, despite not even knowing me. I could only assume

she had some connection with Cole and didn't want me around to screw things up between him and Emma.

"I figured." I nodded, trying to appear unaffected by her hostility. "Since, you know... they're dating."

"They're not dating," Serena's voice chirped behind me. I turned to find her with an umbrella in her hand and dressed in a black bikini that reminded me of those classic movies Emma liked to watch. Her skin was so shockingly white, she almost glowed.

"Shut up, Serena," Peyton snapped. "They're together, and that's all that matters."

Serena shook her head in annoyance. "Will you help me set up this umbrella?" She didn't wait for my reply, but handed me the umbrella and strutted out onto the deck. I remained still for a moment, trying to process what had just happened.

"You shouldn't be here," Peyton grumbled, walking by me and out the sliding glass door.

Wow, I mouthed, thinking Xbox sounded pretty good about now.

"Evan, are you coming?" Sara called to me from outside.

I glanced toward the couch, where Meg sat quietly, pretending to read her book. I didn't think I could feel any more unwanted.

"Yeah," I hollered in return, heading toward the beach with the umbrella in my hand.

I followed the girls to the spot they'd picked for their beach chairs and towels. I angled the umbrella and shoved it in as deep as I could into the packed sand, casting a shadow over Serena to protect her ghostly skin.

They were all set up and ready for an afternoon of sun—or shade— worshipping, and the thought of sprawling on a towel next to them wasn't exactly appealing, considering the mixed hostility.

"I think I'll go for a run," I announced, not intending to come back.

"Really?" Sara asked, but when she looked up at me, she understood and nodded.

I had just taken off down the beach when I heard, "Evan, wait!"

I slowed to a stop and turned to find Serena approaching with a quick stride.

"What are you doing tonight?"

"Have fun with the girls," Cole said, leaning down and kissing me while Sara waited for me at the door.

"Thanks," I returned with a smile, my legs feeling the fatigue of surfing all day. But it was exactly what I'd needed, to be out in the water wrapped in silence, the rush of the waves the only sound. "I'll see you when we get back."

"I'm meeting some friends, so I may not be here. But I'll leave the key under the mat." He kissed me again, pulling me in to him before releasing me with a dizzying rush. "See you tonight."

Disoriented from the kiss, I stumbled out the door where Sara stood on the walkway. "Ready?" she asked with a grin.

"Yeah," I said, trying to breathe normally.

"This is going to be fun." She smiled. "We *need* fun."

"Yes, we do." Serena sat in her vintage light-blue Beetle with the top rolled back.

"Where are Peyton and Meg?" I asked, sliding in the back while Sara held the seat forward for me.

"Still in Carpinteria. They're meeting us there," Serena explained.

When she didn't take the turn that brought us toward the highway, I knew something was up. And when we pulled up in front of the house, I sighed.

"Who lives here?" Sara asked. "This place is incredible."

"Nate," I mumbled, just as Evan opened the door.

I approached the car with a jacket in my hand, smiling when I saw the girls. But the smile disappeared when I saw Emma's face. She didn't know I was coming.

"Hey," I said, looking from Serena's bright welcoming expression, to Sara's confused face, to Emma's avoiding glance. "Uh, you didn't tell them you invited me, huh, Serena?"

"Oh." Serena feigned forgetfulness. "I guess I forgot. But since you're here, you might as well come. Get in the car."

I raised my eyebrow at her demand and looked to Emma for permission. She tentatively lifted her eyes and shrugged. Sara got out of the car and whispered, "Be careful, Evan." She slid in the back, leaving the front seat vacant. I hesitated, heeding her warning, connecting with her for a second to read the seriousness reflected in her eyes. I sat in the front seat as Serena blared a punk song on the radio. I recognized the song, and automatically looked back at Emma, who refused to look at me.

Of course the band that Evan and I had seen together had to be playing on the radio. I shook my head with a humorless laugh. He tried to push the grin from his face after he turned around to catch my reaction, but he couldn't. It was easier not to look at him.

"Are you going to be okay…with him here?" Sara leaned in to ask me as the car picked up speed upon merging onto the highway.

"Sure." I shrugged. "I mean, I promised him two weeks, right?"

"But you don't have to do it if you don't want," Sara assured me. "You've been through a lot this week. You don't have to let him drag you through this guilt trip too."

"I know," I responded, appreciating her protectiveness. I glanced at him as he rested his elbow on the edge of the open window, listening to Serena talk about a band that was coming to the area soon that she was dying to see. His eyes shifted in my direction, and my cheeks warmed. I quickly looked away as his signature amused grin spread across his face once again. I pressed my hand against my cheeks, not having felt their warmth in so long. It was as surprising as it was annoying.

I couldn't keep myself from grinning as the blush crept across her skin. I knew it frustrated her when it happened too, which made it that much more enjoyable to watch. I returned my attention to Serena, who'd caught me watching Emma. I laughed awkwardly as her smile grew. I didn't know how Serena planned to "fix" Emma, but I knew she had expectations that I'd help her. I was afraid I was going to disappoint her, especially since I was barely held together myself.

Serena pulled in to a parking spot and I walked alongside her toward the large waterfront restaurant while Sara and Emma trailed behind us, far enough away so that they wouldn't be overheard.

"I thought we were going to Carpinteria for the movie in the park?" I asked, slightly alarmed to be walking toward a restaurant.

"Yeah, uh, the girls wanted to drink," Sara explained. "I forgot to tell you. But I won't drink…so, you know, that you're not the only one."

"Sara—" I turned toward her, my voice careful. "I don't have a drinking problem. I'm not going to have anything tonight, but I don't want you to worry about me. I've been stupid, no doubt. But it wasn't the alcohol. It was *me*. And I promise never to use it to cope with the shit I can't handle again."

Sara inspected my face thoughtfully. "You know it still scares me…you drinking."

"Because of my mother," I confirmed. "I know."

"But you're *not* her," Sara added quickly. "Emma, you're not. And I should have never said that to you in the motel. I was…angry, and scared. I'd never seen you like that before."

We were standing on the walkway as people brushed past us. I lowered my head and nodded, not really wanting to be caught up in this intense conversation in such an open place. I'd actually have preferred not to be having this conversation at all.

"Sorry," Sara said, realizing the same thing. "Let's go inside." She thrust her arm through mine and said, "We're supposed to be having fun." She revived her vibrant smile and nudged me with her shoulder, leading me into the bustling restaurant.

We spotted the girls…and Evan, at a table on the deck. From Peyton's sour expression I assumed they didn't know Evan would be here either. This was completely Serena's doing. I glanced at her curiously, trying to figure out what she was plotting. She looked up at me with an infectious smile, and I shook my head warily. Her meddling had the potential to make everything worse, despite her obviously good intentions.

After dinner the server came over and set two chocolate desserts on the table. The girls practically melted in happiness as they dipped their spoons in. I started laughing at the inappropriate noises they made while they ate. Then I caught Evan's drawn expression. He looked like he was about to be ill.

I really had ruined chocolate for him. I bit my lip. I knew I should feel awful, but his tortured expression was almost comical. He looked up just as a small laugh escaped. His eyes widened in surprise, and he pushed his chair away from the table and disappeared toward the side of the deck.

"Shit," I grumbled, immediately following after him.

"I'm sorry," Emma said softly, leaning against the railing next to me. "That wasn't funny, I know. But… you should have seen your face."

"Really? Thanks a lot, Emma."

"See. Another reason you should hate me. I'm cruel. Very cruel."

"Yeah." I sighed. Her choice of words made me realize we hadn't had our talk today. So I turned toward her and smirked.

She looked at me suspiciously. "What?"

"While you're here, you might as well give me another reason."

"Now?" Alarmed, she observed the crowded restaurant.

"It doesn't have to be something that dark," I encouraged. "Just give me something. Why should I hate you, Emma?"

I watched her caramel-colored eyes flicker in contemplation. She looked back toward the girls, who were laughing and oblivious. I waited *patiently, bracing myself for what she could potentially say, because I knew she was going to tell me something.*

"Jonathan kissed me," she blurted, holding her breath as she awaited my reaction. "Twice."

I opened my mouth to speak, but the beating in my chest stuttered and I couldn't find a single word to say. She didn't take her eyes off me. It was like she was preparing for me to be angry with her.

"Did you... cheat on me?" I asked, my voice caught in my throat. She kept her eyes locked on mine and shook her head very slightly.

"But I never told you about the kiss," she murmured, her eyes challenging. "Hate me, Evan."

I gripped the wood railing, sickened by the thought of him touching her in any way. I shook my head to rid myself of the image. She waited, her eyes flicking across mine. She had expected more of a reaction. I knew it. And I wasn't going to give it to her, regardless of what was going on on the inside.

"My turn," I said, trying to relax my tensed jaw. "Did you leave with him that night?"

She looked up at me curiously. "No. I didn't. I destroyed him." I was completely unprepared for her answer. She averted her eyes, which were laden with sadness.

It was difficult to talk about Jonathan, and think about what he'd done to us. But if I was going to be able to move on, I needed to understand what had happened between them.

"Emma!" I turned toward Cole's voice, and then he saw who I was with, "Oh, and Evan." His cheeks were deep red as he made his way over to us, bumping the back of a few chairs along the way. He sized Evan up and stated, "You're not a girl."

"Not that I'm aware of," Evan returned mockingly.

"I thought this was a girls' night." Cole turned toward me, dropping his arm around my shoulder and pulling me toward him.

"Cole—" I glared up at him, my voice thick with warning, not caring for his flare of jealousy.

"Oh, right," he remembered impatiently, removing his arm.

"I'm going to eat chocolate," Evan announced sharply, then strode away from us.

"What was that about?" I shot at Cole. "I thought we talked about this."

"We did," he stated, leaning in to kiss me. His sloppy kiss tasted like a whisky bottle. "Doesn't mean I like him here."

I sighed. "You're drunk."

"It does happen." He smiled, blinking lazily.

Emma leaned away from him when he tried to kiss her again, taking her phone from her pocket. He was trying to apologize, but she ignored him as she sent a text, obviously annoyed.

"Wanna shot?" Serena asked, sitting down next to me with two shot glasses in her hands.

"Sure," I answered, picking one up and tapping her glass before swallowing down the bourbon with a wince. "Thanks."

I looked over at Emma and Cole again. She took a step away from him as he reached for her. He was obviously drunk. And she was...

"Serena, what did you mean when you said that they weren't dating?"

Serena followed my focus to Emma and Cole. A devilish smile crept over her face before she leaned in to explain.

21. TWELVE DAYS

I watched Cole lean toward her as she examined her phone again. He said something in her ear, and she smacked his arm with a laugh. Completely different from how they were last night at the restaurant.

I stood inside the house, a beer bottle in my hand, as they leaned against the railing next to each other on the deck, their backs to me. I continued to study them. He half smiled at her, and she shook her head, laughing in disapproval. If they weren't dating, and he wasn't asking for anything more from her, then what were they doing together?

"They have lots of sex," a snarky voice said in my ear. I turned my head to find Peyton. "Thanks for inviting us over, Evan. This is a great house, even if it isn't yours," she said with a false sweetness.

I nodded, still speechless by what she'd said.

"You were trying to figure out why they're together, right? I saw you watching them," Peyton explained, grinning snidely. "They have sex all the time. They can't seem to keep their clothes on when they're near each other. I know... it sounds shallow, but that's what it is. But don't think he'll be that easy to get rid of. He cares for her. And eventually, she's going to let him. So leave her alone, Evan."

"You're friends with him," I concluded, studying the small blonde with eyes like daggers.

"He's my boyfriend's best friend," she clarified.

"Ah." I was beginning to understand. "And you don't like me."

"You hurt her." Her eyes tightened into slits. If she could have punched me, I'm pretty sure she would have.

"What are you talking about? I've barely spoken to her the past two days."

"She was hurting because of you before you got here," she snapped. "And no, I don't like you." She strode off toward the deck, grabbing a beer along the way.

"At least you're honest," I muttered, knowing I was out of earshot. "And she left me, by the way."

"Peyton's a bitch." Serena approached from behind me. "Don't let her get to you."

I laughed, turning around to find her standing at the top of the stairs that led to the lowest level of the house. "I thought you were friends."

"With her?" She laughed like it was absurd. "She drives me fucking crazy. I'm friends with Meg and Emma. I tolerate Peyton, and just barely. Come play foosball with me." She turned around and skipped down the stairs. I chuckled with baffled a shake of my head, and followed.

"You play foosball?" I asked skeptically, setting my beer on the edge of the foosball table.

"No," she said, straight-faced.

"I didn't think so," I replied with a laugh before dropping the ball on the white line.

"I love this house," Sara sighed, dangling her feet in the pool. "Can't we stay here instead?"

"Sara!" I scowled, looking around to see if Cole had overheard. He was still inside, getting a drink.

"I know," she droned, "I'm grateful Cole's letting us stay at his house, but this place is *so* awesome."

"It is," I agreed, admiring the large patio encircling the pool, which included a professional outdoor kitchen. The house itself was three stories, with a walk-out basement and an entertainment room that rivaled Sara's. It was difficult to wrap my head around the fact that this was a vacation home. No wonder the guys had a ton of parties here. Although the last one I'd attended was a bit of a disaster for me.

"Can we please hang out here all the time?" Sara sulked.

"Nice," I shot back. "We can walk right out onto the beach where we're staying. There's no pleasing you, huh?"

"I know. I'm spoiled," she admitted. "How're the two weeks going?" She eyed me cautiously, swirling her feet in the water.

"Hey, ladies," Peyton said from behind us before I could answer.

"Come sit, Peyton," Sara said to her. Peyton kicked off her sandals and sat next to me, lowering her feet in the water. "Are you coming back in two weeks too?"

"I can't. I start my internship tomorrow." Peyton focused on me and said, "But I have nothing to worry about, right?"

I scrunched my eyes in confusion.

"Fuck!" We turned our heads as Serena screamed from the rec room. Meg was leaning against the door frame, watching.

"Serena plays foosball?" Sara questioned, sounding surprised.

"Not from the sound of it," I responded. My heart skipped a beat, hearing Evan's laughter coming from the same room. Then I caught sight of Cole coming down the deck steps, and I turned my attention away.

"I suck!" Serena pouted, spinning the handle in a humorous tantrum.

"You're not that great," I agreed.

"Hey!"

"What? You just admitted you sucked."

"I think I need another beer," Serena sulked. "Meg, what time are we leaving?"

"Probably in the next thirty minutes or so," Meg answered, lingering in the doorway. "But I can drive if you want to get another beer." This offer brought an instant smile to Serena's face, and she scampered upstairs.

Meg sauntered into the room, her arms crossed. I waited for her to say something, but she didn't. Instead, she twirled one of the bars of the foosball table, still not looking at me.

"Do you not like me either?" I asked.

Meg appeared surprised by my directness. "You seem… nice. I'm just… protective of Emma."

"That seems to be the theme around here." I leaned back against the arm of the leather couch and took a swig of my beer. "It's good, though, that you all care so much about her."

"What happens after two weeks, Evan?" she demanded. Her turn to get right to the point.

I stopped before taking another sip, lowering the beer bottle from my mouth. "You know?"

"Sara told me," Meg explained, sliding her hands into the back pockets of her jeans.

"You and Sara are friends?" I confirmed, trying to figure out how they were all connected, and who confided in who.

"Yeah, we talk," she explained.

I nodded in understanding. So, she was Sara when Sara was in New York… or Paris. The only way Sara could truly know what was going on with Emma was to have someone looking out for her on this end. It wasn't like Emma was going to volunteer the information, at least not the information that really mattered to Sara. But, why was everyone so… afraid?

"Why does Emma need you all to protect her?" I questioned. "What's going on with her?"

Meg's shoulders pulled back as she examined me closely. Then she looked away and twirled another foosball knob.

"Meg, I'm not here to make things worse. I just want to understand what happened. Why she left like she did."

"I really don't hate you, Evan," Meg said, completely sidestepping my question. "We're leaving tonight to visit our families for a couple of weeks

before summer quarter starts. We'll be back when your two weeks are up. Just don't leave her any worse than you found her... please."

I was completely thrown by her statement. I wasn't expecting this, to find Emma so... fragile. I knew she had a distorted way of looking at the world and her place in it. She always had—no thanks to the women who made it their mission to destroy her. But she was strong underneath it all, capable of doing anything—if she'd just realize it. So Sara was watching her vigilantly, Peyton basically threatened me, Meg asked me to be careful, and Serena was on a crusade to save her—it didn't add up to the girl who I believed in.

That girl was once full of life and confidence, even if she had a hard time seeing it herself. I had always known it was there. It was what had attracted me to her in the first place. And now... I couldn't see it.

I was starting to wonder who the girl was that had landed in California over two years ago, and who she'd left behind in Weslyn.

Everyone began to leave about a half hour later. The girls were driving back to Palo Alto before heading to see their families. Sara, Cole, and Emma were about to leave for the house when I asked Emma, "Will you go for a walk with me?"

I looked at Cole, who waited for me to answer, his eyes hardening when he looked back toward Evan.

"Come on, Cole," Sara intervened, grabbing his arm. "Walk me home."

I followed Evan to a set of stairs that looked more like a two-story ladder. I held on tightly to the weathered wooden railing and took each step cautiously toward the beach. Evan walked down them as if he were walking on flat ground, and waited for me to catch up at the bottom.

"Serena likes you," I said, shoving my hands in my sweatshirt pockets with my head down as we began our walk. "If I didn't know her boyfriend, I'd think she had a thing for you."

Evan laughed. "I'm sure he's an interesting guy."

"You have no idea." I chuckled.

"She's probably the most optimistic person I've ever met," Evan said, glancing at me quickly. "I like her attitude. She's not who I'd imagine she'd be just by looking at her."

"I know." I grinned. "That's why she's so great."

We continued to walk along the beach, toward Cole's house, which was just around the next bend.

"Nate called me earlier. Since I'm here, he and the guys decided to come down early. They want to throw a party next Saturday, so they'll be arriving on Friday."

I nodded, not certain why this mattered, until he continued with, "But I was hoping we could still have the two weeks, like we originally agreed when I thought they wouldn't be here."

I stopped walking, causing him to turn to face me.

"You don't hate me yet, do you?" Emma asked, her face suddenly drawn.

"I still have twelve days," I quipped, not wanting to see that look on her face any longer. "Why don't you give me another reason why I should?"

"This isn't a joke to me, you know." She sounded agitated. Her eyes narrowed as she stared at me with the wind whipping her hair in her face.

"I know you're serious. I just wish you weren't." Shifting my tone, I repeated: "So tell me, why should I hate you, Emma?"

The anger I had at the sight of his grin dissipated when I looked into his flickering smoky blue eyes. My heart twisted as I took a breath. I needed him to listen. I had to force him to understand why he needed to leave me alone, to move on with his life without me.

"I left you." He flinched. "I left you in that house, alone and hurt. I ignored you when you called for me. Because I heard you. I did. But I didn't stop walking. I left you alone when you needed me, and I never looked back." My eyes stung as the image of him on the floor, barely conscious and beaten, flashed through my head.

Emma was fighting to remain composed, but her voice shook as she delivered the last few words—which was the reason I could never hate her.

Because I could see that what she'd done, the choices she had made, were destroying her.

I was pulled back into that night. The fury that pushed me to take a swing at Jonathan, which only escalated with each ensuing blow exchanged between us. The look in her eyes when he knocked her back onto the floor. And then there was a shooting pain through my head—just before there was nothing at all.

"Hate me, Evan," she begged, her lower lip quivering. It was difficult to watch the guilt shredding her to pieces. "Please, just hate me," she begged.

"I have twelve more days." I forced myself to say this calmly as she twisted my heart a little more. I was still trapped in that memory. I hated him. I hated him for manipulating his way into Emma's life and convincing her to trust him. For being who I always wanted to be for her. For standing in front of Emma's wall, the one I was just beginning to break through. Waking up alone and hurting everywhere didn't even come close to the torment I'd felt when I was convinced that she'd chosen him. "Where did you go when you left me?" I needed to know about the rest of that night, even though the outcome would never change.

"That's your question?" she asked, appearing confused. I nodded.

"Umm..." I swallowed hard and pulled away from the torture reflected in his eyes, even though he remained calm and composed on the outside. He was there in that house, bloody and broken. Exactly where I'd left him. I fought back the emotion that clawed up my throat.

"I drove. I don't know where I went, but I just kept driving." I took a breath, remembering the hysterics I was in as I sped through the back roads of the quiet town, screaming at myself for what I'd done. Tears flooded my eyes with the memory. But I blinked them away. I didn't deserve his sympathy

"I eventually made it back to Sara's. She was freaking out, thinking something awful had happened to me." I paused again as my voice cracked. "Anna was so upset. She couldn't understand what I was saying because I couldn't stop crying." A tear slid from the corner of my eye. I wrapped my arms around my waist to ward off a shiver.

"I told them that I needed to leave. That I couldn't stay in Weslyn. I hated it there, and I was leaving on the next flight out. Anna eventually calmed me enough to talk me into waiting a day or two, to see if I'd change my mind. But I didn't. Two days later I was on a plane to California. Sara tried to convince me that I was making the biggest mistake of my life. She didn't speak to me again for two months."

Emma opened her eyes, and another tear rolled down her cheek. "Does that answer your question?"

I nodded once, watching in silent agony as the light in her eyes faded into darkness. Her pain was all that remained, and I had to look away, unable to witness the suffering without wanting to touch her.

I cleared my throat and took in a breath of the ocean air to clear the ache away. "Well, I don't know about you, but that's about as much honesty as I can handle today." I attempted to smile, but it fell quickly as he continued to scrutinize me. He was so intense in his stillness, I had a hard time looking him in the eye.

"'Bye, Evan," I said, turning away.

"I'll see you tomorrow," he assured me, his voice strained. I didn't respond. I could feel him watching me as I walked down the beach.

When I got to the deck, Cole was sitting in a chair with his feet propped on the railing.

"Hi," I said, sitting down next to him.

"Hey," he responded with a small smile. "How are you doing?"

I shrugged. "Okay."

He scanned my face for all that I wasn't saying. "Do you want to go surfing again tomorrow?"

"Uh, actually, do you remember that friend I tried to help?" I asked, staring out at the water. I gripped my phone in my pocket, still not having heard from Jonathan after I'd called and then texted him from the restaurant yesterday. Talking about him with Evan last night made me think about the night I'd gone in search of him. I couldn't stop wondering where he was now and what he might be going through.

"Yeah," Cole responded hesitantly.

"I think I need to try again," I murmured, glancing at Cole.

He peered into my eyes before asking, "Where are you going to go?"

"New York. But it's not going to go over well with Sara."

"Why?" he questioned. "She doesn't like this friend?"

"Not exactly. So…would you cover for me?" I requested, a twinge of guilt flashing across my face. "I have to do this. I need to at least try."

"How long will you be gone?"

"Truthfully, I'm not sure," I answered. "I'm leaving tomorrow, and hope to be back in just a couple days. But I guess it depends."

Cole was quiet for a moment. "Yeah, I'll cover for you. Want me to drive you to the airport?"

"Yes. Thank you," I replied, my voice soft.

We returned our focus to the ocean as the day faded around us—the sun sinking farther off to our right, leaving a trail of gold with smears of pink and purple stretched across the horizon. The lights from the oil rigs twinkled in the distance, and the sound of the surf was hypnotic. We were once again wrapped in our silence, which used to be so comforting. On the inside, a storm was swirling, uncovering memories and feelings I'd buried over two years ago. My eyes trailed down the beach toward the large house on the cliff. I knew it was only going to get worse.

22. TAKING ME WITH HER

The sun was rising somewhere behind the hills, but it still hadn't cut through the clouds that had settled on the beach. As the fog lingered over the water, I wrapped the blanket tighter around me to fend off the cool morning air.

The yearning for sleep still clung to me. I'd been restless throughout the night, disturbed by the shouting and crying in my head. Eventually I'd slipped out of bed to relieve Cole of my tossing and turning.

My eyes ached with fatigue as I spotted a silhouette coming into view along the beach. I tried to focus through the thick haze. Someone was running along the water's edge. Just the thought of exerting that much energy exhausted me.

As the runner neared the house, he began to slow down. He hesitated, then began jogging my way. I froze, trying to be invisible in the fog, but he knew I was there.

As he came closer, I squinted in confusion. "Evan?"

"Hi," I answered, not certain if I should've just kept jogging and left her alone. But I wanted to know why she was up. She peered down at me, wrapped in a blue blanket pulled up to her nose.

I smiled at the sight of her hair all pushed in different directions. I was still getting used to the short hair. I had to admit, I didn't mind it—the length accentuated the exotic shape of her eyes.

"I knew you were a morning person, but this is ridiculous," she said.

*I laughed at her comment. "I couldn't sleep. Thought running might...
help. And I know you're not a morning person; you pretty much despise
any time with an a.m. after it."*

"I couldn't sleep either."

*"Nightmare?" I asked without thinking, knowing that was the reason
I was running into the fog, and away from the panic that had awoken me.*

*Her eyes darted away and she shrugged evasively. I assumed it was my
fault she was out here and not still wrapped up in the covers... next to Cole.
I forced my shoulders to relax. I'd sworn I wouldn't think of them together,
even after the not-so-pleasant details Peyton planted in my collection of
unwanted thoughts.*

"Run with me."

*Emma looked down at me as if I'd just asked her to go skinny-dipping
in the freezing ocean. I chuckled. "Come on, what else do you have to do?"*

I couldn't believe I was actually thinking about it. I pushed my
chair back. "Fine," I grumbled. "Let me get my stuff."

I ignored the grin that spread across his face, and crept back
into the house. What was I thinking?

When I returned a few minutes later, Evan was sitting at the
bottom of the stairs.

"Don't expect much," I told him, making him stand up quickly
and turn around. Seeing me at the top of the stairs in my running
gear made that smile emerge again. The smile that I couldn't look at
for more than a second without my heart thrusting to life and my
cheeks igniting.

I let my feet carry me down the steps and followed him closer
to the water, where the sand was firm. We eased into a slow run,
and my muscles complained. They weren't fond of being woken
this early either.

"See, it's not so bad," Evan said.

I groaned. "My body is totally freaking out."

Evan laughed, evidently amused by my suffering.

As we continued, the muscles in my legs began to loosen and my lungs didn't fight the air being sucked into them. The fatigue was replaced by adrenaline, and my pace naturally picked up.

"Not tired anymore, huh?"

My heart beat in my ears as I pushed myself to keep up with her. The tiredness in her eyes was replaced by determination; she was fixated on what lay ahead of her. I liked it.

"It's been too long since I've run," she explained, not sounding half as out of breath as I was. "It feels good." Then she tilted her head up at me, wearing a playful smile that I recognized but hadn't seen in a while. "But I still hate mornings."

I laughed. We ran to a set of rocks breaking up the sandy beach and turned back toward the house. As exhausted as this run was making me, I didn't want it to end. For the first time since I'd arrived, she looked at peace, and I didn't want it to disappear when our legs stopped moving.

As soon as the house came into sight, she dug into the sand and her stride lengthened. There was no way I was going to keep up, so I let her go ahead without me. She pushed her body for everything it had, and the sight of it was breathtaking. I almost tripped over a rock, mesmerized by the grace and power that catapulted her down the packed sand, leaving a trail of divots in her wake.

When I caught up with her she was pacing with her hands on her hips, trying to catch her breath. I stood and just watched her, the sweat running along her face, the wind blowing her hair wildly around her. She paused and looked at me curiously, as if trying to read my thoughts. I wished I could have told her what they were.

"I'm going to continue to the house," I finally said. "Thanks for running with me."

She nodded. "Sure."

I picked up my feet, despite their defiance, and continued back along the beach. I looked over my shoulder and faltered at the sight of her pulling her shirt over her head. Still jogging, I glanced back at her dark silhouette wrapped in the grey fog. My pace slowed. I couldn't force myself to look away. I stumbled to a stop when she kicked off her shoes and slid her shorts over her hips. The thick fog provided enough of a curtain so she remained a shadow along the beach. But I was mesmerized by the lines of her thin body. I inhaled, trying to calm my quickened pulse. She walked casually into the water, not reacting to the cold as it rose up her legs until it lapped against her thighs.

She dove under a wave, emerging on the other side. Her head bobbed in the water, dissolving her into the hues of grey. Enraptured, I hadn't realized that I was walking closer until I noticed movement out of the corner of my eye. I was shaken out of the trance when Cole emerged onto the deck with a towel in his hand.

I backed away and broke into a jog, hoping the morning haze had concealed me from his view. My heart rate still hadn't recovered, and I knew I needed to push away what I'd seen if I was going to be around her again. I accelerated into a full-out sprint when I spotted the stairs to leading Nate's.

I rushed back up to the shore, with my arms braced around me and my lips shivering.

"Good morning," Cole greeted me, a towel spread between his arms. He wrapped me up, the warmth of the fabric and his arms staving off the chills. "Not a bad thing to see first thing in the morning."

"Funny," I replied with a sarcastic smile, snuggling against him. "You're up early."

"I'm meeting the guys to go surfing," he explained, squeezing me. I looked up at him and he leaned down, sliding his lips over my wet, quivering mouth. He was so warm. I slipped my tongue into his mouth and he pulled me in tighter. My pulse quickened as he continued to kiss me, the charge rushing through me as I slipped my arms around his neck.

"I could be late," he murmured into my ear.

I laughed and took a step back. "You should go. I'll see you later."

He pressed his cheek against mine and said, "I'll be back this afternoon to take you to the airport. Stay naked for me 'til then?" He pecked my lips, then scooped up my clothes and led me back into the house. I smiled and followed after him.

After Cole left, I headed toward the bedroom to shower and dress before I packed. There was no way I was going to be able to sleep now, though it was still too early to be awake. I had no idea how I was going to leave without Sara knowing. I was riddled with uncertainty about seeking out Jonathan in New York. It had been over a week since he left. I hoped I wasn't too late.

Showered, warm and surprisingly invigorated, I walked into the living area to find Sara's door open. I poked my head into her room, but it was empty. I scanned the deck and the beach, but there wasn't a sign of her. When I turned back toward the kitchen, I noticed a note written in Sara's scrawl on the kitchen island.

Gone to buy Picnic Food! We're having a picnic on the beach today...I may even let you hold my hand. Ha!

I wasn't looking forward to Sara's reaction when I disappeared without telling her where I was going. I sighed and set the note back down on the counter. I opened the cabinet to pull out a box of cereal when the thought struck me: How did she get to the store? She didn't have a car.

"Do you have a car I can borrow?" Sara asked as soon as I opened the door, rubbing the towel against my wet hair.

"Good morning, Sara. Nice to see you," I responded sarcastically. She walked past me into the house.

"I know I haven't been very nice to you, and I'm sorry," she began with her hands on her hips. "I'd like to move past the awfulness of the past two years when you were a total douche to me. And I promise not to be a bitch to you anymore. But only if you promise to back off Emma if she can't handle the whole two-week disaster you proposed."

My brows perked at her forwardness, but I shouldn't have expected anything else from Sara. "What are you afraid she's going to do?"

"I didn't come here to discuss Emma's psyche with you, Evan. I came to make peace."

"And borrow a car." I smirked.

"Yes," she admitted with a bit of attitude, "and to borrow a car."

She crossed her arms impatiently and waited for my assurance. I actually stopped to think about what she'd asked of me. I'd come here to get answers. Now I had to decide what the truth was worth.

I inhaled deeply. "Okay, I'll back off if she can't handle it. And Nate's parents keep the Audi in the garage. The key is in the bowl on the kitchen counter."

"Thank you." Sara smiled in relief. She started toward the kitchen, but stopped and turned back to face me. "Evan, I'm sorry about what happened two years ago. I want you to know that I never agreed with what she did. I still think it was the worst decision of her life. And I think she knows that too, as much as she swears she did it to protect you."

"Protect me? What—"

Sara grimaced. "Uh… thanks for letting me borrow the car."

"Sara," I called to her, "what are you talking about?"

"Shit," she grumbled, closing her hand tightly around the key. "I shouldn't have said that. Sorry. She'll tell you. Just give her time."

I gritted my teeth and nodded, knowing I'd have to hear whatever this explanation was from Emma anyway. But how could she have possibly convinced herself that she was protecting me when she chose to walk away?

"What the fuck, Emma?" I murmured as I stood on the walkway and watched Sara pull the car out of the garage.

"I shouldn't be long," Sara hollered as she came to a stop along the street. She hesitated a moment, then added, "We're spending the day on the beach, Emma and I. I'm going to get food for a picnic... if you want to join us."

I grinned at the peace offering. "Thanks. I'll think about it."

"Well... Emma's at the house now... alone." Sara produced a small smile before speeding off down the street. I laughed at her lack of subtlety.

I tossed the envelope in the small trash can I'd removed from the bathroom, sifting through the mail that Anna had handed me before I left, making room in my tote for two days' worth of clothes. "How many credit cards does a person need?" I sighed and picked up the next envelope, ready to toss it as well. Then I saw the handwriting. I typically would have thrown her letter away, like I had the many others before. But I couldn't. Not this time.

I pulled out the folded white page and opened it. My chest squeezed in around my heart. I let out a quick breath and couldn't breathe again.

I knocked on the front door and waited. Emma didn't answer. I knocked again, and still nothing. I looked around the empty driveway, then put my hand on the doorknob and turned it. It was unlocked. I hesitated for a moment before pushing the door open.

"Emma?" I called, entering cautiously so that I didn't startle her. "Emma?" Silence.

I closed the door and continued into the living room, peering through the glass doors, but she wasn't there either. I was walking toward the bedroom when I saw her foot dangling from the edge of the bed.

"Hey, Emma," I called to her as I approached, "Sara said—"

I stopped at the sight of her, gripping the door frame to keep steady. "Emma, what happened?"

Her entire body was trembling, and her eyes were glazed over, staring blankly at the page she clutched tightly in her hands. Her mouth puckered slightly, taking in erratic breaths that raised her chest in spasms.

"Emma?" I said, trying to reach her. Her chin quivered as she moved her mouth in silent whimpers. "Let me see." I eased the paper from her hands. Her eyes shifted up to me in a quick motion, and I flinched at the screaming pain reflected in them. She didn't utter a sound. Tears pooled in her unblinking eyes. She looked like she was drowning.

I examined the page, and my teeth clenched at the first word written in rushed penmanship: "Emily." I glanced back down at Emma. She remained frozen in torture.

Emily,

Maybe you'll finally read this letter. After all, it is the last.

You should have discovered by now what you did to me. Yes, you did this to me. I couldn't stand the pain anymore. The pain of being alone. The pain of being ignored and not being loved by my only daughter. The pain of losing the only person who ever truly loved me, because of you. The love that you destroyed the day that you were born.

You should never have been born. You have only caused pain in the lives of everyone you've touched. Even the lives of those two innocent children who tried to love you. Look at who you've become. How can you stand to even look at yourself in the mirror, knowing all the destruction you've caused?

You killed me with those cold, hateful words you said to me. You killed me with each letter I sent that you never answered. How could you be so cold and hateful to your own mother? I've given you so much, and it didn't matter to you. I was never good enough for you. Now you'll have to live with yourself, knowing that the reason I can't go on living is because of you.

Love,
Your Mother

I swallowed in disgust. "No," I said, my tone urgent. "Emma, no, no." I shook my head in disbelief.

I sat down next to Emma, but she still didn't respond. Her limbs trembled, and her teeth chattered. I dropped the letter to the floor, not wanting to touch the vile words scribbled across the page.

I slid my arm around her and pulled her in to me. She collapsed against my chest, and I held her tight. "Don't listen to her," I begged. My vision blurred. "Don't listen to her, Emma. Not a single word." But she couldn't hear me.

23. SILENT PAIN

All that escaped her were rhythmic breaths. She couldn't stop shaking, no matter how tight I held her. She didn't resist when I eased us onto the bed. Leaning back against the padded headboard, I shifted her onto my chest, and secured her in my arms. "Emma, you have to know that every word was a lie. Don't let her hurt you," I pleaded, my lips brushing against her hair.

She just continued to quake. I felt like I'd been stabbed in the chest with a flaming torch. I hated that selfish, vindictive woman. She made sure her final act was to crucify the one person who ever tried to love her, repeatedly. I inhaled deeply to push my contempt away. It wasn't what Emma needed right now.

We stayed like this, wrapped in silent pain, until I heard the front door open.

"Emma?" Sara called out. "Evan?"

I opened my mouth to call to her just as she appeared in the doorway. She eyed Emma lying on my chest in my arms and glared at me. "What are you—" She stopped, her eyes narrowing as she examined Emma more closely, then walked cautiously toward us. "What happened? Emma?" Sara looked up at me in alarm. "Evan, what happened to her? What did you do?"

I shook my head at her accusation. "There's a letter. It's on the floor somewhere."

Sara warily took her eyes off of us and searched the floor, bending down to pick up the piece of paper. I couldn't watch her read it.

"Fucking bitch!" Sara exclaimed, startling me. I looked down at Emma. Still locked against me, she didn't flinch. "How could she—" Sara crumpled the paper and stormed out of the room. I heard drawers slamming shut as she muttered, "That fucking bitch," over and over again. I smelled smoke and knew exactly what she'd done.

Sara appeared back in the room, crawling onto the bed on the other side of me so she could see Emma's face. She leaned close to her, peering into her blank eyes, and ran her hand along her cheek.

"Emma," she soothed, "she was an awful person, and all she wanted was to hurt you. You can't let her. Em, you can't let her. You're so much stronger than that. I know you are. Please, Emma."

Sara pursed her lips and tears filled her eyes. She redirected her gaze to me and said, "She can't believe it. Evan, we can't let that woman break her."

"I know," I said quietly, running my hand along Emma's back.

Emma jolted under my touch. I tilted my head to see her face. "Emma?"

She inhaled a sob, her chest heaving. Pulling away from me and curling into a ball, she screamed, "No!"

Sara froze in stunned silence.

"No! No!" Emma balled her fist and punched the mattress repeatedly, her eyes squeezed shut as she screamed the words over and over again. "No! No! No!" She burst into hysterics, crying so hard, her whole body convulsed. Sara looked at me, fear flashing across her face.

I leaned over and gently gripped her shoulder, "Emma. It's okay."

"No, it's not," she cried. "She's dead! She's dead!" She collapsed against the bed and sobbed uncontrollably. Then uttered weakly, "My mother's dead."

"Oh, Emma," Sara gasped, kneeling on the floor next to the bed, her face twisted in pain as she helplessly witnessed her best friend's suffering.

I curled in behind her and held her close, absorbing the spasms of her sobs. She clenched my arm tightly, as if I could keep her from being pulled under.

We didn't say a word. Sara and I stayed by her and let her cry for the mother who didn't deserve her. I knew she was mourning her loss, probably for the first time since she'd learned of her death. All I wanted to do was protect Emma from everything that hurt her. It was reminiscent of the night she cried in my arms as she relived her father's death. I couldn't ease the pain then, and I knew I couldn't do it now. And even though I'd failed time and time again, it wasn't going to stop me from trying.

Eventually the sobs tapered off and her body uncoiled. I felt her back expand against my chest as her breathing deepened.

Sara looked up at me and whispered, "She's asleep." I nodded, suspecting as much. Sara slowly stood up, her body stiff from kneeling as she stretched her arms over her head.

She started toward the door and turned back. "Evan. Come on." She jerked her head toward the door impatiently.

I hesitated, not wanting to leave. But it was evident Sara had something to say that she didn't want Emma to overhear. I eased my arm out from under her, flexing my hand to get the circulation flowing. Emma's body shivered when I moved away. I tucked a blanket around her, reluctantly shutting the bedroom door behind me before following Sara into the living room.

Sara paced back and forth, her red lips pressed tight. She stopped when I walked farther into the room. Her anxiety could've knocked me over. "Evan, I'm scared."

I waited, hoping she'd explain.

"You have no idea what's she's been like for the past two years," Sara continued in a rush. "She is barely holding on, and I'm so afraid that letter may have pushed her over the edge."

"What are you afraid she'll do, Sara?" I questioned. "Turn to alcohol again?"

Sara's eyes flickered thoughtfully before she collapsed on the couch. "I don't know how to describe it." Her voice was quiet and hesitant. "She's just been... existing since she left Weslyn. There's no... light in her eyes. No purpose. No drive. She used to push herself to be more, to want more, and now... now she's barely living." She paused to look at the bedroom door, her eyes watering. "I feel like I've gradually been losing her. Like she's slipping away and I can't hold on. I'm scared that she's going to push us all away for good. I know it doesn't make complete sense, and I don't know how to explain it. I'm just scared."

I sat down in the chair across from her. "What happened to her, Sara?"

Sara looked across at me with sorrow-filled eyes. "She left you."

My face twisted in confusion, but before I could speak, Sara said, "I truly don't understand why she left, Evan. You'll have to ask her."

The sound of the front door opening interrupted us. Sara and I both turned as Cole walked in. He was wet, in a pair of board shorts.

"Hey." He nodded toward us, looking around. "Where's Emma?"

Sara and I looked at each other, releasing a simultaneous breath. She finally said, "I'll tell him."

I nodded and stood from the chair, not wanting to watch his reaction, whatever it was. So I escaped to the deck, closing off Sara's voice with the sliding glass door.

I stared out at the volatile waves and inhaled deeply, exhaustion overwhelming me.

The glass door opened, drawing my attention. Sara stepped out to join me, breathing in the salty air as I had, like it could somehow revive her.

"He went in to see her," Sara told me. She leaned against the railing next to me. After a moment of listening to the ocean, she said, "I'm sure that it's hard for you, to see them together."

"But they're not really together," I countered.

"Still," Sara said, "she's not with you. So no matter what, it must be hard."

"I didn't come here to get her back, Sara. I was being honest about that. I spent the last two years trying to understand what she was thinking, what happened, why she walked away. I need answers. That's why I'm here."

Sara leaned on her elbow to face me. "I don't believe you."

I was shocked by her comment. "What?"

"*Evan Mathews, you can tell yourself and everyone else that you're here to get answers, for closure. But the truth is, you love her. You have always loved her. You will always love her. You're here because you can't walk away. You saw how broken and empty she was back in Weslyn, and you had to follow her. You'll never be able to let her go. You're here because… it's where you belong, with her.*"

My chest tightened; I felt like she'd just delved inside me and sifted through to find what I couldn't admit this entire time. I couldn't speak. I looked out at the water and pulled in a deep breath. I turned from Sara and went back into the house, needing to check on Emma.

Cole sat on the chair, having put on shorts and a T-shirt, and was rubbing his hands together and bouncing his leg nervously.

"*You okay?*" *I asked him.*

He nodded, but the edgy shift in his eyes indicated otherwise. I continued past him and into the bedroom. Emma was still curled up tight in her sleep, twitching every so often. I sat on the bed next to her, smoothing her hair away from her face.

"*I'll stay with her tonight,*" *Sara said from the doorway.* "*You don't have to worry. I'll be here.*"

I left Emma in her haunted sleep and walked into the living room. "*Cole, do you mind if I sleep here tonight? On the couch?*"

I could tell he didn't know what to make of this. But he shrugged and said, "*Yeah, sure.*"

I woke up in the dark. I could hear breathing beside me. My entire body ached, and my head was groggy, like I'd taken cold medicine.

Then I remembered. I clenched my teeth, trying to maintain even breaths. I could still feel the weight of the letter in my hands, the words stabbing me in the heart, twisting the blade.

You should never have been born. You have only caused pain in the lives of everyone you've touched.

My mother had confessed some terrible things in the past, usually induced by the effects of alcohol. She had always known what to say to hurt me. But these words…They were what she wrote before she killed herself. These were the thoughts that carried her to her grave. And she didn't just want to hurt me, she wanted to take me with her.

Now you'll have to live with yourself, knowing that the reason I can't go on living is because of you.

A breathy sob escaped.

"It's okay," he whispered softly, moving closer to pull me in to him. Pressing my face against his chest, I inhaled his soothing scent, letting the tears pour out and soak through his T-shirt. I sobbed in gasps as he held me, my heart aching so bad I wanted to pull it out to make it stop.

"Emma, we're here," Sara said from behind me, her hand rubbing my back. "It's going to be okay. We're here for you, and we're not going anywhere."

Sleep eventually tugged at my punctured heart, and I drifted off into the darkness.

———

I looked around the dark room, still unable to sleep. Emma breathed into my chest, and Sara was curled up behind her, with her hand on her back. Emma would flinch and release a moan every once in a while. I could only imagine what tortured her in her dreams.

Leaving them to sleep, I slipped out of the room and back to the couch that I hadn't slept on. The door to the guest room remained closed, with Cole shut behind it. I sat on the couch and stared out at the dark in a daze, waiting for the sun to brighten the sky.

Sara emerged from the bedroom a couple hours later, as the beach was finally coming into view beneath the blanket of fog. She yawned and stretched her arms over her head, looking exhausted.

"Is she still sleeping?" I asked, trying to decide if I should go back in there so she wouldn't wake up alone.

"If that's what you call it," Sara mumbled, her words wrapped in another yawn. She noticed my indecision. "Evan, she's asleep. You don't have to go back in there right now. Let's make some breakfast or something. Aren't you supposed to be an awesome cook?"

"Yeah, sure," I replied, standing and twisting my body to stretch out my back. "I'll make something."

I remained buried within the blanket but shifted my eyes up at Sara as she sat next to me on the bed. Moving even slightly hurt… everywhere.

"Are you hungry? Evan made omelets. He could make you one," she offered gently.

I tried to shake my head, but wasn't sure if I actually did. I returned to staring at nothing. I was infested with blackness, scorching and marring my insides, feeding on the guilt and hate that had taken root so long ago. It intertwined with every cell, and there was no hiding from it any longer. I couldn't feel. I couldn't think. I couldn't move without triggering an unfathomable pain that would leave me begging to end the suffering, just as my mother intended.

"She's just staring in there. It's like… she doesn't even see me. I don't know what to do," Cole said, sitting in the chair, rubbing his hands together as he looked straight ahead. His voice sounded anxious and panicked. "What are we supposed to do?"

Sara glanced worriedly from Cole to me. We had agreed to let Emma mourn. To let her come to terms with her mother's death as she needed to. But she was closing off, not eating, not talking, and we were all at a loss as to how to reach her.

"Uh, I'm gonna… I'm gonna go out for a while," Cole announced, looking at us guiltily. "Will you be okay if I do that?"

Sara nodded, and he looked to me. I offered a quick nod as well. He grabbed his keys and disappeared out the front door.

Sara continued to stare at the door after he left. "I feel bad for him. He had no idea what he was getting into with her. This kinda sucks."

"Kinda?" I countered, raising my brows. I didn't want to feel sorry for Cole. It was evident that he was in over his head. But that only confirmed that he shouldn't be with her.

"What do we do, Evan?" Sara asked, exhaustion weighing in her voice. "How do we get her back? Should we take her to the hospital?"

I let out a breath and shook my head, feeling just as defeated. "It's been two days. Let's give her another day, and then we'll decide."

Sara rubbed her eyes. "I wish we could remind her how strong she really is."

Then it hit me.

"I got it," I declared, my chest lightening with this revelation.

"What?" Sara's head jerked up.

"I'll be right back," I told her.

I held on to the only thing I had left… hope.

24. WAITING FOR HER

*E*m, I need you to get up."

Her eyes pushed open, barely. She squinted up at me without a word, without showing any inclination to get up.

"I'm serious," I said a little more firmly. "You need to get out of bed and come with me." She just lay there, staring at me like she didn't understand a word I said. "Either get out of bed, or I'm carrying you."

Her mouth dropped open. At least I knew she'd heard me.

"Why?" she croaked hoarsely.

"Because I'm going to help you," I explained. "But I can't do that until you get out of bed."

Her eyes moved in contemplation. It was the most reaction we'd gotten out of her in days, other than crying.

"You're not going to leave me alone until I get out of bed, are you?"

"Nope," I answered, trying not to smile, even though it was getting harder. "Trust me, Emma."

She thought for a moment, took a deep breath, and pushed the blankets back. This time I couldn't conceal my satisfaction.

"Don't look all proud of yourself," she grumbled, sliding her legs over the edge of the bed. I let out a quick laugh at her feistiness. It was a good sign, or a better one anyway.

"Do you want to shower or anything first?" I asked. Her hair was all knotted up on one side, and there were pillow crease lines on the side of her face. She'd been wearing the same clothes for two days, so I figured she'd want to feel... clean.

"Nope," she said stubbornly. "You want me to get up, this is how you get me."

I released a smile. "Okay, then. Let's go."

I turned toward the door.

"We're leaving?"

"Yeah. Are you sure you don't want to wash up or brush your teeth?" I suggested one more time.

She eyed me thoughtfully, trying to figure out what I was up to. I smiled wider, and Emma's eyes narrowed. "No, I'm fine."

Her defiance made me laugh. She was never one to be told what to do, and that was one of the reasons I—

I turned toward the door, cutting that thought off before it had a chance to finish. It wasn't why I was here, and I had to keep reminding myself that—though it wasn't as easy to believe now.

Emma shuffled behind me. Her movements were stiff, probably from being twisted up in a ball for so long. We passed Sara in the living room, reading a magazine on the couch. She was trying so hard to appear casual, but I knew better. She was a wreck on the inside.

"Have fun," she chimed with a smile.

Emma gave her a sideways glance. "Of course you're in on this."

I looked to Sara with a grin. The worry surfaced in her eyes for that second. She obviously wasn't as confident as I was that this was going to work.

The light felt too bright when I walked out the front door, even though it was dusk. My entire body felt like it had been frozen and it was now slowly thawing. My head was still stuffed with cotton, and I felt so tired, I could've laid down on the sidewalk and fallen asleep.

I rolled my eyes at the grin Evan couldn't seem to lose, despite every glare I'd shot at him. I didn't know why I was agreeing to this. But then again, I did. Because he'd asked me to trust him. And I'd never said no before.

I plopped down on the front seat of the convertible, and Evan shut the door after me. We drove the two minutes to the other house in silence. With Evan in the lead, glancing over his shoulder every so often, I dragged myself through the garage and up the stairs.

We continued to the second floor of the house and stood outside a closed door.

"Close your eyes," he requested with a permanent grin.

My brows pulled together. "Are you serious?"

"Yes." He nodded. "Close your eyes."

I sighed and closed my eyes. A moment later I could feel fabric being wrapped around them.

"Really?" I shot at him in disbelief. Evan laughed. I would've rolled my eyes again if they were open.

"Trust me," he said again. I stilled with those words. His words. My heart pounded faster just hearing them.

Evan took hold of my hand. His hand was warm and strong, wrapping mine within it. He gave it a small squeeze before saying, "Okay, take a few steps forward."

I allowed him to guide me, unable to control the fit going on inside my chest.

We passed through the doorway, and I led her to the center of the room before letting go of her hand to shut the door. I waited a moment before I murmured quietly over her shoulder, "Breathe, Emma. Take a deep breath."

She paused a moment, not understanding. Then I watched as she inhaled through her nose, filling her lungs while expanding her chest. She hesitated, as if she were surprised. Then she breathed in again, and the most stunning smile emerged on her face. It was the best reaction I could have hoped for.

Emma pulled the bandana down, and it fell around her neck. She took in the room around her and turned to me. For the first time, I swore I saw a hint of light in the soft brown of her eyes.

"Thank you," she whispered.

I nodded, the lump in my throat making it challenging for me to speak as well. I swallowed and said, "Let it all out, Emma. Find your way back to us."

Emma smiled brighter, causing me to do the same. "Okay," she said, *and turned from me. I went back out the door, leaving her in the room.*

I bit my lip as a tear slipped over my lid and down my cheek. I inhaled, absorbing the calming scents once again. I had no idea how he'd done it, how he'd gotten the room to smell like it did, but it made my heart swell until I felt like it might burst.

Sitting on the stool, I studied the blank canvas, remembering his words. *Let it all out, Emma.* Collecting myself with a quick breath, I twirled the paintbrush thoughtfully in my hand. The rest of Evan's words settled within me. *Find your way back to us.* And a warmth spread through my body. I knew exactly what I was going to paint. I picked up a tube of paint, squirting the green along the palette.

I glanced around and noticed the small cooler with bottles of water and the tray that held a sandwich, a granola bar, and an apple. On the desk were a clean clothes to change into. My chest fluttered—a sensation I hadn't felt in...years. At the same time, my stomach rumbled, and I picked up the granola bar as I continued to squirt colors on the palette. All I wanted to do was lose myself in the strokes of my brush. Gain control over the chaos that was tearing me apart. And find myself in the one place I would forever feel safe.

"I got Sara's note," Cole said when I answered the door.

"Yeah, come on in." I walked back up the three steps into the living room area.

"So...where is she?" Cole asked, glancing around uncomfortably.

"Painting," I told him. He pulled his head back in confusion. *"You didn't know she painted?"*

"I don't think she has in…well, since she left," Sara explained. She was sitting on the love seat with her legs curled under her. She'd paused the movie we were watching when we heard the knock at the door. "Evan thought that it would help her deal with her grief. That she could express herself through a paintbrush. It used to work for her in high school."

"Oh," Cole responded with a nod. " You *thought* of this."

"I did," I replied carefully. "It was a long shot. But it got her out of bed."

"That's good, I guess."

I knew he was still trying to figure out what my motives were, despite our conversation on the first night. And I couldn't get a true sense of what his feelings were for Emma. I did know he wasn't dealing very well with what had been happening the past couple of days.

"She's upstairs, if you want to see her," Sara told him.

Cole glanced up the stairs, his hands shoved in his front pockets. "Have you been up there?" Sara shook her head. "Then I'll just wait too. Will you call me when she comes down?"

"Sure," Sara answered.

"Thanks." He turned and walked out the door.

Sara looked to me with her eyebrows raised, "Umm…awkward." I shrugged and plopped back down on the couch so we could continue watching the movie.

"You can go to bed if you want," Sara said to me as I started to nod off on the couch. The screen was flashing baseball highlights. I hadn't slept much in the past few days, and it was taking its toll. I was fighting every blink to keep my eyes open.

"No, it's okay," I said, shifting to try to appear more alert than I was.

"Evan, you can go sleep in an actual bed," Sara continued. "You don't have to hang out on the couch. It's after two in the morning."

I glanced up at the stairs. She was still up there... painting whatever it was that she was painting. We hadn't heard from her since I'd shut the door, except the couple of times she'd come into the hall to use the bathroom. But neither of us had looked in on her, wanting to give her space to... heal.

"You can go to bed too," I told Sara. "There's more than one guest room." Her red-rimmed eyes made it apparent that she was just as tired.

She shrugged dismissively and turned her attention back to the book that was open on her lap. Neither one of us wanted to leave the couch. It was the best vantage point to hear the door open and close, and to be visible when she finally walked down those stairs.

———

I stepped back to admire the image I'd created and smiled proudly. Every stroke on the canvas pulsed with emotion. My eyes blurred, and my hands shook slightly from the lingering adrenaline that had possessed me, keeping me focused throughout the night.

But when I set down the brush, all of the energy drained from me. I was exhausted. I held up my paint-covered hands. I definitely needed to shower, especially since I hadn't in almost three days. Suddenly I felt disgusting.

I scooped up the clothes from the desk and crept into the hall. I could hear the television and see the light that shone at the bottom of the stairs. Evan must've gotten up early, per usual. I would never understand how a person could enjoy mornings so much.

I jumped up at the sound of the door clicking shut. My feet hit the floor, and Sara jolted awake.

"What?" she blurted, pushing her hair out of her face as she sat up. "What is it?"

The sound of the shower filtered down the stairs.

"She's done," I announced, pushing the blanket off my lap and taking the stairs two at a time.

"Evan, wait for me!"

We entered the office with the huge glass windows that overlooked the ocean. I thought it would be the perfect inspiration for her painting. But when I saw the canvas, it didn't appear she'd needed the inspiration after all.

I looked over at Sara. "I like it," I declared, beaming at the image in front of me. The sun's bright rays filtering through the leaves made me want to squint. With the heavy strokes of the bark, I could imagine dragging my fingertips along the rough texture.

"Of course you do," Sara stated, shooting me a look out of the corner of her eye. "She painted the tree in your backyard with the swing you made for her."

"Yes she did," I gloated.

Sara released a short laugh.

I stood before the canvas, admiring what Emma had unleashed. She'd gone back to the one place that would always be waiting for her.

25. A LITTLE HONESTY

My head was clear and quiet. All I could hear was the deep rhythm of my breathing. My heart thumped at a rapid pace in my chest. If I could just push a little harder, maybe I'd be able to escape, and allow the light to soak through my skin. Maybe it wouldn't be so dark anymore.

I dug my feet into the sand and sprinted faster, ignoring the plea of my burning muscles. I absorbed the calm as the sun cut through the morning gloom. *Just a little faster.*

The stairs climbing up the hillside came into view, and I extended my stride. I gave it everything I had until there was nothing left, fueled by desperation. I picked out a smooth grey rock thrust into the sand. This would be my end point. This would be where I'd find redemption. As I crossed it, I faltered to a stop, my lungs heaving. I rested my hands on my hips and walked back and forth, trying to calm my pounding heart.

As much as I wanted to believe I could outrun the darkness, I knew it was still there, ready to take me. Redemption didn't wait for me here. But the exertion was enough to provide a sliver of the solace that I sought, at least until night fell and the whispers started again.

I turned around just as Evan stumbled to a stop, bending over and resting his hands on his thighs. "Holy shit," he gasped. "You can never convince me you're not a morning person again."

A glimpse of a smile appeared between his panting breaths.

"I'm *not* a morning person."

Evan tilted his head up at me skeptically, sweat dripping from his nose.

"I'm a person who can't sleep," I explained, taking a deep breath to quicken my recovery.

Evan nodded in understanding.

My eyes drifted down, not sure if he really did. I didn't like the restlessness that chased away the sleep. The thoughts that crept into my head when all I wanted was to think of nothing. They weren't nightmares but whispers that haunted me in the dark, not letting me rest, not letting me go, not allowing me to forget.

"Sorry I didn't stop by yesterday," Evan said, redirecting my attention.

"It's okay," I responded, trying to sound unaffected, though I'd spent most of the day wondering where he was. My distraction hadn't gone unnoticed by either Cole or Sara. I'd tried to play it off as still being tired from everything that had happened in the past week. But Sara knew better, although she hadn't confronted me yet.

"You're coming to the party later today, right?" Evan asked, walking toward the stairs.

My cheeks reddened at the thought of seeing his friends again. "Yeah, we'll be over later."

"Okay," he said from the bottom of the stairs, hesitating before turning away.

"Evan," I called to him, making him pause a few steps up. "We didn't get to talk for a few days, so we technically have eleven days left. We can now…if you want to." We hadn't exchanged a moment of honesty since the beginning of the week. I didn't know why I offered. It's not like I enjoyed torturing myself, recounting all of the destructive choices I'd made.

"No." Evan shook his head. "I don't want to do that anymore." I opened my mouth, not expecting his response. "I don't hate you, Emma, and I don't want to. And I'm not going to force you to tell me things that you don't want to tell me. Of course I want to know why you left, and what kept you away. But only if you want to tell me."

"Okay," I whispered, my chest tightening with his concession.

"I'll see you later," Evan said, and began climbing the stairs.

I nodded, then walked back toward Cole's. My feet suddenly felt very heavy. I should've been relieved that he wasn't going to force me to open up anymore. But I wasn't. I didn't understand it. It almost felt like he was...done. I hadn't expected him to give up so easily. But that's what he'd wanted from the beginning—closure. I drew in a quick breath, my heart twisting at the thought of it. I should've been prepared for this. But I wasn't.

"How was your run?" Nate asked, sipping a cup of coffee at the kitchen counter.

"Pretty good," I answered, the corner of my lip creeping up.

"What's that look for?" he demanded, knowing me too well. "Let me guess. You didn't run by yourself?"

"No." I laughed lightly. "I ran with Emma, and it was... good." My mouth released the smile it was trying to hide. "She's amazing out there when she runs. I don't know how to describe it." I got lost in the image of her lean, strong legs propelling her forward, as if she could run forever. It was the only time she ever appeared to be at peace. I pulled my shoulders back in surprise when someone patted me on the back.

"Good morning," Brent said brightly. Brent was always way too awake, no matter what time it was. "What are we doing today?"

"Uh, getting ready for a party," Nate told him like he was an idiot. "The inventory in the closet downstairs is low. We need to go shopping. And I have no idea where the tiki torches went, so we may have to pick up new ones."

"What's the theme?" Brent asked, pouring coffee into a mug.

"Summer," Nate replied simply. "That's a good enough theme for me. But we're starting early, so it'll be a pool party."

"So the ladies will come sit by the pool wearing their bikinis," Brent stated, nodding while wearing an obnoxious smile. "Genius."

"That's all you think about," I said, grabbing a sports drink out of the refrigerator.

"Yeah, it is." He looked at me like I was crazy. "You wait until you see the girls show up wearing practically nothing, and tell me you're not thinking about it too."

Nate glanced at me and smirked. "He won't be thinking about it."

I glared at him. "Shut up, Nate."

"What's going on?" Brent asked.

"Emma's here," Nate said, making Brent choke on his coffee.

"If you're not going to stop sulking, then I'm leaving you here," Sara scolded while curling my hair.

"I'm not sulking. And I want to go." Oddly enough, I did. I twisted my fingers nervously in my lap, anxious about seeing the guys…about seeing Evan again.

"Something happened, and you're not telling me. I know—"

"The two weeks are over," I blurted, watching her reaction in the mirror, hating the fact that I was so transparent to her.

"Uh, no they're not," Sara responded in confusion. "You have like ten days left."

"He said he didn't want to do it anymore," I replied quietly. "So…it's over."

Sara stood still, the curling iron in her hand, examining me in the mirror. "And why does that make you so upset? I would figure you'd be relieved not to have to confess everything you should have told him the first time around."

I made a face and opened my mouth to deny that it bothered me, but I knew she wouldn't believe me. I connected with her blue eyes in the mirror and shrugged. And that's all she needed. She smiled consolingly. "It's not over, Emma."

"Hey," Cole hollered from the living room, causing us both to jump. "What time are we heading over there?"

"Uh, we'll be out in a few minutes," I yelled back, flashing my eyes guiltily at Sara.

"You're not *dating*," she stated.

"Sara!"

"What? They're *your* words," she said innocently.

I sighed. This was about to get even more complicated. "You officially look gorgeous," Sara announced, admiring me through the mirror. "Now let's go and have a ridiculously good time. We haven't laughed nearly enough this summer."

I smiled, inspecting her work. "Thank you, Sara." I turned toward her on the stool we'd taken from the kitchen. "For everything."

Sara smiled back. I jumped down and slid on a pair of wedged sandals. "Let's go."

"Evan, can you grab me more Coronas?" Nate hollered from across the pool. I nodded and excused myself through the bare shoulders and surf shorts toward the downstairs entrance. The crowd parted for me again when I returned a few minutes later with a couple cases stacked in my arms.

"I always love your parties," a girl beside the bar sighed to Nate as I shoved bottles into tubs of ice.

"We like it when you show up, Reese," Nate returned genuinely, not boldly flirtatious. A moment later I heard, "Shit, Evan."

"What?" I stood up, expecting to have to intervene in a fight or something. Nate was staring up at the deck, so I followed his eyes… and lost my breath.

"Dude, you're in trouble," he muttered, still staring.

I couldn't deny it when I saw her walking behind Sara down the stairs. The pink and orange floral sarong hung low on her hips, splitting open to mid-thigh with each step to reveal a sculpted tan leg. The strapless orange top clung to her body, revealing just a hint of bronze skin around her waist. Her usually straight hair was tossed in curls, with one side pinned up by a pink flower. I stared way too long as they made their way toward us—until I felt Nate's elbow in my ribs, jolting me out of my ogling.

My eyes connected with Emma's, and I grinned. "Hi, Em. You look great."

"Thanks," she responded, dipping her eyes while a flush of red flooded her cheeks.

"Hey, Evan," Sara greeted me, a question looming in her eyes. It confused me.

She made me feel like I'd done something wrong. I held my hands up and mouthed, What?

Sara answered with a withering glance. Emma looked toward Sara and back to me, catching the end of our exchange.

"What can I get you to drink, Emma?" Nate finally asked, breaking the awkward tension.

"Umm..." I examined Sara for a second longer, as she tried to hide whatever had just happened between her and Evan. "What's that?" I asked, pointing to a girl behind Sara carrying a pink drink.

"That's a pink lemonade drink we came up with for today," Nate said.

"I'll have one of those," I requested—and saw Evan's eyebrows rise.

My cheeks flared up recollecting the last time he'd seen me drink. "We talked about it," Sara intervened. Sara and I'd made a pact before we left, and I assured her that I could drink responsibly. Now was my chance to prove it.

Nate made Sara and me each a pink drink with a neon green straw and a tiny umbrella. "Thanks, Nate." I couldn't look at Evan for more than a second. My cheeks were about to catch fire when I saw him behind the bar without his shirt on. I was warned this was a pool party, but I wasn't prepared for *that*. It was the first time I'd seen him shirtless since I'd arrived in California, and he'd put on some…muscle in two years. I took a breath to cool my cheeks and scanned the pool. "Wow, there's a lot of girls here. And they're practically naked."

Sara laughed and pulled me after her to find a spot in the shade. We sat on two chairs under an umbrella, sipping our drinks among the oiled bodies splayed around the pool and floating on rafts atop the water. I hadn't realized they made swimsuits that *small*. My eyes widened at the sight of a girl with a string covering only the parts that mattered. Then she turned around, and I realized it didn't cover all of them.

"Does a string up your butt qualify as a bathing suit?"

"Well, she can wear whatever she wants with a body like that," Sara said, unfazed.

Cole joined us after stopping to talk to a few people he knew. He hung his shirt off the back of a chair and pulled it up next to me, but out from under the shade of the umbrella. He was drawing some attention of his own, and the girls weren't exactly being subtle about it.

"Have you been to these parties before?" I asked him, shocked at how obvious the girls around us were being.

"It's California," he replied, unaffected.

"Seriously?" I questioned, making an effort to close my mouth.

Cole chuckled. "This is your first pool party?" I nodded. "Yeah, this is pretty typical around here."

"How can you not stare?" I asked him, having a hard time not staring myself.

"I'd rather not have it blatantly flaunted in front of me, especially when I've seen—" His eyes ran the length of my body.

"Okay, I got it," I interrupted him, adjusting my wrap to cover my exposed leg as Sara just about choked on her drink. Cole laughed, and he leaned over and kissed me gently. Peeking out of the corner of my eye to make sure Evan wasn't watching, I barely moved my lips to return his kiss. Cole pulled back with a confused expression.

I darted my eyes around with a rise of my eyebrows, trying making it appear I was uncomfortable with the PDA.

"Yeah, sorry," he said, leaning back in the chair.

Sara took a sip of her drink concealing her slight grin, but not before I saw it.

I couldn't help but look for her. No matter who I was talking to, or where I was, I'd keep glancing around the room, or the deck, or the patio, seeking her out. Cole caught me more than once, which made it more than awkward.

"You're Evan, right?" I turned my head away from Emma, who was leaning against the railing, sipping the drink in her hand, and focused on the tall blonde in front of me.

"Uh, yeah. Can I get you a drink?" I asked, wondering when TJ was returning to take over for me behind the bar.

"Will you do a shot with me?" she asked, leaning over and setting her elbows on the bar so that I'd get of view of... everything.

I kept my eyes on hers, not tempted to look anywhere else.

"It's still too early for me to do a shot, sorry," I told her, causing her to pout, which was anything but attractive. "Do you want one anyway?"

"I suppose," she sulked. "Tequila." I poured the clear liquid in a plastic shot glass and set it in front of her with a lime. "My name is Kendra, by the way."

"Nice to meet you, Kendra," I responded with a false smile.

"You have amazing eyes," she flirted, slowly licking the back of her hand and pouring salt on it.

"Thanks," I replied, looking past her to find Emma waiting behind her, her eyes darting around uneasily. I grinned.

"Hey, Em," he called to me, despite the fact that the girl was still lingering in front of him. I was convinced she was a model, with her towering lean height and taut body. "Do you need another drink?"

I poked my head around the bony shoulder and nodded. "Please. And a water too."

The leggy blonde leaned over and said, "For later, when you *are* ready." She set a napkin in front of Evan and walked away, moving her hips to accentuate the curves she didn't have.

"Uh…" I fumbled, noticing the phone number she'd set in front of him.

Evan used the napkin to pick up the lime she'd left on the bar and stuffed it in the empty shot glass before throwing it away.

"Having fun?" he asked, not appearing affected by what had just happened. I stood in front of him, beyond uncomfortable. I could only nod, awaiting my drink.

Evan noticed my inability to speak and smiled in that amused way he did. "You saw that, huh?"

I pressed my lips together and nodded again. It was all I could seem to do.

"Not interested." Evan raised a shoulder, grinning at me again. He turned to pull a bottle of water from the tub behind him and prepared my drink. I glanced around to keep from watching him, while I waited. He handed me a cup with an umbrella in it, wrapped in a napkin.

"Thanks," I uttered barely audibly, and walked away.

When I returned to the chair, I peeled off the napkin, which was already getting wet, about to crumple it up when I noticed the blue ink. A phone number was smeared across it, along with For later, Evan. I let out a laugh, drawing Sara's attention.

"What's so funny?" she demanded, studying me carefully.

I couldn't keep the smile from my face as I shook my head dismissively. I folded the napkin in half and concealed it beneath the edge of my strapless top. It occurred to me that I didn't have his phone number saved in my phone, and I should hold on to it. Besides, it was funny.

"You don't want to tell me, do you?" Sara snapped, feigning offense. I glanced at Cole, who was in a surfing conversation with the guy standing in front of him. Sara noticed and nodded in understanding. "Later." I nodded in return.

After a day of drinks and sun, night fell and the party escalated to a new level. Many of the girls opted to change, while others continued to flaunt their bikini-clad bodies. The guys who'd spent the day surfing arrived to provide a little more gender balance, much to Brent's disappointment.

The inside became the dance floor, as intended. I leaned against the wall, taking a look around, and was about to take a sip, when I stopped with the bottle pressed against my lips. Emma twirled under Sara's arm, laughing. My breath faltered at the sight of her body moving to the rhythm, rocking her hips in a pair of low-riding white shorts. She revealed more of her flat stomach, her arms swaying in the air.

"You gotta look away right now," Nate demanded in my ear. I jerked my head toward him.

"What?"

"Dude, he's about to kick your ass," Nate warned quietly, his eyes flicking across the room. I looked over to find Cole glaring at me.

"Shit," I muttered, turning away. "I couldn't help it. I've never seen her move like that."

"Maybe you should get behind the bar," Nate advised. I nodded and cut through to the far end of the room.

"Hey, Evan!" TJ greeted me. "You taking over for me?"

"Yeah," I replied, trying to calm.

"Wanna do a shot with me before I go? You look like you could use one."

"Sure," I answered without hesitation. He poured us shots of tequila.

TJ held up his glass before slinging it back, then shaking off the bite. "Emma looks fricken hot, by the way."

"Yeah, thanks, TJ," I grumbled.

TJ laughed. "That's why you needed the shot, isn't it? Fuck, man. If you're going to try to avoid checking her out, then you definitely need a few more shots. I'll do another with you just to help you out."

I smiled. "Thanks for sacrificing yourself for me." I poured us another shot and swallowed it down, breathing out the tequila through my teeth. "I'm not sure that's going to help."

"Well, it'll take out some of the sting when she goes home with Cole tonight," TJ remarked, laughing.

"Fuck you, TJ," I shot back, making him laugh harder. "You can leave the bar now."

"No problem," he responded, slipping into the crowd.

"Do you want another drink?" Sara yelled to me over the noise of the crowd and the music.

I paused to consider where I was in the spectrum of drunkenness. "Will you split one with me?"

"Yeah," Sara said, taking my hand to lead me to the bar.

Before we neared it, Cole caught my other hand and asked, "Dance with me?"

I looked up at him in surprise and nodded, never having seen him dance before. He led me through the crowd to the middle of the dance floor and held me close. I draped my arms around his neck, and his breath tickled my skin. We slowly moved to the beat, our bodies pressed tight with his hands cradling my hips.

"Are you still planning to find your friend in New York?" he asked with his mouth close to my ear.

"Honestly, I'm not even sure where to look for him," I responded, my eyes dipping toward the floor. "And I think I'm too late...again."

Cole sensed my change in demeanor and pulled me closer, kissing my neck. "I'm sorry."

His hips rocked against mine. I slid my hand down to rest on his chest and could feel his heart beating faster. That's when I realized that mine wasn't. My pulse was even, and my skin wasn't tingling like it usually did when he touched me. I looked up in surprise. His clear blue eyes inspected mine. He knew it too.

Cole stopped moving and dropped his hands. He kept his focus on me, waiting for me to say something. But I remained silent, still stunned with the realization that our connection was gone. And he heard every unspoken word.

Cole shook his head in disbelief. "Really? That's it?" I reached for him, but he moved back a step. "Don't bother." He brushed past me and pushed his way through the crowd, leaving me standing motionless, looking after him.

The dancing bodies filled in the empty space, moving around me as I remained perfectly still, shocked by what had just happened.

"Hey," Sara hollered, parting the crowd with the drink held out in front of her. "Here." She handed me the cup and I took a long sip. "Where's Cole?" She scanned the crowd in search of him.

"He left," I told her.

She drew her brows together. "Why? What happened?"

"Nothing," I answered simply. "Nothing happened." And that was the problem. I sighed guiltily.

"Dance with me," Sara exclaimed, taking my hand and spinning me around to distract me, replacing the guilt with a subtle swirl in my head. Sara offered me the cup again, and I shook my head, not needing to add to it.

I closed the bedroom door behind me, shutting out the laughter and music that was still going on upstairs. I'd pulled the liquor from the outside bar and let the guys take care of the one upstairs, since Brent and TJ were still "entertaining." Nate and Ren had passed out a while ago. *I couldn't recall seeing Ren most of the night, but that's how it usually was with him.*

I stripped off my shirt, threw it in the corner, and emptied my shorts' pockets, dumping the contents on the nightstand next to the bed, along with my phone. I kicked off my shoes and went into the bathroom to brush my teeth.

When I came back into the bedroom, my phone was lit up. I picked it up and found, Is it later yet? *displayed across the screen. I paused, not recognizing the California number. I released a deep breath, wondering if one of the guys had handed out my number.*

Then I realized I had.

It IS later. Where are you?

I waited for her to respond. And my brows raised when my phone lit up again with, Outside your room.

I walked over to the curtain, slid it back and grinned when Emma waved to me from the other side of the sliding glass door.

"Hi," I said when he opened the door, my heart beating a million miles a minute. I'd told myself this was a bad idea for the past half hour, but still found my way from the beach back up to this patio, staring at his room—and eventually texting him when I saw his light turn on. I was convinced I'd die if he was in there with another girl.

"Hi," Evan responded, his breathtaking grin greeting me. "What are you doing out here?"

"Umm…nothing."

Evan laughed. "Are you lost?"

"Most likely," I answered, shuffling my bare feet.

"Would you like to come in?" he offered. I lifted my eyes, having a hard time looking at him without his shirt on. My heart skipped several beats, and my entire face lit on fire. "You don't have to."

"Sure," I finally muttered, averting my eyes to avoid getting lost in the deep curves of his chest and intricate lines of his stomach. I took a breath and forced myself forward into his room while he held back the curtain for me.

Evan slid the door closed and replaced the curtain. I looked around the room nervously, trying to find the courage to say what I'd been saying over in my head for the past hour and a half as I roamed the beach.

She was nervous. Adorably nervous. I had no idea why she was in my room, but I wasn't about to turn her away. The flower was gone and the curls tossed loosely around her head. I glanced at her bare feet and noticed the sand on them. Emma's eyes scanned every inch of the room, avoiding looking at me.

"Emma?"

She turned toward me, darting her eyes from the floor up to my face and back down. I tried not to laugh, but it was quite amusing. "Are you drunk?"

"A little," she admitted shyly. "Are you?"

"A little," I repeated. The shots having done their job.

"That's kinda good," she said, biting at her full lower lip, *which was making it really difficult not to look at it.*

"Why's that?"

"It'll make it easier," she responded cryptically. *She was going to make me pull it out of her, I could tell. I took a shallow breath, recognizing I needed to draw on my patience.*

"Make what easier?" I asked gently.

"Can we, umm, shut off the lights?" she asked suddenly, *taking me by surprise.*

"I suppose," I said in confusion, "but then we'll be standing in the dark."

I frowned at my patheticness. How was I supposed to talk to him without looking at him? And I couldn't look at him if he didn't put a shirt on.

Before I changed my mind or asked if he'd put a shirt on, which I knew was going to sound even more ridiculous, Evan offered, "We

could sit on the bed... in the dark... if you want, so then, well…
what did you come here for, Emma?"

I couldn't breathe. I nodded and moved toward the bed, not
answering his question. My mind was swirling with panic, and I
couldn't form a cohesive sentence. I was going to pass out before I
even uttered a single word, and then all the courage I'd mustered to
walk up here would be for nothing.

I plopped down on the bed and waited for Evan to shut off the
light.

I clicked the light off and noticed she was lying on the bed instead of sitting. I scooted onto the bed beside her. She was perfectly still, with her head on the pillow across from me. It was too dark to see her face, but I could hear her quick breaths, like she was getting all worked up. I knew her brain must be in overdrive, figuring out what to do next.

"Better?" I asked in a whisper.

"Yeah," Emma answered quickly. After a moment, my eyes adjusted to the dark. The glow seeping through the curtain provided enough light for me to see her silhouette.

Emma shifted on her back and began playing with her hands like she did when she was nervous. I waited. She remained silent. Eventually, she turned back on her side to face me, a little closer than she was before. I could feel her breath on my lips.

"Are you still kinda drunk?" she asked softly, making me laugh.

"Kinda," I replied. She was silent again. "Why?"

"Are you more honest when you're kinda drunk?"

"Umm… I suppose," I answered, intrigued by where this was headed.

"Me too," she spouted nervously. "Will you tell me one thing that you normally wouldn't say to me if you weren't kinda drunk, so that I know that you are?"

I smiled at her request. "Okay," I could feel my body respond to her closeness, and drew in a breath. "I'd really like to kiss you," I whispered, my heart thumping louder.

Her breathing faltered as I reached over and ran my hand along her cheek.

I closed my eyes to his touch, unable to breathe properly. I actually wasn't convinced I was breathing at all. "I don't want you to kiss me," I said in a whisper, my heart contradicting my words with its frantic fluttering.

"Okay," he responded, pulling his hand away.

I almost regretted saying it as the warmth of his touch disappeared, but I forced myself to focus, and said, "Because…I came here…to tell you something."

He was quiet. Almost too quiet. I was about to lose my nerve when he murmured, "I'm listening."

I took a breath of courage and said, "I left to protect you."

Evan was quiet again. I could see his outline in the dark, watching his shoulder rise and fall as he breathed evenly. "From what?"

"Me," I said, my voice catching. I had convinced myself I could tell him, to give him the answer he wanted most, and do it without breaking down. But now I knew that wasn't going to be possible.

"I don't understand," he responded, his voice cautious.

"I think I'm doing the right thing. But I never do. Every decision I've made to protect the people I care about has been wrong. And I only end up hurting them." My throat closed in around those last words.

This is what we do. We hurt people.

I fought to regain my composure. "How many times did I have to hurt you, Evan? How many times were you going to keep coming back so I could do it again?" I inhaled a quick breath as the tears broke the barrier and rolled over the bridge of my nose, soaking into the pillow. "I was doing to you the same thing my mother did to me. And I couldn't let you keep coming back for more. I couldn't continue to hurt you. The only way to save you was to leave."

The admission that I was as destructive as my mother twisted my heart. I never wanted to be her. But more of her ran through my veins than I ever wanted to admit. And I needed to push him away before I left him as broken and empty as I'd become.

I tucked my face into the pillow so he wouldn't hear my jagged breaths. My entire body tightened against the ache that crept through my muscles. Honesty hurt.

His silence slowly tortured me as my body shook next to him.

I didn't know what to say. I clenched my jaw as I fought not to touch her, unsure if I should. The muscles along my back were rigid with an anger that I could not deny. I was at conflict with two emotions: the one that wanted to comfort her and keep her from hurting, and the one that was furious that she'd left me, making me suffer all this time without ever taking into account what she was truly doing to me.

Her cries were muffled in the pillow, and I could see her body quiver. In that moment of pause, I knew which side would win. It always would. I moved closer and pulled her in to me, shushing her tears away. She cried against my chest as I wrapped her in my arms and tried to assuage her guilt. The guilt that broke my heart two years ago. The guilt that I would have to fight in order to save us both.

26. LETTING GO

I pressed my nose against her hair and inhaled the soft, clean scent. I'd been listening to Emma breathe since she drifted to sleep. I knew the sun was up on the other side of the curtains, and she'd probably be waking soon. Sleep never happened for me. The rest of my night was spent reliving every second of our life together—trying to find the moment she started to slip away from me. And I kept coming back to Jonathan.

She'd sought me out last night, obviously nervous, to provide me with the answer to the question. That answer still echoed in my head—she'd left to protect me. So she wouldn't keep hurting me.

Emma had always had a different way of processing the world and her place in it. I knew pretty much from the beginning that she was going to be a challenge to understand. But that was one of the things that drew me to her. I wanted to understand, to figure her out.

And she'd been letting me in, a question at a time. It was what I'd always wanted from her. I didn't get what was different now, other than the guilt. The guilt had absolutely changed her.

I looked down at her, wrapping my arm around her waist. She looked so different. It was more than the short hair and thin frame. She seemed so... delicate. My body could surround hers easily, shielding her from whatever harm sought her. But what waited to destroy her was on the inside. And I'd been witnessing the progression of that destruction since the moment I saw her staring out the window of the funeral home.

I didn't know how to save her from herself. I felt helpless. A feeling that didn't sit well with me—but one I'd experienced too often when it came to Emma Thomas. Her question plagued me—how many times did I have to keep coming back to be hurt by her before I'd had enough?

I pulled her in to me and inhaled her again. "But how do I let you go, Emma?" I whispered into her hair. I still didn't know the whole truth.

I leaned over her and pushed the loose strands back to see her face. She looked so peaceful, with her dark lashes hiding the torment that lay beneath. I admired her sloping nose and her soft, full lips. I could never get over how beautiful she was.

"I don't know what to do," I murmured just as my phone vibrated on top of the loose change spread on the nightstand. I rolled back quickly and silenced it, afraid it would wake her, but she didn't move.

Have you seen Emma? I woke up and she's not here. And she's not answering her phone.

I picked up the phone lying next to Emma and pushed the display button; the screen remained blank.

I responded to Sara's text. She's here. Her phone's dead.

I draped my arm back around Emma, about to actually try to fall asleep, when my phone vibrated again. I'm coming to get her.

I sighed, knowing Sara wouldn't stop at the door unless I intercepted her, and I didn't want to hear it from her if she jumped to conclusions about what happened last night. As much as it killed me to do so, I moved away from Emma and rolled off the bed. I covered her with a blanket and dragged my body upstairs. I was hoping I'd be able to put Sara at ease quickly so I could return to bed before Emma woke.

I rolled onto my back when the door clicked shut.

He was letting me go.

I hadn't thought it was possible to be any more broken. I exhaled the little air that was left in my lungs and stared at the ceiling. I needed to leave before he came back. I couldn't face him.

I pushed back the blanket and sat up, shoving myself off the bed. Without looking back, I slipped out the sliding glass door and picked up my shoes on the patio before heading toward the beach.

"Wow, you look like hell," Brent quipped when I appeared in the kitchen.

I ran a hand through my hair and grumbled, "Thanks."

Ren was peeling an orange on the counter. "Rough night?"

"Where'd you disappear to last night?" I asked, avoiding his question. "I swear I didn't see you for more than a minute."

"Met some buddies down on the beach," he answered. This was code for: we sat around, talked surfing and got high all night.

"So you ditched the party?" Brent clarified. Ren shrugged lazily.

"Wanna go surfing?"

"I'm leaving for the airport in a couple hours," I told him.

"I'll go," Brent agreed, true to form.

Nate appeared on the stairs, his body moving clumsily and his eyes almost completely closed. I was half convinced he was sleepwalking until he muttered, "Fuck. This place is a disaster." The house smelled of stale beer and was wrecked, with cups and trash everywhere—the typical after-party effects. I'd seen worse.

"We'll pick up the trash," Brent assured him. "What time is the cleaning crew getting here?"

"Noon." Nate yawned, rubbing his face with both hands.

The front door shook with loud, banging knocks. "Holy fuck! Who the hell is that?" Nate held the sides of his head, pressing it together like the loud noise might split it open.

"I got it." I sighed, knowing exactly who it was.

"Where is she, Evan?" Sara asked impatiently, practically pushing me out of the way.

"She's still sleeping," I told her, shutting the door behind her.

"Who?" Ren asked. Brent and Nate stared at me like I'd confessed to a crime.

"No. Fucking. Way," Brent gaped, shaking his head.

"Don't tell me you did what I think you did," Nate begged.

"Relax." I held up my hands in defense. "We just talked. She fell asleep. And that's it."

"She fell asleep in your bed," Sara snapped. Then she said so only I could hear her, "Sleeping with her is not going to fix things."

I released an annoyed breath. "What the hell? Nothing happened."

Sara disappeared down the stairs. I turned toward the guys, who were still staring at me. "Are we cleaning this place, or what?"

"Emma!" I heard Sara yell. She was shutting the glass door and hurrying across the patio. I waited for her to catch up before continuing down the stairs.

Sara didn't say anything to me until we reached the beach. "Are you okay?"

I shrugged, not knowing how to answer that question. I felt anything but okay. I felt…lost.

"Why'd you go back to see Evan last night?" She watched me carefully. I averted my eyes toward the sand, focused on the receding water sinking into its surface.

"I decided to tell him why I left. He wanted to know. He *deserved* to know. So I told him."

"What did you tell him exactly?" Sara asked.

I repeated what I'd said to her two years ago. "I left to protect him from being hurt by me again." My chest ached repeating it.

"And… what did he say?" Sara coaxed gently, like she was pulling on a fragile piece of string and feared which question would leave her with a broken end.

The constriction in my throat kept my answer trapped. I fought the sting of tears in my eyes, blinking up at the clouds.

"Nothing," my voice strained. "He didn't say anything."

"You don't want him to hate you anymore, do you?" Sara asked simply. I shook my head.

"But I don't think he'll ever forgive me either," I rasped, crushed by the thought of it. "You were right..."

"About what?" Sara asked, the sympathy weighing heavily in her voice.

"Leaving him *was* the worst mistake of my life." I stopped walking, covering my eyes with both hands as I released a silent sob.

"Are you going to tell me what happened?" Nate asked, lingering just outside my bedroom as I threw clothes in a bag.

"No." I shook my head, wanting to keep Emma's confession to myself. "But I have a lot of thinking to do."

"Did it change your mind?" he questioned, crossing his arms as he leaned against the door frame.

"About this trip? No, this has always been my decision. It doesn't have anything to do with Emma," I replied, having committed to this way before last night. "But I'm not sure what's going to happen when I get back."

"That bad?" Nate interpreted.

I shook my head, "No, I just... I need to think."

"Whatever happens, Evan," Nate said, his voice careful, "I won't let you become that guy again. I saw what she did to you, and I'll do whatever it takes to make sure it doesn't happen again, even if you end up hating me."

"I get it," I told him. "And I won't ever be like that again. I swear to you."

He nodded in acceptance. "Hey, isn't your flight taking off kinda soon?" He stretched his arms above his head.

"No, it's this afternoon," I responded, stuffing a jacket in my bag. "I need to stop by and see Emma before we go."

"No problem," he agreed. "But I swear I thought you said your flight was this morning."

"Let me check." I took out my phone and pulled up the itinerary my mother had sent. "Fuck. My flight's in an hour. We've gotta go."

"He just needs time, Em," Sara soothed, sitting next to me on the deck, staring at the waves surging against the sand. I nodded absently. "Evan will forgive you."

I wasn't convinced. Why should he? I'd betrayed him. I'd betrayed both of them. I left Evan instead of letting him in. And I drove Jonathan away, fearful he'd gotten too close. Neither of them had a reason to trust me. Now I was convinced I'd lost them both.

I turned my head toward Sara. She looked back at me sorrowfully, and I began to wonder how long it would be before I did something to hurt her again. She'd always found a way to forgive me, even when I hadn't been completely honest with her. But there would come a time when I would drive her away too.

"I'm going to take a shower," Sara announced, standing.

"Okay," I replied, remaining on the deck. I pushed away the tears and forced the shroud of numbness over me, but I could still feel the ache deep inside despite my efforts.

I reached for my phone to see if Jonathan had responded to any of my messages or texts. I knew he wouldn't, but it didn't stop me from obsessively checking. That's when I realized I'd left my phone at Evan's. I grimaced, not ready to go back there just yet. Maybe Sara would get it for me.

I noticed Cole's door was still closed when I entered the house. It was way past the time he usually got up, but considering how upset I'd made him last night, I decided to leave him alone and continued into Sara's room.

"I left my—" I started to say as I entered the bedroom. Then I caught sight of Sara's slumped shoulders and teary eyes. "What's wrong?"

"Um…my mother called," Sara began. I sat next to her, waiting for her to continue. "My grandfather died."

"Oh, Sara, I'm so sorry," I consoled, taking her hand. She leaned over and rested her head on my shoulder.

"Thanks. He was old. We knew it was only a matter of time."
She sighed. "There always seemed to be something wrong with him."
After a moment of reflection she added, "God, he was a pain in the
ass." Which caused us both to laugh. "But he was my grandfather,
and I loved him."

"I know." I leaned my head against hers.

"I have to leave," she murmured. "My mother's sending a car to
take me to LAX."

I'd met her grandfather a couple times over the years. He made
me uncomfortable, with his cynicism and complaints about every part
of his body failing in some way or another. I didn't think he liked anyone—except Jared, ironically. Sara took a deep breath before releasing
my hand and standing. Although there was a sense of acceptance with
her loss, I wanted more than anything to make her feel better.

"I'll come with you," I told her, hoping to provide even half the
comfort that she had while we were in Weslyn.

"Oh no." She shook her head. "You have enough drama of your
own. You don't want to be around my crazy family, trust me. I'll be
back in a few days."

I nodded meekly.

About a half hour later, she was packed. I was walking with her
into the living room when a honk came from the driveway. "That's
the car," Sara told me. "I have to go." She hesitated a moment to
examine me. "Go talk to him, Emma. Give him a chance to accept
what you said, but then go talk to him."

I gave a slight nod. She leaned in and hugged me. "I'll be back
soon. I'll call you when I get there, okay?"

"Sure," I said, barely audibly. I watched Sara roll her suitcase
behind her and disappear.

Her rejection had stung. The pain zipped through my chest in
a quick streak. I was too messed up to even comfort my best friend.
She didn't need me.

Eyeing Cole's door, I sighed. I didn't have the energy or will to try to explain what had happened last night. We both knew.

But something didn't feel right. I walked to his room and knocked gently. Silence. Hesitantly, I opened the door. The bed was neatly made, and the room appeared…too clean. When I walked in further, I saw my things were hanging in the closet, with some shoes and my tote bag on the floor, but his were missing. I peeked into the bathroom. Everything was cleared out, except for my toothbrush.

I was about to turn around and leave the room when the folded paper caught my eye, resting on the pillow where I slept. I stared at it for a moment, contemplating whether I truly wanted to know what it said, dread twisting in my stomach. I summoned the courage to pick it up and braced myself as I unfolded it.

I agreed to walk away before you hurt me. I won't let you hurt me, Emma.

I lowered myself on the edge of the bed, feeling the impact of those two simple lines.

"Cole, I'm so sorry," I murmured, accepting the unwritten truth. I had hurt him. But that's what I did.

I sank onto the couch and pulled the blanket off the back to try to ward off the chill that had overtaken my body. But the iciness in the pit of my stomach couldn't be thawed as I laid back and stared at nothing.

The sense of being lost seized me again. There was nowhere I belonged. My family didn't want me. Evan couldn't forgive me. Sara didn't need me. The girls didn't really know me. Jonathan was gone. And Cole had walked away, finally seeing me for who I was.

I felt so…tired. Letting the exhaustion pull at my lids, I closed my eyes and hoped the whispers would let me sleep.

I stared at the phone in my hand. The phone Emma had left on the bed, that I was supposed to return to her before I left for the airport. In the rush to make the flight, I had completely forgotten I had it. I plugged it into my charger and set it on the desk.

The door of the hotel room clicked open. I turned to find Jared with a bag in his hand.

"Hey," I greeted him. "What are you doing here?"

"Mom told me to come. She said she'd be here with you, and that she needed to tell us both something."

"She does? Any idea what?" I questioned, I should have suspected Jared was going to be here when I saw she'd reserved a room with two beds. But I was too distracted to give it much thought.

"No clue," Jared admitted. "She told me to be here, so I'm here. Then I figured I'd head back to Santa Barbara with you tomorrow."

"That works," I replied.

Jared plopped down on the other bed, crossing his feet as he leaned against the headboard. "So, how is the master plan coming along? Has it blown up in your face yet?"

"I don't have a plan," I countered in annoyance.

"You always have a plan, Evan," Jared insisted. "That's what you do. You think and overthink everything, strategizing and planning every step of your life. The fact that you took off to Santa Barbara without a plan seems messed up, considering what's at stake."

"I can't plan her," I murmured, staring at her phone again.

I woke suddenly, my eyes scanning the room. I was alone.

I don't want to be alone. Please don't leave me alone.

Needing to get my mother's desperate voice out of my head, I pushed the blanket off me and went out on the deck. The sun was low, spreading golden-orange and red hues across the sky. Although I'd slept most of the afternoon, a tiredness clung to me as I walked along the beach, passing kids running in and out of the water and people sitting along the shore.

I found myself at the stairs along the hill and began climbing. I wasn't sure what I was going to say to him. I just didn't want to be alone, and I had nowhere else to go.

TJ came around the side of the house, carrying a surfboard over his head. He saw me as soon as I stepped onto the patio.

"Emma!" he hollered like he was excited to see me. "What are you doing? Come to visit us?"

"Uh," I faltered, a little thrown by his enthusiasm. "Hey, TJ. Is Evan around?"

"No," he replied, shaking his head like he was confused by my question. "He left."

"He left?"

"Yeah, Nate drove him to the airport hours ago."

"He left," I repeated in a whisper. "Okay, thanks."

Numb, I turned back toward the stairs and let my legs carry me away.

"You can stay," TJ called after me. I raised my hand in form of a wave without looking back, disappearing down the stairs.

"He left," I muttered again, still in shock. He'd decided to let me go.

The darkness crept up and wrapped around my heart. I let it seep in, crushing it until I couldn't feel the thumping anymore. I couldn't feel anything. The whisper of Sara's words echoed through the emptiness.

You can't keep pushing everyone away…because one of these days, you'll wake up and have no one.

I didn't remember walking back to the house. I curled up under the blanket on the couch and closed my eyes.

The whispering words filtered through me, feeding on the guilt and sadness that pinned me down. Unable to fend them off, I waited for the void to rise and swallow me into the darkness.

———

"That was an eventful day," my mother declared, handing her menu to the server who'd just taken our orders.

"Thank you for letting me do this," I said to her, appreciating that she didn't object to my decision, even though I hadn't allowed her to be part of the process initially.

"I understand your reluctance to include me," she responded, "but I told you that I wasn't going to stand in your way, and I won't. I believe you are doing what you think is best."

Before I could continue the conversation, my phone vibrated in my pocket. I removed it, and my mother scowled at me. She forbade cell phones at the dinner table.

"I know," I said before she could say anything, "but I really need to take this. I'm sorry."

I pushed my chair away from the table, answering, "Hi," as I sought a more secluded location down the hall leading to the restrooms. "Is everything okay?"

"I was hoping you could tell me that," Sara said from the other end. "Have you seen Emma today?"

I paused, her question not making any sense. "What? Aren't you with her?"

Sara was silent this time. "Evan. Where are you?"

"San Francisco. Where are you?"

"At my grandfather's funeral in New Hampshire."

"Oh, wow. Sara, I'm so sorry. I didn't know."

"Thank you," Sara said, dismissing my condolences quickly. "I haven't been able to get a hold of Emma. I was starting to worry."

"I have her phone. Sorry. She left it at the house, and I forgot to give it to her. That's why you can't reach her. But she's with Cole, right? You can call him to talk to her."

"I tried," she answered. "He's not answering."

"Do you want me to have Nate check on her? She could use his phone to call you," I suggested.

"It's fine. I'm sure she's okay. I just told her I'd call, and I haven't spoken with her since I left yesterday."

"I'll be back tomorrow. I'll stop by when I arrive," I informed her. "I'm sorry about your grandfather, Sara."

"Thanks, Evan," she replied.

"Talk to you later."

As I was about hang up I heard, "Hey, Evan?"

"Yeah?"

"I know it's really not my place to ask you, but… is everything okay between you and Emma? I mean… I know it's not okay, but you're not going to stop talking to her or anything, right?"

"No," I answered, perplexed by the question. "Uh… why would you think that?"

Sara released a heavy breath. "Never mind."

"Wait, did she say something? Does she think I'm upset with her?"

She hesitated a moment. "Not really. I guess… I just have this weird feeling. I'm probably being overly protective as usual. I'll be back on Thursday. I'll see you then."

Sara hung up before I could question her further. I knew I'd screwed up when I didn't get to see Emma before I left, and for not saying anything after she confessed the other night. Sara's worried tone ate at me. Something wasn't right with Emma, I knew it too.

I made a call to Nate before returning to the table, asking him to stop by and check on her. He didn't understand why I was asking, but he promised to do it anyway.

"Everything all right?" my mother asked as I sat back down at the table, while I replayed everything I did, or didn't do, the night Emma came over.

I redirected my attention to my mother, whose eyes were narrowed in concern. "I'm sorry. That was Sara. Her grandfather passed away, so she's with her family in New Hampshire."

"Are you serious?" Jared interjected. "Gus died? Man, I loved that guy." He glanced between my mother and me, then blurted, "I'll be right back." I saw him pulling his phone from his pocket before he was a foot from the table.

"Why was she contacting you?" my mother pursued, always observant of my subtle reactions.

"I have Emma's phone, so Sara hasn't been able to get in touch with her, and she was wondering if I had. She didn't know I was coming here. No one knew but the guys," I explained. Before Jared returned and before my mother could inquire further, I had to ask, "What did the letter say?"

My mother's blue eyes flinched ever so slightly at the question. "Which letter are you referencing?"

"The letter Emma gave to you before she left. I found the envelope. And whatever it said convinced you to change the course of my life. So what did the letter say?"

My mother paused thoughtfully. "It was given to me in confidence. It's not for me to reveal the content. I'm sorry."

My mother had always had strong principles, and as much as I admired them, at times they could be very frustrating. "I understand."

Jared pulled his chair back and sat down again.

"So how long do we have you?" my mother inquired.

"An hour," Jared answered, appearing anxious.

"Please express my condolences to Sara and her parents," my mother requested before taking a sip of her wine. Jared nodded, but refused to look at me.

"Well, since our time is short, let me share with you the reason we're here," my mother announced. "I have decided to sell the house in Weslyn."

Jared didn't react. He wasn't expected to, since he didn't spend much time there. This statement was directed toward me. Jared was just a buffer for when I said, "You can't."

My mother remained perfectly poised. "I am buying a place in the city, and that house is simply too big now that the two of you are away," she explained patiently. "I'm sorry, Evan."

"No." I shook my head adamantly, my voice rising slightly. "It's the only place that's ever felt like a home to me. You can't sell it."

"Evan—" Jared said in warning, not approving of my tone—filling his role perfectly.

As I paused to collect myself, my mother remained still, silently observing, as she did so well. We'd moved many times throughout my childhood. I never became attached to a house, or friends, with the exception of Nate and the guys.

My parents had offered the private boarding school option that Jared had chosen so he could continue school with the same group of friends. But I liked to travel, and I didn't want to leave my mother alone. Everything changed when we moved to Weslyn.

I couldn't lose the memories I'd made in that house. The thought of never seeing the oak tree again, or walking in the meadow along the brook, was too difficult to fathom. I knew I didn't have Emma, and I was uncertain if that would ever change. But I still couldn't let her go, and that's what I felt would happen if the house was sold. Like everything between us would be erased.

There had to be another way.

"Would you consider letting me buy the house?" I asked.

"Evan, dear, you don't have access to those funds for another fourteen years," my mother reminded me, her expression sympathetic. "It wouldn't be possible sooner without your father's permission and a—"

"I know," I interrupted. I could already hear his condescending words. "But what if we set up payments, or..." She remained quiet. I knew this was not a decision she was willing to support. At least not tonight.

I walked into the hotel room, dropped my jacket on the chair and loosened my tie. I sat down on the bed and propped my feet in front of me. I wasn't ready to give up the house in Weslyn—or what was happening between me and Emma. She was just beginning to open up, and I was slowly finding a way to trust her again. The threat of losing the house made it clear that I couldn't be without her. I couldn't let her go.

A vibration came from her phone. I walked over to shut it off, and the screen lit up to reveal a list of missed calls and texts. They were mostly from Sara, which was understandable. But the one that kept me staring, unable to blink, was the one that just said, Emma?

I knew it was none of my business. I didn't have any right to pry, but I pressed the message, and the previous one showed up under it. It was longer. There was only a phone number across the top, but I knew exactly who it was from.

Got your messages and texts. Sorry—life is complicated right now. Unfortunately we can't go back and change things. Wish we could. I do forgive you. I miss you. Would give anything to hear your voice right now. Won't be able to contact you again after tonight. Phone will be disconnected soon. Please say you forgive me? It would help to know you do. Emma, you deserve to be happy. You deserve to be loved. Hope you believe it.

I wanted to delete it. I wanted to delete him*. But I couldn't. I held down the button to shut the phone off.*

I didn't know what hurt worse. That she'd reached out to Jonathan, asking for forgiveness. Or that she didn't want that from me—insisting that I hate her. Why would he need to be forgiven? What happened between them?

Now I had a choice. I could let her push me away, fearing she'd continue to hurt me. Or I could fight for us. Convince her that we were worth it. Any pain she could inflict would never come close to the pain of being without her. I could never give up on her... on us.

27. GONE

I stared out the window at the grey shroud lapping against the glass. I didn't know what time it was or how long I'd been on the couch. I'd been held captive by the sharpness of tongues that slit my veins with loathing and tainted my blood with hatred.

You're a worthless pathetic tramp.

I shrank away from the disdain that haunted my soul. But I couldn't escape the relentless barrage of maliciousness. No matter how hard I tried to shut them out, their voices were all I could hear now. The scars may have healed, and the bruises faded. But the claws of hate and rejection dug deep within my flesh and never let go. Every spiteful sentiment struck with more force than the most violent of blows. Each degrading remark and estimation of worthlessness broke me in half.

You are not important.

There'd been a time when I was almost convinced that my accomplishments and determination would silence their malice. But I'd given up. I couldn't say the exact moment that it happened. Perhaps it was the second I'd abandoned Evan, leaving him beaten and barely conscious on the floor. Or it may have been before that. But now, in my isolation, the whispers found me.

You don't care about anyone other than yourself.

I stared out into the distance, beckoned by the roaring of the waves, the only sound loud enough to mask what were now sickening screams. I walked down to the beach, through the haze of clouds that swept against my skin.

You took him from me.

I stood at the water's edge, enraptured by the fury rushing to shore. The rolling wave cresting before crashing in on itself in a maddening tumble, sweeping under my feet, pulling me into the shifting sand. The rippling surface seduced with its curling fingers, tempting me.

You can't honestly think he cares about you.

Tears filled my eyes, slipping over my lashes and down my cheeks. I was so tired of fighting. Tired of hurting. Tired of the guilt that would never release me, and the regrets that could not be changed. I didn't want this life. There were only so many times I could hear that I should never have been, before I wished it to be true.

You should never have been born.

I took a step and began walking toward the grey horizon that seamlessly melded with the dark water. My chin quivered as the tears washed over my face. Turbulent waves pushed me back toward shore, but I forged ahead. I dove under them, letting the cold seawater soak into my trembling skin, into my bones, until I was numb.

Don't you realize how much you hurt me?

I swam past the breaking point, to where the water rocked, bobbing me along its surface. I floated on my back, balanced on the hands of the rocking sea with my arms spread wide. Everything became still, and all I could hear was my breathing. I allowed the silence to subdue me. The pain dissipated through my fingertips into the water, carrying the voices with it until I was drained, and all that was left was…me. Accepting the fate that had finally caught up with me, I inhaled my final breath, and then I was gone.

Curling into a ball, I let myself sink beneath the surface. I closed my eyes as the water filled my ears, magnifying the stillness.

All I had to do was give up.

Give up.

The words echoed through my head, begging me.

Breathe, Emma. Just give up, and…breathe.

My lungs demanded the air within reach at the surface. My heart fought for each beat. It refused to surrender to the calm I sought beneath the water. The desperate thumps stammered against my chest. Within the silence, his words were as clear as if they were being whispered in my ear.

Hold on to this life, Emma. You're so much stronger than you think you are.

And I knew. I didn't know how to give up.

Peace awaited me with a single breath. But I couldn't give up. It wasn't who I was. This may not have been the life that was meant for me. Perhaps I was never supposed to be. But while I existed, I would fight for every breath that kept me alive.

I opened myself up and kicked to the top, breaking through the surface with a heart-wrenching cry. The water lapped around my neck and splashed onto my face as I bellowed in pain, my chest caving with each sob.

I forced myself toward shore, crashing my arms through the surface, pulling the water toward me, kicking fiercely. My feet eventually pushed into the sand.

I splashed through the shallow water, moving my legs faster beneath me until I reached the beach. And then I broke into a run, letting pieces of me fall along the way. Shedding the young girl who feared which of her mother's personalities would enter the house each night. Stripping off the belief that if I were perfect, I'd be easier to love. Stomping on the doubts that made me question my worth, never feeling like I was enough. And crushing the guilt that convinced me I would hurt everyone I cared about, leaving me incapable of being loved.

My legs carried me away from that girl, desperate to leave her behind. My stride picked up, and the tears streamed with the water and sweat. I cried for the little girl who lost her father but never had a mother. I cried for the girl who only wanted to be accepted, but was never enough. I cried for the girl who suffered unfathomable pain at the hands of hate. I cried for the girl who deserved to be loved but didn't know how.

In time, my legs just carried me along the water's edge, my breath evened out, and the pain subsided. The tightness in my chest loosened, and the fear and sadness drifted away.

I released a part of me with each step, not knowing who would be left when I stopped running. So I kept going, afraid to find out, though my muscles screamed for rest. After stretches of sand and rocks, my lungs burned, and my vision wavered. My tongue felt pasty in my mouth, and I could barely lift my feet.

I needed to stop. I looked ahead to where the surfers bobbed in the water, sitting on their boards. I drew a line. That's where it would end, and I could stop running—and just be.

I faltered the last few steps over the line and fell upon my knees. My entire body trembled, and a wave of heat floated from my skin. I sat back, but ended up tumbling over onto my back, staring up at the bright blue sky. A face peered over me. I squinted, having a hard time focusing.

"Emma?" I heard the girl say.

I squinted harder, and the blond hair and big brown eyes came into view. "Nika?"

"What are you doing out here? Where'd you come from?" she asked, offering me her hand to pull me up.

I stared up at her, unable to move.

"Cole's," I murmured, my head hazy.

"Did she say Cole's?" a voiced asked. "She must be delusional, because that's fricken far."

"Drink this," another girl said, kneeling next to me and placing a cold bottle in my hand.

Cool water soaked into my tongue, and I wanted to sigh in relief. My hand shook as I tipped it back, unable to take more than a sip at a time.

"Can we drive you back to Cole's?" Nika offered.

I shook my head, my words failing me.

"Where can we drop you?" the brunette beside me asked.

"Nate's," I blurted, still trying to get my bearings as everything swirled around me.

I knocked on the door, and no one answered. I didn't hesitate to see if it was locked, and when the door opened, I kept going. There was something off, and I knew it. I hadn't been able to shake the feeling since last night. And the fact that Nate said no one had answered when he stopped by—

I wished he had just walked in.

I rushed from room to room, but no one was around. When I entered the master bedroom, I hesitated. Cole's stuff was gone. Only Emma's things were here. He'd left.

"Shit," I murmured, returning to the living room. The glass door was open. I stepped out on the deck and scanned the blankets and towels spread upon the beach. I was about to walk down the steps when my phone vibrated.

"Evan, are you back?"

"Yeah, Nate. I'm at Cole's, looking for Emma." I continued to search for her on the beach.

"She's here, with us," he told me. "But, umm… she's a bit dehydrated."

His careful choice of words made me stop moving. "What do you mean, a bit dehydrated? Where are you? And why is she dehydrated?"

"We're at the house. Nika found her on some beach a ways from here and dropped her off," he explained. "Turn up the air conditioning, and make sure she doesn't lie down," he instructed someone in the room.

"What's wrong with her, Nate?" I demanded, anxiety building. I left the house and started running toward Nate's, the phone still to my ear.

"She's not throwing up," he told me, which confused me more. "Evan, she's just really dehydrated and overheated."

"You're freaking me out here," I said loudly. "Is she okay? Does she need to go to the hospital?"

"Shit, did you see her feet?" TJ bellowed from somewhere.

"What?!" I yelled. "What the fuck, Nate?! Does she need to go to the hospital?!"

"He wants to know if we should take her to the hospital?" Nate called away from the phone.

"No hospital!" I heard Emma yell.

"She doesn't want to go to the hospital," Nate repeated.

"I heard that," I said with a sigh, not surprised. "I'll be right there."

When I arrived at the house, I thrust the door open and found Emma sitting on the couch. Her skin was shiny and red, and her hair was plastered with dried sweat. She slouched against the cushions like she'd used up every ounce of energy.

"Hey," I greeted gently, sitting next to her.

She squinted. "Evan?"

"Yeah, I'm here," I assured her.

"You left." She tilted her head back clumsily and tried to focus on me.

"I did."

"You left," she repeated in a pained whisper.

"But I'm back," I assured her, disturbed by her reaction. "And I have your phone."

"Oh. You came back to give me my phone."

"No," I answered quickly. "For you… I mean… " I clenched my teeth with a grimace at the inadvertent honesty. Hoping she was too out of it to pick up on it, I continued, "I was only gone for a couple of days, and now I'm back. Okay?"

"Okay," she answered in an exhausted breath, and repeated with a hint of a smile, "You didn't leave."

The side of my lip crept up at the relief on her face. "No, I didn't leave." I ran my hand along the side of her cheek; fine salt brushed off her skin onto my fingertips.

"There's some of that water with electrolytes in the fridge," Nate told TJ, who went to retrieve it.

TJ offered her the bottle of water, and her trembling hands couldn't open it.

I took it from her and twisted the cap off before handing it back. She pressed her face against the leather couch and took small, slow sips.

I stood up to talk to Nate, who was standing at the end of the couch. "Do you really think she'll be okay?" I murmured, glancing down at her. Before he could answer, I exclaimed, "What the hell?!"

The bottoms of her feet were red and raw, and there was blood splattered on the back of her leg from a cut on her heel.

"I called a friend for advice," Nate said. "One of the girls I race with, she's in her last year of nursing school. I sent Ren to pick up Popsicles and some more drinks with electrolytes. I know you're worried. But I think she'll be fine. I mean, she's going to be sore as fuck tomorrow, but I've seen worse at the marathons I've run."

"I'm not sure that made me feel better, Nate," I answered shortly.

Emma sat on a chair, sucking on a Popsicle. She was showered and dressed in random guys' clothes—Nate's T-shirt, my shorts and TJ's zip-up hoodie. The glazed look was gone from her eyes, and she was more alert.

"Let me see your feet," I requested, with the towel on my lap and the medical supplies on the table next to me.

Emma eased her feet out of the bucket of water they'd been soaking in and gingerly placed them on my lap.

"What flavor is that?" TJ asked Emma from across the table, sucking on a yellow Popsicle.

"Berry," she told him. *"What do you have?"*

"Pineapple. Want a lick?"

"TJ," I scolded.

"Hey, I was just offering to share," he defended, making Emma laugh. *The perfect sound. One that I wished I heard more often.*

Before I could begin cleaning and bandaging the cuts on her feet, my phone vibrated. I grimaced as soon as I saw Sara's name, feeling bad for not calling her sooner.

"Hey, Sara," I answered hesitantly.

"Guilty much, Evan? Thanks for calling," she snipped, making me feel worse. *"Did you see Emma?"*

"Yeah," I responded. *"She's here. You can talk to her."*

I handed Emma my phone and doused the gauze in alcohol.

"Hi," I answered, "Shit! Evan, that fricken hurts!" I yanked my foot out of his hand.

"Emma? What the hell is he doing?" Sara demanded on the other end of the phone.

"I have to clean it, Emma," Evan shot back, grabbing my ankle. "I'll be gentle."

He started dabbing the open cuts, and I hollered in pain, tugging my foot from his hand. "It feels like you're using battery acid and sandpaper."

"Emma!" Sara yelled, fighting for my attention.

"What do you expect if you're going to run a marathon in bare feet," Evan shot back. "Give me your foot."

"At least wait until I'm off the phone," I begged, setting my foot back on the towel on his lap.

"Fine," he said, setting his torture device on the table.

"Sorry. I'm here," I said into the phone.

"Are you going to tell me what's going on?" Sara demanded, beyond frustrated.

I looked down at my lap and twisted my hand in the cuff of the sweatshirt. "You left. Evan left. Cole left. So…I went for a run. A very long run, and now I'm paying for it," I explained simply. Out of the corner of my eye I saw Evan's head turn in my direction.

"Cole left?" Sara repeated. "Oh, wow. And you didn't know that Evan went to San Francisco for a couple days?"

"No," I murmured, unable to raise my eyes from my lap as Evan sat across from me, patiently waiting to resume torturing me.

"I'm so sorry, Emma. I should have brought you with me. I know you wanted to come, but I thought the last place that you should be was another funeral. They suck. But I really do wish you were here. My family's seriously unbalanced," Sara groaned, making me laugh. "Are you okay, really? Because from the sounds of it, it was an insane run."

"Life-altering."

"Umm... okay," Sara replied, sounding confused. "So we need to find another place to stay for the next month, huh?"

"That would be best," I agreed. "Nate knows this real-estate agent, so we're meeting her in the morning to check out a couple places."

"Great. Tell me what you find. Evan's going with you, right?"

"That's the plan," I said.

"Would it be okay if he stayed in the house with you until I get back? It would make me feel better if you weren't by yourself."

I smiled affectionately at her protectiveness. "I'm okay with that, but you'll have to ask him if he is." Evan's eyes moved from the conversation he was participating in with the guys to me. I knew he was listening.

"Let me talk to him. I'll see you on Thursday. And charge your stupid phone!"

"Okay." I laughed lightly, handing the phone back to Evan.

Emma continued to watch me when I put the phone up to my ear. "Yeah?"

"Could you make sure she's not alone again until I get back?" Sara requested. I raised my eyes to meet Emma's.

"I can do that," I responded, noting the slight color change on her sun-burned face.

"Evan, I have no idea what happened, but I don't think it was good," Sara continued.

"I agree," I replied, still holding Emma's gaze. "Don't worry though. We'll find a good place tomorrow, and I won't go anywhere until you kick me out."

"Separate bedrooms!" Sara warned, making me laugh.

"See you Thursday, Sara," I said before hanging up. I tucked the phone back in my pocket. Emma was still watching me. "Ready?"

Her expression changed to that of dread.

"Here, Emma, you can squeeze my hand," Brent volunteered, holding out his hand for her to take.

She wrapped her thin hand around his large rough one, and he grinned.

"Or you could just punch him if it hurts too bad," I grumbled, making Brent shoot me a scowling glance. Emma released a small laugh.

I proceeded to remove the coarse sand embedded in her feet.

"Aahh," Brent complained, when Emma clenched her teeth and squeezed his hand. I chuckled.

"Emma, you're staying here tonight, right?" TJ asked, chomping on the ice chips that were supposed to be for her.

Emma looked to me, "If that's okay..."

Before I could answer, Brent blurted, "Yeah it is."

"Let's sleep on the beach," Ren chimed in. "We'll build a fire, and I'll get my guitar."

Before I could open my mouth to object, concerned about how she would get down there safely and then keep her feet clean, Emma replied with a glowing smile, "I've never slept on the beach before."

I stopped. I wasn't about to wipe that smile from her face. And besides... I couldn't give up the opportunity to be a part of a new Emma experience.

28. FINDING A REASON

"I f you drop her, I'll kill you," Evan threatened as Brent carried me down the steps on his back. I laughed at his warning. The way the two interacted when it came to me was pretty entertaining.

Brent was harmless, and Evan knew it. But he continued to be annoyed by Brent's playful flirting—I found it funny.

My feet were wrapped in a mile of gauze and protected by a pair of Brent's knee-high tube socks. I looked ridiculous, but I didn't care. This had been the most emotionally exhausting and physically demanding day of my life. My stomach hollowed at the thought of how close I'd come to *not* existing.

I'd confronted my demons, and I walked—well, ran—away from a life that I preferred to never look back upon. I feared they'd eventually catch up with me. But right now, I was still here.

"Emma, you okay?" Evan asked, snapping my attention back. His stormy blue eyes searched mine briefly as he walked alongside us on the sand.

"Uh, yeah," I said, trying to keep my voice even. "Just tired."

Brent kept his hands secured under my knees as he carried me down the beach to where the guys had selected a spot along the hillside that blocked the wind. Evan dropped the bundle of logs and two sleeping bags on the sand. Nate set the cooler down to help Ren and TJ unroll sleeping bags, and place them around the fire pit that Evan began digging.

Brent knelt down and gently dumped me off on the black sleeping bag. I scooted my legs inside, my body chilled easily from the sunburn I'd earned during my tour of the California coastline that afternoon.

Ren tuned his guitar while Evan lit the fire. TJ handed out beers, offering me a bottle of lemonade, which I happily accepted. I'd had enough water for one day.

TJ waved a flask at me across the fire. "I could spike that lemonade for you, Emma, if you want."

I laughed at the offer. "Thanks, TJ—I'm all set though. I swore off vodka."

"I did that with Beam," TJ said with a shiver. "Wow, that was a bad night."

Brent laughed in remembrance, settling on his sleeping bag at my feet. "You woke up facedown on the beach, naked."

"Yeah," TJ recalled, "I have no idea how that happened."

"I do," Ren interceded. "We were talking about that guy who liked to surf naked, and you decided that you were going to do it. But that didn't work out so well for you."

"Did I crash and burn?" TJ inquired, oddly ignorant of his own story.

"You didn't even make it into the water!" Ren guffawed. "You fell on your face taking off your pants and passed out right there."

TJ burst out into a cackling laughter, and I couldn't help but laugh along with him. "I can't believe I did that. That's awesome!"

I looked over toward Evan, who was smiling and shaking his head. He noticed I was watching him and didn't move his eyes away. The smile held upon his face. The one that made the blood rush through my body at a whirlwind pace.

I averted my eyes, focusing back on the fire. I brushed at my cheeks with the back of my hand, feeling as if the embers had ignited them.

"That naked surfer dude was weird," Ren reflected.

"That he was," Nate agreed.

"Emma, do you surf?" TJ asked.

I was about to say that we needed to teach her, when she answered, "Yeah. I know I'm not nearly as good as you guys, but I do. I still need my own board, though."

I stared at her in shock. "You surf?"

She smiled bashfully and shrugged.

"I think you just made Evan the happiest guy on the planet," Ren said, making her smile grow brighter.

"We've never had one of our girls surf before," Brent explained. His choice of words drew my attention. He noticed and floundered, "Hey, you know what I mean."

"That's because the girls you're always interested in are too top-heavy and head-empty," Nate shot at him.

I laughed. "When was the last time you even went on a date? Rubbing suntan lotion on someone doesn't count."

"I... date," Brent defended weakly.

"Dude, no you don't." TJ laughed. "You think you're all slick, but you never close the deal. Let's put it this way, who did you hook up with after the pool party last weekend?"

I glanced at Emma, who was observing the exchange with an adorable smile, her eyes dancing between whoever was speaking. She seemed much better than she was earlier today, and I would give anything to keep that smile on her face.

I lay down on the pillow and pulled the sleeping bag under my chin, continuing to listen to the stories shared among the guys. They usually ended with someone defending his actions. I could see why Evan kept them in his life. It reminded me of the girls.

The talking tapered, and Ren played the guitar and sang a relaxing reggae-style song. It was the perfect choice with the sound of the surf in the background.

"Evan, you should've brought your camera," TJ noted. "Dude, I haven't seen you with it since you went off to the Ivy League. You used to never be without it."

"I, uh…" Evan faltered. I turned my head on my pillow to look up at him. "I'm not sure where it is. I haven't really had a reason to take pictures lately."

I felt my heart twinge.

"Maybe you should find a reason again," I murmured, staring at the fire.

I knew no one else heard her except for me, and I was pretty sure she hadn't meant for me to overhear. A small smile crept onto my face as she snuggled into the sleeping bag, staring at the fire, making me recall the first picture I'd ever taken of her. Perhaps I had found a reason.

I watched her fall asleep as Ren sang and TJ joined in. Across the fire, Nate raised his brows, appearing to have read my thoughts.

"Be careful," he said quietly. "Okay?"

Nate was looking out for me. I knew that. He was the only one who truly knew how bad it got after Emma left. I believed him when he said he'd risk our friendship to make sure it never happened again. But I was hoping it wouldn't come to that.

The fire died down, the embers glowing in the sand. Everyone started drifting off. I angled my bag so I could watch Emma sleep until I succumbed to it myself.

———

I shot up in a panic, then stopped and looked around in confusion, not remembering where I was. The guys slept soundly, or in Ren's case not so soundly—dispersed across the sand in their sleeping bags, tucked in deep to hide from the chilled air. It took a moment, but I shook off the panic of the dream that awakened me most mornings. Then I noticed Emma was gone. The panic took hold again, and I jumped out of my bag to scan the beach.

My shoulders eased up when I spotted her seated closer to the water, wrapped in a sleeping bag. "I have to stop freaking out," I mumbled.

I walked toward her, wading through the low-lying clouds until I stood beside her, looking out at the same view of the morning sea.

"I'm still not convinced you don't like mornings," I said, making her jump. "Sorry." I smiled at the familiarity of her response. I always seemed to catch her unaware, lost in her thoughts.

"You love sneaking up on me," she accused, "as is evident by that stupid grin on your face."

I grinned wider, sat down on the sand next to her and crossed my forearms over my knees.

The cool air whipped around me, and I shivered. She noticed and held out an arm, offering a portion of the sleeping bag. "Thanks," I said, wrapping the edge around my shoulder, trying not to think about the heat emanating from her body.

We sat and watched the ocean for a moment, but I couldn't keep myself from asking one of the million unanswered questions that I had when it came to her. "What happened yesterday?"

I could sense him thinking while he was sitting next to me. I was prepared for some sort of question to come out of his mouth, but was hoping *that* wouldn't be the first one.

"I needed to clear my head," I explained evasively.

"What were you running away from, Emma?" he asked, seeing right through my answer.

"Me," I answered honestly, avoiding his gaze. He waited for me to continue. I took a deep breath and said, "I don't want the past to define me anymore. I don't want what happened to me, or all the wrong decisions I've made to keep me from becoming someone better. I want to be better."

Evan didn't say a word, but my heart thrust against my chest when I felt the warmth of his hand slide over mine in the cool sand. The simple gesture made my eyes glisten with tears, and I leaned my head against his arm.

"And did you leave it behind you, Emma? Did you run fast enough?" he asked quietly.

"I don't know." I paused a moment. "But I don't want to look back to find out. I'd rather keep moving into the future, and be grateful that I have one."

His hand squeezed mine.

"Dude!" I heard Nate yell, spinning both our heads around. "I can see you! If you're going to take a piss, do it far enough away so I don't have to see your ass."

My mouth opened in amused disbelief. I whipped my head around before I accidentally saw whoever was offending Nate.

"Sorry about that," Evan offered with a shake of his head.

"It's fine," I assured him, laughing lightly. "It's actually kinda funny."

"Evan!" Brent hollered from behind us, "I'm starving."

I rose gingerly onto my raw feet, my muscles stiff and sore. Evan took the sleeping bag from me and haphazardly folded it in his arms.

"Of course you are!" he yelled back. He looked down at me and asked, "Hungry?" I nodded. "Do you need help walking?"

I shook my head as I took deliberate steps toward the makeshift camp. I eyed the stairs as we got closer, uncertain how I was going to manage. Evan caught me sizing up the climb and was about to say something when Brent said, "Wow, Emma, you look amazing in the morning."

"Really, Brent?" Evan challenged.

Brent laughed, knowing exactly what he was doing. Evan pulled Brent's sleeping bag out from under him, dumping him on the sand.

Nate chuckled in his broken morning voice while Brent jumped up quickly, his legs in a charging stance with his arms spread. I was prepared for him to tackle Evan to the ground.

Evan raised his eyebrows in warning. "You sure about that? You do it, and you don't get to eat anything I cook." Brent lingered in his crouched position for a moment of contemplation, before he finally relented and stood up.

"Fine, but I can still do this," he responded with a devilish gleam and rushed up behind me, sweeping my feet out from under me. I yelled out in surprise when I fell back in his arms. Brent practically ran to the stairs, looking over his shoulder in expectation of Evan's retaliation. Evan rolled his eyes and continued to calmly gather the sleeping bags.

As we started up the stairs, Brent looked down at me with a sparkling smile, "Good morning, Emma."

I laughed and responded, "Good morning, Brent. Are you really going to carry me all the way to the house?"

"As long as I know it's going to piss Evan off, then yes," he replied with a devious smirk. "Besides, this is the most I'll ever get to touch you again."

"He's just trying to piss you off," Nate said, rolling up a sleeping bag.

"I know," I said gruffly, looking after Brent cradling Emma in his arms.

Ren groaned in his sleep and rolled over, completely unaffected by the commotion. TJ grabbed the cooler and trudged up the stairs, still looking half asleep.

"Will you make waffles, Evan?" he grumbled as I followed behind him.

I smiled at his request. "Yes, TJ, I'll make waffles."

I watched Emma laugh at something Brent said, which could have been just about anything that came out of his mouth. I reflected upon her brief moment of honesty while we were alone on the beach. Although she'd shared more than she would have if I'd asked the same question two years *ago, her cryptic answer was still disconcerting. But she was trying, and everything about that felt right.*

"Do you have any houses on the beach, with at least three bedrooms?" Emma asked after viewing the second small house on the realtor's list. Emma continued to scowl at the tiny cottage set on a side street, about a mile from the water.

I saw judgment pass across the agent's face as she eyed the thick white socks and sandals on Emma's feet. But Emma didn't seem to care what she looked like as she awaited the answer.

"Well, I do"—the Realtor smoothed the crisp linen of her sleeveless blue dress and answered slowly—"but I'm afraid it may be well above your price point."

"Really?" Emma responded in amusement. "I'd like to see it." I was surprised by her tenacity.

"Alright, then." The Realtor sighed, flipped her folder shut and led the way out of the house.

"What was that about?" I asked when we got into Nate's pickup truck.

"What do you mean?" Emma asked, although she knew exactly what I was talking about. "I want to be on the water." I let out a short laugh as we followed the gold Mercedes down the street.

We pulled into the driveway of a large white house. My eyes widened at the size of it. I turned toward Emma, and she smirked.

I knew this lady wanted to put me in my place by taking us to this house. But in truth, I didn't care how big it was. She strutted in front of us in her tight-fitting dress, clicking her heels along the stone driveway. She practically snickered when she unlocked the door and stepped aside to let us in.

The wall of glass facing the ocean was the first thing I saw, and that was all I needed. "We'll take it."

"But you haven't even stepped into the house," she stuttered.

"How many bedrooms?" I inquired.

"Three," she answered, looking at me oddly.

"Perfect," I responded, walking farther into the space without taking my eyes off of the view. "We'll need it for a month. I'll give you a card for a deposit so we can move in today and arrange for the rest of the money to be wired to you by tomorrow. You'll be hearing from a gentleman by the name of Charles Stanley. He'll make certain it's all handled."

I finally pulled my eyes away from the ocean and turned to find Evan and the agent staring at me like I'd just recited a poem in Gaelic.

"What?" I questioned, my eyes flipping from one stunned face to the other.

"That's fine," she snapped, taking the card I held out for her. "I'll have the paperwork ready for you to sign this afternoon after I speak with this…Charles Stanley. I'll be in touch."

"Thanks," I smiled and limped past her to the truck.

"Charles Stanley?" Evan asked, still appearing dazed by the entire exchange. "And you don't even know what it costs or what the place looks like. Emma, what just happened?"

"I like the view," I answered simply, clicking my seat belt into place.

"Emma," I said sternly, causing the grin on her face to falter. Reluctantly, she faced me. "What aren't you telling me?"

Emma played with her fingers nervously before swallowing and admitting, "I have a trust."

I blinked in surprise.

"A big trust," she continued, her voice quiet. "My father set it up when I was young, and Charles came to see me before I turned eighteen to let me know it existed. He helps with whatever financial needs I have, whether it's school, or a car, or whatever." She kept her eyes cast down until she was done. Then she cautiously peered up at me, awaiting my reaction.

"O-kay," I said, still trying to take it all in. "I guess we have a house." I wasn't sure what else to say. Perhaps because I was still in shock from this revelation, or maybe because it really didn't matter. The money obviously hadn't affected Emma, or I would have picked up on it before now. Granted, Emma was pissed at the real-estate agent for her arrogant assumptions, but then she kind of had it coming. And the size of the house didn't matter to Emma. That was evident as well. The only thing that she'd seen was the view of the ocean before she made her decision. "Let's get our stuff." I started the truck, and we drove the five minutes back to Nate's house.

I waited for him to be upset with me for not telling him about the trust and the visit from Charles Stanley. But he barely reacted. He was more upset that I'd made such a hasty decision without knowing anything about the place.

Evan never reacted the way I expected, but that was something that had always drawn me to him. And that hadn't changed.

29. NOT KNOWING

I ran my hand along the smooth surface of the marble and tilted my head up at the sun beaming in through the small window set above the Jacuzzi tub.

"Nice place," Evan said from the door, spinning me around.

"Can you believe the size of this bathroom?" I replied, my voice echoing. It seemed more like an elite spa. It even had a television built into the long mirror over the double sinks.

"You're stuck on the bathroom? Have you seen this bedroom? I mean, it has a fireplace and its own private patio."

"It does?" I followed Evan through the master bedroom, past the king bed adorned with a mountain of pillows, and out a glass door covered with a gathered sheer curtain.

"No way." I gawked at the enclosed space, with brilliant pink flowers draping over the fence surrounding it. Two teak chairs and a table sat next to a small fire pit, along with, of all things, an outdoor shower. "Why would anyone need a shower on their patio?"

"To rinse off the sand from the beach," Evan explained, unlatching a section of the tall fence to reveal the main deck and a set of stairs leading to the beach.

"This is insane," I said, shaking my head.

"You picked it." Evan grinned.

"I liked the view."

"And you got so much more." Evan laughed, walking back into the house. I followed him in to the expansive living room with the cathedral ceiling. "I think I'm going to go to the grocery store, if that's okay. You should sit outside and let some fresh air get to your feet. I think I saw a hammock out there."

"That sounds perfect."

"Do you want anything in particular?" Evan asked, grabbing the keys to Nate's truck from the table behind the overstuffed dark blue couch.

"Ice cream?"

"I can do that." He smiled.

I watched him leave. I was trying not to think about the fact that he and I were going to be alone in this house together for the next twenty-four hours until Sara returned. Thinking of it made my entire body rush with panic, despite the rebellious flutter I felt in my chest. I shook away the invasive thought, and decided to distract myself with a book.

I inspected the tall built-in bookcase, jammed with paperbacks and hardcovers of every genre. Then I remembered the book I had in my tote bag, which I hadn't touched since before I left for Weslyn. It was ridiculous to have thought I would be able to read on the plane en route to Weslyn.

I removed the tote from the cavernous walk-in closet in the master suite and sifted through its eclectic contents. I pulled out the book, and a few envelopes dropped to the floor. I scooped them up.

One was a magazine offer. I tossed that on the bed to be thrown away. The other made my insides twist in on themselves. My formal name was scrolled stiffly across the white paper. The return address read, "Boca Raton, Florida." I dropped the envelope on the bed as if it were on fire. The script wasn't George's. I inhaled deeply to keep the nausea at bay. It had to be from my grandmother. I didn't want to hear her brutal accusations of how I'd ruined the lives of her sons and grandchildren. I refused to let one more person blame me for what wasn't my fault.

I grabbed my book and left the room, retreating to the large deck, where a blue canvas hammock awaited me. I carefully unwrapped the gauze protecting my feet and eased back on the swaying surface.

It took some time for my heart to calm as I watched the seagulls gliding above the water's surface. I concentrated on the serenity of the quiet beach and rhythmic waves, attempting to silence the letter that screamed at me from inside the house. Eventually, I opened the book.

When I lifted the splayed pages, something fell out and fluttered to the boards of the deck. I leaned over carefully, fearing I might tip, and reached for it. Rolling back onto the hammock, I twirled the green oak leaf between my fingers and laughed out loud at the flashing image of grabbing it while swinging in Evan's backyard—the night I was forced to stay there. I hadn't realized I'd kept it.

The sun shone through as I held it up to admire it. I felt the same warmth capture my heart as I had the day Evan had revealed the swing. He'd wanted to help me remember my father…and to hold on to him at the same time.

Tears washed over my eyes. I hadn't held on.

"What did you do?" I whispered, forcing back the emotion.

Tucking the leaf into the back of the book, I turned to the first page.

"Emma, I bought—" I stopped on the deck when I realized she was asleep on the hammock, a book resting on her stomach. I couldn't look away as the wind gently blew her hair—strands dancing around her face. The sun lit up her face as deep breaths passed through her slightly parted lips.

"Where do you want everything?" Nate asked from behind me. I turned toward him and he hesitated, taking us both in.

"I'll be right there," I told him.

Nate knew what was happening. I'd heard enough about it in the truck when I picked him up after grocery shopping. He'd made it clear he thought moving in with her for the month was a bad idea. He didn't seem to care that Sara would be here with us… starting tomorrow. And Sara was ten times more protective of Emma than Nate was of me.

When I gently lifted the book to set it on the table next to the hammock, something slipped out of it. I bent over to pick up the pressed oak leaf and smiled as I looked from the leaf to Emma. We seemed to keep circling back to that tree… and the swing. I tucked the leaf into the pages as a bookmark and set it on the table.

As I walked back into the house, I pulled out my phone and sent a text to my mother. You can deplete all of my savings, and I'll sign my trust over to you. PLEASE sell the house to me.

Nate was putting groceries away in random cabinets. I let him continue, knowing I'd end up moving them where I wanted later.

"Do you want to stay for dinner?"

"No thanks, but I'll take a beer," he responded.

"Sure." I pulled a beer from the fridge, trying to conceal the pleased look on my face.

"You really didn't want me here," Nate grumbled, reading me way too easily. "But Evan, do you know what you're doing? I mean, she's obviously going through a lot this summer. Maybe you're going to push her to do something you'll both regret."

"We'll figure it out," I assured him. "I'm not going make things worse. Trust me, they can't get worse."

Nate nodded thoughtfully.

"But I need to let whatever's happening between us, happen. Maybe we can get past everything that we've been through. I have to find out. She's finally starting to talk to me. And she's never really been able to do that before. Not like this."

Nate shrugged in resignation, taking a large swig of beer.

"My mother and her sister are taking my cousins to Disney for the weekend, and they're stopping by here tomorrow on their way. My mother wants you to come over for dinner. You can bring Emma if you want."

"I'll ask her."

"I have to warn you, my cousins are Satan's spawn." His lip curled in disgust. "But you're not getting out of this dinner, no matter what. There's no way you're leaving me alone with these kids."

"The guys will be there." I laughed.

"They're useless," Nate said emphatically. "I'm telling you, you'd better come armed, especially if you bring Emma."

I laughed again. "Sara will be back tomorrow, so Emma may want to stay here and catch up."

"Isn't Jared coming back with her?"

"Why is Jared coming back with Sara?" Emma asked from within the living room. I poked my head through the square cutout between the two rooms.

"Hi," I said with smile. "How'd you sleep?" I eyed her bare feet. "Shouldn't you have your feet protected?"

"I'll wrap them in a minute, but they're not that bad. And you didn't answer my question."

I glanced at Nate, who raised his brows quickly with a silent "good luck" as he finished his beer in a long chug. "Well, I guess I'll see you tomorrow," he declared, patting me on the shoulder as he walked past.

I followed him into the living room. "Emma, this is quite the house," he admired casually. "The guy a few houses down is Mick Slater. He's a big real-estate agent in the area and usually puts on a crazy fireworks display for the Fourth. You should throw a party. The guys and I will help you out if you want."

Emma nodded in stunned silence. I laughed at the thought of her throwing a party. "We can talk about it, Em."

"Okay," she said uneasily.

"'Bye, Emma," Nate said on his way out.

"'Bye, Nate," I replied before he shut the door. I'd noticed he'd been a little more withdrawn around me the last few days, unable to truly look me in the eye. I wondered if I'd done something to upset him.

"We don't have to have a party here," Evan assured me, misreading the concerned look on my face. "But the guys are experts at throwing them without any damages. I think I've seen the fireworks he's talking about, and this guy goes all out. I don't know where he shoots them off from, but they feel like they're going to rain down on the beach. And if you're this close to him..."

"Evan," I stopped him with a stern look. "My question. Why is Jared coming back with Sara?"

Evan rubbed his forehead, keeping his eyes on the floor. "He went to the funeral," he mumbled.

"He what?!" I demanded. "Why the hell would he do that? That's so"—I locked eyes with him—"like a Mathews. Wow, you guys don't care where you're not wanted, do you?"

"Ouch," Evan said, shocked.

"Sorry, sorry," I faltered. "I'm so sorry. I shouldn't have said that."

"Well, I guess it's true," Evan said, recovering. "You really didn't want me at your mother's funeral. And I'm certain Sara didn't want Jared at her grandfather's."

I sat on the couch, my feet throbbing and my muscles aching from standing. I propped my feet up and leaned against the throw pillow to face Evan. "Why would he want to go, Evan?" The image of him and that girl in the paper flashed through my head. "Isn't he engaged? He needs to leave Sara alone."

"Engaged?" Evan seemed to have no idea what I was talking about. Then his mouth rounded. "Oh! Shit. You saw that?"

"Uh, *yeah*. You have no idea what that picture did to us...her. What it did to *Sara*. She was beyond pissed." I clamped my teeth at my slipup, hoping he hadn't caught it.

"I'm sure she was," Evan noted, sitting on the love seat, facing me. "Wow. I can't believe you saw that." Evan ran his fingers through his hair. "Jared tried to tell her, but she never let him."

"Tell her what?! That he was planning to spend the rest of his life with someone else? He should have told her that he was *dating*, forget about getting *married*."

"Hey!" Evan scowled at me. "Sara's the one who ended it with him before she took off to France. She keeps telling him she wants to be with him, but then breaks it off every time they're more than a hundred miles apart. He had every right to move on."

"But he's *engaged*!" I stressed in frustration. "That's a big difference."

"He's not!"

I sat still, staring at him.

"What?" The confusion settled in. My heart was thumping wildly. All I could see was the image of Evan…with Catherine.

"Jared's not engaged, Emma. He never was. There was never anyone for him other than Sara. Believe me…he tried. It didn't take."

"But the pic—"

"Was my father," Evan explained with a disgruntled sigh. "Trina Macalroy was the daughter of a potential client. My father set her up with Jared. They dated for a while, but it was never *that* serious. She would have loved to be engaged to him, and my father's ploy almost pushed Jared into doing it. My brother was never very good at standing up to my father. But my mother intervened, and, well… the engagement never happened. And my parents are in the middle of a divorce because of it."

"Are you serious?" I asked, my head spinning.

"Yeah, it was the last straw," I answered, resting my elbows on my thighs. *"It's pretty much sucked for my mother since. He's not going easily."*

"I'm sorry."

I met her sympathetic eyes. "It'll be fine," I said without conviction, thinking about the house and how owning two properties wouldn't have been an issue if it weren't for the divorce. I knew what my mother wasn't telling me. My father was forcing her to sell it. Emma sank back against the couch, deep in thought.

"Are you hungry?" I asked, standing up and walking toward the kitchen, trying to change the subject. "I bought steaks for that insane grill out there."

"Sure," she answered blankly, still lost in her head.

I stopped at the sound of her fading tone. "What are you thinking, Emma?" I wasn't sure she'd answer me, but it was worth a try.

"Why didn't he like me? Your father. Why didn't he approve of me? He didn't even know me."

I ground my teeth at the sound of the hurt in her voice, anger flooding through me for every selfish thing that man did. How was I going to explain the inner workings of Stuart Mathews to a girl who thought she wasn't good enough and that everything she did was wrong? He'd played on her weaknesses, and he'd gotten to her, despite my efforts to keep them apart.

I walked to the couch, and she pulled her feet back so I could sit at the end. I turned to face her. "You're right. He didn't know you. And you didn't deserve the way he treated you. I never forgave him for that." She lifted her eyes in surprise. "Image and reputation were more important to him than people, than his own family. He didn't come from money—my mother did. He always felt he had to prove something to her family, to be worthy of my mother. But no matter how many times she assured him that they loved him because she did, he couldn't accept that. Once he got the taste of success, he hungered for more, stepping on anyone who got in his way.

"You never did anything. Unfortunately, you didn't fit the image of the girl he wanted for me."

"But Catherine did?" she mumbled under her breath.

My back tensed at the mention of her name. I pressed my lips together, remembering again that Emma had seen the photo in the paper. I connected with her troubled brown eyes and answered calmly. "Yes."

She flinched.

"It's not—"

"I don't want to know," she blurted. "I can't..." Emma pulled her legs in to her, moving as far away from me as she could. She knew there was more to that picture than just me obliging my father. I bowed my head and said, "I never dated her."

"I really don't want to know, Evan," she begged, her voice a whisper.

I didn't want to talk about her. Not now. Not ever. I wanted to forget about everything that had happened after I left. I wished we could just start over again, and let it all go. But I knew that was impossible. I knew I'd have to confront my demons eventually—I couldn't keep running forever.

30. CHOICES

I lay across the love seat with my feet propped on the arm, not really watching the movie that played on the giant flat-screen TV suspended above the fireplace. I looked over my shoulder at Evan, asleep on the couch.

I was trying so hard to be okay. I didn't want to be that girl, drifting in the water, lost and alone, wishing the tide would pull her out to sea. I was fighting to move forward, struggling to be better. But I didn't know how.

Evan stirred, and I looked away from him, pretending to watch the movie.

"Hey," he rasped, sleep heavy in his voice. "You're still awake?"

I tilted my head toward him. "Yes, I am. But *you* fell asleep."

"I did," he admitted groggily. "So movies don't put you to sleep anymore?"

"They still do," I said, grinning slightly. "I haven't really been watching, though."

"What's keeping you awake?"

I spun myself around to face him.

"This has been the most intense two and a half weeks of my life…ever," I confessed. "And considering my life, that's saying a lot."

I leaned over and clicked off the television.

Emma continued, "I guess… I'm overwhelmed and… scared."

"Scared?"

Emma looked down and started fumbling with her fingers. I wanted to invite her to sit with me, so I could be closer to her. She seemed too far away on the love seat. But she was even further away in her thoughts, and I wanted to know where she was and how to get her back.

"There's this letter, sitting on my bed," she explained, her voice unsteady. "I'm pretty sure it's from my grandmother, and I don't want to open it." She closed her eyes to hide her emotions, and I slid down the couch to sit across from her. When she opened her eyes again, they flickered with distress. I fought the urge to reach for her hand.

"Your grandmother?" I questioned, not aware she had any family other than George and the kids.

"My father's mother," she explained weakly. "She disowned him when I was born, because he and Rachel were never married."

I tried to keep my expression smooth as she shared one more thing she'd kept from me.

"Evan, I'm not strong enough to read it, to listen to her blame me for the loss I caused her sons. I can't handle one more person telling me that I should never have been born, or that I'm not worth being loved. I just... can't."

I took a breath, fighting to appear calm for her. These were the insecurities that fed on her over the years, embedded by the women who I despised more than anything. These were her darkest secrets, and she was finally letting me see them. I wasn't about to let someone else hurt her.

"I'll read it for you," I told her. "If it's bad, then you won't ever have to see it. And if I think you can handle it, then I'll give it to you."

"Okay," she replied with a quick exhale, trying to breathe away the anxiety. She continued to twist her hands when I stood up. I started toward the master bedroom and glanced back to find her following me.

My hands were trembling, and I didn't know how to make them stop. I was going to let him go into the room and read it alone, but then I couldn't. I had to be there, to watch his reaction, even if he told me I couldn't read it.

Evan flipped on the light, and I slid onto the bed. He sat on the edge, holding the heavy linen envelope in his hand, and raised his eyes to meet mine. I bit my lip and nodded, encouraging him to open it.

He slid his finger under the seal and pulled out the letter. The paper was thick and folded precisely in half. I could see enough to tell that it was handwritten. As Evan's eyes moved along each line, down each page, my heart pounded impatiently.

"It's not what you think," he said. "But it's still going to affect you. Would you like me to read it to you, or would you rather read it yourself?"

I hesitated before answering. "I'll read it." I held out my hand. "But stay. Please?" Evan scooted beside me, my shoulder pressed against him.

I took a deep breath and unfolded the paper.

Dear Emily,

I hope this letter finds you well. I apologize that our first encounter must be so impersonal, but I thought it would be best under the circumstance. My name is Laura Thomas. I am your paternal grandmother.

After what transpired in Weslyn, George thought it was best to move here to live with me in Florida. I was pleased, since I had not had much time with my grandchildren. The circumstance surrounding their relocation was unfortunate, but I was determined to make them feel loved and welcome all the same.

During this time, the children spoke of you often. They asked about your well-being and when they would see you again. As you can imagine, it is a sensitive subject, and something we could not knowingly answer. George has avoided addressing any questions pertaining to you, and I, unfortunately, do not know you well enough to answer them myself.

Jack, in time, has ceased his questions. However, Leyla has persisted, constantly creating drawings for you, and has even begun to make up stories about you to her teachers and classmates. Both children have been *under the care of a wonderful therapist to help them adjust to a life without their mother, and the therapist is concerned.*

I have asked if it would be beneficial to request communication with you, and the suggestion was encouraged greatly. George does not know of this correspondence, and would not favor this idea. But Leyla is very important to me, and you, Emily, are very important to her.

So, I am kindly asking if you would consider reacquainting yourself with your cousins. We could begin by correspondence, either written or electronic. Then perhaps we could work up to phone conversations, and in time, if you are willing, visits.

I will understand any reservations you may have regarding this request. I am sending this in the best interest of Leyla. You are welcome to respond to the e-mail or mailing address printed at the bottom of this letter.

Cordially,
Laura Thomas

I folded the page in half and set it on the table next to the bed, my hands continuing to shake. I leaned against the pillow and let the sterile words of my grandmother sink in. She wasn't contacting me because she wanted to meet me, or because she was sorry for missing out on so much of my life. After the sting of that abated, the true message tore at my heart.

I could tell Emma was trying to fight it, to lock out the emotion that was making her chin tremble.

"It's okay," I consoled her. "Just let it out, Emma."

She collapsed, leaning into me, and I pulled her against my chest. She didn't sob like I expected, but her cheeks were slick with tears.

"I miss them," she finally murmured, her voice broken. "I miss them so much. All I ever wanted was for them to be happy."

"I know. They miss you too. Em, that just means they love you as much as you love them."

I held her while she cried for them. When she'd caught her breath, she eased away, wiping her flushed cheeks.

"I don't want to cry anymore," she said, blowing away the tears. "It feels like all I've been doing is falling apart and crying."

"You can't keep it all inside, Emma. Cry. Scream if you have to, but don't let it destroy you. I wish you wouldn't underestimate your strength." I raised my hand to the side of her face and ran my thumb over her damp cheek.

"Thanks," she said, attempting a smile—meeting my eyes and lingering until I felt the compulsion of our connection in every part of my body. I let my hand fall, needing to look away from her before I did what I wanted to do. Emma turned and pushed the decorative pillows to the floor, adjusting a pillow and lying down on her side, facing me.

Evan followed my example and knocked the small pillows on his side to the floor before shifting down to lie across from me.

"Feeling any better?" he asked, his silver-blue eyes focused on mine, trying to see inside. I didn't look away to hide my conflicted emotions. I let him in.

"I don't know what to do," I said, tucking my hands under the pillow. "I want to see them so bad. But I'm afraid it will make things worse. I need to think about it."

"Okay," he said quietly. I could tell there was so much more he wanted to say.

"You want to tell me to do it, don't you?" I prodded. "That seeing Leyla and Jack is the right thing to do, and that there's nothing I could do that would hurt them more than ignoring this letter and staying out of their lives."

A grin crept across Evan's face. "Didn't have to tell you that, did I?" He laughed when I reluctantly smiled. "Either you're really good at reading my mind, or you already knew what you wanted to do."

"Okay, you can stop talking now," I admonished, trying my best to stifle a smile. "But I *really* don't want to cry anymore. It's so exhausting."

Evan laughed. "I understand. But I'm here if you need to."

"Thanks." I smiled gently. "And if *you* ever need to cry..."

Evan started laughing. Evidently, the thought of me consoling him was comical.

"What?! You don't cry?" I shot back, shoving his shoulder.

"Have you ever seen me cry?" he asked with an oversize smile.

"Once," I answered automatically. His grin faltered and we stared at each other, lost in the memory of that night. The night in the meadow under the stars. The night we asked each other for forgiveness. The night I gave him everything.

I held my breath, unable to look away from the intensity in his eyes.

"Yeah, once," I murmured, still connecting with her, refusing to look away. My eyes drifted toward her lips and my heartbeat picked up its pace.

Her eyes were wide and uncertain.

I was about to lean toward her when she asked, "Will you do something with me tomorrow?"

Her voice caught me by surprise, and I eased back, trying to calm my pulse. "Whatever you want."

"Will you help me pick out a surfboard and a wetsuit?"

I couldn't have smiled any bigger. "I'd love to."

We continued talking about surfing until her lids got heavy, and eventually didn't open again. Reaching over her, I shut off the light. I was about to crawl off the bed when her hand grabbed my arm. She didn't say anything, just rolled over sleepily and wrapped my arm across her stomach—and didn't let go. I tucked in behind her and held her against me, breathing her in until I fell asleep.

I shivered and reached for the blanket, but there wasn't one. I opened my eyes and blinked in the dark. I could hear breathing behind me and felt the pressure of Evan's body along my back, our hands intertwined. I slipped my fingers out carefully and eased off the bed to use the bathroom and get a drink of water.

I walked cautiously in the direction of where I thought the bathroom was, feeling blindly along the wall. I eventually pushed the door open, and shut it behind me before clicking on the light.

As I brushed my teeth, I considered whether I should sleep on the far side of that large bed, so we weren't so close.

He'd considered kissing me twice tonight, and I'd almost let him. But I'd gotten scared and backed away. There was still so much pain between us. It was easy to forget in these vulnerable moments when we found ourselves drawn to each other.

So why is he in your bed, Emma? I looked at myself in the mirror, sighed, and filled a glass from the vanity tray before walking back into the bedroom.

When I opened the bathroom door, Evan suddenly shot up in bed. "Emma?" My breath faltered at the sudden movement.

"Evan? Are you okay?" My heart raced as I took in his rigid posture.

He appeared confused. "Em?"

"I'm right here," I said to him, gripping the glass tightly as I stood within the frame of the door. He'd had a nightmare. It was strange seeing it from this side, panic followed by confusion and heavy breathing. Then, with the realization of where he was, his shoulders slouched in relief.

"Sorry," he said, as I remained unmoving, my hand on the light switch.

"It's okay," I assured him quietly. "Do you mind turning on the light next to the bed so I can shut off the bathroom light?" The lamp clicked on, and I noticed his hand trembling when he removed it from the switch.

I shut off the bathroom light and got back in bed. He moved over and lay on his back, his arm resting across his forehead. I continued to watch him. His chest rose and fell as he struggled to recover.

"What was it about?" I asked, knowing it was a question *I* never answered.

"You," he whispered.

It slipped through my mouth, and as soon as I said it, I wanted to take it back. I turned my head toward her, and she remained perfectly still. Now I needed to explain. "It's a little different each time. But in some way, you're always gone. And I wake up in a panic."

She looked as if I'd crushed the air out of her. "Don't, Em. Don't blame yourself for this too."

"But... how can I not?" she murmured. "You wake up from a nightmare each night because of what I did to you. How can I not feel it's my fault?"

Her eyes dipped sorrowfully. She sunk farther into the bed as the guilt pulled on her. I wished I had the strength to lift it from her.

"You've worn guilt like an iron mask, welded to you, because you're convinced that you're to blame for what happens to everyone else. You martyr yourself for things you're not responsible for. And you end up hurting the people you care about because you push them away, believing you're protecting them." Emma remained quiet. "You can't continue to carry that guilt anymore. You can't keep shutting everyone out. That's not living, Emma."

"I know," she whispered, swiping the tears away.

"Living in the mistakes of your past isn't going to do anything but destroy your future."

The truth in his words shook me, and I held on to them with my fists tight, letting the tears seep into the pillow.

I thought I'd concealed the darkness so well, but he'd seen through my facade—the forced smiles and the evasive answers. He knew me.

I wished he didn't.

I focused on his eyes. "I'm sorry, Evan. I'm so sorry for leaving you on the floor of that house. For not saying anything when I left for California. It was the worse choice I ever made."

"Taking away mine."

I scrunched my eyes slightly, not understanding.

"You never gave me a choice, Emma. I think that's why it's so difficult to forgive you. You chose for me. Just like my father did most of my life—until I was finally able to stand up to him. But with you, it was different. I would've done anything for you."

The weight on my chest got heavier the more he spoke, until I felt it would splinter my bones. To be compared to his father made me want to dissolve into the mattress.

I never gave him a chance to decide if I was worth loving. I'd taken that choice away from him—because I feared what it would be.

"Then be mad at me, Evan," I finally pleaded. "Please. Yell. Be angry. Do *something*. Stop accepting all the times I fuck up. Quit being so understanding. If you'd gotten pissed every once in a while, and hadn't just avoided me or left, then I would've had to choose too. I thought I was doing the right thing by protecting you, as insane as that sounds now. I have such a fucked-up life; I didn't want you to know…I didn't want you to see that side of me."

"What side?"

"The side that I hate," she shared with a strained voice. She'd reached her limit, and rolled over, unable to face me anymore. I was speechless; her honesty and raw vulnerability thrust into my chest like a sledgehammer. Struck with an equal rush of awe and exhaustion, I clicked off the lamp.

I moved closer to her and said quietly, "I will get mad at you, I promise. But not tonight. I'm too tired." She let out an emotional breathy laugh. "But right now, I'm going to hold you, because you need it, and so do I. Okay?"

"Are you giving me a choice?" she asked, a hint of sarcasm breaking through the tears.

I laughed. "Yes, Emma, I'm giving you a choice."

"Okay," she replied, scooting back a little until she felt me. I wrapped my arm around her, and she slid her fingers between mine. I pressed my face into her hair. She whispered, "I won't take your choices away from you again. I promise."

31. TRUCE

The ivory curtains that hung on the glass doors did little to block out the bright morning light. I rolled over and pulled the pillow over my head, not ready to be awake.

"Hey, Em," Evan called to me. I grumbled under the pillow. "Good to see you hate mornings again. Do you want breakfast?"

I lifted the pillow, about to tell him I could make my own breakfast, when words failed me completely. Evan stood with the door partly open, slicked with sweat, in just a pair of running shorts. I forced my eyes to stare at the ceiling rather than his carved body. What had he been doing the past two years?

My heart was beating so fast, my entire body was flushed.

"Emma?"

"I, um…whatever," I said without looking at him.

"Is there something wrong?"

"Evan, put a shirt on," I blurted, my cheeks burning intensely.

He laughed. "Really?"

"Shut up." I pulled the pillow back over my head.

"Would you listen to me if I asked you to wear pants?" he asked, taking me by surprise.

"What?" I shot back, sitting up. I felt my hair floating around my head and flattened it behind my ears. "Cover my legs?"

He grinned and walked away. I grumbled and pushed the covers off me, trudging to the bathroom.

When Emma finally came out of the bedroom, the spoon completely missed my mouth, smearing milk along my chin.

"What the hell?" I exclaimed. "Those barely qualify as underwear." Emma sauntered into the room in a pair of the shortest denim shorts I'd ever seen. Her tan legs, defined with lines of lean muscle, crossed in front of me as I sat on the couch.

"What do you mean?" she said, playing the innocent. "They're shorts. It's summer."

"Did you just cut them? Because I know you'd never buy a pair of shorts that short. Seriously, they're… revealing." As soon as I said it, she tugged at them slightly, her cheeks turning red. I grinned, hoping she would change.

I glared at him. He sat on the couch, his hair wet from the shower. And *still* without a shirt. He was doing it to get to me. So I decided not to play fair, except now I was worried I'd cut too much off the jeans. I could feel the material riding up. I wanted to pull them down, but knew he was waiting for it. So instead, I continued outside.

"Emma!" Evan hollered, practically jumping off the couch. "Okay. I'll put on a shirt. Now please come inside and put on a pair of shorts that cover what shorts are supposed to cover."

I smiled proudly and stalked past him as he shoved his head through his T-shirt. "Truce?"

"Truce," he mumbled, lowering his shirt over his taut stomach. "Do you still want to go to the surf shop?"

"Yes," I hollered, closing the bedroom door behind me.

When I stepped out of the house, I was surprised to find a red, boxy-looking truck with a black canvas top. I flipped my eyes toward Evan curiously.

"Whose is this?" I asked, stepping up and pulling myself onto the seat. A waft of worn leather filled the cab. I examined the shiny red metal and black leather interior, with its small round instruments and bucket seats.

"Mine," Evan answered, shutting the door behind me.

"Where'd it come from?" I asked when he entered his side. Despite the obvious age of the vehicle, it was in really good condition and appeared to be newly painted.

"The garage dropped it off this morning," Evan explained, starting it. "They were converting it to biodiesel, so I had to wait awhile."

He began to pull out of the driveway. "Evan, stop," I demanded. He braked and put it in neutral. "Explain. Now. All of it."

"Explain what? Biodiesel?" he said with a devilish grin.

"Evan!" I scolded. The smile dropped from his face.

His eyes flickered in deliberation. "Just say it," I pushed.

"I needed a vehicle because I transferred to Stanford, and I start classes next quarter. And I went to San Francisco earlier this week to meet my mother because she wanted to see the place I'd picked out before I signed the lease."

I blinked. That's all I could do. The rest of me was stunned into paralysis. I finally asked, "Why are you going to Stanford?"

"It was my first choice," he answered. He continued out of the driveway, leaving me staring at him from the passenger seat.

"Okay," I breathed. "Okay. It was your first choice. Okay."

I was expecting yelling, or at least some sign of annoyance. But she just sat there repeating "Okay" over and over, like she was trying hard to accept it.

"What's your major?" Emma asked about five minutes into the drive.

"I have a double major in business and education," I told her. "I haven't decided yet."

"Oh." She nodded thoughtfully. "Education, huh? Serena's boyfriend is an education major. I think he's coming up tomorrow. You can talk to him."

My shoulders relaxed. A small smile eased onto my face as we drove into town.

I was trying to remain calm. I didn't know if I was actually pulling it off, but maybe asking questions would keep me from freaking out.

"So you got a place off campus?"

"Yeah," he answered. "A studio. It's small, but I won't have roommates. This guy converted the space above his garage to rent out."

"Nice," I responded, with a casual nod that I hoped hid my turbulent thoughts. He'd sworn he hadn't come here to get me back. And I knew the transfer deadline was months ago, so this had to have been something he planned to do way before seeing me again.

That's when it all fell into place. Stanford *was* his first choice, and I'd screwed that up when I left. When I'd given Vivian that letter... And this was yet another choice I'd taken away from him.

"I think you're going to like it here." I smiled softly, rubbing my damp palms on my cargo shorts.

"I think so too."

We pulled into the lot at the surf shop. "Ready?"

She laughed at me. "Excited much?"

"You have no idea." I grinned stupidly, jumping out of the truck.

I walked around toward her side, but she'd already opened her door. As she climbed out, I noticed her bandaged feet.

"No socks today," I noted.

"It's getting better," she explained. "They're not as tender, so I figured Band-Aids were enough."

I held the shop door open for her, and we headed to the front counter.

Evan's face was beaming as we scanned the racks of surfboards. I smiled at his excitement.

The inventory was overwhelming at first, but when I found a design by a local artist, I knew I had to have it. Much to Evan's disappointment, the only longboard with that design was in their shop in Cardiff. We'd have to wait a few days for it to be delivered.

After I found a wetsuit that fit and selected a few rash guards, Evan and the guy behind the counter continued talking "surf," so I decided to browse the bathing suits, wanting to find a better style for surfing.

I selected a few that looked like they wouldn't fall off if—when—I wiped out, and then I came across the dental floss suits. I held up a hot pink one, trying to understand what parts all the strings covered.

"You're not serious," Evan said from behind me. I grinned before turning around.

I laid it across the front of me as if sizing it. "What do you think?"

"You can't wear that surfing," Evan said with a shake of his head.

"Of course not." I laughed. "For the pool parties."

His mouth fell open. "No, Emma. That's not a good idea at all."

I smiled wider, continuing to taunt him. "I think I'm going to try it on. Do you want me to model it for you?"

"Nope," he responded, his neck turning red. "You don't need to model it for me or anyone else. In fact, if you wanted to keep it on the hanger, that would be just fine too."

I laughed again and walked away, seeking out the dressing area with the suit still in my hand.

I slid the curtain shut and hung the suits, trying on the ones I was truly interested in and making a selection. Then I picked up the one that was a breeze away from nudity. Seeing his reaction to the thought of me wearing it was more than entertaining.

I hung up the suits I didn't want—including the hot pink mess—and continued to the register. "And I have the board, rash guards and wetsuit too," I reminded the guy.

I glanced around. Evan was on the other side of the store, checking out sunglasses.

"The board's already paid for," the guy informed me. "We're closed on Sunday, so it'll be here for you to pick up on Monday morning. We open at seven."

"Oh…thanks," I replied.

After I was done at the counter, I grabbed my bags and headed toward the door.

"Evan—" Emma scowled as we walked through the door. "Why'd you do that?"

"I wanted to," I replied. "Let's just say it's in celebration that you surf." I wasn't about to tell her it was a gift for the day she never celebrated. It would arrive two days early, so officially, I was giving it to her before her birthday.

When we arrived back at the house, she hung the wetsuit in the entry closet before continuing into the bedroom. I followed her, knocking on the door to get her attention. "Do you want to go with me to Nate's for dinner when Sara and Jared get here?" She was folding the black swimsuit in her hands. "What? You didn't buy the pink one?"

A mischievous grin spread across her face. "You wish. But I would've loved to have taken a picture of your face when I held it up." She laughed, and… didn't stop.

I would let her laugh at my expense all day just to hear the lightness of it.

"Speaking of which," Emma said when she eventually stopped. "Do you have your camera?"

I hesitated—still not convinced I was ready to pick it up again. "Somewhere."

"Well, if you choose to, the sunsets here are stunning. I was thinking of painting for the afternoon, hoping to capture the colors by the time the sun sets."

The corner of my mouth rose. "That might be worth taking a picture of."

"The sunset?"

"No," I answered, awaiting her reaction as I paused a second. "You painting." The softest flush of pink filled her cheeks. I could never get enough of that either.

He walked away, leaving me staring after him with warm cheeks.

Evan continued upstairs while I dragged out a stool from the bistro table onto the deck, and set up the easel. I sat on the stool and breathed in the salty air. It was a perfect day.

And when Evan emerged with his camera, messing with the lens, I was convinced it couldn't get any better. He went for a walk along the beach with his camera while I visualized the scene I wanted to create and began spreading a base of color along the canvas.

Completely focused on what I was doing, I never noticed when Evan returned. I actually didn't notice much of anything until I heard the front door close, and spun around on the stool.

"Hello?" Sara called through the house. "Emma?"

"Out here," Evan responded, lying on the hammock, reading the book I'd left on the table. My heart skipped a beat when I noticed the oak leaf resting on his chest. I bit my lip with a slow grin at the sight of it. When I raised my eyes from the leaf, he was watching me with a knowing look on his face.

There had always been a connection between us, since the first day I saw him—a delicate tether of energy that bound us together. But something was different. With each bout of honesty, I was letting him in deeper, exposing the most vulnerable side of me. I could feel us getting closer, with every touch, every glance and subtle smile.

The screen door slid open and I turned quickly to face Sara, slipping down from the stool. She stepped onto the deck, radiant in a green and yellow floral sundress, a vibrant smile on her face. I would have thought she was returning from vacation, not a funeral—and then I saw her hand clasping Jared's.

Sara released him to hold out her arms, but she reconsidered when she saw the paint on my hands and gave me a quick kiss on the cheek instead. "Hi! I'm so happy to be back. This house is perfect, Em! I can't believe we're staying here for a month. The only thing we're missing is a pool."

"It's on the roof," Evan blurted before I could say anything. "Really?!" Sara practically squealed with excitement.

"No," Evan laughed teasingly.

Sara shot him a look. "You're an asshole, Evan." This caused Jared to chuckle. She stepped behind the stool to look at my painting, "Wow. That's powerful."

"It's not done yet," I said in a rush, fidgeting as her eyes scanned the strokes, swirling in apparent chaos.

"But I like it," she said with a smile.

"I know you guys just got here, but we're going over to Nate's. His mom invited us for dinner, if you want to come with us," Evan announced.

"We are?" I questioned. He clenched his teeth in apology, realizing we hadn't truly discussed it.

"We'll go," Sara declared happily. "Come on, Em. I'll pick out something for you to wear while you clean the paint off your…body."

I glanced down and found paint splattered across any exposed skin between my shoulders and my knees. Evan laughed at my amazed reaction. "You are probably the most intense painter I've ever seen. I'll clean up your stuff so you can get ready."

"Thanks," I said, and followed Sara into the house, trying not to touch anything.

"Holy shit!" she exclaimed upon entering the master bedroom. "I could live in this room and never leave."

"Pretty nice, huh?" I agreed, bumping the bathroom door open with my hip. "Tell me about New Hampshire." I hollered to her as I shed my clothes to shower.

"We'll talk about it when you get out," she bellowed from somewhere deep within the closet. "You need dresses!"

"No, you need me to need dresses!"

When I returned to the bedroom, wrapped in a towel with blotchy red skin from scrubbing the paint off, I found Sara seated on the chaise with her ankles crossed, texting. She set down her phone when she saw me. I inspected the white linen shorts and light blue halter top resting on the bed, and the wedge sandals on the floor beneath.

"I wish you'd go dress shopping with me."

"Sara, please," I pleaded, not wanting to have this conversation.

"I'm not giving up on you, Em." Her brows arched as her glossy lips quirked slightly.

"Nice to have you back, Sara," I said, dressing in the clothes she'd set out for me. "Now talk."

Sara sat on the end of the bed, peering up at me with twinkling eyes. "He showed up at the funeral." Her smile shone across her face.

"I know that," I said impatiently, "but what happened? What did he say?"

"We didn't really get to talk until yesterday, because my father just about threw him out of the church when he saw him. So he basically harassed me with a million texts, begging to talk to me until I finally agreed to meet him at a bookstore. I think he wanted to meet there so I couldn't scream at him.

"Anyway, he told me about his dad, always putting business before everything else. I knew that. I mean, look what he did to you." My face tightened. "Sorry, that was a bad thing to say..."

"Just keep going," I encouraged, not wanting to dwell on the fact that Stuart Mathews didn't like me.

"He was dating this girl, which made me want to throw up. But then you should've seen his face when I told him about Jean-Luc. So I guess we were both pretty stupid. His father kept dropping hints that Jared and this girl had a great future ahead of them together. Jared kept shrugging it off. But that's what Stuart wanted, and so did the bitch in the photo. I should've known she was a conniving whore-bag when I saw that she was friends with Catherine Jacobs, who's the biggest skank of them all."

Sara noticed the color drain from my face.

"They didn't date, Emma," Sara assured me in a rush. "Okay?" I nodded, my skin still crawling at the presumption of them being intimate in any way.

"She wanted in, and Stuart was giving her an in, scoring a pretty sweet deal with her father while he was at it. She made certain she wore her grandmother's ring on her left hand at the party, and Stuart arranged for the reporter. The news of an 'engagement' was leaked upon sight of the ring, and it took Vivian a week to clear it up—but only after it was printed, thanks to Stuart's influence. He's such a dick." Sara clenched her teeth in disgust.

"I'm so glad Vivian forced him to leave. And Emma, she was so upset after what he'd done to you. My mom told me she and Vivian went to lunch last summer, and you came up. Vivian always questioned whether she did the right thing by keeping Evan close to home, away from you. But she blamed Stuart for his part in your leaving."

I fought to keep my face even while she spoke, but my breath rippled with emotion. "What now?"

"So…we're together. And it's amazing!" Sara practically bounced on the bed. "Em, I was so paranoid to think that we wouldn't be able to handle the distance. I mean…he's it. He's the only guy that makes me feel like I could do anything, and that I'm the most important person in the world. I'd never been in love until I met him. And I haven't loved anyone since."

She emanated happiness, and it looked beautiful on her.

"That's the best story you've ever told." She jumped up from the bed and hugged me, catching me off guard. I wrapped my arms around her, squeezing just as tight.

"Now, tell me about you," Sara insisted, trying to be serious, but joy soaked through her like light. "What happened with Cole? What did he say?"

"Nothing," I shrugged. "He left a note." I turned from her and started toward the bathroom. "I should dry my hair. I think the guys are waiting on us."

"Emma," Sara chided, following me into the bathroom, "I'll dry your hair. You talk."

I sighed, sitting at the vanity while Sara reached for the round brush and hair dryer. "There's not much to say. It was only two sentences. You know I'd asked him to leave before I hurt him, so that's what he did. He wasn't going to let me hurt him."

"Shit," she replied. "He knew, Em. He knew as soon as Evan stepped off that plane that it was over."

"Evan?" I questioned in surprise. "*I'm* the reason he left."

"Whatever," she said dismissively. "You don't always have the clearest perspective on things, Em. Either way. He left, so how are *you?*"

I averted my eyes. "Fine."

"What?" she demanded. "Are you upset that he's gone?"

"I hate how it ended," I admitted. "He was a good guy. Really."

"I know," Sara acknowledged. "I liked him."

I nodded. "I knew it was going to happen. I knew there would be an end eventually. I just didn't want it to get…complicated."

"Yeah," Sara scoffed. "If you don't want complicated, then stay away from guys."

I made a face at her advice.

"Now what about Evan?" she continued. "How have you been getting along? Was it weird to be alone with him here last night?"

I shook my head, trying to keep my body temperature from rising. But the heat rushed to my cheeks anyway.

Sara switched off the hair dryer. "What happened?" I glanced up, and she was staring at me with large eyes. "Did you have sex with him?!"

"What?! Omigod, no!" I answered quickly, my entire face now red. "We've been talking, that's all. And...well..."

"Emma," Sara said in her familiar lecturing tone. "What did you do?"

"He stayed with me, in here, last night," I explained quietly. "We talked until we fell asleep."

"And you didn't exactly sleep on opposite sides of that huge bed, did you?" She knew the answer when I couldn't meet her eyes. "What's happening between you two?"

"I'm not sure," I answered honestly. "We really are *just* talking. And it's good, I guess. It's honest, anyway. And I cry *way* too much. It's kind of pathetic."

"I'm sure it's not pathetic," Sara comforted me. "You probably haven't cried enough in your life, so you're making up for it."

"Great," I grumbled, wishing I knew how to find the off switch again. "But—"

"Are you almost ready?" Evan hollered into the room.

"We'll be right out," Sara answered, turning on the dryer to finish my hair. "This conversation isn't over." She gave me a stern look, and I nodded meekly.

Sara walked out of the bedroom before Emma with a smile on her face that wouldn't quit. I glanced over at Jared, who stared at her with an I've-been-hit-on-the-head-with-a-hammer look on his face. Their reconciliation was bound to make things a little awkward around here, especially when Emma and I didn't even touch... except when we went to sleep.

"We need to talk," Sara said between her smiling teeth.

"What did I do now?" I asked. She looked behind me, and I turned to find Emma with her leg bent behind her, using the wall as support to slide on a pair of dress sandals—her feet still covered in bandages. The

white shorts were short enough to show off the legs that made me weak. I realized I was staring when her cheeks glowed red, and she smiled at me awkwardly.

"Uh, ready?" I confirmed, noticing that Jared and Sara were already at the door. I reached out to grab her hand, but caught myself and ran it along the side of my khakis instead, hoping she hadn't noticed. Maybe inviting her wasn't the best idea. It felt like a date, and despite the connection we were feeling, we weren't ready for that. I started for the door as she grabbed a sweater out of the closet.

"You look nice," she said, turning me around. "I like that shirt on you."

"Thanks," I responded, completely taken by surprise. "You look... amazing."

She smiled shyly and said, "Thanks," as she walked by me out the door.

"Sweet Scout," Jared admired, climbing in behind the driver's seat. "What year is it?"

"'Sixty-nine," I responded, waiting for Emma to climb in so I could close the door behind her. I noticed Sara's eyes scrunch slightly, like she was trying to figure out the same thing Emma had earlier. I decided to let Emma tell her about me transferring, not certain what her reaction would be. Sara wanted Emma to be happy, but I knew she was still worried about her. I didn't know if she was still concerned about my motives, or just the emotional turbulence that had swept into Emma's life this summer. Either way, I knew I was part of it.

If I'd heeded Nate's warning about his Satanic tweener cousins, I would never have exposed Sara and Emma to them. I don't know how, but somehow we survived dinner without anyone ending up stabbed in the eye or floating facedown in the pool, although I could tell by Jared's menacing glare that he was thinking it. We escaped as soon as we could, making an excuse about a movie. Nate and the guys disappeared to a party to save themselves.

"I think I have barbecue sauce on my back," Emma said as we drove home. She was trying to wipe it off her shoulder blade, but was unable to reach it. "I didn't know anyone could be so annoying."

"Dude, I am never having kids," Jared declared. I glanced in the rear-view mirror and noticed Sara staring at him. He quickly added, "Like that. Those two kids were hatched by gremlins, I swear."

I reached over and ran my finger across the brown streak on Emma's back.

"Thanks," she said, turning her head to look out the open window.

"What time are Serena and Meg arriving tomorrow?" Sara asked. Emma turned toward her, and I grinned at the flush of color that my touch had caused.

"Late tonight. So we won't see them until the morning. James is supposed to be coming too," Emma told her, then appeared alarmed when she noticed my expression. "What?"

I shrugged innocently, but couldn't keep from smirking as we pulled into the driveway. This only made her redder. I exhaled a quick laugh.

"Just tell me," she demanded. "Did that little brat write his initials on my back or something?"

"No." I shook my head.

"But he was trying to look up your shorts every time he purposely dropped his fork under the table," Jared shared.

She looked to Sara for confirmation. "Did he?"

"He tried," Sara affirmed, "until I dug my heel into his hand. I think I may have scarred him for life."

"Nicely done," Jared said proudly. He pulled her into him and kissed her on the forehead. I looked away from the mirror. Their couple status was definitely uncomfortable to witness.

"Sara, you're cruel," Emma accused playfully.

"Yes, I am," Sara gloated, causing Jared to laugh loudly.

When we entered the house, Sara announced, "We're going to bed," practically dragging Jared up the stairs behind her.

Emma and I exchanged glances, very aware that they were not going to sleep. And just to make it obvious, Sara leaned over the railing at the top of the stairs and said, "You may want to put on music, or the TV, and turn it up."

My eyes widened as Jared laughed, trailing after her.

"Wow," I said, "that was..."

"Awkward," Evan finished for me. "Uh, so..."

"Want to go for a walk?" I suggested. We both looked down at the Band-Aids on my feet.

"What if I built a fire on the patio instead?" Evan suggested.

I glanced at the clock—it was later than I thought. And in truth, I really didn't want to talk, which I knew would happen if we sat out on the patio.

"You know what, I think I'm going to go to bed," I declared. "I'll read until I fall asleep."

"Oh," Evan replied with disappointment. "Okay. Well..."

Sara's exuberant laughter carried down the stairs. Evan eyed the second floor in dread.

"You can stay in my room...if you want," I offered.

"Are you sure?" he asked cautiously. "I don't want it to feel like we're—"

"I know," I responded. I was very aware of what we weren't, and I didn't need to hear him say it.

"I'll be right down," he told me. "I need to get my bag."

Evan rushed up the stairs, probably not wanting to be within earshot of them any longer than he had to. I continued to the bedroom to prepare for bed. Evan knocked lightly on the bathroom door while I was brushing my teeth. "I'm changing out here, so give me a minute before you come out."

"Okay," I responded, my voice garbled with a mouthful of toothpaste. And of course, the only thing I could think about was Evan changing.

I rinsed my mouth and washed my face, patting it dry just as
he knocked again.

"You can come in," I announced. Evan opened the door, dressed
in a pair of shorts and a worn T-shirt that left little to the imagination about what was concealed underneath. I let out an exasperated
breath as I passed him.

"What?" Evan laughed, obviously reading my expression.

I got into bed without responding and clicked on the bedside
lamp. I could hear the water running as Evan brushed his teeth.
Eyeing his bag on the chaise, I wondered just how many nights he
planned to spend in this room.

I opened the book as Evan emerged from the bathroom, setting
the oak leaf on the pillow next to me. He slipped under the covers
on the far end of the bed.

"That's a good book so far," he noted. "I was reading it earlier
today."

"Want to read it with me?" I offered, without really thinking it
through.

"Have you ever done that before," he asked, "read a book at the
same time as someone else?"

"No. Have you?"

"No." He laughed lightly.

"Come here," he beckoned, gently picking up the leaf and scooting toward the middle pillow. I eyed him suspiciously. "Don't worry,
just come here."

I moved over, and he opened his arm and patted the shoulder
closest to me. "Lie here, and I'll hold the book."

I hesitated, contemplating.

"Emma, just come lie down."

I sighed and rested my head on his chest, fitting perfectly along
the dip of his shoulder. He handed me the leaf, taking the book
from me. I could hear his heart beating under my ear. I didn't know

where to put my arm, so I rested my hand on his chest, listening to his heart pick up its pace at my touch, knowing mine was doing the same thing. I took a slow breath and tried to concentrate on the words as he held the book above our heads.

"I'm a couple pages behind," he told me. "Do you mind if I catch up real quick?"

"Go ahead," I said, pinching the stem of the leaf that was still in my hand, brushing it gently against his chest.

I lay there silently as he read. I could feel the heat from his body along my skin. I could hear the erratic beating of his heart. I was being pulled to him, and it was becoming too much for me to resist. Just as I was about to move away, Evan said, "I'm going to miss that house." His gaze was focused on the leaf I was nervously playing with.

He rested the open book on his stomach and brushed his fingers along my arm. I propped up on my elbow so I could see him, still closer than I should've been.

"What do you mean?"

"My mother's selling it," he told me, his voice heavy and quiet.

"She can't do that," I said passionately, my heart convulsing at the thought of it belonging to anyone else.

"I'm working on it," he assured me with a deflated breath. "But it's not looking good."

I lowered my head back on his chest, reflecting.

"I love this tree," I said in a hush. "And the swing." I stared at the leaf so he wouldn't see the emotion surfacing.

"Me too," he muttered softly. "And the barn. That was such a great place to escape to."

"Yeah." I flipped the leaf over on his chest. "If those walls could talk, right?"

Evan laughed. "I would listen." I smiled fondly at the thought of what they'd say.

"Those woods freaked me out though," I recalled. "Or maybe it was your driving."

"Hey," he balked defensively. "I thought I was pretty good on that bike. You didn't trust me?"

"Only when my eyes were closed," I teased.

"I *love* that kitchen," Evan stressed. "I set it up exactly how I wanted it."

"The kitchen, really?" I laughed. "Of course you'd love the kitchen."

"If I remember correctly, you loved that kitchen too."

"It was more about the food than the kitchen," I corrected. I paused, mentally walking the halls of the house, inhaling the scent of wood and polish. "You never did play the piano for me."

"No," he said quickly. "That never did, or will, happen. My parents forced me take lessons, but these fingers are most definitely not meant to play the piano." He splayed his fingers in front of him, and I grinned, lying back against his shoulder to look up at them.

"Yeah, you're right; they don't look worthy of a piano," I mocked.

"I wish I could've swam in that pool at least once."

"I still don't believe there was a pool. I think it was just a hole, because why else would it never get uncovered?"

"Guess we'll never know," he sighed, his voice heavy. "I can't believe she's selling it. The best moments of my life happened in that house."

"Mine too," I whispered, lost in the remembrance of all the life changing moments that had happened while I was protected within the borders of that property. Evan was quiet. I suddenly realized what we were *really* saying.

"Have you caught up?" I asked, clearing my throat.

Evan picked up the book again. "Yeah."

We began reading. I'd nod when I was done with the page, being the slower reader—or maybe he wasn't really reading anymore.

At one point he shifted, and I could feel his breath along my cheek. I couldn't concentrate. My heart raced, and my body flooded with heat.

I closed my eyes, pushing away the desire to tilt my head up toward him. I knew he was right there; I could feel him. I pressed my lips together and inhaled. When I opened my eyes, the book was gone, and Evan had carefully removed the leaf from my hand.

"I know this is hard," Evan said in an exhale, rolling on his side with his arm still under my neck. I kept facing up, staring at the ceiling, trying to breathe. I knew I should move away, but I couldn't. "I feel it too. And I'm having just as hard a time resisting, Emma. Because I don't want to do anything we're not ready for."

I closed my eyes, my chest tightening, knowing *I* wasn't ready. But the firmness of his body against my side and his scent held me captive, keeping me from moving a single muscle. I was afraid to lose this—his touch, his warmth. His hand ran across my stomach, and I inhaled quickly.

"Oh, Emma," he murmured in my ear, making me bite my lip. His fingers coiled into a fist on my stomach, and his arm tightened in restraint. "Maybe I should go upstairs."

Just as he turned on his back, I uttered, "Don't go." He was suddenly very still. "You're right. We're not ready. And I don't know what's happening between us. But…if you can, will you just lie with me? If you can't, I…"

"I can do that."

He exhaled deeply. I realized he needed some distance, so I rolled on my side and shut off the light. A few minutes later, Evan slid behind me and I found his hand, gripping it tightly in front of me.

"Good night, Emma," he whispered in my ear just before he kissed the top of my head. My breath faltered. I squeezed his hand, and as impossible as it seemed, I fell asleep.

32. RELENTLESS

I thought I heard voices. I tried to ignore them, but they were… giggly and almost shrieking. I shifted and Evan mumbled something behind me, his arm still draped over me. "Evan?" Still deep in sleep, he didn't respond.

I listened again and heard, "I'm so glad you're here. We're going to have the best weekend." I shot up in bed, forcing Evan to roll over.

"Evan, wake up," I urged in a panic.

"Yeah, Emma's still in bed," Sara said to one of the girls. "Her room's right there, if you want to wake her."

"Shit, Evan." I shoved him. He blinked his eyes open. "The girls are here. Get out of my bed."

"What?" he mumbled, rubbing his eyes.

"Get out, now." I pushed against his shoulder. "They're coming into my room."

He finally caught on just as a knock sounded at my door. Evan scrambled out of the bed and practically fell over, tripping on the sheets in his dazed state. He disappeared behind the bathroom door as Serena poked her head in.

"Emma?" When she saw that I was awake, she smiled brightly. "Hi."

"Hi," I said, smiling in return and trying to calm down from panic mode. I glanced at the bathroom out of the corner of my eye, and had to force myself to keep smiling when I noticed the door was cracked open. I wanted to throw something at him, but I redirected my attention to Serena before she caught on.

"Good morning," Meg said as she entered the room. "You slept late."

"What time is it?" I asked, fighting the urge to look at the bathroom again.

"Ten thirty." Meg sat on the edge of the bed.

"How was the drive?" I asked, my heart beating so hard I could feel it in my ears. I needed to figure out how to get them out of my room without it seeming obvious.

"Not bad," Serena said, sitting on the bed in the spot Evan had just left. "This house is insane by the way. Nice find."

"Thanks," I responded, twisting the sheets under the covers. "I was just—"

"Finally!" Sara interrupted, coming into the room and shutting the door behind her. I wanted to groan, knowing I wouldn't be able to make them leave now. "I thought you'd never wake up. Now that the girls are here, we can finish that conversation we started last night." I opened my mouth to argue, but she stopped me. "Don't you dare. This is a big deal."

"What's a big deal?" Meg asked, looking from Sara to me.

"What's going on between you and Evan?" Sara began the interrogation.

I braced myself for the heart attack that was about to happen. I actually hoped it would, so I could avoid this conversation.

Serena pounced. "Why? What happened?"

I couldn't help it—I glanced at the door—and even though I couldn't see him, I knew he was listening.

"Umm...I don't know really," I answered evasively, trying to keep my voice quiet. "We're...talking."

"There's more than talking going on," Sara said. "I mean, I saw you guys last night at dinner."

I swallowed. *Please let me vanish right now. Please!*

"Has he kissed you?" Serena demanded.

"No," I answered quickly, trying not to think about the kiss he'd given me on the top of my head last night. My cheeks flamed in betrayal.

"Are you lying?" Sara accused. "Did you kiss him and not tell me?"

"I swear, I didn't kiss him," I answered adamantly.

"So how do you feel about him?" Meg asked. The girls quieted, leaning closer in anticipation. And I could have sworn the door opened wider.

"I'm not sure how to answer that," I said honestly, resigning myself to the conversation…and Evan listening. "It's been intense. A lot's happened, and I'm just trying to figure things out. It wouldn't be fair to either of us to start anything without fixing what went wrong to begin with."

"And what was that?" Meg asked.

"Me," I answered quietly, unable to look at any of them. "He doesn't trust me. And I have to earn that back if I want to try again."

"Do you—want to try again?" Serena asked excitedly.

I didn't want to answer this question, so I said, "I'm not ready." It was the only thing I knew to be true.

"Okay. What are we doing today?" I did my best to sound cheerful as I redirected the conversation. "I have to kick you guys out in a minute, because I really have to use the bathroom. But what's the plan, so I know what to wear?"

"We're going shopping," Sara announced. "And don't you dare sulk. You need some dresses."

"I disagree, but…whatever."

Meg stood, "Hurry up and get ready. We're going to brunch before we shop."

Serena hopped off the bed and followed after the girls. She turned to me before she left and said, "I like him, Emma...a lot. And I think you know exactly what you feel for him. Stop fighting it."

She shut the door behind her, leaving me staring.

The bathroom door eased open, and Evan stepped into the room just as I threw a pillow at him.

"Hey!" He caught it with a quick laugh. "What was that for?"

"You didn't have to listen, Evan!" I hissed, trying not to raise my voice.

He chuckled. "You were talking about me. Of course I was going to listen."

Her face was flushed all the way down her neck.

"They're relentless, aren't they?" I noted with a shake of my head. "I'm glad I'm not a girl."

Emma whipped the blankets back and got out of bed. "I can't believe you heard that."

It was hard not to laugh at her dramatic reaction. "You knew I was listening, Emma. And it's nice to know they don't hate me."

"Why would they hate you?" she asked. "You didn't do anything wrong."

I shrugged. "I know, but they're protective of you, and if they didn't like me it would suck."

She grinned. "Why do you want their approval?"

I'd said too much. "No reason."

"Liar."

"I'm going out through the patio to take a walk on the beach," I announced suddenly. "We don't want them to see me sneaking out of your room, do we? They may think we kissed or something." She threw another pillow at me.

"Shut up, Evan." Her cheeks were bright red.

I laughed, picking up my camera from her dresser.

"Have fun shopping." She stuck her tongue out at me just as I took the shot. I smiled at her small tantrum as she shut the bathroom door with force, adoring the fiery side that I had a tendency to bring out in her.

I was surprised that the girls hadn't spotted my camera on the dresser or my bag sitting on the chaise. They were probably too intent on drilling Emma to even notice.

Easing the gate open, I peered around the corner of the deck to make sure no one was outside. I quickly crossed to the steps and reached the beach just as I heard the screen door sliding open.

"Hey!" Sara called out, stopping me in my tracks.

I reluctantly spun around, knowing I'd been caught.

"You just came from Emma's room, didn't you?" she accused, her hands on her hips. I shrugged guiltily. "Evan, can we talk?"

"Sure," I said with a heavy breath.

Sara hopped down the steps, and I began walking alongside her, bracing myself.

"Did anything happen between you and Emma while I was away that I should know about?"

"No," I answered. "Nothing you should know about."

"Evan"—she scowled—"you know I just want to make sure she's okay."

"I know, Sara. I do. I heard everything."

"Why did you stay in her room? I don't understand what's up with you two."

"Neither do I," I replied. "And I'll tell you the same thing Emma did— we're just talking. That's it. And I have no idea where it's going, but please don't force her to figure out what she feels for me. I don't want to push her away again, especially when I'm getting to really know her for the first time ever."

Sara drew her brows together. "What does that mean?"

I considered how to explain it. "Emma's not the same as she was a couple weeks ago. Her eyes aren't vacant anymore. She doesn't look like she's about to break apart at any second. I can't really say what happened, but she's finally opening up and—"

"Becoming the Emma we used to know?"

"No." I shook my head. "She's not her either. I don't think she'll ever be her again. But I think she's trying to heal, to be better. She's letting me in, and she's never done that before. She's actually trusting me, and I don't

want to lose that because she's afraid of what might or might not happen between us. I know you care about her, and so do I. But I'm just asking you to back off a little. Let us figure it out."

"Do you trust her?" Sara asked.

I stared out at the ocean as we continued to walk. "I want to," I answered. "I really want to."

"But you don't," Sara concluded, hearing the reluctance in my voice. "That's not right Evan. You need to trust her enough to tell her what you went through when she left. If you don't tell her, then you're doing the same thing she did to you. She should know."

"She's already about to collapse from all the guilt that's been dumped on her her entire life," I argued. "She already knows I have nightmares. That's enough."

Sara's eyes tightened slightly. I hoped she wouldn't ask...

"But you can't expect her to open up and trust you with emotions and thoughts she's probably never expressed before, and then not trust her in return."

I hated it when Sara was right.

I about freaked when I saw Evan and Sara returning together. She knew he'd been in my room. I could tell when she shook her head at me as she climbed the steps to the deck. I sunk down in the chair, averting my eyes. I didn't get a chance to ask Evan what they talked about before he, James and Jared left for Nate's to help set up for another of their infamous parties.

When I returned from shopping with the girls, we spent the day on the beach. I threw on a pair of jeans and a tank top, along with my black Converse for the party. Sara scanned me up and down.

"We just bought some amazing dresses today, and you're wearing this? What am I going to do with you?" she sighed.

"Love me for who I am," I replied with a smirk.

"I do," Serena chimed in.

"Serena, don't encourage her," Sara said. "Besides, your wardrobe consists of black…and black."

I interceded. "I think Serena is very fashionable."

"So do I," Serena added defensively.

"Okay, I apologize, Serena. You do know how to mix up your black. But I'm sorry, Em. You need an intervention."

"Did James take your car, Serena, or did they go in the Scout?" Meg asked, avoiding any contribution to the attack on my fashion sense.

"Whose car is that anyway?" Serena asked. "It's pretty cool."

I hesitated, not wanting to answer her. Sara's eyes tightened when I spent way too much time tying my shoes.

"Emma Thomas, talk," she demanded impatiently.

"It's Evan's," I muttered, slowly standing up.

"I was wondering when we went to dinner last night," she said. "But why would Evan need a car in California?"

The fact that I was holding my breath said everything.

"No way."

"What?" Meg demanded, completely confused.

"Yes!" Serena practically leapt. "He's staying!"

"He's what?" Meg questioned, gawking at me.

"Evan transferred to Stanford," Sara stated, still staring at me. I nodded tentatively, waiting for her to explode. "Of course he transferred to Stanford."

"Why did you say it like that?" I questioned.

"Because, it just makes sense," she said, nodding slowly. "The conversation my mother had with Vivian last summer, about whether she should've allowed him to go to Stanford when he wanted to. She also said that she wasn't going to stand in his way this time, like he was going. But that was last year, so when he didn't switch schools last fall, I didn't think too much about it."

"So, he's been planning to move here for a while now?" Meg concluded.

"It was his first choice," I explained.

"So were you," Sara said, interrupting my breath. "Don't look at me like that, Emma. I think he would've come out here sooner if his parents hadn't basically locked him up."

"What are you talking about?" I demanded.

"They didn't allow him access to his money," Sara explained. "He didn't have a car on campus. They essentially put him under state arrest."

"They wouldn't let him travel?" I asked in shock, knowing how much that must have pissed him off. Evan traveled. That's what he did, every opportunity he had. So to be confined to Connecticut must have felt like prison.

"Not for a while, I guess. Not until last summer, from what my mother told me."

Wow, I mouthed. I'd interfered with his life so much more than I'd intended.

"Emma, you didn't do that to him," she consoled. "That was his parents' decision, okay? It's not your fault, so stop thinking it is."

I nodded, trying to release the winding guilt.

"But he needs to be the one to tell you all of this"—Sara sighed—"not me. He still should, even if you already know. If you decide you want to start over with him, he has to be honest too."

My shoulders sank. "You're right."

She usually was.

33. THE POOL THING

The street was already lined with cars when we reached Nate's that afternoon. Our conversation about Evan had delayed our departure.

"I love this already," Serena declared, shuffling through the crowd in the house to locate the source the guitar riffs out back.

"Hey, Emma!" Ren yelled from the bar across the room.

"Hey, Ren!" I waved without stopping, trying to keep up with Serena.

We stepped onto the deck to discover girls in various state of dress surrounding the pool.

"Wow, some of these girls have no shame," Meg surmised, scanning the oiled skin glistening in the sun.

"I think they have confidence," Serena countered. "Why be ashamed?"

"This coming from the girl with flawless alabaster skin," Meg teased.

"Who isn't afraid to walk through the house naked," I reminded Meg.

"She just does that to piss Peyton off." Meg laughed.

"Emma!" TJ hollered from the patio on the terrace below with a ridiculous smile on his face. "You're here!"

"Yes, I am," I hollered back, laughing.

"One of Evan's friends?" Sara noted.

I nodded.

"Finally, a party with decent music," Serena admired, bobbing her head to the band set up on the patio. "C'mon. Let's find the guys." She grabbed my hand to lead me down the stairs.

"Do you want a drink?" Meg asked when we reached the patio.

"Yes," Sara answered for all of us, heading toward the bar.

"Hey, guys," I said to Nate and Brent when we finally reached the front of the line.

"We were wondering when you were going to show up," Nate said, then noticed the girls next to me. "Hi, I'm Nate. And this is Brent."

Brent revealed his flirtatious smile and held out his hand when I returned the introduction.

"Emma, you look stunning," Brent complimented.

"Thanks," I replied, smiling back. The girls eyed me curiously.

"What can I get you lovely ladies to drink?" Brent offered, rubbing his hands together.

"Surprise us," Serena requested.

"Evan's with James and Jared. They're around here somewhere," Nate informed us after Brent lined up our drinks on the bar.

"Thanks!" Serena replied. She grabbed my arm with one hand while holding a blue-hued drink in her other.

We didn't have to look too hard. They were the guys every girl seemed to be staring at. It helped that they were also taller than just about everyone around them.

"Hey," I said, approaching Evan.

His breathtaking smile appeared as he said, "Hi. Glad you're here."

"Oh, we *have* to dance to this song," Serena exclaimed, taking the drink out of my hand and giving it to Evan before dragging me through the bodies toward the small stage. I glanced back at him in apology. Evan grinned and shrugged. In seconds the rocking crowd had swallowed us up.

Serena picked a spot in front of the band and began jumping to a cover of a popular alt rock song.

Uncertain how tender my cuts and blisters still were, I tentatively started bouncing on the balls of my feet.

"C'mon, Emma!"

Realizing I could handle it, I pushed off with more force, jumping alongside Serena as she thrust her arms in the air. Sara bounced her way toward us, her red hair flailing around her. Meg, who preferred her feet on the ground, laughed at our exuberance while rocking her hips.

"I'm not sure we're going to see them again," Jared said, watching Sara as she pogoed, tossing her head from side to side.

"The band will take a break eventually," I assured him.

"What are they drinking?" James asked, holding up the blue drink Serena left with him.

"It's a girl drink," I explained. "The guys come up with a special drink for the girls each party. It's usually super sweet and full of alcohol."

James took a sip and cringed. "Yeah, I'll stick to beer."

I laughed.

"How are things going with Emma?" Jared asked, not taking his eyes off Sara.

"It's complicated," I answered, taking a sip of my beer.

"Usually is with her," Jared said, making James chuckle.

"You're not surprised?" I asked James.

"She's… different," he responded, choosing his words carefully. "But I like her. She's not predictable."

"That she's not."

"That's why Evan likes her," Jared commented with a half smile. I let out a short laugh, recognizing the truth in his statement. "Well, whatever you've been doing, it seems to be working, because she doesn't look so messed up. She looks pretty good actually."

"Uh, nice, Jared," I said with a shake of my head. But he was right. I watched as her cheeks glowed pink, laughing at Serena jumping beside her.

I couldn't deny that she was beautiful, even in just jeans and a tank top. But then again, I thought the same thing when she woke up in the morning with her hair sticking up and pillow lines on her face.

"Hey, Evan," TJ bellowed across the pool, drawing my attention away from Emma. "Ren could use your help upstairs."

"I'll be right there," I yelled back. "I'll see you guys later." I looked down at the drink in my hand. "Could you give this to Emma?" I handed it to James, who balanced both drinks on the palm of his hand.

I left them and headed into the house, where the demands of the party kept me busy for a while. More people showed up for this party than for any of the others so far. Somehow, I'd gotten suckered into helping once again, even though I had nothing to do with planning this party. In fact, I wasn't even staying in the house anymore.

Emma came over to say hi, but I wasn't able to talk to her because it was so busy. I tried to break away several times, but it just didn't happen. I scanned the room in search of one of the guys, getting more irritated by the minute.

"Hi." A slender blonde greeted from the other side of the bar.

"Hi," I said without really looking at her as I continued to keep an eye out for someone to take my place. "What can I get you?"

"I'll have a beer," she requested. As I was reaching into the tub, she continued, "You're Evan, right?"

"Yeah," I confirmed, flipping the top off the bottle and handing it to her.

"I'm Nika." She took the bottle from me. "I know you guys from surfing."

I finally focused on her, and vaguely recognized her dark brown eyes and sun-bleached hair. I was pretty sure she was one of the girls Brent kept trying to get a number from. "That's right. Glad you could make it."

"Me too." She smiled. "Maybe I'll talk to you later."

"Sure," I replied, looking past her to the guy in the baseball hat.

"Nice, Evan," Ren nudged, emptying ice into the tub.

"What are you talking about, and where the hell have you been? I need to be done here."

"Come on," he said with a chuckle. "That girl's totally into you."

"Whatever. Will you cover for me?"

"I need to get some more ice, and then I'll be right back," he promised.

When I was finally relieved at the bar, I cut through the tightly packed room to the deck. I searched the faces until I located Emma and Meg on the far side of the pool, talking and laughing about something. I made my way down the stairs toward them.

Nika suddenly appeared in front of me when I stepped onto the patio. "I was wondering if you were ever going to come out from behind the bar."

"Oh, hey, it's good to see you again," I told her, glancing around for Emma in the dense crowd around the pool.

"Are you staying at this house with the rest of the guys?" she inquired, apparently determined to have a conversation.

"I'm staying at a place about five minutes from here."

"Is it just as nice?"

"Um, it's a great place, right on the beach," I explained, trying to give her enough eye contact so that I wasn't insulting her, while subtly tracing along the pool's edge for a purple top and short brown hair.

"I'd love to see it," Nika stated.

She was a very attractive girl, and if I were Brent, I'd be thrilled she was giving me the time of day—but I wasn't Brent, and she was the wrong girl.

"Maybe we'll have a party sometime," I told her. "Do you know Emma Thomas… from surfing?"

"Uh, yeah. I actually just brought her here a few days ago, after we found her on the beach."

"Well, I'm glad you were there to help her out."

"She's dating Cole, right?"

"No. She's not," I replied. My jaw twitched slightly just thinking about them together. "She's staying at the same house I am. Does she have your number?"

"I think she does," she responded, with an undertone of disappointment. "Are you—"

"Evan!" Serena beckoned from behind Nika. Serena's eyes flickered between the two of us, silently assessing. "We were looking for you."

"Sorry, I've been stuck upstairs," I told her.

"Hi, I'm Serena," she said to Nika, sliding in beside me and wrapping her arms around mine. Not waiting for Nika to be introduced, she continued, "I'm going to steal Evan now."

Before she could drag me away, I heard a quick yelp, followed by a splash in the pool.

"Oh no," Serena groaned, pulling me after her.

"I can't believe I didn't see that coming," I gasped as Meg popped up next to me.

"I think you were a little distracted," Meg teased. "And now I'm one up on you."

"I don't know what you're talking about," I defended, my face flaming up at being caught watching Evan talk to Nika.

A spray of water interrupted us when someone else jumped into the pool. TJ surfaced, wearing his charismatic smile.

"Want some company?" he asked, swimming across to us.

And just like that, bodies began crashing into the water with hollers and cries of resistance. Guys wrestled each other into the pool, landing on screaming girls. I ducked under the surface, trying to reach the ladder and remove myself from the chaos.

I reached for the rung of the ladder just as someone grabbed my ankle and pulled me back under. I kicked to the surface, and when I spun around to see who'd done it, I noticed Brent swimming away. I turned back toward the ladder and came face to face with Evan. He seemed just as startled as I was.

"Hi." He smiled, causing my heart to stutter as the water dripped from his disheveled brown hair down his chiseled face.

"Hi," I said, with a blushing grin.

"I heard you did this," he said, nodding toward the havoc in the pool.

"This one was Meg!" I defended myself. I was nudged toward Evan by two guys who were struggling to dunk each other. He slid back to the corner to avoid them. I floated after him.

"Meg doesn't seem the type to start trouble." He moved over to allow room for me along the wall.

"Oh, and I am?" I said, trying to sound offended.

Evan smirked. "Yeah, you have a reputation. And this isn't the first time I've ended up in the pool with my clothes on because of you."

"True," I replied, a flush rising to my cheeks. I couldn't look away from his steel-blue eyes as he drifted closer. He lingered in front of me, scanning my face like he was looking for an answer… or permission. My pulse raced when he set his hand on my hip. I gripped the side of the pool to keep afloat. I couldn't breathe as he moved closer—and then he was gone. I whipped around in search of him.

"Hey, Emma." Brent smiled from where Evan used to be. And then he was dragged under himself. This was my cue to get out of the pool, needing some distance after yet another *moment* with Evan.

"How did you not get thrown in?" I asked Serena and Sara, who sat in chairs around a table, observing the bedlam.

Sara's eyes glinted. "They know better."

"But *you* look ridiculous," Serena laughed, pointing to the jeans that hung from my hips, the weight of the water stretching them over my shoes. I attempted to pull them up, but it was useless.

"Time to go?" Meg confirmed from behind me.

"I think you've made your contribution to the party," Serena stated, handing her keys to Meg. "But I'm going to stay a while longer."

"Me too," Sara added.

"Well…have fun," I said. Meg and I left the girls and walked along the edge of the house.

"Are you leaving?" Evan called after us, running to catch up.

I indicated my uncooperative jeans with a slight tug and said, "I can't stay like this. We're heading back to the house. We'll see you there."

"I'll come back with you. Actually, I'll meet you out front. I'm going to give my key to Sara so she and Serena can get back later with the guys."

"Okay," Emma replied, continuing toward the front of the house.

I found Sara and Serena seated by the posts of the deck, laughing at the spectacle.

"Sara, use my truck whenever you want to drive back," I told her, handing her the key.

"How are you getting there?" she questioned curiously.

"I'm leaving now with Meg and Emma."

Serena grinned. I could only imagine what she was thinking.

"Okay. I guess we'll see you in a bit," Sara replied. I took off to find Meg and Emma, but stopped short when I reached the sidewalk. The girls were removing their jeans and placing them in a black trash bag.

"Hey, Evan." Meg noticed me. "No wet pants in the car—it's our rule."

"Huh?" I responded, having a hard time taking my eyes off Emma's exposed legs. I blinked and focused on Meg's face.

"You need to take off your pants if you're getting in the car," she explained.

I raised my eyebrows.

"Or you don't have to drive back with us," Emma stated. She had to know exactly what seeing her standing in just a tank top and her underwear was doing to me. This ride might kill me.

"No, it's…okay," I conceded reluctantly. I took a quick breath and peeled off my jeans, dropping them in the bag Meg held open, and placing my shoes in the trunk among the cleats and soccer balls. With my eyes on Emma, I said, "You know what, you might as well as have this wet shirt too."

Emma stared at me with her mouth open. Meg looked between us, shaking her head. "Whatever."

"You're evil," Emma grumbled.

"Hey, you broke the truce," I grinned, stripping my shirt off. I laughed when Emma turned her back to me, concealing her flushed cheeks.

"You can drive," Meg said, handing me the key before throwing the trash bag in the trunk.

Emma sat on the passenger side, waiting. I caught a glimpse of her lean, muscular legs leading up to the black fabric of her underwear. Meg climbed into the back while I held the seat forward. I was oblivious to her revealed skin as she scooted by me, too distracted by the half-naked body in the front seat.

"Why are you driving?" Emma demanded in a panic when I got in the car.

I shrugged. "Meg asked me to."

"Meg!" Emma groaned.

"What did I do?" Meg asked, completely confused. "What is wrong with you guys? It's not like you're naked. Stop acting weird and just drive, Evan."

Emma turned her attention away from me.

The radio blared when I started the car. Emma whipped around and shouted at the same time as Meg, "David Bowie!" but then Emma finished with, "'Young Americans.'"

"You suck," Meg shot back. "I couldn't get the song out fast enough."

I had no idea what just happened. All I knew was that Emma's thigh was suddenly inches from my hand on the stick shift —and I couldn't breathe. I forced my eyes to remain on the road. Any diversion in my current attire would not be good. "What was that about?"

"It's what we do when the car starts or someone changes the station, we see who can name the artist and song the fastest," Meg explained. "It's just something between Emma and me."

"Like the pool thing?"

"Exactly." Emma laughed. "Like the pool thing."

Her laugh made me glance over at her—bad idea. All I could see was skin. I tightened my grip on the steering wheel, fighting for control. What the hell was I going to do when I saw her in a bathing suit?

When we pulled into the driveway, I released the air in my lungs. I let Meg and Emma go in ahead of me, offering to get the bag of clothes from the trunk to give myself time to recover. The girls were in the living room by the time I'd changed into dry clothes.

"Evan, do you want to watch a movie when everyone gets back?" Meg asked.

"Sure," I responded. "Are you guys hungry?"

"What are you cooking?" Emma asked excitedly.

"Nothing," I answered with a chuckle. "Thought we'd order pizza. Or maybe you could cook."

"Pizza!" Meg declared. "Emma will burn the house down."

"Hey!" Emma shot back. "I've mastered grilled cheese."

"That's a feat," I teased. Emma picked up a pillow and threw it at me. I easily caught it, laughing.

My mind wandered to the pillow fight Emma and I'd had years ago. I was tempted to retaliate to make it happen again.

"So, Evan, I heard you're a Stanford boy now," Meg said, redirecting my attention.

Evan turned toward Meg, taking his taunting grin with him. I had a feeling I knew what he was thinking about, clutching that pillow in his hand. "Yeah, I guess I am."

Everyone else arrived right after the pizza did. And thankfully we'd ordered a lot. Jared and James practically ate an entire pizza each.

I sat on the plush rug in front of the couch after we'd finished eating, while Evan stood in front of the TV, flipping through the movie titles on the screen.

"Come on, Meg," Serena called to her, plopping down on James's lap on the love seat, hanging her long legs over the other side of the arm.

Sara giggled at something Jared whispered in her ear—which was exactly why I'd chosen the floor. Meg plopped down next to them with a huge bowl of popcorn as Evan selected the movie.

"You can sit on the chair," he encouraged when he turned to find me on the rug.

"I'm comfortable," I assured him, clutching a pillow to my chest. Evan hesitated, then sat down in the chair himself and clicked off the light.

The images from the television filled the room with moving light. There was another low giggle behind me, and I scooted closer to Evan's chair, leaning against the space next to his legs.

As the movie progressed, exhaustion settled in. I dozed off with my face leaning against Evan's leg.

When I woke, the room was dark, and I was lying on the bed. I felt Evan's breath on my neck, and with my lips turned up ever so faintly, I settled back to sleep within his embrace.

34. JUST DON'T THINK ABOUT IT

I don't think I should sleep in here anymore," Evan announced as soon as I stepped out of the bathroom.

I stared at him in confusion. "You don't want to sleep with me anymore?"

Evan let out an awkward laugh. "That's the problem."

"What do you mean?"

Evan smoothed the covers over his lap, leaning his head back against the headboard to scan the ceiling, struggling with how to explain it to me.

"Just tell me." I sat on the edge of the bed next to his feet.

"It's...difficult," he muttered. "We're still figuring everything out...this thing between us. But when the only time I get to touch you is in this bed, listening to you breathe, smelling your hair, feeling your...it's...not easy."

"Oh," I uttered, hit in the face with his meaning. My heart thrust to life at just the thought of his warm body pressed against my back. "Yeah, I know."

"So, it would probably be best if I slept upstairs from now on," he repeated.

"Um, okay," I said hesitantly. "If that's what you think."

"You don't?" he questioned in surprise. "Am I the only one being tortured here?"

Heat spread across my face as I shook my head.

"It's hard enough not to kiss you..." Evan began.

"Okay, I understand," I said in a rush, not wanting him to continue, not wanting the thought of kissing him in my head. I clenched my eyes closed—too late.

"So, I'll take my stuff upstairs." He said it as a statement, but there was this hint of questioning in his tone that made me look up at him.

"Yup," I answered awkwardly. Evan grabbed his bag from the chaise and his camera from the dresser.

He hesitated at the door, gave me a tight smile, and shut it behind him.

I collapsed on the bed, relieving my lungs with the air they were deprived of during that exchange. What had just happened? We basically admitted to wanting each other, without saying we wanted each other. That was the most awkward moment...ever.

Sara entered without knocking and closed the door behind her. She sat down next to my sprawled body.

"So, I just saw Evan walk by with his bag," she said. "Did you get in a fight or something?"

"No." I sighed.

"Then what's going on?"

I stalled a moment. "Do you remember in high school when you asked me if I thought I'd have sex with Evan, when we first started dating? After you asked, that's all I could think about, because *you* made me think about it."

Sara started laughing. "Yeah, that was hysterical. You couldn't even function around him for like a week, and I was convinced your face was going to remain red forever."

"Yeah," I mumbled. "Anyway..."

"Wait, did you have sex with Evan?"

"No," I shot back loudly.

"But you want to?" she blurted again, not allowing me to explain.

I buried my face in the blanket and screamed in frustration.

"Omigod, you do," Sara concluded. "Wow. I didn't think you two were *there* yet."

"We're not really *anywhere*…yet," I argued. "It's just…well, he won't be sleeping in here anymore."

Sara produced a wide smile. "Right."

"Sara, stop looking at me like that."

"You two are ridiculous. Figure your shit out so you can get on with your lives together already." She gave me a weirdly sympathetic look, then got up from the bed. "The girls will be here soon. We figured we'd spend the day on the beach."

I nodded faintly, still stunned by how forward she was with things that I still couldn't admit to myself.

And just like that… we were back in high school again. I couldn't look at Evan, or be within three feet of him, without my body kicking into hyperalert. I couldn't stop thinking about him, even when he was standing right in front of me. And basically, my conflicted brain wasn't capable of doing anything about it.

"Emma?" I called to her again as she stared off in the distance. She blinked her eyes, snapping out of it.

"Huh?" She gazed up at me with her brown eyes wide and cheeks pink.

"The girls were looking for you," I told her. "They're in the kitchen getting lunch together."

"Okay, thanks," she said quickly, shifting her eyes away from mine before slipping off the hammock. She ran her fingers through her hair to flatten it, still unable to look at me. I watched her curiously as she entered the house.

"Emma," Sara said impatiently, "go shower and then come help us."

"I'm going," I heard Emma reply.

As I walked into the house, I could hear the sound of the cabinets closing in the kitchen.

"They're going to be okay, right?" Serena asked.

With the music playing in the living room, they obviously hadn't heard me come in. Not sure what to do, I turned and started for the stairs.

"They'll figure out they can't live without each other eventually," Sara concluded. They were oblivious, not realizing that their voices carried through the kitchen opening, echoing off the tall ceilings. They had no idea how well they could be heard out here.

"Really? You think they're going to forgive and forget?" Meg questioned skeptically. "I think they're only going to keep hurting each other if they can't just be fricken honest. Emma's two steps from going over a cliff if she doesn't open up and let someone help her."

I grabbed the railing as I tripped on a step.

"That's not true. She's getting better. I can tell," Serena said passionately. "Besides, it's obvious they love each other. I mean, look at them. She was only half a person when they were apart. She's different now."

"And what happens if he doesn't forgive her? And ends up walking away?" Meg challenged.

"Dude, what are you doing?" Jared asked from the top of the stairs. I stared up at him and clenched my teeth, silently begging him to keep his mouth shut. We both overheard Sara say, "I wish we could force them to be completely honest with each other."

Jared laughed. "You're listening to them talk about you. Nice."

I rushed up the stairs, convinced they'd heard him. "Shut up, Jared. I wasn't doing it on purpose."

"Yeah, right," he chided. "You were totally eavesdropping. But I don't blame you. I mean, if they were talking about me, I'd absolutely listen. Wait. Were they talking about me?"

"No," I said, with a shake of my head. "You're evidently not as fucked up as Emma and me. Besides, I wouldn't stick around to listen to Sara go on about how incredible you are."

"She said that?" He grinned proudly.

"No," I scoffed.

"If you're done eavesdropping, I brought that huge duffel bag with the sports gear that you asked me to bring. Wanna toss a football around or something? I think James is out on the beach already."

"Sure, but let me see if the girls are all set first." I headed back down stairs noisily, so that this time they knew we were coming.

The girls were eerily quiet when I poked my head into the kitchen. "Need any help?"

Meg and Sara kept their expressions neutral, but Serena's eyes sparkled mischievously. I looked at her questioningly. A smile broke across her face, which prompted a sharp elbow jab from Meg. "Ow! What was that for?"

"No, we're all set for now," Sara told me. "You guys can bring everything out in a little bit."

"We'll be on the beach," I said, leaving them to continue contemplating our fate.

I eyed the dress Sara had hung on the back of the bathroom door. I used to enjoy raiding Sara's closet, and letting her style me—as terrifying as it was at times. But now it wasn't the same. I wasn't the same. I hadn't worn a dress since *that night*—except to my mother's funeral. And considering I could barely function, I didn't exactly have a choice.

I knew she was trying to reach me, to make me better somehow. "Oh, Sara." I sighed, pulling it off the hanger. "I'll wear the dress."

After drying my hair and tugging the short skirt one more time, I found the girls in the kitchen.

Sara's eyes lit up when she saw me—and that look was worth the discomfort.

"So, what do you need me to do?"

"Take this out to the table," Meg instructed, handing me a pitcher and cups.

"Hey," Jared said from the patio door. "Sara, I got your text. What do you need help with?"

"We're getting ready to eat, so can you and the guys bring every-thing out to the table? And can you put the umbrella up?"

"No problem."

I walked up the stairs after Jared told us lunch was ready. I just about fell over when I saw Emma leaning up on her toes, helping Jared secure the umbrella with the pin. She was wearing a white strapless dress with yellow flowers printed on it. I ran my eyes down her slender arms, extended above her, to the soft angles of her shoulders. The fabric clung to her curves until it flared out to reveal the length of her sculpted legs.

I finally got "Do you need help?" out of my mouth. But they were done. Emma turned toward me; her cheeks perked in color and she smiled slightly. I grinned and got caught in her eyes before I heard Jared say impatiently, "Evan? Hello? Go inside and get food."

"Alright," I said. "I like the dress," I whispered as I passed her. She ran a hand down its skirt, trying to add another inch to its revealing hemline.

"Evan, bring out the tray of sandwiches," Sara instructed. Each of the girls passed me with something in her hands. By the time I'd returned with the tray, there was only one place left to sit—and I shouldn't have been surprised that it was the one next to Emma.

If this was their way of backing off, the girls needed a few tips on sub-tlety.

Emma leaned away from me when I sat down. I glanced at her out of the corner of my eye, and she kept fidgeting, like she was nervous to be near me. It reminded of that time in high school…

I started laughing.

"What's so funny?" Serena asked.

I shook my head. "Nothing. Would you mind handing me the pitcher?"

We were clearing the table after lunch when his chest brushed against my back as he leaned over to pick up the bowl of chips.

"Excuse me," he said in my ear, sending a thrilling shiver down my spine. I glanced over at him, and he grinned that amused grin that sent a shot of adrenaline straight into my heart. I leaned away, needing space between us before my knees gave out. He smiled wider.

"Are you going tell me what's so funny?" I asked.

"You," he answered and walked away.

I scowled and watched him as he left, not liking his answer.

"What's wrong?" Meg asked, following my gaze. I shook off her question and handed her a stack of plates.

When the girls came back out, Sara was gripping the handle of a small metal case. Evan exited with James and Jared a moment later, spinning a football on his palm.

"You girls want to play football?" Evan offered.

I opened my mouth to accept, but Sara intercepted with, "No, you guys go ahead. We're having girl time."

"Girl time?" I questioned warily.

"Yes," Meg replied. "Pedicures. What color polish do you want, Emma?"

I watched enviously as the guys continued down to the beach, Jared jogging out for a pass.

"How about pink?" Sara suggested.

"I don't do pink anymore," I blurted quickly. And Sara knew this.

"Maybe it's time you gave it another try too," she said, looking me directly in the eye.

"I think you would look good in pink," Serena noted sweetly.

"I think you would look good in color," Sara said, directing her attention to Serena. "Would you please let me do a makeover for you?"

"No thanks, Sara," Serena replied. "I'm fond of my monochromatic individuality."

Sara sighed. "Will you at least let me paint your toes red?"

"Yes, that you can do." Serena smiled.

"How about purple for me?" I suggested to Meg, who was filtering through Sara's caddy of polish. "And Sara, who brings a box of nail polish on vacation?"

"What are we doing tonight?" Meg asked.

"Let's see if the guys want to hang out," Sara said. "We can play cards or something."

"Or we could play truth or dare!" Serena suggested.

"Because we're twelve?" Meg responded, shooting her down.

"Why not poker?" I offered, sitting back in the lounge chair to give Meg access to my toes.

"Oh, and Meg, I'll do your toes. Emma sucks at it," Sara announced.

She was right. I couldn't paint my toes without getting it on the surrounding skin, no matter how much I concentrated. I could paint the smallest details of a tree on a canvas, but I couldn't master my toes—as pathetic as that was.

"What about strip poker?" Serena chirped.

"What is it with you and these games?" Meg demanded. "You have a boyfriend. Why would you want to get naked in front of other guys, or see them naked?"

"It's more about the truth part," Serena said carefully.

Sara suddenly stopped what she was doing. "Come with me, Serena," she ordered. "Em, you stay here and finish your toes. We'll right back."

"I'll be right there. I'm going to get James," Serena replied.

"What the hell just happened?" I asked, completely lost and slightly annoyed.

"We forgot we were going to make dessert, and since you suck at cooking too, just hang out here." Meg lied terribly.

They were up to something. That much was obvious. I was just afraid to find out what it was.

Jogging up the steps in search of water, I found Emma with her knee bent and her short dress tucked between her legs, concentrating on painting her toes. She grimaced in frustration and wiped the toe clean with a damp tissue.

"Stupid toes. Who cares if they're painted anyway?" she huffed under her breath. The corner of my mouth rose.

"Where are the girls?"

"I don't know," she griped. "Conspiring or something."

"Need some help?" I asked, nodding toward her toes.

"You really want to paint my toes?"

"I could probably do a better job than you are," I teased, making her narrow her eyes at me.

"Go for it," she said, thrusting the purple bottle at me.

I sat at the bottom of the lounge chair. "Purple, huh?" I noted. "Not pink?"

A rush of color filled her face. "I haven't…" She looked away. "Pink's my chocolate," she whispered.

I raised my eyes to meet hers. The sorrow that reflected in them was difficult to witness. I nodded in understanding and looked back down at her feet, not knowing what to say.

I gently set her foot against my leg and dabbed the brush on the lip of the bottle. "Here," I said, handing her the bottle so I could hold her toe. I bent over and concentrated on her feet, doing my best not to glance at the legs attached to them.

When I looked up to get more polish, Emma was watching me, intent and perfectly still. I grinned and her cheeks pinked. The color still looked stunning on her, regardless.

"You can breathe, Emma," I teased. "Stop thinking about me naked and breathe."

"Evan!" she hollered, yanking her foot away. I started laughing. I knew if she'd had something to throw at me, she would've. Then I eyed the nail polish bottle in her hand and jumped up.

"Don't throw that at me," I begged. "I was just messing with you. You've been so tense since our talk this morning. I figured I'd make you relax a little."

"That's not how you do it," she lectured, crossing her arms defiantly. I chuckled.

"Stop thinking about it," I told her, trying to keep my tone light. "It'll only make it worse. Think about every reason why I won't kiss you."

Her eyes dipped. "Right," she whispered, her shoulders sinking.

I grimaced. Wrong thing to say. "I didn't mean it like that. I just meant—"

"It's okay," she said, raising her eyes to me. I smiled apologetically. "Will you please finish my toes?"

"Sure. I only have a couple left." I sat back down and eased Emma's foot onto my thigh.

"What the hell are you doing, Evan?"

I looked up to find Sara glaring at me like I was violating some girl code or something. "Finishing what you started," I told her, painting the last toe. I eased Emma's foot onto the chair before twisting the brush in the bottle. "There you go. All… purple."

Emma smiled softly, meeting my gaze. "Thank you," she said sincerely. I nodded and took off into the house.

"Hey, Evan," Meg called to me as I passed her and Serena on the couch. "Do you think the guys would be up for playing cards tonight?"

"I can ask."

They looked at each other in a mischievous exchange. Emma was right. They were up to something.

35. BRUTAL HONESTY

TJ, we are not listening to that shit all night," Jared threatened, setting a speaker from the entertainment room on the patio.

"We'll let the girls decide," TJ stated. "And where are they? Thought you'd show up together."

"They're on their way. And you're going to be outnumbered, TJ," I told him. "Meg's the only one who's going to be on your side."

"Sara—"

"Has a wall of electric guitars," Jared finished.

"Whatever. We'll put your music on when they get here," TJ conceded reluctantly.

"Welcome, ladies." I could hear Brent in the kitchen, greeting the girls in his ineffectively flirtatious tone. "Hope you're ready for margaritas and poker."

"Which is now." Jared smirked at TJ, and the music instantly changed.

The screen on the deck slid open, and Brent led the girls down to the patio, carrying two pitchers. I was pushing in chairs around the poker table when Emma came into view. I knew I should keep my distance. But it was virtually impossible. I was drawn to her, needing to be near her, whether it was the right thing or not.

"Hi," I said with a grin when she reached the bottom step.

"Hi." She smiled brightly.

"I still think we should play strip poker," Brent announced, setting a pitcher of margaritas on each table.

"I like that idea!" Serena declared. Emma looked at both of them like they were crazy. "What, Em?! Regular poker can be so boring if you suck. This could make it more interesting."

"I've told you how much I love you, right?" Brent told Serena, putting his arm around her shoulder. Then he eyed James staring him down, and moved away. "Sorry, man."

"You actually want to play strip poker?" I asked, waiting for James to react. He didn't.

"Serena has no objection to walking around nude," Meg offered as an explanation.

"Strip poker?" Jared questioned, not exactly sold on the idea either.

"With a twist," Serena suddenly added.

"We play five-card draw. You can replace all of your cards except for one, then everyone lays them down, and whoever wins chooses two people. These people can elect to remove an article of clothing or answer a difficult question," James suddenly explained.

"You're in on this?" I blurted.

"Serena brought it up, and I suggested a few rule changes so there's an option to keep clothes on," he said nonchalantly. "Not exactly stoked about having my girl naked in front of these guys, no matter how comfortable she is in her skin. And another rule: if you touch a girl, I break your face." He stared at Brent, whose eager smile deflated.

"Sure, why not." Emma and Jared both didn't look very happy with Sara agreeing to this. "Don't worry. I'm good at poker, remember?" Sara assured Jared.

"You'd better be prepared to be very honest tonight," Jared said. Sara kissed him on the cheek and smiled.

"I told you they were up to something," Emma mumbled under her breath.

"We don't have to play," I offered.

"It's okay," she assured me. "Everyone seems to want to do it, so why not? I can answer questions, I guess."

The honesty part was probably going to be harder for Emma than taking off her clothes.

"Are you sure?"

"Yeah, it'll be fine," she responded without conviction.

"TJ!" Two girls squealed from the top step.

"Hey!" TJ hollered back. "Perfect timing. We're about to play a new game. It's a version of strip poker, with truth or dare thrown in."

"Strip or truth," Nate presented.

"Ooh, sounds fun!" the girl with the high ponytail exclaimed with way too much excitement.

"See, they do sell shorts that short," Emma murmured next to me.

"They looked better on you," I said automatically. She smacked my arm and walked away.

"Who are those girls?" Sara asked Meg as I approached them by the poker tables.

"I don't know. Friends of TJ's, I guess," Meg said. "Do we still want to do this?"

"If this is your idea of making things somehow better between us, then it sucks," I interjected.

"It's just a game," Sara said, trying to convince me. "It won't be some tortured confess-your-sins thing, I promise."

People began to sit while TJ made the introductions. "This is Darcy and Kim. Darcy and Kim, this is… everyone."

"Hi," they waved in unison, flanking TJ.

"Would it be okay if we shut off the lights?" Emma requested.

Nate shut off the patio and pool lights, plunging us into the dark of the hills until he lit a couple of candles. This allowed everyone's faces to be seen, only giving a hint to what lay below the shoulders.

"Better?" Sara asked. "Are you going to play?"

I bit my lip, and nodded. But I wasn't sure what was going to be more torturous, seeing Evan without a shirt, or having to be completely honest about humiliating moments in my life.

"Will you just answer questions with me?" I leaned over and asked Evan, who was seated beside me.

He grinned. "Yeah, I can do that."

I was trying to counter the girls' not-so-subtle attempts to interfere with what was happening between Evan and me. As much as it was comforting that the girls cared and wanted me to be happy, they really had no idea just how complicated things were.

"A five-articles-of-clothing limit, and we have to alternate seats, boy girl," Serena explained.

"But I only have on one," the blonde in the yellow dress pouted.

Sara opened her mouth to say something, and from the glint in her eyes, it wasn't to offer her more clothes. TJ interrupted her assault with, "You can count shoes and earrings, Kim."

"Oh, good idea. Thanks TJ!"

Emma covered her mouth, trying to stifle a laugh.

Nate shuffled two decks together, and I noticed Emma bouncing her leg anxiously, biting at her lip.

"Here, this will help." Brent handed her a margarita, pulling in his chair so it about touched hers. Emma hesitated, then took a large gulp.

I shot Brent a warning glance, and he scooted his chair toward Kim.

TJ's "friends" seemed more interested in taking off their clothes than answering questions, so in no time, they were stripped down and in the pool, with TJ and Brent in quick pursuit. So far, the questions hadn't been horribly invasive, but then again, I hadn't been asked any either.

Then, with Serena's first win, she asked, "Emma and Evan, strip or truth?"

I braced myself. "Truth."

"Truth," Evan concurred.

"What was your favorite high-school moment?" Serena asked, eyeing the two of us.

She was really doing this to me, wasn't she?

"That's not a very revealing question," Darcy complained.

"Hey! No feedback from the naked losers in the pool!" Sara hollered.

I knew what she was doing, trying to get me to recall a moment with Evan, but I wasn't going to give in to her ploy. "The night of my first football game. I stayed at Sara's, and she performed one of her notorious makeovers. I even let her cut my hair."

"You did that?" Evan said to Sara.

"Yes, I did," Sara said proudly.

"Nice." Evan nodded, his eyes distant in remembrance. "The night pink became my favorite color."

I sat very still, trying hard not to react. Sara smiled, her eyes twinkling. "My fault."

Evan laughed lightly.

I needed to cool my cheeks with the frozen drink. Evan was playing right into their meddling.

"What are you doing?" I pleaded. His eyes flickered in confusion.

"Evan?" Serena prompted, pulling him away from trying to read my expression. "What was yours?"

"My favorite moment wasn't actually at school. It was the night of SATs." Before I could elaborate, Emma started coughing, loudly. When she excused herself from the table, I went after her.

As soon as I got near enough, her coughs ceased.

"Evan, seriously, what are you doing?"

"What? You said to answer questions."

"But you don't have to be so honest," *she said in a yelling whisper.*

"Emma, they'll have no idea what I'm talking about. Besides, I think honesty might do us some good right now," I pointed out. "What do we have to lose?"

She stared at me in shock, unable to believe I'd just said that. I was wondering where it came from myself.

"You want honesty?" she challenged. She walked over to the table, gripped the back of her chair and announced, "I want to retract my answer."

"I knew I wasn't your favorite high-school moment." Sara grinned knowingly.

"I was in the Art room, and Evan had just returned from San Francisco and—"

"That's all they need to know," I interrupted, suddenly understanding her aversion to too much honesty.

"I get it," I whispered as we sat back down.

"Thought you would," she teased.

"Okay, then," Jared intercepted. "Whose turn to deal?"

"I'll deal," I said.

Meg won the next hand and chose Evan and Jared. Jared took off his shirt, and Evan opted to answer a question. The way the questions were going, I thought I'd rather deal with him taking off his shirt.

"If you had to choose between Jared and Emma, who would you choose?"

Evan stared at her in disbelief with his mouth open. "What kind of question is that?"

"A difficult one—that's the point."

Evan stalled, flipping his eyes between me and Jared. Every time he opened his mouth, nothing came out.

"Meg, that's an impossible question," Sara accused, trying to take the pressure off Evan.

Jared was struck with the conflict that Evan was having about the same time I was, and we stared at him in amazement.

"It's your brother, right?" I prodded, my voice low. "It's okay, Evan."

But he continued to struggle with the answer.

"Well, it's a good thing we aren't trapped in a fire." Jared laughed. "We'd both be done for if Evan was standing outside, deciding who to go in after."

"Forget that one, Evan," Meg said, her eyes smiling. "We don't want you to give yourself an aneurysm deciding. How about this—what was your first impression of Emma?"

"Meg!" I yelped. She grinned.

Serena leaned in closer, awaiting his answer. I flipped the card that was in front of me over on the table, unable to make eye contact with anyone.

"More margarita?" Nate offered, holding out a fresh pitcher to top off my glass.

"Thanks," I accepted, starting to feel the effects of the first two glasses, but not enough to ease the anxiety in my stomach.

"The first time she spoke to me, she told me off," Evan said.

"I didn't tell you off," I defended myself.

"Yes, you did," Sara said, followed by laughs from the spectators. "It was the first time the class had ever heard you argue with anyone. It was crazy." She looked to Evan and said, "Sorry. Go ahead."

"She had me from the beginning. Her tenacity intrigued me, and I wanted to know everything about her," Evan said. "Still do," he added under his breath so only I could hear him. I took a sip from my glass.

Meg won the next round too, still completely clothed.

"What's something you know about Sara that no one else knows?" she asked Jared, who was down to his shorts.

"She has a birthmark on her inner thigh," Jared blurted without hesitating. Sara shrugged.

"Sara, what's one thing about Emma that no one else knows?"

Sara studied Emma, contemplating all the secrets she knew as Emma's cheeks turned red in anticipation.

"*In seventh grade, right after she moved to Weslyn, she accidentally caught Ms. Flynn's sweater on fire when we were working in the bio lab for extra credit after school.*" Emma sank in her chair, shielding her eyes in embarrassment. "*She put it out before Ms. Flynn returned to the classroom. The best part was that she hung the sweater on the back of her chair like nothing happened, and the next day Ms. Flynn wore it in class with a burn hole on the back.*"

Jared laughed. "*How the hell did you catch her sweater on fire?*"

"*She was trying to show me how to burn off lint balls, and it was pretty cool at first, then it just started burning.*" Sara giggled.

"*Yeah. That happened,*" Emma admitted, glancing at me out of the corner of her eye.

"*It made me laugh so hard,*" Sara recalled, "*I knew I had to be friends with her after that.*"

"*Wow,*" I said with a grin. Emma bit on her lip.

We continued playing, and I won the next hand, selecting Meg and Sara, who nonchalantly removed their shorts. As retribution, Jared selected Emma and Serena when he won his next hand. When Serena removed her shorts, revealing the length of her ivory legs, James protectively set his hand on her pale thigh.

"Truth," I selected, relieved that Jared was doing the asking.

"If you could get away with one illegal thing, what would it be?" he asked playfully.

In a flash, all I could see was blood, and the disfigured face lying motionless on the floor. I felt the blood rushing from my face. Meg looked at me curiously. I rubbed my damp palms on the skirt of my dress.

A cold sweat broke out along my spine. I pushed away from the table and walked away without saying a word.

"Emma!" Sara called after me.

I didn't look back. I needed to shut down the rush of images. Jonathan punching the guy over and over again. The blood smeared on the floor when he picked him up. My hands clutching the steering wheel as Jonathan wiped the car of fingerprints. It was the one secret that I'd been able to keep closed off, locked in the deepest bowels of repression—only to be released by one harmless question.

"Emma!" Sara yelled again, running to catch up as I reached the sidewalk. "What was that about? What's wrong?"

I couldn't. I shook my head and kept walking, shutting everything out.

"Emma, stop," she requested desperately. "Please. Please tell me what happened?" She reached for my arm, and I spun around. Sara flinched when she saw the hardened look on my face. "Please tell me what happened?"

I caught a glimpse of Evan watching us from the sidewalk.

"I'm walking back to the house," I said in a rush, turning away. "I'm not playing anymore."

"Okay," she answered. "Can I come with you?"

"If you want. But I'm not talking about it," I told her firmly.

"Alright," Sara agreed. She hollered to Evan, "Emma and I are walking back."

He nodded but remained on the sidewalk, watching after us. I kept walking, and Sara accompanied me in silence.

Just when I thought there was a chance to shed myself of all my horrible choices, I was painfully reminded of the one that I could never outrun.

36. ALWAYS YOU

S ara had come out of Emma's room hours ago and told me she was going to be okay. That was it. Then she went upstairs with Jared.

There was nothing okay about the horrified look in Emma's eyes when Jared asked that question. He'd apologized over and over, but I still couldn't talk to him. Of all the questions he could've asked, he had to ask the girl who'd survived being strangled that question. The girl who had been tormented for years at the hands of a sadistic woman.

I couldn't stay mad at him. He wasn't thinking of Emma's past, just of the hilarious answers any other person would have come up with. He had no idea she was going to react that way. When she'd pushed her chair away, her whole body was trembling. Sara had reached her before I did, and so she was the one who was there for her. And I stayed away, and let her.

But now I couldn't sleep. I wanted to check on her. To lie next to her and hold her. I knew I could keep her safe, if she'd just let me. But something kept me on the hammock, staring at the stars, instead of knocking on her door. There was still too much we hadn't told each other.

I pushed my foot against the deck, rocking the hammock gently as I scanned the dark sky, the stars shifting beneath the swift veil of clouds. I wasn't looking forward to telling her what had happened when she left. I knew she needed to know, but it didn't make it any easier. But maybe if I opened up to her, she would do the same—and tell me what she was still keeping from me.

Jonathan's text made my stomach turn. I hadn't been able to get the words out of my head since I'd read them. I do forgive you. I miss you. Would give anything to hear your voice right now.

I never did like him… or trust him. Apparently, I'd had a good reason not to. She'd confided in him. She'd trusted him in a way she couldn't trust me. But there was more to it than that… Please say you forgive me?

Something had happened, and before we could move on, before we could completely forgive each other, she had to tell me what that was. He wasn't here for her now. And from the sounds of it, he wasn't planning on being in her life. But whatever he'd done, it had changed her.

I couldn't sleep. I stared into the dark, thinking about Jonathan. My heart thumped loudly in my chest, the lingering violence I'd witnessed clinging to me. For two years I'd pushed it away, refusing to confront what we'd done. I wanted to believe that protecting him was the right choice. I'd held Jonathan's secrets as my own, as I'd promised I would—convincing myself that my silence was justified. My body shuddered at the memory of the charred remains of the house where his family had died, burned alive. I could still see the torment in his eyes when he confessed to the arson. There wasn't any punishment that could destroy him more than his own guilt and sorrow. I knew what that hate did to a person. That venom still tainted my veins.

Needing fresh air, I grabbed a throw from the end of the bed and went out to the patio. I pulled the blanket tightly around me, but it did little to ward off the shivers. I focused on the overcast sky, wondering where Jonathan was now, and if their screams still haunted his dreams. There was an anxious part of me that couldn't let him go. A part of me that still needed to find him, even though I had no idea where to start.

My ears perked at the squeaking sound. I listened intently and heard the squeak again. Pushing the gate open, I walked quietly around to the main deck. Evan was lying in the hammock, slowly rocking back and forth.

"Hi," I said, startling him. He jumped up and practically tipped the hammock over. I cringed. "Sorry."

"It's okay," he assured me, trying to shake it off. "Now I know how you feel when it happens to you."

"Funny," I commented, making a face. "Can't sleep?"

"No. Thinking," I explained. "And you?"

"Same," she answered, moving closer, a light-green blanket wrapped around her shoulders.

"Want to talk about what happened tonight?" I proposed as she came into full view, standing next to the hammock.

Her darkened eyes flickered in contemplation. "I'm not sure I can."

"You can sit at the other end if you want." I scooted farther up on one side of the hammock.

Emma eased herself over the edge, maneuvering toward the middle so she wouldn't tip us. She leaned back and bent her knees, her feet by my side.

"Will you tell me something I've always wanted to know?" I asked, having thought about it so many times over the years.

"What's that?" Her voice was careful and quiet. I could feel her tensing. She drew the blanket in tighter as if to protect herself.

"What were your nightmares about?" I asked, reflecting on the nights I'd been by her side when she'd awoken in a sweat, screaming. Her torment had always haunted me. I couldn't protect her from what waited for her in her sleep.

Emma released a smooth breath, blowing it out through slightly pursed lips.

It had been over a year since I'd had a nightmare. Their disappearance coincided with the increase of the emptiness. I couldn't be tormented with images of my death when I was no longer afraid of dying.

"They were about dying," I explained, trying to keep my voice calm. "About being killed in some way over and over again, and I'd wake just before my last breath. But it felt so real, the fear and helplessness, not being able to get away from her."

"Her?" Evan repeated, with a bite in his tone. "They were about *Carol*?"

I shivered, her name slicing through me like a smooth blade. "Usually."

"I hate that woman," he said with an edge in his voice. "I can't tell you how close I came to hurting her that night."

I propped myself on my elbows, jostling us slightly.

"George knew. He saw it in my eyes and stood between us, afraid I wouldn't be able to control myself. I made myself concentrate on you to keep calm.

"But if you *hadn't* breathed. If you had—" He swallowed. I could feel his entire body stiffen against the hammock.

"Hey." I redirected his attention. "But I'm here." I set my hand on his leg.

"Why did she hate you so much? What made her want to hurt you?"

I filled my lungs with the cool, damp air. "I don't know."

"Don't you want to know? Don't you want to understand what made her such a psychotic bitch?" Evan's words were weighted with pent up anger.

"No," I answered, my voice low. "There isn't an excuse or explanation in the world that would make it right, that would help me understand why she hurt me. I don't need to forgive her. I need to figure out how to keep living—otherwise she *should* have killed me."

I raised my head. "What? Why would you say that? You don't think you deserved to die? Do you, Emma?" I asked, my chest pounding.

"I wouldn't say it like that exactly," she replied, her voice monotone and distant, like she was speaking about someone else. "I'm not sure what I deserve. But I know I'm not doing a very good job living."

I was disturbed by her defeatist tone, but before I could say anything, she added, "I have a tattoo to remind me. I drew it when I was still suffering from the nightmares. It's supposed to keep me from getting lost. To help me hold on."

"Can I see it?"

Emma sat up, and I straddled the hammock, pressing my feet on the deck to keep us steady. She scooted between my legs with her left side facing me, pulling up her T-shirt to expose the ink inscribed under her ribs. I pulled my phone out of my pocket to provide enough light to see the intricate details of the waning moon with a sleeping male profile. The entire outline was the same words repeated over again: "It's only a dream." The script was fine and ran together in a cyclical chant, until the lowest point. A set of words disrupted the perfection. "Open your eyes and live."

I reached out with my finger and traced the swing hanging off those words, small and delicate. Her skin erupted into a chill of goose bumps at my touch.

"Maybe I should get one that says, 'She's still breathing,'" I murmured as she lowered her shirt. She turned toward me in a sudden motion.

"When you said that you have nightmares that I was gone, you meant that I died?"

I preferred not to reflect upon the many nights when I'd arrived too late, finding her limp and pale. "Not always," I admitted reluctantly. "Sometimes I can't find you at all, no matter where I search. I usually wake up in a panic. The others…when I'm not there in time…feels like someone's tearing my heart out."

I couldn't get in a breath as his eyes sifted through those nights of despair. I could only imagine what it was like to be forced awake by a nightmare, only to find that it was true. I ran my hand along his cheek, and his eyes focused on mine, surprised by my touch.

"I don't want you to hate me. I want you to forgive me," I gasped. "I want you to love me again." His eyes shone. "But I don't know how to let you if I can't forgive myself." I paused, my lip trembling. "It always comes back to forgiving, doesn't it?"

"It does," he sighed, cupping my hand and holding it against his warm skin. "I never stopped loving you, Emma. I just don't know how to love you enough."

A tear spilled over my cheek. "Why would you say that?"

"If I did, you'd trust me with all of you."

I bowed my head, pulling my hand away. "I'm afraid. So afraid that if you see who I truly am, you'll hate me. And I can't let that happen. I only exist because of you, Evan. You've saved me more times than you know. I'm so afraid I'm not worth the breath you gave me. I want to be so much better than this girl in front of you. I *want* to deserve you, to let you love me. I just don't know how."

"You don't have to *let me*, Emma. I already do. You just have to love me back. With everything you have. And that's all I need. I need *you*. *All* of you."

The raw intensity of our unfiltered words was consuming. I was terrified and exhilarated all at once. She was finally opening up, exposing herself to me, and I couldn't have asked her to be any more honest. But at the same time, I was disturbed by what she was saying. And I was fearful about where this was heading.

There was a heartbreaking sadness in her eyes. Emma slid away from me and off the hammock. I watched her walk toward the stairs, where she turned and waited for me. I followed her down to the beach, accompanied by the sound of the volatile waves crashing to shore. We walked for some time, our eyes on our feet.

"I need to be honest with you." My voice finally broke through the silence. "If we're going to have a chance of moving forward, then I have to tell you everything that happened after you left. It's not going to be easy to hear, but I need you to listen… to all of it."

"Okay," she said quietly, her voice nearly swept away in the ocean breeze.

I sat on the sand, and she lowered herself next to me. Feeling the pressure of her body huddled tight against my arm, I stared out at the coursing waves.

"When you left me like that, in that house. That awful house. I was so angry. I couldn't understand how you could disappear from my life without a word. That anger overpowered any other feelings I had for you. I wanted to let you go. I was convinced you'd chosen him."

"Jonathan?"

"Yeah," I replied, trying to relax my shoulders. "I didn't know what to think. But after what he said that night, about how you confided in him, with secrets you could never tell me... I just assumed."

"It wasn't like that," she insisted.

"Then what was it like, Emma? What happened between you two?" I begged. "Did you love him?"

"No, I didn't love him." Her eyes glistened as they flickered in the dark.

"But he loved you," I said in a whisper.

"He thought he did." She looked away. "And I do care about him."

"Still?" I asked. She didn't answer. My fists clenched against my knees, the text flashing through my head.

"Why does he get to forgive you, when you didn't want that from me?" I asked, the edge in my voice rising to the surface. Emma turned toward me, her eyes flashing with shock. I wanted her to tell me. I needed her to. "Are you going to tell me what happened?"

Emma's eyes pooled with tears. She shook her head slightly and looked back out at the water.

I closed my eyes to collect myself and asked another question that had been plaguing me. "What did that letter say, Emma?"

Anger still lingered in Evan's voice.

"You know about the letter?" My stomach hollowed. Evan knew way more than he was supposed to...about everything.

"I found the envelope, and I tore my mother's office apart looking for the rest of it. We never talked about it, and she never told me. Not until last week, when she admitted that it existed. That letter changed my life. I think I deserve to know what it said."

I pressed my forehead against my bent knees. "It doesn't matter anymore."

"I don't want to be angry, Em. I *want* to forgive you. But first we need to be honest…about everything. I still don't understand how you thought that leaving wouldn't destroy me. Because it did. You couldn't have hurt me any worse."

I stifled a sob and clutched my knees harder.

"I know this is hard. But I need you to keep listening, okay?"

"I'm listening," I murmured, barely audible.

"After you left, the school made up some lie that you chose to leave for Stanford early, and wouldn't be at graduation. But everyone knew. They were all at the party where we never showed. They saw my face when I came back from Cornell a few days later. My cuts were barely healed by graduation. No one knew the details, but they figured that whatever happened to me had something to do with why you left. And then…I had to give that fucking speech, the valedictorian speech *you* were supposed to make."

"What about Ben? He was the salutatorian," I questioned, feeling increasingly ill the more he spoke.

"He refused." Evan shrugged. "I don't know the exact details, but I ended up having to give a speech that was supposed to encourage everyone to go after their dreams. How was I supposed to convince them to look forward to their futures when I couldn't see two steps in front of me? It was a disaster.

"And then I went to Yale. I wanted nothing to do with you, so I didn't fight it at first. It wasn't in me to care anymore. I'd go to classes during the week, and spend the weekends at home…with Analise."

"Analise?" My voice broke.

I lifted my eyes toward the shifting sky and gathered myself. Knowing how much I was hurting her was killing me, which was the reason I didn't want to share this with her to begin with. But I was convinced it was the only way we'd finally be able to heal.

"She was always a friend. She cared about me. And so we'd hang out, and she'd try to take my mind off you. And I let her. By Christmas, the worst of my anger had disappeared. But then I wanted answers. I needed to see you, so I could ask you why. I tried to come out here over break, but my parents wouldn't let me touch my savings, and my father eventually took my car away when they realized how determined I was.

"I couldn't reach you. The McKinleys were as evasive as everyone else, and Sara didn't even pick up my calls. I was so cruel to her after you left, basically taking it out on her, forcing her to avoid me completely—even while she and Jared were still dating. I wasn't myself, and I was dragging everyone down with me in my misery."

I paused to look over at her. Emma was clutching her knees tightly to her chest as her body trembled.

"Are you okay?" I asked, wanting to comfort her. But I couldn't bring myself to touch her... not yet.

"Keep going," she murmured, her voice strained.

This was torturing her. Guilt was her poison, and I was pouring it down her throat. I continued with the honesty, hoping in the end she could let it all go.

"Analise tried to rationalize with me, about how it was your choice and that I needed to respect it and leave you alone. But she didn't know you—not like I did. It was hard for her to see me go through it. I think it was right around the beginning of the next year that we started dating. She was finishing her senior year, and I was... I wasn't doing much of anything. If she wasn't there to make me, there were days I wouldn't get out of bed.

"I can't even imagine what that was like for her. I have no idea why she wanted anything to do with me."

The thought of her comforting him, convincing him to let me go, made my chest want to cave in on itself. I squeezed my legs tighter to keep from falling apart.

"She tried," he continued, as much as I wished he'd stop. "But she wasn't you. And as long as you were out there somewhere…I couldn't let you go until I got the answers I needed. At least that's what I convinced myself. When she saw the transfer application to Stanford, that broke her. She thought I was going after you. And on some level, I guess I was. She had every right to hate me. But then, inexplicably, she forgave me.

"Something went wrong with the transfer. I should have suspected something, but I didn't. She eventually confessed to withdrawing the transfer because she wanted to keep me from getting hurt again. I was furious. She'd become yet another person making decisions for me. So I stopped talking to her, and we never saw each other again…well, until she showed up at my house the day of Rachel's funeral."

"She did?" I asked in shock. "Why?"

"She knew you were in Weslyn for the funeral. Maybe she wanted to be there for me, in case I…But…I wanted to be there for you."

"Did you…love her? Forget it. I don't—" I stopped, clenching my teeth together. "I don't want to think of you with *her*."

"I'm sorry," he said soothingly. "I know subconsciously that's why I did it. To hurt you. And that's so messed up. But she was a good friend, Em, as much as you didn't like her."

"I know," I muttered.

"So I'm not perfect in all of this. I've done some pretty awful things to people I cared about. I ruined a good friendship with Analise. I slept with Catherine, even though I never cared about, or even liked her. She was just another in a line of catastrophic choices. All because I was desperate to get over you. But they were *my choices*. Your choice was to leave. The rest were mine."

My body shook as I bent over and cried into my arms.

I didn't want to hurt her anymore. There was only so much honesty a person could take, and she'd reached her limit. But I wasn't done. I knew if I didn't finish now, she wouldn't understand, and I'd risk losing her for good.

"The nightmares started last summer when I realized I wasn't going to Stanford in the fall. I'd broken things off with Analise, and I was convinced you were never coming back. I wanted to move on, to try to live a life without you, but I wasn't living. Emma—" She lifted her tear-stained face. *"I'm not supposed to live without you. And you're not supposed to live without me. We're in this life together. Without each other, we're not really living."*

"Why did I have to know?" I asked in a broken voice. "Because it hurts to think of you with...them, to know what I did to you. It's like you're squeezing my heart with your bare hands. I know I deserve it. But why tell me?"

"Because we need to always be honest, even when it's hard. And you need to know that I'm not perfect either. I've screwed up, and I'm so sorry. But it's done now. And whatever you're holding on to that makes you think I'll hate you, I want you to be able to tell me, and know that even if it hurts me, I'm not going anywhere."

"You can't say that," I argued. "Evan, what if I did the most awful thing you could imagine? I don't know if you could still love me."

"But I know you, Emma. I do *know* you. Your heart won't let you do anything that could make me not love you. And I've seen your vicious side. I was there when you confronted Rachel. I've seen how ruthless you can be. It's a side I don't like, but *you* don't either. So I'm not afraid that's who truly you are. Because it's not. It's the hurt and pain lashing out, needing to make someone else feel the way you did all those years. It's not good, Em. But it doesn't define you."

My heart was pounding erratically. He was offering a safe place for us to open up and tell each other what we knew would hurt, owning up to our faults with the expectation of letting go and moving on. An exchange of our most awful mistakes. But I was holding on to something far darker than he could imagine, and it *would* change the way he looked at me. I couldn't do it. I knew if I did, I'd lose him forever, and then I'd be worse than nothing.

"I'm not ready," I whispered. "I'm sorry."

I could see her fighting with it, the decision to tell me whatever it was that still held her captive, keeping her from me. I knew in every muscle of my body that it had to do with Jonathan. Something did happen between them. But she had to be the one to tell me. And as long this secret still loomed between us, I wouldn't be able to completely forgive her. I also knew I couldn't breathe without her.

"I'll give you time. But we're not going to be able to move on if you can't tell me everything." Her eyes dipped sorrowfully. "Come here." I held my arms open, and she moved between my legs, leaning her back into me so I could wrap my arms around her. She laid her head on my arm, and I kissed the top of her head. "We'll get through this. I believe in us."

Emma wrapped her arms around mine and squeezed. "I want to believe."

"Look at me."

She twisted around to face me. Her eyes were raw from crying, and her breath trembled with each inhale. I ran my finger along her damp cheeks. "I love you."

I peered into his intense blue eyes. They bared all that was vulnerable and pure in him. The part that just wanted to protect me, to encourage me to be better, to make me happy. He revealed it so plainly, my chest swelled with a flittering warmth. If I knew anything, I knew he loved me.

"And you love me." He stated it as the truth it was.

"I do. Loving you is the only certainty in my life. I will never stop. But it was because of how much I love you that I ended up hurting you so badly. I only wanted you to be happy, and be rid of my destructive life. And you're so beautiful and perfect—even with your flaws. I couldn't destroy you too."

Evan laid his hand on the side of my face. "Stop trying to protect me from your life. I knew exactly what I was getting into. I never doubted you loved me, not ever. All I want is for you to trust me, Emma. *Please.*"

"Trust isn't going to save me," I told him, pressing my forehead against his chest as he hugged me tight.

"Let's go back to the house," Evan said, nestling his chin into my hair.

I helped her off the sand and held her against my side as we walked back into the house. Disclosure was draining. Every part of me ached.

"Will you stay with me tonight?" she asked in a hush, leaning in to me. I could feel the energy seeping from her.

"I wouldn't be able to sleep unless I did," I said, pulling the smallest smile from her exhausted face. I led her into the room, and she practically collapsed on the bed, kicking her shoes off with her toes. I slid the covers out from under her and after removing my shorts and shoes, slid in behind her, pulling her to me so I could feel her heart beating against my chest. "Emma?"

"Hmm," she murmured, already half asleep.

"When can I kiss you?"

I was too exhausted to move, but that one question released an unexpected surge, and I was suddenly very much awake. I rolled over to face him, and he grinned at me. "Hi."

"Hi." I smiled softly, running my hand into his hair. "You can kiss me now."

My heart stammered as his lips pressed against mine. So familiar, but different at the same time. Our passion increased as he pulled my lip into his mouth and slid his tongue in mine.

Heat surged through me as her lips teased mine, her tongue caressing in a slow sensual pace. I gripped her tighter, having wanted, needed, to taste her for so long. My pulse raced as I leaned into her, sliding my hand along her back. She gasped as the pressure of our bodies intensified. I opened my mouth and teased the spot below her ear with my tongue. She released a small sound of pleasure that drove me crazy. My breathing picked up as I found her lips again, pressing against them with urgency.

I knew that we needed to stop, but the more she breathed in quick pants, the more my body responded, not wanting to pull away. She dug her fingers in my hair, and I was consumed by the softness of her lips, the touch of her tongue—her subtle floral scent intoxicating me. Emma wrapped her leg around me and tilted her head back to expose her throat, inviting me to take it. I trailed my mouth along it, tasting the sweetness of her skin.

She reached for my boxers, and that's when I knew this wasn't that moment. We were raw and hurt, and this wasn't going to heal us. I gently moved her hands away and whispered in her ear, "I want you so bad, but we need to stop."

I sank into the bed. "I know," I breathed, trying to recover. I was so caught up in the need for him, wanting him, that I couldn't stop even when the resounding voice told me, *Not yet.*

I leaned over to see his face, to run my hand over his cheek and caress his lip with my thumb. I stared into the depths of his eyes, and my entire world steadied as I lay there in his arms—exactly where I belonged.

37. ALL ABOUT TOMORROW

"What do you want to do tomorrow?" Sara asked from the hammock.

"Evan went to go pick up my surfboard, so I'd like to go surfing," I answered, leaning back on the stool to scrutinize the painting in front of me. I picked up the fine bristled brush and tapped it into the dark blue paint.

"Didn't you buy that last week?"

"Yeah, but they had to get it from another shop. We were supposed to pick it up yesterday, but something got screwed up with the delivery. Evan was beyond disappointed when it wasn't in." I smiled, remembering the crushed look on his face when the guy at the surf shop told him he'd have to come back this afternoon. You would have thought he'd just been told there wasn't a Santa Claus.

"I'd love to watch you surf," Sara said, a magazine shading her face.

"Sure."

"Then want to go out to dinner after? Just the four of us?"

"That's fine," I agreed, not really wanting to think about tomorrow. It wasn't a day I ever wanted to think about.

"I have it!" Evan bellowed through the house, his voice full of excitement.

He came out to find us, his eyes lit up with a gorgeous smile. "You officially have your first surfboard."

"Great." I laughed lightly. "We'll go tomorrow."

"Tomorrow?" His shoulders slumped in disappointment.

I smiled wider, adoring his fixation with seeing me on a board. "It's already late. We'll go first thing in the morning. I promise."

"Tomorrow," Evan repeated in defeat, coming up behind me and placing his hands on my waist, sending a tingling along my skin. He leaned over and kissed my bare shoulder before setting his chin on it to examine the painting. I leaned back against him as he encircled me with his arms.

"It's not done yet," I rushed to explain, my cheeks as red as the hues on the canvas. I could feel him interpreting every stroke.

"It's intense."

It was a powerful piece, but unsettling at the same time. I wasn't going to say that to her, but I'm sure she knew. The desperation she released with her brush was impossible to miss. A swirl of color and textures, abstract images of hands reaching out through turbulent seas, blending with the motion of the waves. It fed the disturbing sense I had that there was some deep-seated desire in her to give up on this life. It wasn't the first time I'd experienced this fear.

"I was hoping to talk to you about something," I murmured into her neck before pressing my lips against her warm pulse.

"What's that?" she asked in a breathy voice that made me want to push her up against the railing of the deck and make her entire body flush the way it did when she got excited. Then I noticed Sara reading on the hammock and eased away, needing to tame those thoughts.

"When you're done, we'll go for a walk," I said.

"How about a run? Soccer conditioning starts in a few weeks, and I need to be ready."

"That's fine," I agreed. "But you have to run with me so we can talk."

She laughed. "I'll slow down for you."

I crouched down to tie my shoe when Evan came out wearing shorts and sneakers.

"Evan," I scolded, the sight of him sending heart palpitating flutters through my body. "You have to put a shirt on."

"We're still doing that?" he argued. "Really?"

"I'm going to fall on my face if I have to run next to you looking like that."

"I don't look any different than most guys on the beach," he tried to persuade me.

"It's *you*," I stressed. "Any other guy could look exactly like that shirtless, but it's *you* shirtless that makes my brain go all stupid."

He laughed.

"What? I'm just being *honest*," I shot back, my confession drawing color to my face.

I stood up, and Evan pulled me in by my hips. "Then if we're just being honest," his words tickling my lips, "I'd rather—"

"Really don't need to see that," Jared announced, walking out of the kitchen.

"Let's go," Evan said, grabbing a shirt he had lying on the back of the couch.

We eased into a run along the surf. I waited until we were at a comfortable pace before I started talking, wanting to make sure I could have a conversation and keep up with her at the same time.

"So, I was thinking about going to see someone about my nightmares." I watched for her reaction out of the corner of my eye. "I was hoping it was something we could do together."

I'd been going over how to present this to her since I'd made the phone calls yesterday, knowing how much she despised talking about her feelings, especially to strangers. It was hard enough getting her to open up to me and Sara.

"Couples counseling?" she teased.

"Uh, no, but that may not be a bad idea for us." I chuckled. She shoved my shoulder. "It's a therapist who works with people who've experienced trauma. I thought it might be easier if we did it together for a few sessions."

She was quiet, keeping her eyes on the sand.

Just the thought of a therapist made my stomach twist into knots. I'd seen a couple in my lifetime and hadn't found the process useful at all. Granted, the first time I was young and it was right after my father died, but talking about it didn't bring him back. So I told the woman with the big front teeth who smelled like cherries exactly what she wanted to hear until she told my mother that I was adjusting.

Looking back, it surprised me that my mother had sent me. I couldn't imagine her caring for anyone else's feelings other than her own. Maybe there were brief moments in my life when she was actually a mother, or perhaps the school counselor had recommended it. That seemed more likely.

The second therapist I'd visited after being discharged from the hospital, during my junior year, when my world was upside down and inside out. I couldn't bring myself to tell her anything. It was like my mind shut down and wouldn't let me divulge any emotion or recollect a single traumatic moment—except in my nightmares. I went through the motions, fulfilling the court-mandated visits, and left her office just as defective as when I'd entered. So I was skeptical, to say the least.

"Will you consider it?" Evan asked when I was silent too long. "You'll be helping me too."

I glanced over at him, my anxiety swarming. But I couldn't dismiss his request after he'd said that. "I'll think about it."

"Thank you."

"Was that The Talk?" I asked with a small grin.

"It was."

"Then I'm going to run faster now," I told him with a quick raise of my eyebrows. "Keep up if you can." I pushed into the sand and propelled forward, needing to be filled with the rush of adrenaline that calmed me and made everything clearer.

"*Thanks for running with me!*" *I bellowed as the distance lengthened between us. Her "think about it" response was better than what I'd expected. I watched her push herself down the beach, knowing our conversation had probably fueled her strides.*

She waited impatiently for me in front of the house, her hands on her hips. I shook my head with a laugh.

"*Am I too slow for you, Emma?*"

"*It's not your fault you can't keep up,*" *she taunted.*

"*I may not be able to keep up with you, but I can still catch you,*" *I said, not slowing down as I lowered my shoulder and lifted her off the ground.*

"*Evan, put me down,*" *she hollered, her voice broken in laughter.*

I held on to her thighs, which were slippery with sweat. My steps faltered as I ran into the water, not getting very far before a wave knocked us over.

Emma emerged with her mouth agape, wiping water from her face. "I can't believe you did that!" She splashed me, unable to keep from smiling.

I stood up to reach for her as she tried to escape toward shore with a laughing squeal. The knee-deep water slowed her down.

"*Not so fast now.*" *I flung my arms around her waist. Her forward momentum dumped us on the sand at the water's edge.*

I rolled her over, her hair splayed across the sand. Her eyes sparkled as she smiled up at me.

"*You've got a little sand...*" *I brushed my hand along her cheek. Her breath faltered. Gripping her waist, I drew her closer. She closed her eyes as I bent to taste the salt water on her lips. I could spend the rest of my life kissing her and never get enough. The heat from her breath parted my mouth, and I caressed her lip with my tongue, pulling her against me.*

Evan held me to him and I wrapped my leg around his, the water running under us as we lay on the coarse sand. His hand slid along the back of my thigh. I let out a small moan, tilting my head back—looking directly into a pair of big brown eyes. I pushed

Evan away, and he pulled his head up, instantly letting me go as a small boy holding a yellow pail continued to stare at us from a foot away.

I sat up, smoothing my hair back, my entire face on fire.

"We're, uh, pretty sandy." Evan looked down at the sand clinging to his wet clothes and skin. "Maybe we should get back in the water."

My pulse still erratic from his kiss, I turned to him with a grin. "Outdoor shower?"

His lips parted to reveal a vibrant smile. I scrambled up to race toward the house. He grabbed my ankle, causing me to sprawl on the sand. Evan let out a chuckle as he sprinted past me.

"Hey!" I hollered, pushing myself back up and racing after him.

I could hear her coming up behind me, and dug in a little faster with a low laugh. She could outrun me in distance, but I could take her in a sprint. I leapt up the steps, toward the gate to the patio. I had enough time to kick off my sneakers and socks before Emma slammed the gate behind her.

She stood before the fence, panting. A sexy smile crept across her face. I turned on the water to let it warm up as she deliberately flipped off her sneakers and peeled her socks from her feet without a word. I watched her move toward me, still with that seductive grin on her face, pulling her wet, sandy shirt over her head.

She reached for her waistband and stopped—looking at me, questioning. I shook my head, knowing that if she removed her shorts, my restraint would go with them. Emma stood before me, her eyes not leaving mine as she slipped her hand under my shirt, the brush of her fingers on my skin making the muscles along my stomach constrict.

I reached over my shoulder and pulled my shirt off, dropping it on the wood slats. She pushed up on her toes as I bent to kiss her, my hands gripping her waist. Her skin was hot against my stomach as she pressed against me. I carefully backed up, leading her to the shower—hoping the temperature wasn't going to disrupt our connection.

The water was warm on my back, so I guided her in with me. The water cascaded over us as our lips parted, exchanging the air between us. Dragging my mouth along her neck, I tasted the saltiness of her skin. She tipped her head back with a gasping moan. My back tightened as my body reacted to her.

Emma ran her mouth along my chest, and I dug my fingers in her hair, tilting her head and kissing her wet lips with such want that I was having difficulty remaining in control. I felt the edge of the stone bench against my calf and pulled her right leg up, setting her foot on the ledge.

I inhaled at his touch as his hand eased up my thigh, under my shorts. A flush of heat rushed through my chest. I closed my eyes, overtaken by the sensation. My breath broke into uneven bursts as I buried my face in his neck, teasing his skin with my tongue and brushing my lips along his jaw until I found his mouth, moaning into his parted lips as his touch pushed me over. I gripped his back and tightened around him, lost in the rippling current coursing through my body. I collapsed against him with a drawn breath.

"I can still run faster," I murmured, my lips pressed against his smooth skin.

Evan laughed softly in my ear and whispered, "But you'll never lose me."

———

A pillow plopped against my head. I grumbled, not wanting to open my eyes.

"Get up, Evan," Emma insisted.

My lids cracked open slightly. It was still dark. "What time is it?"

"It's technically morning," she said, sounding way too awake for that to be true.

"Why aren't you sleeping?" I mumbled, pulling the covers up around my chin.

"Because I couldn't, so I decided we're going surfing."

I blinked my eyes open. "What?"

"I thought we could be the first ones on the water. Just you and me," she explained, already dressed in a sweatshirt and shorts.

It took me a moment to register what she was saying. Then when it hit me I pushed the blankets off. "I'm up. Give me five minutes."

"I thought so." She beamed.

I shut the door to the bathroom, groggy but elated by her enthusiasm, realizing that this was a bigger deal than even she knew, especially today.

I was fidgety, wanting to get out of the house. When Evan finally came out of the bedroom, I tossed him a granola bar that he barely caught and left him trailing after me.

"Wow, you really have a schizophrenic relationship with mornings," Evan noted, shutting the door behind him. "You already loaded everything?"

"I couldn't sleep," I explained again. But sleep was never possible on this day.

"Do you want to tell me why?" he asked, as I knew he would.

"I'm anxious about today," I replied. "I need it to be a good day."

He nodded, not asking for more, and said, "It will be." Evan spread his arms, and I stepped closer, squeezing him tight. He tipped my chin and kissed me gently, "Good morning, Emma."

"Good morning." I smiled because it truly was.

I handed Evan the keys, and he drove us to the remote surf spot the guys had found. We carried our boards and wetsuits over our heads along a path lined with vegetation until it opened up at a rocky beach. The jetties were what made this place an excellent surf break.

The sky was still grey as the morning haze settled on the dark water. It was still too foggy to surf, so I leaned my board against a boulder, along with my wetsuit. I ran my fingertips over the captivating design of the female figure breaking through the surf in an arching motion. As soon as I'd seen it, my heart leapt. There wasn't another board I wanted, despite Evan's efforts to convince me otherwise.

Unzipping my sweatshirt, I stripped it off to reveal my swimsuit underneath. "What are you doing?" Evan asked.

"Going swimming," she said simply, like it was the most obvious answer.

"The water's freezing, remember?" I argued as she dropped her shorts to the ground. Then I couldn't say anything at all.

"Stop staring and come in the water with me," she said, slapping me in the stomach. "It'll wake you up."

She jogged in without hesitation and plunged under the waves.

"Shit," I groaned, knowing this was going to be painful—and it was. I let the water rush up to my shins, not committed to going in farther. My toes were already numb.

I searched for her. The darkness and haze made it difficult to see anything. But I found her floating on her back, riding the rippling ocean.

I took a breath and rushed in, diving under the water. Fighting for breath as I resurfaced in the frigid water, I swam out to where Emma lay, and admired her peaceful posture. She glided along the surface with her arms splayed. Her eyes were closed, and she was breathing calmly through parted lips, like she was lost in a dream. She must have sensed my presence because she popped her head up, her body sinking.

"Hi," she said, her face glowing despite the lack of sun. "Was wondering if you were going to come in."

"This water is freezing, Em," I said. "Warm me up." I pulled her close, the bare skin of her stomach sliding against mine. "Your lips are already turning purple."

"Really?" she asked, searching my eyes. "So, should we get out of the water?" She wrapped her arms around my neck, running her fingers into my wet hair.

"I think I'm starting to warm up," I told her, my chest thumping as she crushed her body against mine to reach my lips.

I pressed my shivering lips to his, and he inhaled in shock. "Your lips are frozen."

"Warm them up," I requested, brushing them along his jaw. Evan turned his head to intercept me, but before he could kiss me, he uttered, "Hold your breath." I could feel a wall of water hovering over us. Inhaling quickly, I sank under the water. The powerful current separated us, and I was carried away with the wave. When I popped up again, I spotted Evan farther from shore. My muscles ached from the icy water, so I rode the next wave to the beach.

When I emerged, I heard, "How's the water?" A few other surfers had decided to be the first ones in the water too, interfering with any plans I'd had of warming up on the beach with Evan.

"It's freezing," I told them as Evan walked out of the surf. He greeted them and eyed me. The disappointed look on his face told me we'd been thinking the same thing. "Guess it's wetsuit time."

"Guess so."

The skies remained grey for a couple of hours, but the waves were ideal. I couldn't get up on my board at first, too distracted by the sight of Emma sitting on hers, waiting for a wave. And then when she dropped in on her first one, I couldn't take my eyes off her. She looked incredible in her stance, weaving along the wave like she'd been doing it for years.

"Are you going to sit there all day?" she teased when she paddled back out.

"Just admiring your skills," I told her. "I have to admit that I'm a little disappointed that I didn't get to teach you."

"This is better," she assured me with an awkward smile, since we were inadvertently talking about Cole. "This way we just surf. It took me a while to be able to stand, forget about ride. So I prefer this."

I nodded, appreciating her answer. This was perfect, just her and me—and, well, a few other guys we didn't know. This was an experience I couldn't have planned if I tried. And for that, I had to be a little grateful to Cole for teaching her. But not for dating her.

Emma must have realized what I was thinking about because she paddled over and grabbed my leg. "I'm sorry about him—that you had to see us together. It hurt just hearing about you and…Well, I can't imagine seeing it."

"I won't lie. It wasn't easy to be around him, even though I like the guy. Except I knew it wouldn't last," I told her with a grin, dismissing the ill feeling brought on by the thought of him kissing her.

"What?" she asked in surprise. "We weren't dating, Evan."

"Whatever, you were together. It doesn't matter what you call it," I said dismissively. "But you're supposed to be with me, so any other guy is doomed to failure."

I leaned over carefully and kissed her. When I pulled back, she said, "I love you." Those three words coming out of her mouth made me feel like I could conquer anything. I smiled back and said, "You and me, Em—no matter what." I got caught in the light reflected in her eyes—the eyes that had been so vacant I was afraid I'd lost her. She sat up on her board with a gorgeous smile on her face and repositioned herself in preparation for the next wave.

We continued to ride until my arms felt like they were going to fall off and my legs were shaky. The guys, along with Jared and Sara, met us midmorning as the sun was breaking through the grey. They'd packed a cooler for lunch, allowing us to spend the day on the beach. Nothing else mattered today. I lived within the minutes I was in—not dwelling on the past, or fearing the future. I just let the day present itself as it would, and it couldn't have been better.

Sara took hold of my hand and rested her head on my shoulder as we left the quaint restaurant hidden in a grove of lit trees.

We'd had dinner, just the four of us, as she'd wanted. We'd sent Evan and Jared ahead of us so we could use the restroom, basically to talk about them.

"I'm happy for you," she said, pulling her head back and smiling. "That you finally have him." She looked affectionately at the two of them in conversation by the car. "This is the way it should've always been... Wow, we were stupid girls."

"I know," I said, smiling softly.

She squeezed my hand and added, "More than anything, I like seeing you like this. He's the only one that can make you glow. I've missed that ridiculous look on your face."

I blinked back the emotion with a laugh. "Thanks, Sara. And thanks for putting up with me. I know the last two years weren't great for you either."

"That's what sisters do," she chimed, bumping my shoulder with hers.

Her laughter turned me around. Emma caught me looking at her. I walked toward her. She released Sara's hand and took the one I offered. I kissed the top of her head.

"So how was your birthday, Emma?" I asked, taking a chance mentioning it.

She stopped. I turned to face her, fearing her reaction. Emma leaned up on her toes and kissed my cheek, allowing me to smile. She wrapped her arms around my neck and said softly in my ear, "It's the best birthday I've had in thirteen years. Thank you."

38. THE PROMISE

A shiver danced down my back with his tickling touch along my neck.

"The girls are about to come in here and jump on the bed," Evan said, his voice low in my ear. "You may want to think about getting up."

As his warm lips pressed against my shoulder, mine curled into a reluctant smile. I squirmed back to feel him against me, still refusing to open my eyes.

"Emma!" Sara pounded on the door. "Get up! You need to help us get ready!"

Evan laughed as I swore into my pillow.

"Told you."

"Why did I think this party was a good idea?"

I inhaled quickly when his hand slid under my shirt, along my stomach.

"No one talked you into it," Evan murmured, teasing my neck with his tongue. "You were all excited about it last week, on your birthday, remember?"

"That was…a weird day. I mean…a good day." I sighed, unable to concentrate on the conversation. "The Fourth of July… shouldn't start… 'til after dark." I grabbed Evan's hand, squeezing it when the warmth of his mouth sent shivers through my body.

"Emma!" Sara hollered again. Evan chuckled and rolled away.

"I'm up," I called back, then mumbled, "Unfortunately." Evan slid off the bed as I pulled back the blankets. He was already dressed in a pair of shorts and a T-shirt.

"I've been volunteered to pick up ice." I sat up on the edge of the bed and flopped my head against his stomach. "I'll be back in a little while, okay?" he said, running his hand over my hair.

I nodded. He pulled me off the bed into a hug. I dragged my feet to the bathroom as he made his exit.

"Please tell me she's up," Sara said as soon as I came out of the room.

"Yes." I laughed. "She's up."

"Hi, Evan," Serena chimed with a sparkling smile. "Do you have an iPod? Sara's put me in charge of music."

I looked toward Sara, who shrugged. "Yeah, it's out in my truck. I'll bring it in when I get back from picking up Nate."

"Can you buy some lemons too?" Meg called from the kitchen.

"Sure," I answered on my way out the door.

"How's everything at the house?" Nate asked as we drove to the store.

"Sara's in charge of... everything," I stated. "Serena's selecting the music. Meg's getting the food ready. And James and Jared are setting up tables and a volleyball net outside." Which left me and the guys in charge of drinks.

"What about Emma?"

"Um..." I chuckled. "She's wishing it was tomorrow already."

"I wondered why she decided to have the party. I saw her face when I mentioned it."

"We caught her on a good day when we brought it up last week," I explained.

Nate's looked to me curiously.

"It was her birthday."

"Oh." He nodded. "I didn't know. How come we didn't—" He stopped, suddenly remembering why no one knew it was her birthday, and why she *didn't celebrate it. Because it was also the day her father died in a car accident, thirteen years ago. "Forget it."*

"How's it going between you? I know it's gotten more serious. Have you told her... everything yet?"

"Yeah," I answered, not entirely ready to have this conversation.

"And has she been completely honest with you?" That question was precisely why I didn't want to talk about us.

"Not entirely," I said evasively.

"Dude! Really?! What are you doing then?"

"Giving her time," I told him.

"She's had two fucking years," he declared heatedly.

We pulled into the parking lot, and I got out as soon as I shut off the truck, ending the conversation... for now. Nate wasn't convinced that Emma wouldn't still destroy me. And I'd never admit it to him, but... I wasn't either.

"What do you want me to do?" I asked.

"Cut up the watermelon?" Meg requested as Sara stood out on the deck, instructing the guys where to put everything.

"Emma, where's your iPod?" Serena asked from in front of the entertainment unit.

"It's in my room," I told her, "somewhere in the tote bag that's in the closet."

Serena disappeared into the bedroom while I prepared to slice watermelon. I'd never done it, but how hard could it be? I stuck the long knife into the rind and... couldn't move it—leaving the blade sticking out of the green flesh at an awkward angle. I pushed again and it slid down a fraction of an inch.

I looked behind me, and Meg was staring at me in disbelief.

"Really, Emma?" she said, both amazed and amused by my ineptitude. "I truly thought you could handle that."

"I can do it," I argued, making a futile attempt to move the blade.

"Don't stick it in so far, and use more of a sawing motion," Meg instructed.

"Emma!" Serena called to me from within my room. "Will you come here a second?"

"I've got it," Meg assured me when I scrutinized my predicament, not certain I could just leave the watermelon with the knife protruding out of it. Meg took my spot, and before I'd even left the kitchen, the watermelon was falling into halves.

"I loosened it for you," I insisted as I passed the opening in the wall.

"Yeah, that's it," she agreed, with a shake of her head.

When I entered the bedroom, Serena was standing with her arms crossed, waiting for me.

"Hey," I greeted her warily. "What's up?"

"What's this?" she snapped, holding up The Letter. My mouth opened to speak, but nothing came out. "Are you planning on ending things with Evan? What's going on, Em? I mean, I thought you two were finally together again." She sounded like I'd betrayed *her*.

I released a slow breath. "I wrote that two years ago, before I left. His mother sent it back to me a little over a year ago. She said there'd be a day he'd want to know what it said, and it was my decision whether to share it with him or not."

"You just left him with a letter?" she asked in shock. "You didn't say anything?"

"Not exactly." I sighed, averting my eyes. "And yes. I was wrong to leave like that. But I thought I was doing what was best for him."

"You should have never left him, Em," Serena said sadly. I bowed my head in acceptance of the truth. "Are you going to show him this?"

"I don't know," I said softly. "Why would he want to see it now? I mean, we're trying to move on."

"Because he should know. You promised to be honest, didn't you? Besides, you didn't say anything that you didn't believe to be true."

"I know," I whispered.

After Nate and I had loaded the freezer in the garage with the bags of ice, I walked into the kitchen. "Where's Emma?"

"Sara sent her to take a shower and get ready," Meg explained. "You should probably do the same. People will be here in an hour or so."

"iPod, please," Serena requested, holding out her hand. I pulled it from my pocket and passed it over. "Thank you."

I continued into the bedroom to find Emma sitting on the bed, wearing a blue-and-white dress and strapping on a pair of red sandals. Hearing me enter, she tilted her head up, and my mouth instinctively spread into a smile. When her response was hesitant, I peered deeper and recognized the distraught shift in her eyes.

"Hi," I greeted cautiously. "Everything okay?"

She didn't say anything, only nodding slightly. She stood from the bed and smoothed the short skirt around her. I stood in front of her as she averted her eyes and slid my finger under her chin to redirect her gaze.

"You can tell me, you know," I coaxed gently.

"I know," she murmured. "I will. Later, okay? After everyone leaves."
My eyes tightened, not liking the way she said that.

"Okay," I responded, bending down to kiss her. She received me tenderly, sliding her hands into my hair, pulling me deeper into the give of her lips, but then she pulled away briefly, her eyes flickering with emotion.

I struggled with what I saw for a moment, until she pulled me down onto the bed with her, kissing me like her breath depended on it. My body responded to her touch as she ran her hands along my back, under my shirt. I pushed against her, kissing her soft skin, down her neck and over her shoulder, peeling back the strap.

"Emma, are you ready yet?!" Sara shouted from the other side of the door. Breathing heavily, we didn't move for a moment. "Emma?"

She looked up at me in apology. "Coming!"

I offered her my hand to assist her to her feet. "Later?" I asked, having a hard time recovering.

Emma's mouth curled up seductively as she nodded. "Later." There was still a hint of sadness in her eyes, but her smile seemed genuine.

"Emma!" TJ hollered in his overly emphatic way, dumping ice in the bin at the bar.

"Hey, TJ," I responded with a smile. James and Brent were messing with the volleyball net, tightening the lines.

Ren and Brent arrived a few minutes later with boxes from the liquor store, and a bucket full of some red drink they'd come up with for the day.

Once the guests started to arrive, I realized quickly that I never wanted to throw a party again. I was so busy refilling food, letting people know where the bathrooms were, and bringing the guys at the bar bags of ice, I wasn't exactly having fun. It didn't help that Evan had been assigned grilling duty, not giving us more than a passing second together.

I caught a glimpse of Evan standing at the grill with Nate and Jared when I brought out another salad to set on the long table. The sun reflected off the light brown strands of his neatly trimmed hair, which was becoming more golden as the summer progressed. His short-sleeved plaid button-down brought out the shades of blue in his eyes. He laughed at something Jared said, revealing his heart-stopping smile.

"Em?" Serena beckoned, catching me staring. She grinned when she saw who held my attention. "He won't be at the grill all afternoon."

"Emma, can you get the bag of rolls from the kitchen?" Meg requested.

I sighed, and Serena laughed as I walked into the house.

Evan was on his way in as I was heading out with my hands full of rolls.

"And I'll see you when?"

"I'll find you," he promised, intercepting me with a hand on my waist. Before he could lean over to kiss me, the front door opened and more people came in. He gave me a brief kiss and continued on his mission.

"Evan, come play volleyball with us," Jared hollered from the beach. I had just shut off the grill and was about to find Emma, having lost track of her with the influx of arrivals. I was pretty sure we'd invited about forty people, a number that had been surpassed within the first hour. "Evan, come on, we're one short!"

"I'll be right down," I called to him, looking around one more time for Emma.

I made my way down to the volleyball net, joining Jared, a few other guys and a girl. I unbuttoned my shirt and tossed it on the sand, prepared to play.

"Hey, Evan," the girl said. It took me a moment to place her, and just as I recalled, she reminded me. "Nika. I met you at Nate's. So this is your place, huh?"

"Oh. Hey," I replied. "Yeah. This is the place I was telling you about."

"It's really nice," she admired.

Jared called for everyone to take positions and got ready to serve. Nika took a position next to me. Brent was across the net, and he couldn't keep his eyes off her. I was tempted to switch teams, but with Jared's serve I was caught up in the game.

"Just you and Emma staying here?" she inquired.

"No," I responded, watching TJ run off to get the ball that he'd batted twenty feet out of bounds. "There's another couple here too."

"Oh, you're dating?"

I nodded, glancing at her surprised expression before setting up for the next serve.

I noticed the blue-and-white dress on the deck out of the corner of my eye. Emma was watching from against the railing, and next to her was a guy... standing a little too close.

"Evan!" Jared hollered, as the ball whipped by me. "Focus!"

"What do you study at Stanford?" Paul asked, hovering a little too close, despite my blatant lack of interest.

"Premed," I told him, keeping my eye on the game and the lines of muscles flexing along Evan's back as he set the ball up for Jared to spike over the net. They pumped their fists when Brent missed and it landed on the sand. Nika raised her hand for a high-five that Evan delivered. She was talking to him...a lot.

"That's pretty intense," he noted, having already gone on about his celebrity access as an assistant at a talent agency in LA.

"Hey, Emma." I turned to find Nate behind me.

"Nate! What's going on?" I greeted with near-TJ enthusiasm. He looked at me oddly, then noticed as Paul scooted in closer.

Nate's eyes perked in understanding. "I was actually hoping to talk to you," he said, fulfilling his rescue role.

"Sure," I responded almost too eagerly. "It was nice talking to you." I followed Nate without looking back.

"Thanks," I stressed. "I've been trying to ditch him for a while, but he doesn't know how to take a hint."

"Glad I could help. But I did really want to talk to you."

"Um, okay," I said, surprised by the request. We ventured away from the crowd and headed farther down the beach, my stomach twisted with nerves. He wanted to talk to me about Evan.

"Ren, have you seen Emma?" I felt like I'd been asking that question all day.

"I think I saw her walking down the beach with Nate." Ren was lying in the hammock with his arm draped over the side, holding a beer.

"Nate?" I asked in confusion. Then it struck me. He was going to say something to her. Emma wasn't going to handle being questioned by my best friend very well. The past week with her had been amazing. But we weren't going to be fixed instantly, and I didn't need Nate forcing her to reveal anything before she was ready. He wasn't as patient as I was.

"Where'd they go?"

Ren pointed, and I rushed off in that direction.

I walked beside Nate, anxiously waiting for him to say something. My phone buzzed while we were walking. I pulled it out of my pocket to find a text from Evan: Where are you?

I looked at Nate. "Sorry. Evan's looking for me." I texted him back. After I hit *Send*, I clicked back to my list of messages, and my step faltered when I saw, Emma?

"Emma, are you okay?" Nate asked, pulling my attention away before I could open the text.

"Yeah," I whispered, my mouth suddenly dry. "What did you need to tell me, Nate?"

"I shouldn't say anything, but…but I can't watch it happen again."

Nate shifted his gaze above my head, peering up at the darkening sky, calculating his words. I couldn't calm the pounding in my chest, starting to feel a bit light-headed—I feared my legs might give out.

"Evan's a planner. What I mean is, he's always trying to plan for what's next, almost like a chess game. Everything he does has a reason behind it. He's thought it out, sometimes three steps ahead of where it will lead him. Except when it comes to you." He paused, glancing at me quickly. I remained still, holding my breath… waiting.

"You're like…speed chess. He has no idea what you're going to do. No matter what he thinks his next move should be, he may have to come up with another one in a hurry. You do the unexpected. You challenge him, and that's definitely one of the reasons he's drawn to you." Nate took a deep breath, shifting uncomfortably until he finally met my own nervous gaze.

"He wasn't good that first year. I'd never seen him like that, and I never want to again. He submitted to being at Yale, and told everyone that he was moving on with his life without you. But when he started the transfer to Stanford, I knew it was because of you. No matter what he tried to convince everyone else, he could never get over you."

Nate paused in thought before continuing. "The reason I'm telling you all of this is because the more time you spend together, the more hopeful he becomes. But Emma, don't do this if you aren't planning to be completely truthful with him. He deserves that much. I don't know what you haven't told him yet, but he needs to know. If it's going to make him never want to see you again, then that's the risk you have to take. I'm not going to let you gut him like you did two years ago."

I met Nate's determined expression and nodded feebly. "I will be honest with him. I promise." And I knew exactly what that promise meant. My knees weakened.

"Thank you," he said sincerely. "Hey, we should start heading back. The fireworks should be starting soon."

"I'll be there in a minute," I rasped, knowing that if I moved, I'd collapse. I pulled my phone out of my pocket and stared down as Jonathan's words lit up on my screen. My heart stopped.

"There you are," I declared as soon as I came around the bend. "I was..." *Nate quickly passed me without a glance. Behind him, Emma was staring at her phone.*

"Emma?" She collapsed to her knees. I was too late.

39. NO MORE SECRETS

I held Emma's trembling hand as I led her back to the house. Nate had picked up his pace, so he was already submerged in the crowd. He knew I was pissed, but I didn't want to get into it with him in front of Emma. She was having a hard enough time looking at me.

Her steps faltered as I cut through the crowd and into the house. I shut and locked the bedroom door behind us while Emma continued out to the patio. I found her seated on the end of the teak lounge chair, her gaze fixed on the ground and her arms wrapped around her waist.

"What did he say to you?" I asked quietly. "Whatever he said—"

Her heartbreaking dark eyes peered up at me, coated with tears.

"He just wants me to be honest with you. That's all. He didn't say anything wrong, Evan. Don't be mad at him. He was only being your best friend. And he didn't ask me for anything that you don't deserve."

I hugged myself tighter and drew in a quivering breath. "I'm scared." I swallowed against the lump in my throat. "I'm going to lose you, Evan."

"Hey," he soothed, crouching in front of me. "No, you're not. I'm not going anywhere. I promise."

"You can't promise that. You have no idea..." My voice trailed off.

"Then tell me, Em. Please just explain what happened and stop torturing yourself," he implored passionately. "I'll understand, whatever it is."

I raised my eyes to let him in. I wasn't going to fight it anymore.

Her eyes delved into me with an intensity I'd never experienced before. They were steady, full of conviction. "I want you to see. All of me. Like you've always wanted. But you're not going to like it. There's a part of me that's dark and… angry. And I don't know if I'll ever be rid of it."

She paused, like she was trying to prepare me. But this wasn't what I'd expected.

"I'm more like my mother than I ever wanted to admit. I'm just as hateful. Just as self-destructive. And just as broken. She was right when she said I should never have been born."

"Emma, don't say that."

"It's your turn to listen, Evan," she said calmly, her voice distant and coated with ice. "I hated her. I hated my mother, and I'm glad she's dead." I flinched at her words, but I didn't say anything. "She can rot in hell where she belongs. I don't give a fuck."

I stood up and backed away a step, startled by the loathing in her hardened, dark eyes.

I didn't react when he withdrew from me. He wanted to know, so I wasn't going to hold back. He shook his head, as if denying this was really me.

"Jonathan understood. He knew what it was like to be tortured by hate until it becomes a part of you. Our pain bonded us—allowed us to be honest with each other. He didn't judge me when I told him I hated her. He didn't look at me like you are now. Like I'm detestable. And I am. I know I am. That's why *you* should hate me, Evan." The emotion broke my resolve. "You're supposed to hate me as much as I hate myself."

The torment cut through, shattering her icy tone and dissolving the hatred in her eyes. I took a step toward her, prepared to console her, to convince her that I didn't hate her, and never could. It crushed me knowing she was convinced that she was worth all the hate that had ever been unleashed upon her.

"I almost gave up."

I froze. "What?"

"That day… of my run. I almost gave up." My heartbeat picked up. "I walked out into the ocean, and just kept going. I wanted it to take me. To drown the guilt. I didn't want to hurt anymore. I didn't want to be hated anymore. I didn't want to keep breathing."

Her words stole the air from my lungs. "Emma." She crumpled onto her knees. I caught her, wrapping her in my arms. "You don't get to quit on me. Because if you do, you'll take me with you. And you can't do that to us."

Tears stung my eyes as she collapsed against me. "I can't…" Her voice broke. "I can't do this anymore."

"Then I'll do it for you," I rasped, my throat closing. "Let me love you. Let me love you enough for the two of us, until you can accept that you're worth it. Because you are, Emma. I don't know how to convince you. But I'll spend the rest of my life trying. You can't give up on me now. I won't let you."

I couldn't catch my breath. I buried my face in his shirt. He was my reason for existing. It was his words that pulled me to the surface. His breath that saved me. And now, his arms that held me within this life, unable to give up. He was my strength, and the love I didn't have for myself. And I couldn't live without him any more than he could let me go.

I pulled my head away from his chest, and he loosened his hold on me. I placed my hand over his damp cheek as he bent toward me, capturing my breath with his. The sudden pressure of his firm lips on mine filled me with an overwhelming surge of affection, rushing through every pore of my body. He kissed me as if his touch could make me whole again. And in that moment, I was convinced that it did.

I let my mouth linger over hers, needing her to feel how much I meant every word I'd said. I couldn't let her go, not now, not ever. She gasped at the intensity as my lips continued to slide over hers. She curled her fingers into my hair. My heart thrust at the touch of her warm tongue tasting my lips, teasing my tongue.

I couldn't get enough of her, needing to seep into her skin and feel her heart beat within my chest. There was a pounding within me that convinced me that I had. That we were sharing the same pulse. Her fingers trembled as she faltered with the buttons of my shirt. I slid the straps off her shoulders and peeled the dress from her smooth skin. I let her push the shirt off me, sweeping her hands down my chest. The look in her eyes, full of love and fear, held me captive.

"I love you, Emma Thomas," I whispered. "There'll never be another second of your life that you don't know it."

A silent tear trickled out of the corner of her eye and into her hair as she lay against the dark blue cushion. I ran my thumb along her skin, brushing it away.

A sudden explosion overhead startled us, diverting her attention to the fireworks spreading in the sky. I kept my eyes locked on hers, watching the colors reflect in them. She inhaled at the tickle of my gentle touch as I trailed my fingertips across her stomach.

I continued down her bare legs, releasing the strap around her heel, letting her sandals fall to the ground. Her breathing deepened as I kissed every inch of her along my return. I unbuttoned my shorts as I continued to make my way back to her soft lips. Her breath faltered when I unclasped her bra, exposing her to the chill of the air.

She gripped my shoulders as I moved down her body, tasting her skin. Removing the last of our clothes, I pulled back to admire the slopes and curves of her, feeling the emanating heat as I brushed across her inner thigh, her legs shifting slightly with a gasp.

My pulse quickened as I watched her lips part with her eyes closed, consumed by the sensation of my touch. Even in the dim light, I could see the flush spread from her chest up to her cheeks. I bent down to kiss the color. She turned her head toward me, and I felt the give of her mouth as her breath panted against my lips. She quivered beneath me, with her back *arched ever so slightly. Her eyes blinked open heavily, her beautiful full lips puckering.*

Not taking my eyes off hers, I positioned myself over her. She wrapped her legs behind my thighs, gently guiding me into her. I tensed at the connection as she surrounded me, and all I could feel was her. I buried my face into her neck, kissing it as her head rocked back in pleasure.

She exhaled, pushing her lips against my shoulder with one hand behind my neck and the other dragging down my back. I tightened my hold on her hip, absorbing every movement, scent, and feel of her. I couldn't remember needing her more than I did at this moment—or her giving more than she was right now.

As the heat escalated and the demand grew stronger, she inhaled sharply and tilted her hips into me. Her legs trembled as she fought to find her breath. Forced to close my eyes, overcome by the waves that crashed through me, I became lost in the breathless surge and pressed my face into her shoulder, inhaling her sweet scent until I couldn't hold anything back.

I lowered beside her and held her, pressing my lips into hair. When I pulled away to look at her, her eyes shone.

He lay beside me as I nuzzled against him, unable to find my voice. I was overcome with every possible sensation—it was a moment I'd hold on to for the rest of my life.

We remained in our silent embrace, watching the vibrant sparks drizzling down the night sky. I shivered, and Evan eased away just long enough to get a blanket.

"Are you okay?" he asked as he held me.

I turned my head toward him and swept my thumb along his bottom lip, and said, "Every breath I breathe is because of you." His eyes flickered, still peering into mine. "Even when you weren't there to save me, you were my reason to breathe. And for that I will always love you. Always."

———

"Emma?" Evan called to me from within the dark room. I closed the bedroom door, my heart shattered and my body weak.

He clicked on the bedside lamp. Confusion ran across his face at the sight of me dressed and standing at the end of the bed.

"What time is it?" he questioned.

"It's early," I told him with a wavering breath.

"Emma, what's wrong?" he asked, his face tight with apprehension. "What is it?"

"This is the part where I break your heart," I whispered. "And you finally get to understand why you should hate me."

I ran up the stairs, every muscle tense. I banged on the door.

"Sara!"

A moment later, Jared opened it, rubbing his eyes. Sara sat in the bed behind him, still groggy and half-asleep.

"Evan? What's the matter?"

I moved past Jared into the room. "I need you to call your father. Emma left."

"What?!" She whipped the covers back. "What do you mean, she left?!"

"She just told me something—" I had to pause, my stomach filling with acid at just the thought of it. "She confessed to something, and I don't know what to believe. I need to know if it's true. And your father is the only one I can think of to tell us."

"What are you talking about?" she demanded, her brows pulled together. "Where did Emma go?"

"To New York," I told her. "To find Jonathan." I took a deep breath and proceeded to recount exactly what Emma had finally confided—the last piece of honesty that sliced a wound so deep, I was bleeding out.

"Emma, you're not making any sense." I pushed the covers off. "What haven't you told me?" Then I noticed the phone clutched in her hand. "The text."

"You knew?" she asked, her eyes flinching slightly. "How? I mean ...
why didn't you tell me?"

"I thought you'd see it when I returned your phone," I explained.
"I couldn't bring myself to say anything. I don't know what happened
between you and Jonathan, and why you need to forgive each other,
but..." I stopped and put my hand over my face. "I despise him, Em. I
honestly regret that you ever met him."

She bowed her head with her eyes closed.

"This is about him, right?"

She nodded.

"Why did he need to forgive you?"

"Because I hurt him ... just like you. I took his trust and used it
against him, knowing I'd break him. And I did."

*"He's making a phone call," Sara told me, interrupting my pacing. "I'm
sure there's something more to this."*

*"So she never told you?" Sara shook her head. "She's kept this to herself
for over two years?" I clenched my jaw and began pacing again.*

"Evan, let's just figure out what really happened first, okay?"

"The night that the guy broke into my house," she began, her head
still slumped forward, "Jonathan did fight him off me. But he beat him
so bad, he stopped moving. And when I finally got Jonathan to stop,
he didn't even look human anymore. There was blood ... everywhere."
Her voice faltered and her hands trembled. I remained on the bed next
to her, trying to keep my breath even.

"I helped him get rid of the body after, and we lied to the police to
cover it up."

"He was dead?" I questioned. She nodded.

*"Jonathan didn't kill him," Sara announced, hanging up the phone over
an hour later, exhausted and shaky. "He beat the shit out of him, but the*

dealer was found in that parking lot with a bullet in his head. They ended up matching the gun to another shooting about six months later. I guess there was another douche bag at the bar, and this dealer didn't exactly have the best reputation. So the douche took it upon himself to shoot him and take off with a trunkful of money and drugs."

"She thinks she helped kill him. She thinks she's an accomplice to his murder."

"Is that why he asked you to forgive him, because he killed this guy?" I asked, every inch of me rigid with anger.

"No," she answered, her voice so low, it barely made a sound.

"He did kill his family," Sara told me, and I clenched my teeth in revulsion. "He pleaded guilty to lighting the fire that burned his mother, father and brother in their sleep. The trial was expedited, and he just got sentenced three days ago. My dad said that he was abused by his father pretty bad most of his life and suffered psychological damage. His psychiatrist testified on his behalf, and he ended up being sentenced to twenty years for first-degree manslaughter, required to serve ten. He's at a medium-security prison in New York."

"You knew, and you didn't do anything?!" My voice grew louder. "You were going to let him get away with it?!"

"I promised. And I know he'd do the same for me."

After a deafening moment of silence, she stood up from the bed.

"Where are you going?"

"I have to find him. I know something bad has happened, and I couldn't live with myself if I don't go look for him. I'm sorry, but I have to leave."

Emma had kept Jonathan's secret to herself, as she'd promised she would—until tonight. I thought I hated him before. The rage I felt now was about to incinerate me.

I sat down on the floor, against the wall, with my hands cradling my head. "She knew," *I murmured.* "She knew and chose to protect him, to keep his secret. He killed his family, and she didn't say a word."

"Evan," *Sara implored. I refused to look up.*

"What kind of person does that?"

"I'm not the girl you fell in love with. She's gone. You have to decide if you can still love me. It's your choice now."

And then she left.

"Sara, you should call her, to tell her about the drug dealer. And where Jonathan is too."

"You don't want to call her?" *she asked.*

"I can't talk to her." *I left the room, slamming the door behind me.*

40. WHAT IS YOURS

I *pulled at my jeans as I sat at the table, waiting for him to enter. My heart was beating so fast, my head was spinning.*

When the doors opened, the entire room shifted in anticipation. I scanned the faces of men in green jumpsuits. Men who I would never want to be in the same room with alone. When I saw Jonathan's face, I stood, and his eyes lit up when he spotted me.

"Hi, Jonathan," I said awkwardly, not certain what I was supposed to do.

"I can't believe you're really here," he said, relief washing over his face. "I thought you hated me."

A quick pang shot through my chest at the choice of his words. "No. I think it's about time we start forgiving."

The visit with Jonathan had been a relief in some ways, but seeing him in that oppressive prison was still weighing heavily on my mind. My phone beeped, pulling me from my thoughts. I picked it up to find a missed call from Evan. A rush of nervousness ran through me at the sight of his name. I hadn't heard from him since I'd left Santa Barbara five days ago. Knowing what the call meant, I gripped the steering wheel tighter. He'd made his choice.

I pulled in to the rest stop and parked the rental car. Then I took a deep breath and listened to his message.

"Hi, Em. Please call me." His voice was quiet and sad.

I closed my eyes. The quick patter of my heart filled my ears. I tried to calm it, to relax. But that was impossible. I was about to listen to the only person I would ever love tell me that he couldn't be with me. There was no recovering from that.

There were no more secrets. He knew everything. I was exposed. Letting Evan completely in was the hardest thing I'd ever had to do. It left me vulnerable to his judgment and rejection. I might as well have splayed my ribs and handed him my heart. I didn't need it if I wasn't going to be with him.

I stared at the phone in dread. I had been preparing for this call since the moment I'd walked away from him…again. I listened as the phone rang, concentrating on each breath.

"Hi."

"Hi," I responded faintly.

"I'm glad you called. I was afraid you wouldn't."

"I figured you'd made your decision," I faltered, my heart continuing to pound fiercely.

"I did. I…had to think. I was so angry. I couldn't understand why you kept something that horrible a secret. I'm still not over it."

My chest squeezed tight. I closed my eyes and waited.

"Emma, there was never a choice. I will always choose you. Always."

I couldn't speak for a minute. "What?"

"I don't agree with what you did," he explained. "And I'm pissed that you didn't tell anyone. You screwed up, Em. But you knew that. That's why you were torturing yourself. And I'll get over being angry. But I could never get over losing you again. We can get through anything if we're honest, if you let me in. Can you promise me no more secrets? No matter how much you think it'll hurt, you'll tell me everything?"

This wasn't what he was supposed to say.

"Emma?"

"I don't understand. You still…love me?"

He released the slightest chuckle. "Yeah, I do. And I know you're not the same girl. But I'm in love with *you*, Emma. I fell in love with you all over again this summer. People change. I know this. And we'll continue to change. That just means I'll get to fall in love with you again. Because no matter what happens in our lives, what I feel for you will survive anything."

I was so afraid I'd lost him—that he could never love me. It had never occurred to me that he could forgive me. That he could love me as much as I love him. There was no way he was saying this. There was no way he was forgiving me. But he was.

I collapsed on the steering wheel and sobbed, the phone slipping from my hand.

"Emma?" I heard him call to me, and I fumbled to pick it up. "Emma?"

Between broken breaths, I responded, "I'm here."

"You need to have more confidence in me," he said lightly.

"Sorry. I just—"

"I know," he interrupted. "But don't ever doubt me again."

"Never," I said, releasing a calming breath. "And no more secrets."

"No more secrets. So where are you?"

"At a rest stop, somewhere in Oklahoma," I answered, looking around the busy rest area.

"Oklahoma? Why are you there?"

"I just felt like getting in a car and driving."

"How long were you planning on doing that?"

"Until I found something worth stopping for," I answered, wiping my damp face and sinking back against the seat.

"And you're stopped now, right?"

I smiled. "Yes."

"I'll take that as being worthy," he teased, making me smile wider. "Are you planning to drive all the way here?"

"I was thinking about it," I responded. "I figured I'd be back by this weekend."

"I'm flying to Connecticut this weekend," Evan informed me. "I have to pick up my things. My mother sold the house, and everything has to be out by this Sunday."

"Really?"

"Yeah," he murmured. "But it doesn't matter anymore. I have you." Then he paused. "Right?"

I laughed, swiping at my eyes. "Yes. You have me. "

"Good. Call me when you stop driving tonight, please?"

"I will," I promised. "'Bye, Evan."

"'Bye, Emma." I let out a long breath, relieved she'd called me back. I held up the letter she'd left on the bedside table, and ran my finger over the ink with a soft smile. The letter that had once again changed my life.

I love him more than he will ever know. And because of that, I choose his happiness.

Those two lines were all that she'd written. And it took a phone call to my mother to understand. She repeated Emma's vow back to me, "I love him, but I would walk away before I'd ever let anything jeopardize his happiness." My mother claimed that this letter forced her to make one of the hardest decisions she'd ever had to make.

I walked into the living room where Sara sat on the couch with her phone in her hand, texting. She eyed me curiously, then beamed. "You just spoke to Emma." I nodded, unable to hold back the smile. "Good."

"Thank you for talking to me. I don't know if I would've been able to take a step back and understand what she was going through if you hadn't helped me."

"You were angry, which was understandable," she explained simply. "It's hard to see clearly through that much anger. Believe me, I've been friends with Emma for a long time. I'm kind of an expert by now."

———

I pulled in to the driveway and looked up at the large white farmhouse with a heavy chest.

I used my key to open the door, the key I was supposed to leave on the kitchen counter before I left today. My footsteps echoed through the stark kitchen. The room seemed even larger now that everything had been removed.

I ran my hand over the marble countertop, recalling all the conversations and meals shared there—not only with Emma but with my family too. I continued into the empty sitting room, with just the small crystal chandelier dangling in the middle of the room. Shadows of twilight stretched across the floor through the large picture window.

I didn't bother turning on the light as I walked down the hall, allowing the dimness to reflect my somber mood. The piano sat in the same spot, mocking me—the last item left behind, besides what was in my room. The piano movers weren't expected until the next day. I climbed the spiral stairs, the stairs I'd carried Emma up when she'd hurt her knee. I smiled faintly, remembering her irritation when I'd scooped her up unexpectedly.

I stood outside my bedroom door and hesitated. This was the first house where I'd unpacked every single box, wanting to stay. All because of a girl with a fiery attitude and a blush that let me know exactly what she thought of me. That's all it took, and I was hers. And now I had to leave the only place I'd ever considered home.

I pushed the door open and flipped on the lights in the dark, cavernous room, but I remained within the door frame, looking around curiously. It looked exactly how I'd left it. Unpacked.

I walked over to the tux lying across the bed, with a note set on top.

Put me on and come out back.

I grinned.

When he finally came outside I was sitting on the swing with small twinkling lights glowing above me, like a thousand fireflies spread out along the wiry branches. It was enchanting. Exactly as I'd intended.

I smiled brightly at the flawless guy dressed in the fitted tux. His golden-brown hair was swept neatly to the side, and he wore a smile that made my entire body ignite in rampant flutters.

"Hi," he said, the lights sparkling in his eyes. "I'm glad you're here. I've missed you."

"Hi," I responded, swinging gently on the swing. "I've missed you too."

There was no use trying to breathe when I saw her sitting on the swing in the strapless pink dress that floated around her. Her short brown hair framed her stunning face, and the lights in the trees illuminated her skin. I was mesmerized by the girl in front of me.

"A guy once told me that a girl needed time to prepare for something like this," she said. "I think we've waited long enough. Evan Mathews, will you go to prom with me?"

I laughed, my ears suddenly picking up the music coming from the pool area. "Yes, Emma, I'd love to go to prom with you." She hopped down from the swing and took the hand that I held out for her. I wrapped her securely in my arms, my nose pressed into her hair. After everything that had happened this summer, I just needed to hold her. And she needed to know she was mine, and that I was still hers. We remained in the embrace until her shoulders relaxed and she melted against me.

I eased away, peering down at her radiant face. "You did this?" I asked, nodding toward the tree.

"No," she said with a light laugh. "I hired people to do it. I'd break my neck. But I planned it. Are you surprised?"

"Very." I laughed, about to kiss her when she swung open the gate. The fire reflecting on the water caught my eye, and I turned my head.

Emma beamed. "See. There is a pool."

Candles floated along the surface, and the entire patio was softly lit with colorful paper lanterns, reminding me of the ones she'd told me her father would hang for her in the backyard on her birthday.

Wow, I mouthed. "This is amazing, Emma."

"I know. I'm pretty impressed with myself."

Evan laughed, sweeping his arm around my waist and guiding me closer. He leaned over and kissed me so gently it felt like a whisper against my lips. My eyes remained closed when he pulled away.

"Breathe, Emma." His voice drifted in the breeze. I opened my eyes, and exhaled. He didn't let me go, and we began swaying to the hypnotic sounds of female vocals swirling through the air.

"Thank you for doing this," he said, kissing my temple. "It means a lot to have you here, to share the last night in this house with me."

"Last night?" she remarked, tilting her head up at me. "Why would tonight be your last night?"

I scanned her face as her eyes twinkled in the soft light. "What aren't you telling me, Emma?" She revealed the most dazzling smile. "Tell me."

"Well… let's just say that I made an investment in my future."

"You bought this house." We were no longer moving to the ethereal singer.

"Technically, you own a portion of it," she explained. "Your mother accepted part of your savings as your offer, and Charles arranged for payment of the rest. So essentially you own your bedroom." She laughed. I

wrapped my arms around her waist and swung her around, making her
yell out in a joyous laugh.

I kissed her neck. "We have a house."

"You have a room," she teased. "I have a house. Umm…the piano's staying."

"I'm not playing it," he said quickly, causing me to smile.

"I guess I'll have to learn," I said, laying my head on his chest as we began to sway again.

Elation seeped out of him like he might burst, and I was smiling so big it almost hurt. I was grateful that Vivian hadn't accepted any other offers before I met with her last weekend—although at the time I didn't know I'd be the one living here. She'd shared a reflective moment with me regarding choices and love.

Love was easy. All I had to do was look in his eyes and know that.

In the uneven balance of my life, I'd experienced love and loss. The loss challenged me to be strong, but it was the love that supported me when I was weak. I was a survivor. And now I wanted to focus on *living* my life.

This was just the beginning of our healing. Of being forgiven. I knew I would struggle with it at times, and feel like I was fighting for every breath. I just had to remember, there was always a choice. And I chose to live. I chose to love. I chose to breathe.

EPILOGUE

I twisted my hands in my lap. My heart felt like it was going to pound right out of my chest.

"Stop!" I hollered, practically panting. "I can't do this. I can't."

Silence. No pep talk. No coaxing. No trying to convince me.

I closed my eyes and took a breath. If my pulse kept this up, then I'd be sweating right through my dress. And that was not the impression I wanted to make. I took another breath.

I can do this. I can do this. All I have to do is walk. And smile. And maybe talk. I can do this.

I opened my eyes again, and said, "Okay. I'm ready."

Evan glanced sideways at me. "Are you sure this time?"

"Shut up and go," I pleaded, making him chuckle. My shoulders relaxed as we slowed to a stop.

The large, soft-coral-colored house sat before me. My breathing evened, and the panic subsided. Before I could step out of the car, the front door flung open, and a little girl in a frilly pink dress came running out full force. "Emma!"

She crashed against me, her arms wrapping around my stomach. "Hi, Leyla," I said, my eyes watering as I hugged her tight. "You look so beautiful."

"I knew you'd wear pink," she exclaimed joyously. "It's our favorite color."

"Mine too," Evan chimed in, making her giggle.

"Jack, why don't you go help Evan bring in their things," the woman with the coiffed grey hair instructed gently.

The young boy with the round wire glasses approached Evan hesitantly.

"Hey, Jack," Evan said, holding out his hand. "I'm Evan." Jack grasped it, and a small smile emerged as he shook it. "You can take in this box, since it's yours anyway." Jack's eyes lit up when he accepted the gift wrapped in festive Christmas paper. "And I had to wrap it because Emma can't fold a corner to save her life."

Jack laughed.

"True," I sighed.

"Hello, Emily…" My grandmother paused. "Emma. It's nice to finally meet you in person." I raised my head to view the woman before me, who I easily resembled. The woman who had given me back my family.

My grandmother began to reach out with her hand, then stopped, undecided how to greet me. I slid away from Leyla.

"Thank you," I said, wrapping my arms around her. She folded her thin strong arms around me and held me tight.

ACKNOWLEDGMENTS

Nearly four years ago, a story came to me that demanded to be told. Over the years, I opened up and let a part of my soul pour out onto the pages. I was left vulnerable and exposed, giving everything I had to allow the story to be exactly what it needed to be. And I'm proud of the part of me I left on the pages. During the process I learned so much more about who I am—the most important being, I'm so much stronger than I ever thought I was.

I did not, and could not, do this alone. There are many people in my life to be grateful for. For loving me, believing in me, and being exactly who I needed them to be along the way. I love them all, and they know who they are.

And then there is this select group of people who contributed their time, patience and affection for the story to help make the final chapters of this series spectacular...

First, I must thank Emily, for having such belief in me that she changed her life to be a part of mine. There isn't a truer friend, or a more loving human being.

Elizabeth, my partner, my tether to sanity, and the voice I can never live without—Thank You! I am so fortunate to have such a beautiful person and devoted writing partner in my life, who is also so very talented at everything she does.

Faith, who never let this story be less than sincere and true, and in turn, I have become a better writer.

Courtney, for making certain every emotion is genuine and every word is as powerful as it needs to be.

Nicole gave me more than she knew she did—her friendship and love above all else.

Amy, my awe-inspiring guru, for sharing the beautiful art of writing and allowing me to view it from a different angle.

Jenn, my destined friend, with whom I share my passion for storytelling, and who helped me find Emma's voice when she needed to be heard.

Sarah, without whom I would never have found my way back to the beginning to make this a story that is so much more than just "a story."

Tracey, Colleen and Tammara, my inspiring and talented friends, for reading my words and sharing theirs in return. They have each touched my life more than I can ever express!

The dedicated team at Trident Media Group, especially my agent Erica, who has been by my side every step of the way; even when I felt I was about to fall off the cliff, she kept holding on.

Tim, Amy and the entire crew at Amazon Publishing for listening to my words and embracing all that makes me a passionate writer. I am grateful for all they have committed to this venture.

I had the privilege of meeting and befriending many talented and fabulous authors over the past year, along with some vivacious bloggers. I am a better person for having them in my life. We live in a world in which we create, and invite readers in with us to share in the vividness of our imagination. How fortunate are we to be able to touch someone we've never met, inspire with words and invoke emotion with the flip of a page. I am honored to be among them.

And that leaves me with the reason for all that I do...my readers. If they were not there to share in my world, it would not truly exist. I am thankful to have them as a part of my life—it will never be the same.

Lastly, I must express my admiration for the strength and perseverance of every survivor of abuse. There is hope. There is love. There is help. You are not alone.

Rebecca Donovan, a graduate of the University of Missouri–Columbia, lives in a quiet town in Massachusetts with her son. Excited by all that makes life possible, Rebecca is a music enthusiast and is willing to try just about anything once.

Web: www.rebeccadonovan.com /
Facebook: thebreathingseries /
Twitter: beccadonovan